Utopian Literature

Advisory Editor:
ARTHUR ORCUTT LEWIS, JR.
Professor of English
The Pennsylvania State University

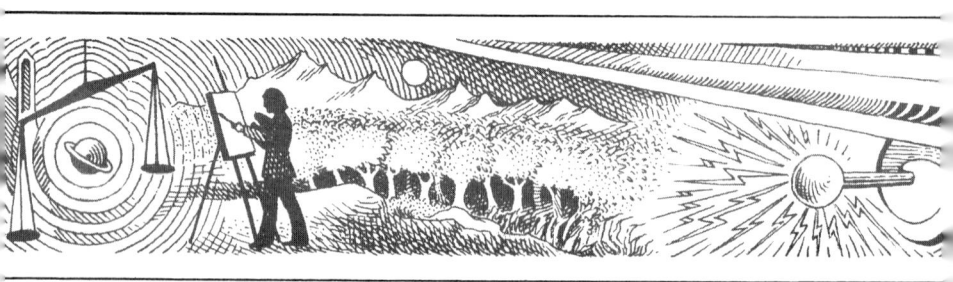

The First To Awaken

*Granville Hicks,
with Richard M. Bennett*

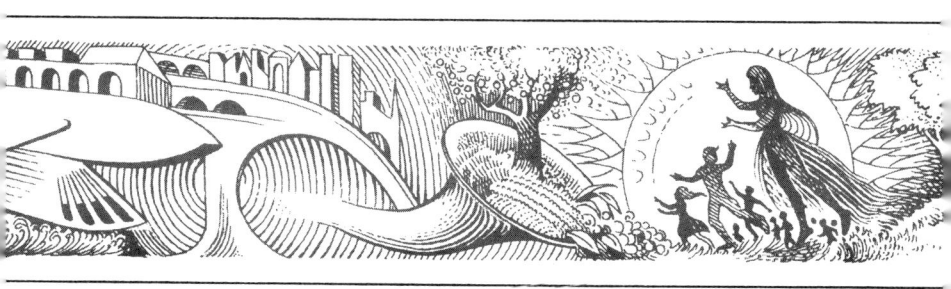

ARNO PRESS & THE NEW YORK TIMES
NEW YORK · 1971

Reprint Edition 1971 by Arno Press Inc.
© 1940 by Modern Age Books, Inc.

Reprinted from a copy in The Pennsylvania State University Library

LC# 70-154446
ISBN 0-405-03529-2

Utopian Literature
ISBN for complete set: 0-405-03510-1

Manufactured in the United States of America

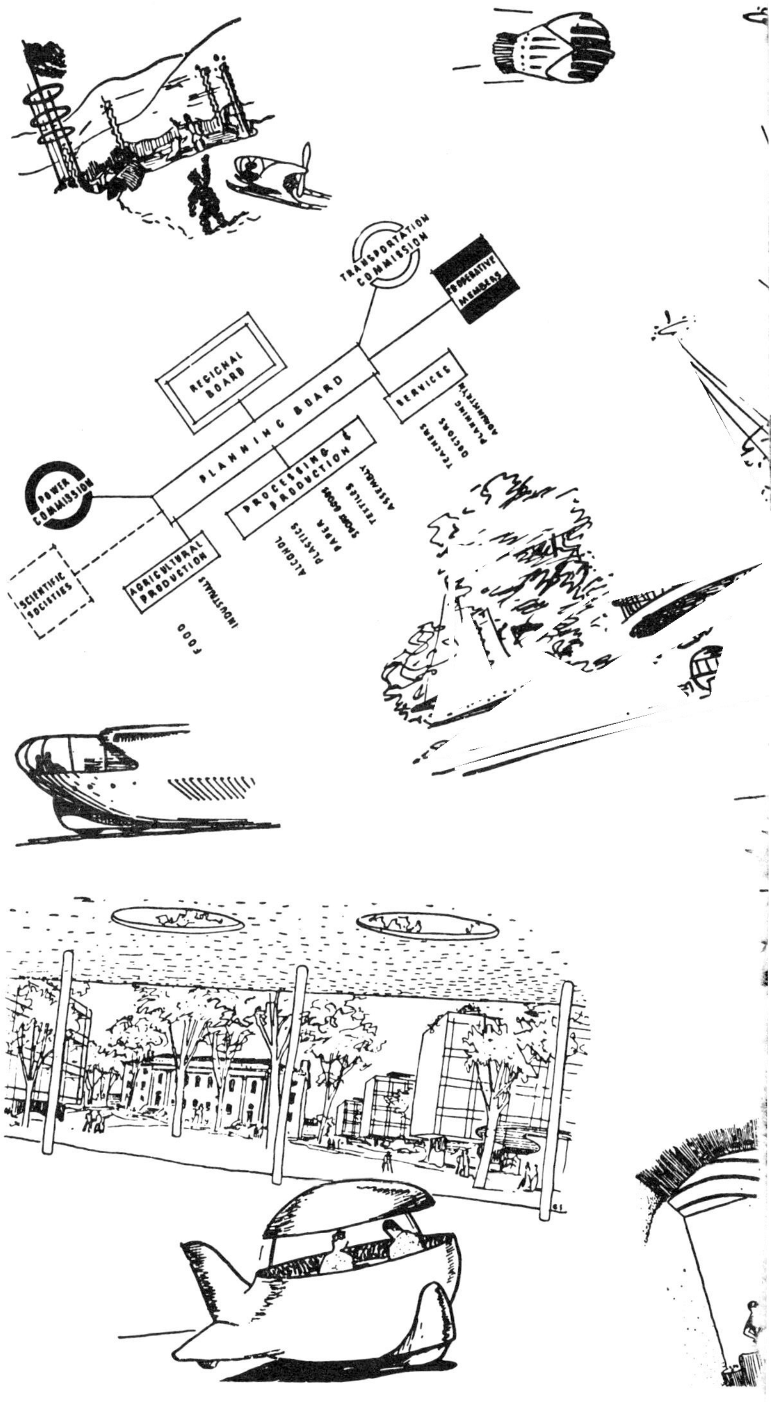
TRANSPORTATION COMMISSION
COOPERATIVE MEMBERS
REGIONAL BOARD
PLANNING BOARD
SERVICES
TEACHERS
DOCTORS
PLANNING
ADMINSTRTN
POWER COMMISSION
PROCESSING & PRODUCTION
ALCOHOL
PLASTICS
PAPER
SPORT GOODS
TEXTILES
ASSEMBLY
SCIENTIFIC SOCIETIES
AGRICULTURAL PRODUCTION
INDUSTRIALS
FOOD

ALSO BY GRANVILLE HICKS

The Great Tradition

John Reed: The Making of a Revolutionary

I Like America

The Letters of Lincoln Steffens (Co-editor)

Figures of Transition

THE FIRST TO AWAKEN

THE FIRST TO AWAKEN

By Granville Hicks
With Richard M. Bennett

New York, 1940

MODERN AGE BOOKS

COPYRIGHT, 1940, BY GRANVILLE HICKS

PUBLISHED BY MODERN AGE BOOKS, INC.

All rights in this book are reserved and it may not be reproduced in whole or in part without written permission from the holder of these rights. For information, address the publishers.

Edited and produced under union conditions by contract with the Book and Magazine Guild, Local 18, UOPWA, CIO, and printed and bound in union shops affiliated with the AFL.

DESIGNED BY BRUCE GENTRY

PRINTED IN THE UNITED STATES OF AMERICA, BY H. WOLFF, NEW YORK

FOR

ALICE, DOROTHY, AND STEPHANIE

HOW THIS BOOK WAS WRITTEN

SEVERAL years ago, before Modern Age Books existed, I discussed with Louis Birk, now vice-president of that company, the possibility of a book about life a hundred years from now. Though Mr. Birk repeatedly urged me to write it, other books got in the way, and *The First to Awaken* remained only a vague plan—a book that might some day be written. That it became something more than this is to the credit of Richard M. Bennett, for it was a conversation with him that made me see why the book should be done and how I might do it.

As other conversations followed, and we became collaborators in the making of plans, it was inevitable that he should do the drawings. But these were only a small part of his contribution. Every chapter was discussed with him before it was written and after it was in rough draft, and now it is impossible for me to say how much the book owes to his knowledge and his imagination. Although I did the actual writing and must accept the responsibility for the final shaping of the book, in every other sense it is as much his as it is mine. In our pleasant partnership we have talked of it as "our" book, and I hope that is how the readers will think of it.

GRANVILLE HICKS

Grafton, New York
February 22, 1940

CONTENTS

	Introduction	xi
I	I Go to Sleep	3
II	I Wake Up	33
III	The City of the Future	60
IV	Conversation at Midnight	84
V	Return to Braxton	111
VI	I Find a Home	140
VII	How It All Happened	169
VIII	Progress of an Education	198
IX	The Course of Justice	225
X	I Speak My Piece	252
XI	Design for Divorce	281
XII	Adventures of a Globe Trotter	303
XIII	Hail and Farewell	333

INTRODUCTION

By David V. Wilson

RESEARCH FELLOW OF
THE NORTHEAST DISTRICT
AND PERSONNEL CONSULTANT
FOR THE BRAXTON COOPERATIVE

MOST OF MY READERS will recall the peculiar circumstances under which it was discovered, some two years ago, that between 1940 and 1947 eight persons submitted themselves to cryogenic treatment, as developed by Waldo Richard Carr, M.D. To speak in the vernacular, these persons went to sleep for one hundred years.

The first to awaken was George Swain, who returned to consciousness on March 12, 2040, one hundred years to the day after animation was cryogenically suspended. As a psychologist, I undertook a study of Swain's response to his new environment, and my conclusions will be published, presumably within the next year, by the Continental Institute for Social Psychology.

The average citizen, however, will be more interested in Swain's own account of his experiences. This account, despite its many inaccuracies, is of great value for the insight it gives into the life of the first half of the twentieth century. Particularly when he is writing about our period, Mr. Swain reveals the character of his own. A document of major historical importance, his story is also, I venture to say, more interesting than fiction, chiefly because of the freshness with which he approaches what is commonplace to us.

When we urged Swain to record his observations, it was with the therapeutic value of such activity uppermost in our minds, and, as his own narrative makes clear, he did not write with contemporary readers in mind. I make this statement to explain the manner in which the book is written and especially its vocabulary. When publication was proposed, he wished to revise the manuscript, but the task was obviously too much for him, and we saw that more would be lost than could possibly be gained.

At his request, however, I undertook to edit the book. I have used footnotes as sparingly as possible, for I believe that the reader will have little difficulty in deducing the meaning of unfamiliar terms from the context. I have also been restrained in suggesting books and articles that would help the reader. Since Swain has also seen fit to introduce some further comments, the authorship of each footnote is indicated by the use of initials.

I do not want to close this brief preface without thanking George Swain for the good will he showed while I was carrying on my observations and for the compliment he paid me when he asked for my editorial assistance. The reader is about to become better acquainted with George Swain, and he will understand why I value him as collaborator and friend.

Braxton, N.E.D.
Minervary 12, 2040

THE FIRST TO AWAKEN

I

I GO TO SLEEP

"WHEN I open my eyes," I said to myself, "it will be the year 2040."

That is what I had repeated, over and over again, as I lay on Dr. Carr's operating table, slipping gently into unconsciousness while he and his assistant administered the anesthetic.

It was just as it had been in childhood. "When I open my eyes, it will be Christmas Day." "When I wake up, it will be the Fourth of July."

Now as then I shivered a little: I might be wrong. But mostly I was confident—I had only to open my eyes and the miracle would be performed.

"Three things may happen," Dr. Carr had said. "Perhaps you won't wake up at all; perhaps you will wake up before I intend you to; perhaps you will go through the century. I think everything will be all right, but you're taking a chance."

It is strange that I was so calm. We were sitting in his office the morning after he had made his extraordinary proposal. He had asked me to sleep on it, and I had—slept well, too, certain that I would do what he suggested. And now he sat opposite me, smiling a little tensely over the corner of the big, old-fashioned rolltop desk, his drawn, yellow face solemn but eager.

"You understand," he continued, "that the experiment must be protected, and therefore your death will be announced and all the forms gone through. That has been planned for, and there will be no hitch. But have you considered the effect? So far as your world is concerned, you will be dead. What about your family, your friends, your job?"

"I have no family," I answered impatiently, "and no friends to whom my death will make the least difference. As for the job, why should I care about the Braxton National Bank? Anyway it will go on well enough without me."

I was a little bored, for I had thought of all this in the first five minutes after I heard his suggestion, and it seemed a waste of time for him to ask and for me to answer questions that had no importance. My mind drifted away, and I began to think how strange it was that I had never been in this office before. For nearly fifteen years I had been seeing Dr. Carr at least once a month, but he had never invited me or any of the others to come and visit him. For a time that had surprised me, but then we had all grown used to his idiosyncrasies, and it was only now that I plucked the mystery out of the back of my head and began to re-examine it.

If it had not been for the Tavern Club, I should have known Dr. Carr only as the rest of Braxton knew him—as a not ill-natured recluse who lived in the great house that had been his father's, had no local practice, and yet somehow was famous throughout the world. Braxton knew he was famous, for

I GO TO SLEEP

periodically reporters came from Boston and New York and tried to interview him. Their lack of success did not prevent them from writing astounding articles.

We of the Tavern Club knew little enough, but more than that. The Tavern Club was founded a few years after I came back from the war. The war was for me, as for so many other young men, the great divide in my personal history. Before 1917 I had known exactly what I wanted to do. From the time I understood what words meant, my mother impressed it upon me that I was going to college. My father had been a Dartmouth graduate, and I would go to Dartmouth. Then I would go to Harvard or Columbia and become a teacher, not a high school teacher as my father had been but a college professor.

We did not have an easy time of it. We were left a little insurance, and the town fathers[1] gave my mother a position in the clerk's office. The job paid enough for us to live on, if we were frugal, but it left no margin for college. I did odd jobs, mowing lawns, taking care of furnaces, beating rugs. Summers I worked on neighboring farms. But in spite of this, when I graduated from high school in 1915, I did not have money enough saved. The shoe factory was booming then, and I got a job, first as stockboy but later as a regular machine operative.

[1] Town fathers, i.e., selectmen—the elected administrative officials of a New England town. In general such terms, of which there are a great many in this chapter, will not be explained. The interested reader is referred to Samuel Bettinger's *The Politics of Capitalist Decay* (Boston, 2027), Mary L. Tilden's *Folkways of the Twentieth Century* (Albany, 2012), and the more popular *Life in Old New England,* by Dirk and Laura Stroopscaller (Manchester, 2036). There is some discussion of problems of vocabulary in Chapter 13 of the report mentioned in the preface.—D.W.

THE FIRST TO AWAKEN

By the beginning of 1917 I was sure that I could enter Dartmouth in the fall, but then war was declared, and college seemed a little foolish. For a long time I thought of enlisting, but in the end I waited to be drafted.

Meanwhile I had been going out with Elsie, and when I left for Camp Devens we were engaged. Elsie's father was cashier of the Braxton National Bank, and one of the town's substantial men. That does not mean, however, that he was rich. The only people who ever grew rich out of Braxton were the big stockholders in the corporation that had taken over the shoe factory, and they lived heaven knew where—not, certainly, in Braxton. Mr. Harrington had what seemed to me, in 1917, a luxurious home, and he could well afford to send the two boys to Bowdoin and Elsie to Mount Holyoke, but he was not rich and not, in the worst sense, snobbish. He would surely have resented it if Elsie had wanted to marry a French

The Tavern in Braxton

Canadian factory hand, even if the man had been skilled and highly paid, but he would not have thought of objecting to the son of a high school teacher, no matter how poor.

When I came back from France, Elsie and I wanted to be married, and in any case I felt that I was too grown-up for college. Mr. Harrington offered me a job as teller in the bank, and I took it. We were married a year later, spent a fortnight in the White Mountains, and then settled down.

I suppose I am the kind of person who does settle down. I accepted the bank routine and rather liked it. Everyone who came to my window knew me, and most people called me by my first name. Elsie's father never said that I was brilliant or promising; he said that I was steady.

My mother had died in the great flu epidemic, while I was in France. That left no one—or almost no one—in my world but Elsie. It is not easy for me to write about her. I know that even in Braxton she was not an exceptional girl. She was only moderately good-looking, had done only fair work in college, was superficially like most of the young matrons of the town. When we were first married, she did all the obvious things—played bridge once or twice a week, belonged to a literary club, took part in the women's activities in the church, went occasionally to country club dances. She liked the books and the movies that everyone else liked, wore the clothes that everyone else was wearing, and, I'm afraid, held the opinions everyone else held—acquired, mostly, from the Boston *Herald* and the Braxton *Voice*.

Afterwards, as I shall tell, she became less conventional, but then she was pretty much a conformist, and I would not have had her otherwise. That, however, was not the Elsie I was in love with. I knew that really she was different from that, just as, of course, I knew that I was different from what I appeared to be. When we were engaged, we used to read aloud together and take long walks, and after we were married we continued, a little furtively but at the same time with pleasure in doing what no one else in Braxton cared to do. I had always liked to sketch, and Elsie, who had had drawing lessons, encouraged me, saying that my drawings were better than hers.[1] (I knew this was true, though I always denied it.) This companionship was our real life. It was the way Elsie's face would light up over a line of poetry or the sight of a waterfall in the sunlight or a flight of birds that made me know why I loved her. At first we were afraid that we would have children, for bank tellers are not well paid in Braxton, and then we were afraid we wouldn't. Yet in the end our childlessness did help us to keep something alive that might not have survived the burden of raising a family on a salary like mine.

I have said that there was almost no one in my world but Elsie. The qualification was necessary to make a place for Everett Wilson. Everett was at Camp Devens with me, and we went to France in the same transport ship and saw our first action together. Thinking now of my friendship with Everett, I realize that I must have been a somewhat more rebellious youth than, after twenty years in a teller's cage, seems possible. But whatever of unconventionality I had in me, it was Everett who released it. My boldest ambition was to be a

[1] Dr. Carr preserved, along with other material that he thought might interest posterity, a small portfolio of Swain's sketches. Some of these have been reproduced in connection with this chapter. The full set has recently been exhibited at the Braxton Cooperative and is now on file in the Braxton library.—D.W.

history professor; he talked of being a poet and novelist or perhaps an actor. For a time he had lived and gone to high school in New York City, which I had never even visited, and later he had worked on a ranch in California and as a lumberjack in Oregon. He had spent a year in college, and had been expelled for a daring and irreverent demonstration against the authorities.

What made Everett so important to me was his articulateness. He was an atheist; he had been a Socialist and was at the moment a disciple of Nietzsche; he had heretical views on sex; he even ventured to throw doubt on the purity of the motives of our allies in the war. I discovered, to my amazement, that I had opinions on all these subjects. I also found that I knew far more about history than Everett did, though I knew little enough, and had more knowledge and perhaps better taste in literature. It was I, for example, who introduced him to the poetry of A. E. Housman, who immediately supplanted Kipling as his favorite poet.

The long talks with Everett are all that I remember pleasantly of the war. Except for a certain number of hours, I was not consciously unhappy, and it was not until afterward that I realized how hateful the whole experience had been to me. But as I looked back, I increasingly resented the fact that eighteen months of my life had been devoted to a silly and brutal business. It made me furious to think that anyone had the power to pick me up in the little town of Braxton, put me into an uncomfortable and ill-fitting uniform, set me under the orders of stupid officers, force me to engage in hour after hour of mechanical drill, and then ship me across the ocean to kill and perhaps be killed. I never said this to anyone, though Everett knew and perhaps Elsie guessed. At least she defended me when her father was indignant at my refusal to join the Legion.

Everett, though he was more outspoken in criticism both of the aims of the war and of the way it was conducted, felt little of my kind of resentment. In fact, if it had not been for his personal slovenliness and his discreet but unmistakable insubordination, he would have made a good soldier. When we went into action at Château-Thierry, I was numbed by the sense of being a helpless part of this machinery of slaughter, but his mind actually seemed to be quickened.

After the Armistice I was eager to get home as quickly as possible, but Everett said that this was his first visit to Europe, and he wanted to see something besides barracks and trenches. He talked of applying for permission to study in Paris, but Captain Merriam said flatly that he would not recommend him, and so he asked to be transferred to the Army of Occupation and was sent to the Rhineland.

For four years after we separated in France I heard only occasionally from him. When he wrote, his letters were enormously long, but they were always more speculative than autobiographical. On his return to the United States in 1920 he got a job on a New York paper, and I gathered that he was working on a novel, or perhaps it was a play. He seemed to have made many literary friends, though few of them were persons I had heard of. Repeatedly he promised to come to Braxton, but he never came.

Elsie and I had often talked of spending a week in New York together, going to theatres and museums, but my vacation came in the summer, of course, and we always chose to

I GO TO SLEEP

go to her father's camp in the mountains, for the fortnight there meant a great deal to us. In the summer of 1923, however, we spent only a week in the mountains and saved a week for a New York trip in the autumn.

It was a good trip all right, but my pleasure in it was dulled by my realization of what had happened to Everett. His newspaper job, though he did not seem conscious of the fact, was as purely routine as my work in the bank. In compensation he spent much time with fifth-rate people in the Village, drinking large quantities of what I now know was very bad bootleg liquor,[1] and talking about the novels and plays he pretended—to himself as well as his cronies—to be writing.

When we got back to Braxton, Elsie and I talked about Everett and what could be done for him. She didn't admire him as I did, and, after the first disappointment, I knew I never should have expected she would. To her he was a shabby, hard-drinking newspaperman who talked a lot of nonsense. But she knew that he was the best friend I had, and she tried to be sympathetic. In fact, it was she who suggested my getting him a job on the Braxton *Voice*.

The *Voice* wasn't wholly a bad newspaper, as smalltown newspapers went, for, however objectionable its editorials were, it more or less adequately covered our town and the

[1] Alcoholic beverages illegally manufactured and sold from 1919 to 1933 when all intoxicants were prohibited by constitutional amendment. See Chapter V, "Bootleggers and Speakeasies," of Tilden's *Folkways,* cited above. The term is supposedly derived from the fact that, at an earlier period, smugglers concealed the contraband goods in the legs of the high boots they wore. This, however, is denied by Schmitt (*Sprachverbesserung,* CLII, 972), who thinks the word comes from a corruption of bottle. For an interesting extension of its use, see below, page 95.—D.W.

surrounding countryside. I had reported high school events for it, and I knew that George Winfield was no fool. Elsie's father was one of Winfield's buddies, and may have had a small interest in the paper. Winfield was nearly sixty then, and had been talking for a long time about bringing in a new man. As it was, he and Deak Carpenter got out the whole paper, with the aid of two or three score of country correspondents, one press service, and considerable syndicated boilerplate.[1]

When Elsie had succeeded in convincing her father, and her father had succeeded, to the surprise of all of us, in convincing Winfield, I took on the job of convincing Everett. I have never worked harder over a letter, for I wanted to let him know what I was feeling without making him angry. I couldn't tell him there was a great career before him, but I did allude to Ed Howe, who had been one of his heroes, and I mentioned all the other smalltown editors I could think of. Mostly, however, I talked about the human interest of the work and the opportunities he would have to write.

In spite of my care, I hurt his feelings, and he wrote back a twelve-page, single-spaced letter, bitterly saying that he knew as well as I did that he was a failure, but ending by accepting the job. I think he knew he had to get out of New York, and I imagine he expected to stay about three months in Braxton.

It didn't take long for both Everett and me to realize that we were disappointed in each other. He can never have felt about my talents as I felt about his, but he had expected more

[1] See Leon Bayle, *The Vanishing Newspaper* (New York, 1956), for a nearly contemporary account of the state of journalism.

of me than the routine of a bank and Braxton domesticity. Yet our mutual disillusionment brought us closer together in a way, and in time we were almost as dependent on each other as we had been in the army. We did not talk as wildly as we had done a few years before, for both of us had changed, I in the direction of conformity, Everett in the direction of cynicism, but we were still interested in each other's ideas, and there was a solid bond of understanding between us. As Everett gave up the pretense of literary ambitions and accepted his role as smalltown journalist, he found it easy to mingle with all kinds of men, and he became a popular figure in the town, but he spoke his mind to me and to me alone.

Elsie did not come to like Everett any better as time went on, but she grew tolerant of him, and he spent some time at our house. When, however, to our complete amazement and consternation, he married her closest friend, the whole relationship changed. Everett and I remained friends, and so did Carlotta and Elsie, but it was impossible for the four of us to be together without tears on Elsie's part, profanity on Everett's, hot temper on Carlotta's, or sullenness on mine.

It was then that he and I formed the habit of spending Thursday evenings at Riley's Tavern. Because Braxton had been dry for many years, prohibition made little difference to most of its citizens. The same bootleggers continued to function, and Riley continued to serve illegal beer in his back room. We usually took the table in the alcove, and there we could talk and drink at our leisure and with some privacy.

Riley's was mildly unrespectable, and the town's best people, if they drank at all, as mostly they didn't, drank in each other's homes. The back room was filled with factory hands and the gayer young men of the town. I knew most of the people there, and Everett knew them all, for that was his job. Soon after we started going there, Carl Tagus, whom I had always thought of as one of the sports, began to sit with us every now and then and join in the conversation. Later Clement Stevens, who was being marched along willy-nilly in his father's footsteps as the town's leading lawyer, got wind of our gathering and attached himself to it. Soon there were six of us, and we began to refer to ourselves as the Tavern Club, though I understand that among the shoe operatives we were known as the Windbags.

Everett, of course, was the leading spirit. Though so much of the old fire had gone out of him, he could still talk, and his talk could still move men of the right kind to controversy and speculation. In this period he was, naturally enough, a disciple of H. L. Mencken, and he collected from the papers in the office many an item for the Americana column in the *Mercury*. He constantly adduced from his own experience further evidence of the imbecility of the booboisie,[1] and what he said about the leading citizens of Braxton was as amusing as it was unfair. He was at his best, however, or so it seemed to me, when he forgot his cynicism and launched into some reckless flight of speculation. Then he could start us all talking, and I still believe that sometimes the talk was good.

Of course people in Braxton knew something of our sessions, and there was one occasion when Mr. Harrington called

---

[1] The word is formed, obviously, from "boob" (a stupid fellow) plus "bourgeoisie," and was coined by H. L. Mencken to express his opinion of his less sophisticated contemporaries. See his *The American Language* (New York, 1937), p. 560. Mr. Mencken was a well-known humorist of the period.—D.W.

I GO TO SLEEP

me into his office and lectured me on bad company, quoting the Bible on the subject of mockers and scoffers. I think I convinced him that we were harmless, and indeed we were, as the town, so far as it took any interest in us at all, really knew. And I, the polite, shy teller at the bank, was the most harmless of all.

We had been meeting in this way for more than a year when, one Thursday night, Dr. Carr appeared in the doorway. I do not yet know how he happened to hear of us or quite why he chose to join us. He was, as I have said, Braxton's only famous man. His father, once the owner of the shoe factory, had sent him to Exeter, to Harvard, to Johns Hopkins, to Germany and Austria. Then stories reached Braxton that the young man was a brilliant surgeon. A few years later, while I was still in grammar school, he suddenly moved into the family mansion on the edge of town. Braxton was wide-eyed. He was a failure, some said, and was coming home to practice. He had made a mistake and killed an illustrious patient, said others, supplying names of various famous men who had recently died. He had been insulted, according to a third story, by the head of the medical school in which he gave a course.[1] So the stories went.

There was little enough for gossip to feed on, for Dr. Carr completely separated himself from the life of the town. Often

[1] This is the most nearly accurate of the three versions. The full story of Dr. Carr's fight for academic freedom at the University of Franklin was not known until recently. It is ably presented in an article by J. C. Wingfield in the *Annals of the Northeast District Historical Society* for March, 2040. Many discussions of his contributions to medical knowledge have appeared in the *Journal of the Cooperative Medical Association* and elsewhere. It is understood that a biography is now in preparation.—D.W.

he was away, sometimes for only a few days, sometimes for six months. And when he was at home, he was only seen working in the garden or walking along some country road. He had a housekeeper, a man-of-all-work who drove his car for him, and at times a young man who appeared to be a sort of research assistant. All three members of the staff were subjected to frequent inquisitions, but all were discreet. No one in Braxton had the least idea what the doctor was doing until stories of his cancer research began to appear in the papers.

And there he stood in our doorway, diffident, a shabby gray hat in his hand, a bashful smile on his thin, sallow face. "May I join you gentlemen in a glass of beer?" he asked.

Everett jumped up. "Charmed," he said. "My name is Wilson, Everett Wilson, reporter on the *Voice*." And then he went round the table introducing us and called to Jimmy for another glass of beer.

Dr. Carr sat down rather tentatively and said, "I'm afraid I'm interrupting you. Won't you go on?"

Clement Stevens had, as it happened, been commenting in a most unfriendly spirit on the medical profession. We were all embarrassed, and there was a stupid silence until Everett saved us. "We were discussing the relationship between pure and applied science," he said.

"What do you mean by pure science?" Dr. Carr asked in a voice that was full of challenge. He didn't wait for an answer, but went on, drawing upon the whole history of civilization to support his argument. I can't remember all that he said, and it doesn't matter now. For thirty minutes he talked as I had never heard anyone talk. Then he fell silent, making only the most laconic answers to our questions. Perhaps an hour later he left, rapping out his pipe, paying for his beer, and crushing the battered hat on his head. Before he went, he bowed formally, saying, "Thank you. May I come again? Good night."

This is how he always behaved, appearing suddenly, edging to a chair, ordering his beer. After a time we sufficiently recovered from our awe to be able to continue whatever discussion we happened to be engaged in. Sometimes he would remain silent all evening, but more often there would be some point at which his interest would be roused. Then he would talk himself out, finally lapsing into silence. I have never known a man who was less capable of taking part in a conversation nor one who could talk so brilliantly when he had the floor to himself. Even Everett granted his supremacy and accepted a place in the background when he was there.

Of course we were all flattered by these visitations, but more important was the sense they gave us of participation in a larger world of ideas. I think we came to realize that all of us, including Everett, had simply been smalltown rebels. I know for myself that, even when Dr. Carr was not there, I wanted the conversation to be on a level of which I would not be ashamed in his presence. Even in my routine at the bank I acquired a new kind of self-respect.

Outwardly my life went on as before. Mr. Harrington had twice raised my salary, and Elsie and I bought a car, in which we explored the neighborhood. Our social life grew a little gayer, with more dances at the country club, and more drinks and more wearing of dress clothes. Occasionally a group of us drove the one hundred and fifty miles to Boston, went to a show, and were back in time to doze a little before breakfast and the job. Two or three times, when a holiday came on a weekend, we went to New York, spending more than we could afford on hotels and theatres and speakeasies. There were even members of our little set who had spent vacations in Bermuda, though that was an extravagance to which Elsie and I never aspired.

In 1928 politics was the chief subject of conversation of the Tavern Club. For my own part, I voted for Herbert Hoover. Perhaps I was motivated by some remnant of anti-Catholic prejudice, very deep in our town, where the Irish and the French Canadians were the people who were different from us; but I thought it was because I respected Mr. Hoover's talents as an engineer, because I found embodied in him the scientific mind for which I had acquired so much admiration. Everett, as one might have supposed, was for Smith, and so, in the privacy of our back room, was Clement Stevens. Carl Tagus amazed us all by coming out for Norman Thomas, chiefly, I suspected, because he hated Hoover's fat jowls and yet could not bring himself to vote for a Catholic. Arthur Burdick and Bob Winship argued at one time or another on all sides, but I imagine they voted Republican.[1] Dr. Carr was seldom with us during these political discussions, and when

[1] Although I realize that the election of 1928 is adequately discussed in history courses that everyone has taken and in a number of widely read books, I cannot resist the temptation to call the reader's attention to an excellent but somewhat neglected monograph, *Psychological Implications of the Regional Distribution of Democratic Votes in the 1928 Election*, by Eleanor Tagus, a descendant, as it happens, of the Carl Tagus referred to above. This was published in 2028 by the Continental Institute for Psycho-Historical Research.—D.W.

he came he said little. We were irked by his indifference but confirmed in our sense of his superiority.

The winter of 1928-29 was the gayest Braxton was to know for a long time, and that summer Elsie and I varied our routine and spent a luxurious month on an island off the coast. I have always been glad that we did.

Being in the bank, I was immediately conscious of the effects of the Wall Street panic. I argued with the best of them that it was a temporary phenomenon, and that stocks would soon soar again, but I could not fool myself. Fortunately my innate timidity had kept me out of the market. Long years of rigorous economies had made me unwilling to risk our meager savings. But I knew that most of our friends were not so lucky. I knew how many of them had pledged everything they owned to cover their losses. I was not surprised when the principal of the high school committed suicide or when a deacon of the church went to jail.

Our club members suffered with the rest. Everett, who had always scorned the stock market as a booby trap, had weakened in September, buying stocks at the very peak. He was cleaned out in a few days. Carl Tagus, having apparently acquired a small fortune by buying on margins over a period of years, was so hard hit that he fell ill and ceased coming to our meetings. The others took losses they could afford but bitterly resented. They all praised my caution, which they had hitherto derided, and, knowing that Elsie's father had remained conservative in spite of considerable pressure, I felt secure.

It was not until almost two years after the crash that Braxton as a whole began to feel the depression. The wages of the

Blaine and Kittery Streets in Braxton

shoe workers had twice been cut, but work remained fairly steady until the summer of 1931. Then the shop was completely closed for three months, and it re-opened on a part-time basis.

I had never realized what can happen to a town that depends on one industry. Some of our friends had managerial or clerical positions, and they had had their salaries cut not twice but four or five times. Every grocer and druggist, every doctor and lawyer suffered when the factory was closed. One movie house was shut, and the other did badly. Even the ministers had their incomes reduced. Mr. Harrington began to show his age, and my salary was back to what it had been when I first entered the cage in 1919.

With the factory paychecks averaging eight or ten dollars a week, there was not a working-class family in Braxton that could hope to save money, and when the factory again closed in the fall of 1932, the problem of relief was staggering. There was something a little panicky in the Community Chest drive that autumn, and I must say that most of us gave all we could afford. For across the tracks there was actual starvation.

I GO TO SLEEP

Elsie was doing volunteer relief work now, and she would come home at night exhausted by hours spent in heatless company houses, trying to take a professional tone with mothers whose babies were obviously dying of malnutrition. In a larger community people like us might have been able to overlook the consequences of the depression; in Braxton they stared us in the face.

The Tavern Club continued to meet, but it had changed. Carl Tagus no longer came, and Bob Winship had left town. On the other hand, two young business men had joined us, and the new Methodist minister, defying public opinion, took a glass of ginger ale with us every Thursday evening. Our talk was now political and economic. Everett had rediscovered his Socialism, and in the privacy of our sessions he cited Marx rather than Mencken. Clem Stevens had become an ardent technocrat. Even I had learned to jeer at Hoover. All of us supported Roosevelt, and Braxton went Democratic in November, for the first time since the Civil War.

Dr. Carr continued to drop in, and, as before, took part in conversations when they interested him, and otherwise was silent. He and Reverend Miller struck up a surprising friendship, and the robust young minister, with his booming evangelistic voice, could usually start our guest talking. Reverend Miller was probably the most radical of us all, more radical than Everett with his revolutionary formulas or Clem with his startling figures and charts. He genuinely believed that men could establish a heaven on earth if they would attack social problems in the spirit of Jesus. I must say that he made that spirit a much more explosive thing than it had ever seemed when I heard about it from Mr. Harrington's pew in the First Congregational Church.

Dr. Carr agreed with him about the heaven on earth, but it was the spirit of Charles Darwin he urged upon us. I don't mean that he believed the scientists in their laboratories would bring utopia. On the contrary, he used to laugh at Stevens' faith in a revolution by technologists. He used to say that the people would have to liberate the scientists and then the scientists would liberate the people. But he always shook his head when Everett mentioned Marx and Lenin.

I liked Reverend Miller's passion. I felt that something must be done at once, and while the others speculated, I pinned my faith on Roosevelt. There were bad moments during the bank holidays, but we knew that the Braxton National was solid, and the people believed us. Then came the NRA. What saved Braxton, however, was federal relief, first the FERA and then the WPA.

That is a long story, and one that I know well, for Elsie worked for a time in the office of the administrator of the FERA and subsequently had charge of women's work for the WPA. She had once thought of being a social worker and had taken some courses in college, but more important were her highly systematic mind and her great tact with people.

Slowly Braxton recovered. Stores and movies began to do something like normal business, and doctors were able to collect some of their bills. In 1935 the shoe factory began to operate on a full-time basis, though still with low wages and frequent layoffs. The business men of the town grew cocky once more, and talked about "that man." I remember a dinner at Mr. Harrington's, at which Delbert Adams, manager of the shoe factory, told all the vilest stories about Mr. and Mrs. Roosevelt. I sat there actually shaking with indignation, but it was Elsie who spoke up, and spoke very well too. "I'm afraid," Mr. Adams said to Mr. Harrington in his most patronizing manner "that your daughter is a bit of a Socialist."

It was in the spring of 1937 that the CIO made its appearance in Braxton. Several times in the past the AFofL had tried to organize the factory, and certain of the skilled workers were members, but on the whole the union movement had made little impression on the town. That March Everett brought a guest to one of our meetings, a young man named Schwartz. He was dressed like a worker, but he turned out to be a graduate of Yale, and he was exceedingly well informed on labor problems and the condition of the shoe industry. I suspected, even before Everett told me, that he was an organizer for the United Shoe Workers.

Schwartz did his work well, and it was not long before the town was full of talk about the CIO. Almost immediately an organizer appeared from the AFofL, and it was apparent from the outset that the management was giving him every opportunity to enroll the men. Nevertheless, when the NLRB election was held, the CIO had a good majority.

In the negotiations that followed, the management very skillfully gave the impression that the closed shop was the only issue, though actually the company rejected the most reasonable proposals for an increase in wages. Negotiations dragged on until it was dangerously near the slack season, when the company could easily afford to close down for a few weeks. Schwartz understood the danger, and so did the workers. They waited as long as they could afford to, and then struck.

THE FIRST TO AWAKEN

It was Braxton's first strike. At the outset probably ninety percent of the town was on the side of the strikers. We had never wasted any love on the out-of-town corporation that had taken over the factory, and most of us knew from experience what the workers' wages meant to us in terms of our own economic well-being. And, if I may say so, a lot of us were fair-minded enough to see the essential justice of the strikers' cause.

That was before Major Willis came to Braxton. I understand that the major's record was revealed by the La Follette committee, but I have never read the report. All I know is that he was a handsomely dressed, exceedingly plausible gentleman, who could pray with Reverend Billings of the Calvary Baptist Church, or drink with our own Mr. Cross, or play poker with George Winfield, the now aged but still energetic editor of the *Voice*. It took him just two weeks to set up the Braxton Citizens' Prosperity and Peace Committee.

I must say to Mr. Harrington's credit that he was not one of the first to succumb to the major, but he could not resist Mr. Cross, who was after all the president of the bank, even though he had always been a good deal of a figurehead. Harrington was one of the forty-two signers of Major Willis' ringing appeal to the citizenry of Braxton. The people of Braxton, it said, were warm friends of labor, and none doubted the right of workers to form unions of their own choosing, but no well-wisher of the town could permit the destruction of its peace and prosperity by outside agitators under orders from Moscow, nor was it thinkable that the solid workingmen of the town, who asked only for a chance to return to their jobs, should be denied this fundamental

I GO TO SLEEP

American right. The appeal was promptly followed by a mass meeting in the Baptist Church, at which Major Willis, Mr. Cross, Mr. Adams, and others spoke, with all the solid men of the town on the platform or in the audience.

Elsie and I were there, gripping each other's hands in anger and fear. How well I could explain the presence of nine out of ten of these solid citizens. Here were a group of well-to-do owners of real estate, terrified at the threat of the factory's moving.[1] Here were storekeepers, their properties heavily mortgaged to the bank. Here were the lawyers whose livelihood the corporation could destroy, either directly or through the Braxton National or through the politicians. As for the politicians themselves, two out of three selectmen had always been at the company's beck and call, and the chief of police was a former company employee—still, it was said, drawing his salary.

I cannot believe that it all happened: the attempt to open the factory, the calling of the National Guard, the vigilante raid on union headquarters, the tarring and feathering of young Schwartz. The Tavern Club ceased to meet, for we were ashamed, I think, to look each other in the face. Reverend Miller was the only one to stick to his guns, speaking against the Citizens' Committee from his pulpit—which he lost soon thereafter—and organizing a soup kitchen for the strikers' children. Everett wrote some of the foulest editorials in the *Voice*. Clement Stevens signed the manifesto. Carl Tagus,

---

[1] I have subsequently learned that the factory was organized in the spring of 1940, and none of the threatened evils occurred. On the contrary, the town was more prosperous than it had been for years.—G.S. (The prosperity was, of course, partly due to war orders.—D.W.)

who had got a job with the company, was said to have taken part in the raid.

I gave a little money to the strikers and kept my mouth shut. With Elsie to encourage me, I might have spoken out and lost my job, but Elsie fell ill at the beginning of the strike. She had become more and more forthright, and I had become prouder and prouder of her. When his associates turned so bitterly against Roosevelt, her father had objected to her working for the WPA, but she had continued so long as the job needed to be done. After the funds were cut, she organized a volunteer women's project of her own. It proved of great help to the strikers' wives, but by then it was in other hands than Elsie's. Perhaps because she had spent all her strength, what seemed an ordinary enough cold developed rapidly into pneumonia, and through most of the bitter weeks of the strike she was fighting her own losing struggle.

The Center of Braxton

I GO TO SLEEP

Elsie's death and the defeat of the strike were never quite separate in my mind, and together they explain almost everything that has to be explained. Whatever happened after that merely intensified the mood they had created. A year later, for example, when Coughlinites smashed the windows of Joel Frank's store, I felt little but a sense of complete hopelessness. I resented the indecency of anti-Semitism—as well as its absurdity in a town like ours where there were not a dozen Jews. I saw also the sinister implications of Coughlinism as it spread among the workers and threatened their precarious unity. But I could not be shocked more than I had already been.

Even the war did not move me as once it would have. The events of the summer of 1939 brought the members of the Tavern Club together again for the first time since the strike. Everett, on whom I had once more come to depend, admitted frankly that he was, as he put it, a son of a bitch. Stevens made the same admission in words more appropriate to his profession. We three, who confessed our ignominy, formed a kind of nucleus, and gradually three or four others joined us. There were innumerable theories about the Soviet-German pact, the conduct of the war, the aims of the belligerents, and the probable role of the United States. Personally I felt little more than a deadened hatred of the whole business, but I was willing to listen to the speculations of the others.

One night early in October Dr. Carr made an appearance as abrupt as his first arrival. Every now and then in the preceding two years he and I had met, by accident it seemed, and had a drink together. Without referring to my loss, he had offered his companionship, no less welcome to me because we usually sat in silence.

Now he talked as he had on earlier occasions. His theme was the philosophy of history. He argued, as nearly as I can recall, that progress came, but came always in the most difficult way. Scientific development, he maintained, had foreshadowed a revolution by the end of the nineteenth century. By the beginning of the twentieth the revolution was inevitable. Yet here we were, close to 1940, and men were still trying to avoid the consequences of their own ingenuity. "I sometimes wonder," he said, "what further stupidities they can devise to thwart their own intelligence and will."

"Well," said Stevens cheerfully, "it makes an exciting period to live in."

"Not for me," I insisted.

"Come, come. You wouldn't miss it for anything."

"Wouldn't I, though! Probably Dr. Carr is right; progress is made in spite of all our blunders; but I'm good and sick of the blundering. I wish I could go to sleep tonight and not wake up for a hundred years."

"I wonder," said Dr. Carr reflectively, as if it were somehow more than a theoretical question. Then he changed the subject.

He met with us often during the next four or five months, and more than once the same theme was introduced. Always I maintained that I would be perfectly happy if I could sleep through what Stevens called the period of transition and wake up on the other side. And whenever I said this, Carr looked at me with such speculative curiosity in his eyes that I was half prepared for his proposal when at last he made it.

He walked to my room with me that blustery March night,

I GO TO SLEEP

and sat on my bed, calmly telling me that he could put me to sleep for a century. I was as calm as he. "This is a kind of by-product of my major line of research," he explained, "but I confess that it has fascinated me for twenty years.[1] Of course, it has long been possible to suspend even fairly complicated forms of life for a matter of three or four days, and in a sense there have been only mechanical problems in the way of extending the period indefinitely. Practically, however, the difficulties have seemed insuperable. It was in trying to develop some economical mechanisms for my own research that I first came on the clue. I went ahead and experimented, and the results have been good. Three months ago a rabbit awakened from a ten years' sleep. Fairly conclusive tests show that he is in better condition than he was when the experiment began. With human beings I have been able to experiment only over shorter periods of time. But if you understood the method, you would know that, if it works for a week, as it does, else I would not be here at this moment, it could work for a century."

He smiled. "Why a century? Well, it's your own figure, my boy, and I suppose we all feel the old magic of numbers. The only important thing is that, if my historical analysis is anywhere near sound, it's long enough. You'll wake up in a new

[1] The reader must realize that Swain did not have sufficient scientific knowledge to understand Carr's methods. The classic treatment of the subject is Mordecai Tennyson's *The Chemistry of Life and Death* (Los Angeles, 2012), but Dr. Tennyson wrote before Carr's researches were known. These involve no fundamental change of theory but do show an amazing anticipation of later experimention. The best discussion of them is Lasswell's "W. R. Carr and Cryogenic Anabiosis," in *Journal of the Cooperative Medical Association*, LXXVI, 942.—D.W.

world. If, that is, you wake up at all. I have the greatest confidence in my method, but I guarantee nothing. Even if it is perfect, an accidental dislocation of the mechanism would be fatal. An air raid on Braxton, say, and a lucky hit—poof. It's a chance I could advise only a desperate man to take. Don't say anything now. Sleep on it, and come to my house tomorrow morning."

The housekeeper let me in, and showed me to the office with all its old-fashioned furniture. The doctor laid down his pen and shook my hand. He argued a little, but when he saw that my mind was made up, he led me into a small white room. There was a single bed in the corner, tanks such as I had seen in my dentist's office, and two straightbacked chairs. "This," he said, "is where the anesthetic will be administered." He opened another door, and we stood in his laboratory. I suppose I had expected the kind of equipment one sees in a movie laboratory, for I was disappointed by the simple bench with its microscopes, test tubes, and bunsen burners. In a moment, however, I was staring at a black box, about eight feet long and three feet wide and raised at one end.

Dr. Carr smiled. "That's it," he said, "and you might remember, a hundred years from today, that it cost a pretty penny." He walked over and flung open the lower part, which was exactly like the inside of a coffin. He pointed to a small lever, just where my right hand would come. "If you are inside the box when you wake up, pull that. Then lie still until the cover opens. After that it's up to you."

He went on, "There's just one more thing that I have to show you." He led the way down a long flight of stairs and into a tunnel cut in solid rock. He swung open a heavy steel door and showed me a bleak tomb, large enough for a dozen coffins such as mine. "The door," he said, "can be opened from the outside only by someone who knows the combination, but from the inside it can be opened like any other door. It is my intention to leave a communication so that the men of a century hence will be on hand with a welcoming committee. But if something goes wrong, you can make your way into the tunnel, and here is a shaft that leads to the surface. There will be tools with which you can dig your way through any accumulation of debris." He shook his head apologetically. "I don't really believe Wilson when he says civilization will be destroyed within the next century, but we might as well be prepared for whatever happens."

His quiet, almost pedantic manner would have soothed harassed nerves, but I needed no such sedative. What I felt was the simple longing one has to go to bed after an exhausting day. And I was very grateful to Dr. Carr. I doubt if I could have committed suicide, but for many months I had understood why men did. What he offered me had all the advantages of suicide, with the blessed possibility of another chance.

Back in the little room with the white walls and the simple bed, I undressed and put on a hospital nightgown. Dr. Carr returned with a surgeon's tunic and cap, and framed in the glistening white his taut face seemed almost saintly. He brought with him a man he introduced as his assistant, Dr. Bedlow—"the only other person who knows, and presumably the only other person now alive who ever will know." I had seen Dr. Bedlow once or twice on the street, and thought of him as the ugliest man I had ever looked on, with the almost classic ugliness of Abraham Lincoln.

I stretched out on the bed, and Dr. Bedlow began to adjust the valves of the tanks. Dr. Carr casually felt my pulse. "Good boy," he said. He adjusted the mouthpiece. "Best of luck!"

I breathed deeply, and almost at once my body, light as a feather, was soaring away. "When you wake up," I told myself, "it will be the year 2040."

II
I WAKE UP

HALF-DREAMING, half-remembering, I lay there in the comfort that comes between sleep and waking after a good night's rest. Suddenly I felt with my right hand for the lever, and it was not there. I opened my eyes.

Panic smote me as I looked about the little room with its white walls and its two white chairs. Certainly this was the room in which Dr. Carr and his assistant had anesthetized me, and I had slept but a few hours. The thought called up a picture of Bedlow's badly matched features as he had bent over me tube in hand. I looked at the nurse standing by my bed, as pink-cheeked and pretty a girl as had ever graced a white uniform in a *Saturday Evening Post* illustration, and I burst out laughing.

She laughed back. "It is the twenty-first century, isn't it?" I exclaimed.

Still laughing she said, "It is March 12, 2040.[1] How does it feel to sleep a hundred years?"

[1] Actually I went to sleep on March 8, 1940. The discrepancy in dates is due to the adoption of the thirteen-months calendar.—G.S.

"It feels very good. Can I get up?"

"Oh, yes. Why not? Breakfast is ready."

"Am I in Braxton?"

"Yes, indeed."

"Well," I thought to myself, "you never came from around here." There was only the faintest trace of New England in her speech, though I should have been hard put to say what section she did belong to.

I threw back the cover and was surprised to find myself in pajamas of a color and fabric wholly new to me. I sat on the bed a moment, stretching and smiling. "Do you want to wash?" she asked, and opened a door into a bathroom. When I came back, breakfast was waiting—orange juice and cereal and toast and eggs.

I could do nothing but smile as I began to eat. I knew it was silly, but I felt so exceedingly well. She watched me with pleased sympathy, neither officious nor ingratiating. "Is everything all right?" she inquired, as I took a second piece of toast.

"Delicious."

"We were a little worried about the cereal. There were so many kinds of breakfast food in your day. Dr. Peabody, the dietician, went through some of the magazines, and he said it was impossible to know what kind you would want. In fact, he couldn't even imagine what some of them were like from the advertisements. We have only four or five kinds today."

For a moment I was puzzled, and then I smiled. "We had only four or five kinds then, I guess, but they were put up in a lot of different boxes by a lot of different companies. This tastes fine to me."

I WAKE UP

I finished my egg, and fumbled automatically in the pocket of my pajama jacket. Then I looked. Yes, there were cigarettes in a box on the tray. I am not a great smoker, but I do like a cigarette with my coffee in the morning. The nurse was smiling again. "There are various types," she said.

I looked in the box and saw that the cigarettes were numbered. I took one at random—it happened to be number 3—and lit it. It was good, though later I learned to prefer type 2.

As I started to get up, the nurse glanced at her watch. "Do you mind sitting there just two or three minutes longer?"

"I don't know why I wanted to do anything else." Strange as it appears to me now, I had no impulse to ask questions. I felt little curiosity and almost no self-consciousness. I remember one morning during the war, the morning after my first night on leave. I had slept twelve hours, and had got up to the kind of Sunday breakfast that, as my mother knew, I liked best. Then as now I felt physical well-being as a kind of positive force that was throbbing through me.

Just as I finished my cigarette, the door opened and two men came in, one dressed in white, the other in light brown with a crimson scarf at his throat. "Dr. Rosenthal," said the nurse, "and David Wilson."

Both of them shook hands with me. "Everything went splendidly," the doctor said, "splendidly. We'll have the full reports ready very shortly. I take it you feel well."

"I've never felt better in my life," I said, smiling at the thoughts the words roused in my mind.

"Would you like to dress and step outside?" Wilson asked.

"Good idea," said the doctor. "Then, I imagine, you'd better leave." He turned to me. "The resident research staff of the Cooperative Medical Association wants to examine you. They can't, of course, do anything we can't do here, and I shall be surprised if they add to our findings. But you understand—the oldest and most honored of our medical societies—we must defer. And I suppose you won't mind seeing New York." He spoke with the same clear, sharp enunciation as the nurse.

Wilson led me to a room where suits of half a dozen different colors were laid out. "Take your choice," he said, "and if there's nothing here you like, we'll see what we can do."

For the first time since my awakening I was a little ill at ease. This was the unknown, opening suddenly before me. These were the garments in which it clad itself. Till now I had been George Swain, a New Englander of the twentieth century. What would I become when I had put on this clothing?

I fumbled with the suits, my hand touching a deep chestnut, a sparkling gray, a rich crimson. Then I looked up and caught my reflection in the long mirror. There I was, looking all of my forty-three years, a little bald, a little pot-bellied, more than a little stooped. The lines still puckered on my forehead. The eyes—my best feature, Elsie had always said—were still brown and sober and rather timid. The mouth might have been called sensitive, but the chin could never have been called strong. I looked like a teller in the Braxton National Bank. Who was I to be beginning this adventure in the twenty-first century?

Then the sense of health came back over me, and I grinned at the not very impressive figure in the mirror. I chose the least conspicuous of the suits—gray heather I think it could be called—not only because it was the most sedate but also because it reminded me of a suit of mine Elsie had liked. There was a simple undergarment, over which I drew trousers. Imitating Wilson, I chose a blue scarf and knotted it around my neck. The design and texture of the socks puzzled me, but I put them on, and fastened the sandal-like shoes. The jacket felt and fitted like a sweater, but the lines were as neat as those of a well-cut suit-coat. There were several caps, and I picked up a blue beret that matched my scarf. On the whole I rather fancied what I saw in the glass, but I felt as if I were going to a masquerade.

As Wilson led me down the corridor, I realized what of course I should have known all the time, that I was in a hospital. But there were no hospital smells, nor sights, nor sounds. The corridor was brightly decorated, and the rooms, I noticed, were only on one side—where, I suppose, they would get the maximum of sunshine.

We took an elevator to the roof, and Wilson said nothing as I gazed about me. I could not convince myself that the city I saw before me was Braxton, and it took a few minutes' study of the contours of the countryside, the hills Elsie and I had so often tramped, to tell me where I was. At last I got it. This was Cobb's Hill, the sightliest place in the whole region. It had been a private estate in my day, and the big old house, occupied by the Cobbs only two or three months a year, had been a landmark. The grounds had been posted against trespassers, but every once in a while Elsie, bolder than I, had led me up here. Here we could turn our backs on the town and look across the lovely rows of hills to the mountains beyond.

Now I turned from the mountains to look at the town. Yes,

there was the river, as clear and blue in the heart of Braxton as I had ever seen it far up in the country. I looked for the smudgy red of the factory, for the rows of freight cars in the yards, for the long tenement blocks beside the tracks. They were all gone. The eye fell instead on a group of buildings along the river, steel and glass shining in the sun. Some of these, David told me, were apartment houses, others factories; at the distance I could not distinguish between them. There was a variety of sizes and shapes, and, with parks and large open spaces all about them, they composed an impressive pattern, strange in my sight but orderly and strong. So often, standing on that very spot, I had turned my back on the squalor and tawdriness of the old Braxton, and now I was gazing upon this spacious design.

Gradually I began to see the rest of the town. In my day one climbed the social ladder as one climbed the hill from the river. A little higher than the company-owned blocks, so dingy and comfortless, were almost equally flimsy but more pretentious two and three story frame houses. Our belt, the zone of the aspiring middle class, had an abundance of single houses, some of them old, but most of them new and close-packed. Above us were the homes of the relatively well-to-do —old Victorian mansions, neat white houses with two-car garages, and an occasional pseudo-villa in stucco.

Now all that was gone. There seemed to be no solid residential area on the hillside, but here and there, along winding roads, in the midst of many trees, were houses in many strange designs. They could be seen on the hills on both sides of the river, stretching all around the town as far as my eye could reach.

I WAKE UP

Until that time I had been too excited, physically at too high a pitch, to ask myself any questions. Now I realized that there had been a question in my mind as I went to sleep and as I woke up. I sighed and turned to Wilson: "It's good." That was what I saw and saw beyond any doubt. Whatever else might be true, the new Braxton was better than the old. Civilization had not declined during my long sleep.

I must have shivered a little, for Wilson said, "March in New England hasn't changed any. Come inside." We went into a kind of penthouse, and there was an old man with a long gray beard, writing at a desk. He took off his glasses when Wilson introduced me, and bowed politely. "Oh, yes," he

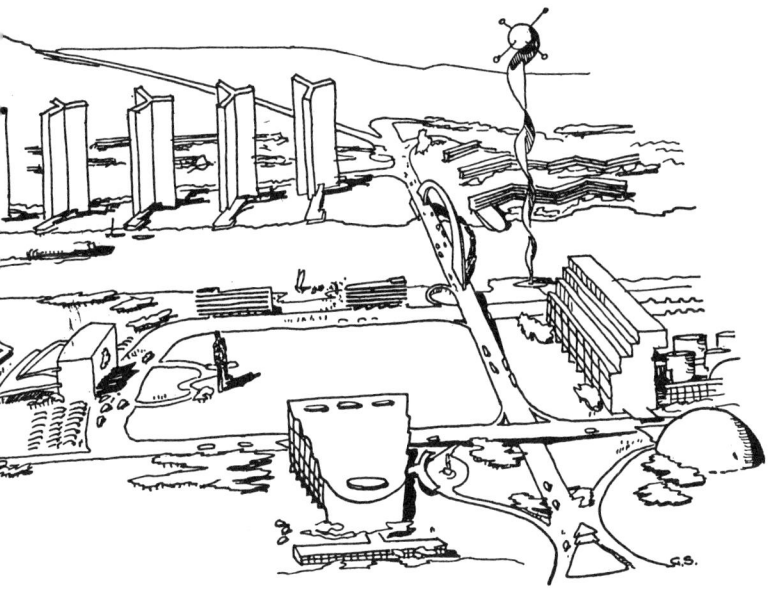

View from the hospital in the new Braxton—auditorium in foreground, assembly plant at right, airport at left, apartments across the river, wartime safety tower at center right.

said. "You and I are almost contemporaries. I am very glad to have the chance to speak to you. Can you tell me whether the young man who was tarred and feathered in 1937 spelled his name S-c-h-w-a-r-t-z or S-h? The newspapers are inconsistent."

"S-c-h, I think."

"Thank you very much."

He put on his glasses and began to write again. Wilson smiled. "Are you warm now?" he asked. And when I told him I was, he showed me how to fasten my socks around the bottoms of my trousers, tighten the cuffs of my jacket and close the collar, and adjust the trouser-top and the jacket-bottom.

"Now," he said, "you'll be as comfortable as if you had on an old-fashioned overcoat." And as we stepped outside I was, though the wind was raw.

"Professor Middlebury," he said, "is ninety-seven, and used to be one of the world's leading authorities on pre-Homeric Greece. A few years ago his heart was affected, and he had to be hospitalized. He is kept very comfortable, and, as you see, remains active. After he had been here a while, he began to write a history of the labor movement in New England. Now he wants to live to finish it, and Dr. Rosenthal says he probably will."

I said, "You don't practice euthanasia, then?"

He hesitated as if reflecting. "No, we don't practice it, though I don't suppose anyone is opposed in theory. You see, there are few diseases we can't cure and no pains we can't deaden. Under such circumstances most people want to live, and that settles it. And even from the point of view of society, how can you say when a man is useless?" He grinned. "Far be

Professor Middlebury at work, aided by service panel over desk which includes television connections with research libraries and archives.

it from me to be a Philistine but I think Dr. Middlebury is doing the most important work of his life right now." [1]

"But isn't this exceptional?"

"Oh, very. Not many persons live into the nineties, and few of those are as vigorous and useful as the professor."

I was staring at Braxton again. Some distance to the south I could catch glimpses of a great highway. Directly below me, on the roads leading to the hospital, were automobiles, shaped rather like polliwogs and largely—or so it seemed to me—made of glass. An airplane was landing between the apartment houses and the factories.

---

[1] It should be understood that Swain's reporting of my remarks—and presumably of the remarks of other persons—is by no means wholly dependable. I cannot be held responsible for certain opinions attributed to me in this book.—D.W. (Quite right. I am merely trying to indicate what I got out of these conversations. However, I must say that my reporting gives a better impression of what D.W. is really like than do the footnotes he has supplied for my text.—G.S.)

The airplane reminded Wilson of his duty. "I'm sorry," he said, "but you can come back. We ought to get the ten o'clock plane for New York."

We went down in the elevator. I had expected Wilson to stop for packing and other preparations, but he led the way straight to a row of cars parked near the door. Looked at closely, the cars were even more extraordinary than I had thought. The front, glass-enclosed, was almost a hemisphere, and behind this was a curious flat tail. There was a large single wheel in front and two small ones in the rear.

Wilson got in one of the cars, and I sat beside him. He moved a lever and at once we were in motion. "Don't worry about the examination," he remarked. "It will amount to no more than the one you've already had. I wouldn't call you a first-rate physical specimen, but there's no doubt that you've come through the long sleep beautifully."

I had been trying to study Braxton as we drove through it, but I was piqued by what he said, partly because of his all too accurate reference to my physique, chiefly by his pulling my leg about the examination. "For heaven's sake," I exclaimed, "what is all this business about my having been examined?"

He smiled at my irritation. "You have been examined, whether you know it or not."

"Before I woke up?"

"Before and since." He paused, as if to make up his mind where to begin. "The trouble with the old-fashioned examination was that the patient, being very conscious of what was happening to him, couldn't behave normally. So doctors have found ways of examining the patient when he doesn't know what's happening."

"But what kind of examination?"

"Well, in your case, at least three kinds. In the first place, the room in which you woke up is a kind of laboratory in itself. That is, it is equipped with apparatus that tells exactly what you do with the air you take into your lungs. The nurse, of course, has already been measured, and there is an adjustment made for her."

"That's why you and Dr. Rosenthal didn't come into the room right off?"

He nodded. We were in the center of town now. Children were playing in the park, and a few men and women were working in the shrubbery. Through the transparent sides of a factory I caught glimpses of machinery and groups of people. Wilson continued, "In the second place, your excretions have been analyzed. Finally, moving pictures were taken of your digestive processes while you ate your breakfast."

He drew up at the flying field. "Please forgive me for lecturing. I was a teacher once, and we teachers still have bad habits."

As we boarded the plane, I asked, "What happens to your car."

"Oh, it will be used." We found seats. Suddenly he turned to me. "I'm sorry. I keep falling down on my job. I'm a psychologist, and I ought to know that everything you say has to be translated. When you spoke of 'my' car, I understood you to mean what a contemporary would have meant—that is, the car I had been riding in. But you were speaking of 'my' car as you would have spoken of 'my' hair or 'my' teeth. In that sense the car isn't mine at all. It is one of the several

THE FIRST TO AWAKEN

thousand maintained by the Braxton Cooperative for the use of its members."

It was just ten o'clock, and a slight vibration showed that the motors were turning, though we could not hear them. There were twelve of us in the plane: a young man and woman and their two children; a couple of middle-aged men in rougher clothing than ours, who were starting a game of checkers; an elderly lady, reading a book; two girls, one wearing slacks and the other a skirt; and a boy of ten or twelve, whose face was pressed against the window between us and the pilot's compartment.

The plane spiraled to what I, who had flown only once before in my life, thought a great height. As it rose, I watched the changing perspective of the town and the surrounding hills, but in a few minutes we were so high that I could see little to interest me. As the plane leveled off, it proceeded so smoothly that I became as indifferent to its progress as my companions.

David sat quietly until he saw that I was ready to listen. "Are you still worried about 'my' car?" he asked. "I want to tell you whatever you want to know."

I sighed, rubbing the back of my head in the gesture that Elsie always said was responsible for my baldness. "There is so much I want to know. Go on, tell me about the car."

He explained that there was no such thing as private ownership of an automobile. "There is," he said, "a system of long-term leases that amounts to ownership—for those, for example, who live in the country. Such cars are marked, and I would no more have taken one of those than you would have stolen a machine in your day. But within the limits of a community such as Braxton most cars are common property. Let us say that, in the course of a day, twenty cars drive up to the hospital and twenty cars leave. Does it matter whether a person leaves in the car in which he arrives? So at the airport: the cars left by departing passengers are used by arriving passengers."

There were a dozen questions I wanted to ask him. Was there, then, no such thing as private property? What happened if, through some mischance, a man badly needed a car and none was available? Suppose a man just plain left a car in some out of the way spot?

The questions all started to pour out, but then I suppressed them. When I went into the army, I had wanted to know everything at once, and as a result I had been hopelessly confused. My first day in the bank I had insisted on being told the whole story, until finally Silas Derek, the veteran teller, had said, "Take it easy, George. Don't try to learn everything before you know anything." It was good advice, particularly, I decided, for the twenty-first century.

"It seems a sensible arrangement," I said stiffly.

David smiled, almost as if he had been following my thoughts. I liked his smile. In fact, I liked his whole appearance. He was an inch or two shorter than I, but much better built, with a full chest and muscular arms and legs. He had thrown back his jacket, and, perhaps because his clothing seemed more like what we had worn for sports than anything else I could think of, I felt as if he had just come from the tennis court or the golf links. His skin was tanned, but ruddy rather than a deep brown. His face was singularly open and boyish, with a suggestion of diffidence, but his bearing was self-confident.

"I could give you a lecture on the whole system of production and distribution," he said, "but I honestly doubt if you'd take much of it in right now. If I were you, I'd meet problems as I came to them. But have it your own way."

"I'll wait."

"All right. Just remember that, wherever you find a car without a blue seal, you can use it."

The boy had got bored watching the pilot and came back to sit opposite us. "I know who you are," he said abruptly; "you're the man who's slept a hundred years." I was nonplussed. I suppose I had figured that, if people knew who I was, they would make a big fuss. "Gee," the boy went on, "that Dr. Carr must have been a smart fellow. I'd like to have seen the statues pop." My bewilderment must have been obvious, for he said, "Gee, don't you know about that?"

I turned to David. "Go on," I said with resignation, "tell me about it."

"It's a good story. I guess you haven't had time to wonder why you came to life in a hospital bed instead of in Dr. Carr's cave. As Paul says, Dr. Carr was a smart man. He wanted to be sure that you and the others—"

"The others!"

"Why, yes. Seven others, put to sleep at various intervals before Dr. Carr's death in 1948."

"But why so many?"

"He was playing safe. He wanted at least one to get through. As a matter of fact, now that you're here there is every reason to believe that the others are all right."

"He thought of everything," said the boy solemnly.

"He did, Paul. Three others were buried here in Braxton, two in Arizona, two in Winnipeg. He started here, of course, because he lived here, but then he got worried for fear the whole East might be raided by bombers, and so he found two other places."

"And then he fixed it up so that we'd know about it," Paul interposed.

"That wasn't so easy as you might think. He didn't dare leave any kind of public record, on account of the newspapers,[1] and he had no idea what might happen in a hundred years. He wanted to be prepared for any emergency. Dirk Bragin, the sculptor, was a friend of his, and when he died he bequeathed a Bragin statue to every important museum in the world. He figured that, whatever happened, not all the museums would be destroyed. Some of them were—London, Paris, Berlin, and Leningrad. But the statues in Cleveland, San Francisco, Mexico City, Melbourne, Cape Town, and so forth were safe and just a year ago, on exactly the same day, the heads popped up everywhere."

Paul burst out laughing. "I wish I'd seen them."

"How did he do it?"

"Some invention of his—measured corrosion. The amazing thing is the skill with which Bragin incorporated this device in each statue, so that no expert ever noticed anything strange."

---

[1] Dr. Carr's message characteristically begins, "Lest some ghoulish reporter exhume the bodies I have concealed, killing these men and women and ending our experiment, I have seen fit . . ." etc. It is almost impossible for us to realize the extent to which the newspapers of the early twentieth century invaded the privacy of the citizen. Individualism in our sense of the word did not exist in Swain's time.—D.W.

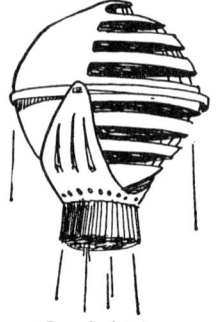

Gymbal Planes

"And they all opened the same day?"

"Well, someone has discovered that there was an explosion in the Madrid museum in the fifties, and it seems pretty clear that it was one of these statues. But at the time there was just a lot of newspaper talk about a radical plot."

"What was Dr. Carr like?" the boy broke in again. "He must have been wonderful."

I realized that to Paul's hero-worshiping mind I was merely someone who had been fortunate enough to know Dr. Carr. "He was the most wonderful man I have ever met," I said.

"Gee, why didn't he put himself to sleep?"

"Perhaps he intended to," David suggested. "He died rather suddenly."

"I doubt it," I said.

Paul shook his head in disgust, and David went on, "You ought to read the directions he left.[1] He told just when it would be safe to remove the case from the underground hiding place and when it could be safely opened. As a matter of fact, you were still in the case at six o'clock this morning, and Dr. Rosenthal followed Carr's directions in every particular."

Paul had drifted away. Now he came running back. "Look," he said, "a gymbal plane."

---

[1] First printed in the Continental Bulletin for March 14, 2039, Dr. Carr's message has since been widely published. A carefully annotated text appears in the *Proceedings* of the Regional Research Council, May, 2040.—D.W.

I WAKE UP

Some distance away a great ball, with what seemed to be a scaffolding dangling from it, was rising higher and higher into the air. When it was almost out of sight, it appeared to pause for a moment and the tail swung up and pointed to the east. Then it shot away westward and immediately vanished.

"Transcontinental," David said. "Three hours and twenty minutes to San Francisco. Rocket propelled in the stratosphere."

I fell silent for a time, thinking. I had deliberately allowed myself to be put to sleep for a hundred years, partly because I had been curious about the future, chiefly because I was not unwilling to escape from a world in which I had personally found little but frustration. Miraculously, I had survived. I was starting a new life, in good health and apparently in pleasant circumstances. I was lonely, but loneliness was not new to me. I made up my mind to learn all that I could, to plunge deeply into this new life, to wrest from it more than the old life had given me.

David was looking out of the window, apparently as absorbed in his thoughts as I was in mine. His tact so far had been unfailing. "Have you been assigned by the state to look after me?" I suddenly asked him.

"The state? That word doesn't mean quite what it used to. But let that go. The state has nothing to do with my being here. I am a psychologist, working in the Braxton cooperative and carrying on a research project of my own. When the first announcements of your awakening were made, I got permission from the council to observe you. That's all."

I must have frowned, for he quickly said, "No, that isn't all, and it's foolish of me to say so. You don't like being the object of psychological research, and I don't blame you, though you must see it's a fascinating problem. But I also have a personal interest: you see, my great-great-grandfather was Everett Wilson."

The strangest shiver went up and down my spine. "Your great-great-grandfather!" I hadn't thought of it quite like that. Everyone I had known was dead, had been dead for scores of years. Their children had died and their grandchildren. This was the measure of the gulf between my past life and that on which I had been embarked for the past three or four hours. I thought of Everett then, of those long harangues at Camp Devens, of his face when our trench was shelled in France, and of the evenings at the Tavern Club.

"Your great-great-grandfather," I said, "was my best friend."

"I know. My grandfather has his letters and scrapbooks.[1] I had known of you long before the statues opened. I know about the Tavern Club. Everett admired you a great deal, more, propably, than you ever realized. He thought you were wasting yourself in Braxton, and what he believed to be your death was to him a tragedy."

"What happened to him?" I asked hesitantly.

"He became editor of the Braxton *Voice* after Mr. Winship retired."

"Winfield," I corrected.

"That's right, Winfield. He was not a happy man, I should say, nor a good editor. But during the rebellion he fought on

[1] At my suggestion, Swain is preparing some of this material for future publication. It usefully supplements the first chapter of this book.—D.W.

the people's side. And he was killed in the siege of Springfield."

With a wrench I changed the subject. "And you're a psychologist? Psychology, I suppose, has made great advances."

At the moment I did not care much whether it had or not, for I was thinking of what Everett had said to me last night—yes, literally, so far as my consciousness was concerned, the very night before. David talked animatedly, but I paid little attention. He quarreled, it seemed, with the dominant schools of psychology—over what I haven't the least idea. Somehow his observations of me were going to clinch an important point.

He talked for five or ten minutes, I suppose, and then became embarrassed. "I'm sorry," he said. "Please don't think of me as a psychologist. Think of me as the relative of a friend. I want you to know that we value friendship—even we psychologists—unless we're damn fools, which some of us are."

I was touched and, not wanting to embarrass him further, asked a question at random: "How did you happen to become a psychologist?"

David smiled and called Paul. "What are you going to be when you grow up, Paul?"

The boy answered without hesitation, "An agricultural engineer."

"How's your physical aptitude rating?"

"A-1. And say, you ought to see our project. We got wonderful cucumbers. We're testing S72 fertilizer, and Mr. Hill says it's a big success."

"How's your arithmetic?"

"Not so good," Paul replied cheerfully.

"You'll get on top of it."

"There's Long Island Sound," the boy shouted, and ran to the window on the opposite side.

"You see: at ten Paul knows what he's going to do."

"Pigeonholed already."

Puzzled and then perhaps a little irritated, he replied evenly, "I don't think so. Paul probably won't be an agricultural engineer. He may turn out to be a plain farmer. That isn't so different as you might think, but it isn't the same thing. Or he might become a biologist or an executive. That will depend on him and on the way the community is shaping up. But one thing is pretty certain: he won't grow up to be a square peg in a round hole, as you would say."

He went on to say something of the way aptitudes were tested. "It's just a matter of finding out what the child wants to do and can do. You know, we can work two ways—we can make the individual fit society or society fit the individual. We try to do both."

This didn't make much sense to me. "I should think it would be a lot easier to change the individual."

"In the short run, it is. If we take a child young enough, we can do almost anything we want to do with him. And fifty years ago there was something that might be called pigeonholing. The country needed certain kinds of workers very badly, and so education was tied up with economic planning."

I frowned.

"It wasn't as bad as it sounds," David assured me. "It would have been horrible, of course, in a system of private property, for then people would simply have been conditioned to be slaves—and to like it. But privileged classes had been done away with."

"Why didn't you go on that way, then?"

"Because the psychiatrists and the technicians and the planners weren't really the bosses. And because the system, good as it was, wasn't good enough. No matter how cleverly they were conditioned, people knew they were being regimented. They had fought for freedom, and they weren't going to put up with anything less."

"Was there a revolution?"

"There didn't have to be. It's a complex story, and one you can't take in just yet. It's all tied up, for instance, with regionalization and the end of the super-city. The reconstruction period was over, and there was no more need for drastic measures. It took time for the controls to break down, and in some areas there was quite a lot of trouble, but that's all past now."

"So you don't try to mold children to fit the grooves any more?"

"All education is a process of shaping, isn't it? But we do try to turn out healthy, happy, well-rounded human beings. We want all the capacities in the child to have a chance, not just one or two. And that means that the responsibility falls on the community as well as the school. We have to have the kind of community that can use what people are able to give. Whatever job he has, Paul's talents won't be wasted."

This meant little enough to me at the time, though I was subsequently to see quite clearly what David was talking about. I was more interested when he went on to tell me about his own career. He had intended to become a protein chemist, and had studied the subject until he was twenty-one. Then he had suddenly left the university to join the Arctic Reclamation Corps. Apparently he was tired of study and wanted a vigorous, adventurous life. And then there was something about a girl—something he muttered with a good deal of embarrassment.

The Arctic, I gathered, was one of the new frontiers, and the Reclamation Corps was largely made up of young men like David who wanted toil and hardship and excitement. There must have been girls there too, though in what capacity I don't know. Anyway, David got married. His wife was an economist, and she took a job with the Pacific Coast regional planning board.

David, meantime, had become excited about the social sciences, for which he had hitherto had a good deal of scorn, and he began to dream of bridging the gap between them and the physical sciences. That was how he turned to psychology, and he spent three years of study in western universities.

"We had two children by then," he explained, "and I had the curious feeling that I wanted them to grow up in New England. There is still a kind of regional patriotism, you see. Nathalie, on the other hand, has roots in no one place, and she didn't care. So I established connections with the regional research board in the Northeast District about two years ago, and when there was a vacancy I became a personnel consultant in Braxton. That's the usual thing, you know—to combine research with a job of some sort. Nathalie had no trouble getting a position with the cooperative planning board.

I WAKE UP

It's not good enough for her; I mean she's capable of handling something much more difficult; but she has her own studies, and it works out all right. For the past year and a—"

"New York!" Paul shouted.

I peered out of the window. We were dropping gently, and in the distance I could see the gleam of metal and glass. Rapidly the city took shape, and I gasped. Braxton had been neat and clean and comfortable, and the bigger buildings were impressive as nothing in the town had been in my day. But this was the future, an imposing island of broad avenues and mighty towers. This was what the bolder imaginations of my day had dreamed of. It was the perfection of the whole that staggered me. There was not one dirty, scrubby little building. From the air it was exactly like a model—a model, indeed, of the metropolis of the future—flawless as, it had seemed to me, only a model could be.

I could see the parks around the island's entire rim and down the very center, and, as we passed just above the towers, I looked into the great courts framed by high buildings. Then we were settling down in what I recognized as Central Park, with other planes all about us. The great bulk of a gymbal plane rose with incredible speed, and flying beside us was what seemed little more than an enormous pair of wings, with a puny skeleton in back.

We landed without a jar—not a man had been disturbed on the checker board and the players were still absorbed in their game. As soon as I was outside, I stared about me. The buildings around the field rose in terrace upon terrace to a height of thirty or forty stories, with here and there a tower soaring to twice or three times that height. Many of the walls

THE FIRST TO AWAKEN

were entirely of glass, but others were made of what seemed to be vari-colored stone—actually, as I learned, some sort of translucent material. Much as I had admired Rockefeller Center and the Empire State, they had always seemed cold and inhuman, but these buildings were warm and animated.

"It's magnificent," I said to David.

"Yes, isn't it?" he answered politely, looking at his watch. "I think, if we're to get to the examination before lunch, we'd better be going."

Planes were landing and leaving all the time. People got out, made their way to low kiosks, and disappeared. David led me to the kiosk nearest us, and down two flights of stairs. We followed an arrow marked "east."

It all seemed simpler than the subways of my day, and I noticed that there were no crowds, no turnstiles, no noise, and no dirt. Instead of the long platform I had expected, we turned into a narrow corridor. The couple just ahead of us sat down in a pair of seats, which immediately moved away. Another pair took its place. Seated in them, we slipped between gently lighted walls for a moment, and then I saw that we had become part of a long line of such seats, stretching as far ahead and behind as I could see. The apparatus was almost noiseless, and I could hear a gentle murmur of conversation. The speed was moderate, and there was no wind.

"Do you want the news?" David asked, and turned a lever. There was a soft voice at my ear. "11.15, Shanghai: Dr. Hung-kang-lo announces that he has finished his survey of tuberculosis in the Yangste Valley. He predicts its complete disappearance by 2056. 11.15, Dublin: A riot has been reported in Cushcamcarragh, County Mayo. 11.15, Baton Rouge: George

I WAKE UP

T. Berman of the Baton Rouge cooperative has established a new continental record for the one hundred yard dash. 11.10, Belgrade: Michael Shuskewitz, head of the Balkan Planning Board from 1995 to 2018, died this morning at the age of eighty-nine. 11.10, Tucson, Southwest District: The New World Rocket Society announced that it had postponed its 375th attempt to send a rocket to the moon. 11.10, New York City: George Swain, who has been in a state of suspended animation for the past one hundred years, arrived here for examination at the Cooperative Medical Association hospital. 11.05, Lobengula: Members of the Matabele tribe met in council today to decide whether to—"

Without my noticing it, our car had detached itself and come to a stop in the station, and the radio had turned itself off.

As we got out and climbed the stairway, David said, "Amusing gadget, isn't it? Better than the old habit of reading newspapers in the subway."

We got into a southbound car, and David switched on the radio again. "11.20, Paris: Members of the Société des Gourmets are enraged this afternoon at the discovery that most of the food served at their annual dinner last night was synthetic. It appears that the delicacies they had imported from all parts of the world were spirited away by students at the Institut Polytechnique and synthetic foods substituted. Until the secret was revealed, the dinner had been praised as the finest in years. 11.15, Shanghai: Dr. Hung-kang-lo—" David turned the switch. "11.05, Lobengula: Members of the Matabele tribe met in council today to decide whether to affiliate with the South African Union for Progress. The

THE FIRST TO AWAKEN

Matabeles have been one of six tribes to maintain their native customs. 11, Portland, Northwest District: Children in the southern cooperative school—"

The radio stopped again. David led the way to an elevator. "You get the idea," he said. "It's a kind of phonograph that records the radio news broadcasts. They run backwards. That is, as you see, the latest news comes first. But you can set it for any time in the past four hours. I call it a gadget[1]—a wonderful word that I learned from reading my great-great-grandfather's papers.

The elevator took us directly to the twelfth floor of the hospital, and David led me to an enclosed sunporch. "I'm afraid we'll have to wait a few minutes," he said. "Do you mind if I make a telephone call? I'll be right back."

To tell the truth, I was glad of the opportunity to be alone for a while. I dropped into an easy chair, and gazed out over a series of terraces, where people were sunning themselves, and over the park, with broad highways stretching through it, to the East River. "Take it easy," I told myself, "take it easy."

I tried to review what I had thus far experienced, but it was useless, and I let my eyes and my mind wander. "Elsie would have liked this," I thought. "She always said there was no reason why a hospital couldn't be as pleasant and run as much for the patients' convenience as a first-class hotel." How she had hated the little dark room, the tasteless food,

---

[1] Mencken, *op. cit,* 211, groups "gadget" with "jigger," "dingus," and "doodad," all words used to describe "novel contraptions." A gadget is a device whose ingenuity exceeds its importance.—D.W. (I should say a gadget was something you got along without all right but found indispensable once you got it.—G.S.)

I WAKE UP

the awful smells, and the harassed nurses in the Braxton Hospital! "I wouldn't mind much being sick here. I wonder if there is anything really wrong with my liver. They could probably fix me up. Maybe they could make my hair grow." I smiled. "And certainly they could do something for my teeth. I'm getting hungry again. Probably I just press a button and a turkey dinner appears on the arm of my chair."

I went on in this silly way, and perhaps was half asleep when David opened the door. "Here's Dr. Reilly," he said.

The doctor, who towered above both David and me, came forward smiling. "There," he said, "the most important part of the examination is over."

I sighed and rubbed the back of my head. David laughed. But if it was the most important part, it was certainly the easiest. Not that I was ever uncomfortable or even very nervous, but for an hour one doctor after another appeared, and one fantastic instrument after another, and my anatomy was thoroughly, if painlessly, explored. "Now," said Dr. Reilly at the end of it, "you're a free man."

"Come on," David called, "let's eat."

III

THE CITY OF THE FUTURE

THERE were no automobiles on the streets. People sauntered across at any point that suited them. Dogs ran here and there, unthreatened except by boys and girls and occasional adults on bicycles.

"No cars," I said to David, "no delivery trucks, no taxis?"

"Nowhere on the island," he replied, "except for the circumferential highways."

We slanted across the roadway and followed the gravel walk under the trees in the center strip. I gathered we were about where Third Avenue had been. The hospital occupied a block, and beyond that was the parkway along the river.

"But these streets," I protested; "they must have been built to take care of thousands of cars."

I watched the people we met. The majority were dressed as we were, but there were women in dresses of various lengths and designs, and once I saw a bearded old gentleman in a flowing cape.

THE CITY OF THE FUTURE

"You're quite right," David answered. "The city was rebuilt in the last quarter of the last century—what we sometimes call the Technological Era. At that time every family in the city either had a car or was bound to get one. Many had two or three. So the engineers got busy. But in spite of all the broad streets and the new bridges and the vehicular tunnels and subterranean parking places and all the rest of it, traffic congestion got worse and worse."

We stood aside as a band of boys in bright colored shirts and shorts, their faces and knees red from the March wind, came trotting evenly along the gravel.

"This, you understand, was before the organization of the self-sufficient block had been perfected. Well, I'll explain about that later. At first cars were banned by law in certain districts. There were many complaints, but children were safer and most people were happier. In the other districts people stopped using cars because they were such a nuisance. Then, when the blocks got to functioning and the belt-line system, they realized they didn't need to go dashing all over the city. By that time it would probably have been all right for those who wanted to use cars to go ahead and use them, but what was the good of it? No matter what was done, lives were endangered, and sometimes streets were blocked. So a referendum was passed by a big vote."

"It's all right with me, though I can't help looking both ways before I cross a street. What about the delivery of goods? What about trucks?"

"I'll show you the answer to that one. Maybe tonight."

We walked along slowly, for I was trying to see all the buildings and all the people at the same time. The buildings bothered me. "David," I said suddenly, "there aren't any stores."

"Oh, yes, there are. You'll see them. I thought we might eat at the Research Center restaurant. It's only a couple of blocks from here."

I realized that one block was now about three of the old north-and-south blocks. I guessed that we were somewhere near Forty-second Street. "Do you recognize that?" David asked, pointing to a tower.

"No," I said positively. Then I reconsidered: "It isn't the Chrysler Building?"

"It is. That's a funny thing. Engineers in your time were worried about the staying power of the steel they used. As a matter of fact, the steel girders in most of the big skyscrapers of the early twentieth century are as good as they ever were. Of course we've stripped off all the stonework they had to support, and used glass and the new translucent materials, and we've got rid of Mr. Chrysler's fancy spire. But there's the essential building, still on the job. It's been incorporated in a planned block, but it's there. So's the Empire State, most of Rockefeller Center, and a good many other buildings."

Because most of the buildings fell back, story after story, from the street, and because the streets themselves were so wide, I had none of the sense of being at the bottom of a canyon that used to trouble me in New York. Everywhere there were broad terraces, some of them bright with unseasonable flowers. Children played in the sunlight high above our heads. "What are all these places?" I asked.

"Apartments."

THE CITY OF THE FUTURE

I sighed. "This used to be a working-class district. Where are all the workers now?"

David smiled his sober smile, with just that touch of triumph that I liked. He swept his arm to include the people on the street and those in the houses. "They're all workers."

There was nothing for me to do but sigh again. Then I thought of another problem. "I haven't any money."

David turned, a little startled. What I fully expected him to say was, "You don't need any." Instead he snapped his fingers in irritation. "I ought to have thought of that. You wait a minute."

As we crossed the street, he said, "This is the Research Center." I stared up at the great tower, then looked left and right at the expanse of glass. I could see into laboratories, offices, schoolrooms. We walked through the building and into a court. Now I realized what David had meant about stores, for here they were. The court was almost as big as an ordinary city block, and there were lawns, just beginning to show a touch of green, low trees, and various little buildings. And on two sides of the court were shop windows.

David walked into an office, and we sat down at a table in a comfortable booth. Picking up the phone, he called Braxton and Manchester. Both calls had something to do with me and a card, but I could gather little more than that, and I understood for the first time what an extraordinary effort David must have been making to use a vocabulary I could understand. When he hung up the instrument, I said, "Where's the television?"

"What?"

THE FIRST TO AWAKEN

"Everybody was convinced in my day that before long it would be possible to see the person you were talking to."

"I imagine it is possible, but why should you want to?"

There was a small case at the end of the table. David opened it and looked inside. A few minutes later he opened it again and pulled out a card. "There," he said, "that's better than being able to see Redtape Rogers."

The card read: "George Swain is a member of the Braxton Cooperative, Northeast District. Robert E. Rogers, Secretary. George Swain is a student without affiliation of the Northeast District. Elizabeth Marinetti, chairman education committee, Northeast District."

"It's useful to be able to send documents by wire," David pointed out, "more useful than being able to look at somebody's face. It isn't ordinarily so simple, though, to get a card. Even in your case it took a little arguing."

"But what's this for?"

"Blueprints, a set of figures, drawings, photographs, anything of that sort."

"I mean, what's the card for?"

"You could get along without it, but it means food and clothing and a place to sleep. And a D-rating income. We'll go and collect tomorrow, and then you'll have a little change in your pocket."

"What's a D rating?"

"What do you say we get some food? I'll explain all about it then."

As we crossed the court, I noticed the children. There were a dozen or so playing around, little kids of five or less, good, healthy looking youngsters. David, following my glance, said,

THE CITY OF THE FUTURE

"It's still no place for children, but they're not so badly handicapped now."

From outside, the restaurant looked immense, and David said it could seat two thousand people. But once inside, I found it so broken up into alcoves and recesses, so skillfully built on various levels, that I didn't think of it as big. We found a table in a corner, with only a few other tables round us, and I forgot about all the other people. Somewhere out of sight an orchestra was playing softly—an orchestra, according to David, made up of members of the cooperative—and that and the voices of the people near us were the only sounds.

As I studied the menu, looking for items I could recognize, I wondered where the waiters were. "Direct table service," David explained. Asking me what I wanted, he wrote our orders on a kind of teletype, and then said, "I think you're due for a lecture."

It was a good lecture, too. The substance of it was this: [1] "As you have already seen, we get medical attention free, transportation free, telephone—and also telegraph and postal —service free. We also get housing free, food free, and clothing free. These are services provided the useful citizen by the community. All this is a logical extension of practices in your day. It was an easy step from uniform postal rates to free postage, from the general distribution of water to the general distribution of light.

"This didn't happen all at once. It began with the nationalization of the basic industries, which you will read about in

[1] The minor inaccuracies in Swain's summary of my remarks will be apparent to everyone. He wanted to omit these paragraphs, but it seems to me that they are valuable because they show what aspects of economic life impressed him.—D.W.

the history books. It also began with the development of large-scale cooperative enterprises. But for a long time the various services, though they were provided by the government or by the cooperatives, were paid for by the individual. Gradually, however, one service after another fell into the category of social supply. So today some seventy or eighty percent of a man's wants are taken care of without any money transaction."

"But isn't this wasteful?" I interrupted to say. "Don't people use more food, for instance, if they don't have to pay according to what they use?"

"Why, yes, it's somewhat wasteful. But look at the way it works out. I dare say that when you were growing up your family was careful to put out every light that wasn't actually in use. Isn't that so? Well, in later years people stopped watching the lights so carefully. That was chiefly because, even under capitalism, electricity had become so much cheaper that one light more or less didn't make a great deal of difference. Now it's true that, if electricity is supplied free, people aren't going to run around turning off lights, but it's also true that the cost is not excessive. And the waste is actually much less than the cost of bookkeeping that's involved in measuring each individual's consumption and charging him for it.[1]

"The matter of food, of course, is not quite so simple, for people can spoil food, and sometimes do. I could refuse to

---

[1] Swain has given a clearer illustration of my point than I was able to make, though I did try to speak in his language. The reader will see, however, how completely foreign the whole concept is to our way of thinking. For our purposes, electricity makes a very bad example, for we should not know how to waste it if we wanted to.—D.W.

eat this lunch I've ordered, and insist on having another. That sort of thing happens now and again, but not often enough to count. And when weighed against the efficiency of the whole system, it doesn't really matter."

I began to see another point. These were people who had never had to go without, and were perfectly confident that there would always be enough for them and for everybody else. Two or three generations of plenty had evidently wiped out much of the desire to grab. There was no reason for grabbing when you knew that tomorrow's wants would be taken care of.

"I take it everything isn't free," I said. "How do you decide what is to be a service and what isn't?"

"Roughly speaking, whenever a demand is widespread and is statistically predictable, the meeting of it becomes a service. That takes care—"

He stopped and opened a cover in the center of the table. There were his fruit juice and my soup. "That takes care," he continued, "of seventy or eighty percent of the economy. That is to say, seventy or eighty percent of our energy goes into these basic necessities."

"Luxuries, I would say." The soup was excellent. "Could you pause just a moment to tell me a little bit about this restaurant?"

He did, after producing our meat and vegetables, well cooked and steaming hot. "It's just a system of carrier belts and dumb waiters," he said, "with these vacuum containers. Some restaurants still have waiters, and there are a few cafeterias, which I dislike because they make conversation almost impossible. You'll find a good deal of variety here in New York, but I must say this system seems as efficient as any."

I overheard a few words of vigorous discussion from a table near us. A young woman of twenty-two or twenty-three, who wore the conventional blouse but with a flaring crimson skirt, was arguing with two older men. "Geologists, I judge," David explained.

"Are all these people students?"

"They're research workers. This is headquarters for the

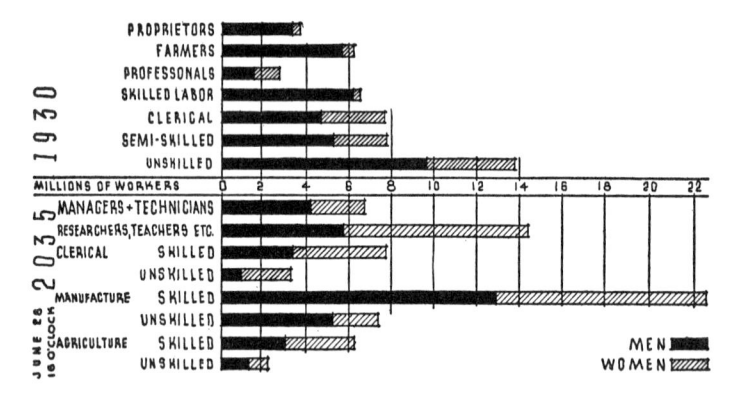

North American branches of most of the international research councils in the physical sciences."

"You mean this whole block?"

"Yes. The first eight floors are occupied by laboratories and offices, the rest by apartments." He went on to explain what I had begun to gather, that each block constituted a cooperative unit of from fifteen to twenty or thirty thousand people. They worked there, lived there, ate there, played there, sent their children to school there—found, in short, a complete community life.

THE CITY OF THE FUTURE

"But why so many researchers?"

"We need an awful lot of them, George. We've done the thing you were starting to do, and we've done it thoroughly. But the more you save manual labor, the more you depend on science. A restaurant the size of this would once have required hundreds and hundreds of workers, whereas today it uses only a few score. But I suppose it employs dozens of experts of one kind or another. And back of those experts stand a host of research workers. Research is the very foundation of our society." [1]

"Now what about this rating business?"

He explained that anyone who did useful work was a useful citizen and entitled to belong to a cooperative, which looked out for his fundamental needs. Over and above that he was given a certain income, and what it was depended on his rating. The most dangerous and arduous and unattractive types of work had an A rating—for example, mining, though I gathered that it had become much less perilous, and large-scale construction. Most factory work, transportation, and the more monotonous types of service had a B rating. Work that could be supposed to bring its own satisfactions—teaching, medicine, managing, planning, and the like—had a C rating. The D category included not only students but also other kinds of privileged individuals.

"Does it sound completely topsy-turvy?"

"No, it makes good sense. I have always thought I would

---

[1] I may as well give here two charts that illustrate Wilson's point. The 1930 chart is adapted from *The Structure of the American Economy* (Washington, 1939); the 2035 chart from *A Primer of Social Organization* (Wichita, 2036).—G.S.

have to be paid more to be ditch-digger than to be a bank-teller."

"That's just the point. Everyone receives a pretty good education, and there's almost no one who couldn't fill what you used to call a white-collar job. Of course, there are people who crave a certain amount of physical exertion, and there are others who would naturally avoid any work that involved thought and initiative. But there aren't enough to take care of the hard jobs. So the community holds out special rewards in the form of a higher income, and thus we manage to keep a balance."

"Don't the experts look down on the workers?"

"Not very noticeably, especially in a place like Braxton where they all mix together. It's true that the expert has a good deal of honor, which he deserves. But the lines aren't sharply drawn, and probably they will become less so as time goes on. The man who runs a machine has to know almost as much as the one who designs it. You'll see how it works out."

I had kept David talking so constantly that he had only eaten half his dinner when my plate was empty. He devoted himself to his food, and I looked about. So far, the system had been easier to understand than I had feared. So many of the problems of my day had been solved. People were well cared for, which was more than you could say for the majority of my contemporaries, and they had jobs they liked and were sure of. In about five hours—and I could not believe it was so short a time—I had learned enough to feel that Dr. Carr was right. Mankind had at last been forced to put intelligence to work.

THE CITY OF THE FUTURE

A light glowed, and David, raising the cover again, handed me my ice cream and coffee. Then he paused, with an expression of dismay, half-humorous and half-serious, on his face. "Good Lord," he exclaimed, "if this is Vermont Delight, I'm one of the Green Mountains." He drew out some sort of sirupy concoction, stared at it, thrust it back into the container, and scribbled on the teletype. Almost immediately there came back: "I was born in Vermont, and I know. If you don't like it, try something else."

With a kind of boyish indignation, David seized the menu, looked it over, and began writing a message of several sentences. Before he had finished, the mechanical pencil was racing over the pad. "I'll make it just the way you say, but don't blame me if you have a belly-ache."

Calmly David turned to me, proceeding in his best pedagogical manner. "As I was saying, since the community controls production—"

"In other words," I interrupted, "socialism."

"Sure," he said impatiently. "Since the community controls production, it distributes goods in whatever is discovered to be the most efficient way. For most kinds of goods, this means the complete elimination of the market. But this is efficient only because the unit of control is small enough to respond to consumer demand. The development of the cooperative and systematic decentralization were essential."

He reached into the service box, bringing forth a pastry soaked in maple sirup. He looked at it reflectively for a moment, and then doggedly ate it.[1]

---

[1] For obvious reasons I have not seen fit to suggest the elimination of personal anecdotes of this kind. Doubtless they are not wholly irrelevant.—D.W.

"What do we do now?" I inquired.

"I thought we might rest a little."

At the moment nothing could seem more preposterous. I didn't feel tired, and there was so much I wanted to see and learn. "Listen," I said, "I've been sleeping for the last hundred years."

Warm water sprayed through the service box, and we rinsed our hands. David looked at me earnestly. "You'd better go slow, George. I suppose no one has had an experience quite like what you've been through in the last few hours since the first Indians were taken to Europe. You can't learn everything at once, and you've got plenty of time. Take a little rest now, and you'll have a much better time this evening. Besides, I wouldn't mind a nap myself."

"So I've worn you out. I don't wonder."

He filled and lighted his pipe. "I do feel it a little, and that's why I'm sure you are more tired than you realize. But I often take a nap after lunch. I think we all ought to sleep more—or at any rate more often—than we do."

We rose, but he went back and scribbled, "Many thanks, it was delicious." Before we could get away, there was a reply: "I admire a man who sticks to his guns. Don't give me away to the doctor."

As we went out, I said, "Do most women work?"

"Practically speaking, all women."

"What about kids?"

"There are nurseries and schools."

"But isn't there any family life?"

"Why not? The working day is four hours. No child is

going to suffer much if he's separated from his mother for four hours."

I wondered what happened if a man and woman were in different lines of work, but David pointed out that, in an ordinary community, there would be places for both of them. In New York, it was true, they might work in opposite ends of the city, for the blocks were specialized. "New York," he said emphatically, "is an outrage."

I had thought there was a critical tone in David's voice whenever he spoke of the city, but I was not prepared for so dogmatic an outburst, nor could I understand it. New York seemed to me a marvelous achievement, and I said so. "You'll see," David replied with conviction.

"We could just as well sleep here," he commented as we entered a kiosk in the court, "but you'll be interested in the Clothing Center."

As we took a chair car going west, I asked him if there were no regular subways. "Five high-speed lines running north and south. Another product of the Technocratic Era, but still necessary. You can't put even two million people in so small a space without making transportation problems. The chair cars do well enough for east and west traffic, and for shorter trips up and down the island, but for long distances you need speed."

He showed me how to manipulate the levers, so as to get either music or news. It was soothing to lean back and listen to a string quartet.

"I do like New York," I insisted, perhaps rather pathetically.

"I know. It is impressive. It is the kind of city some of

THE FIRST TO AWAKEN

your prophets dreamed of, and the engineers surpassed their dream. But the whole urban tendency was wrong. You'll understand that later. New York is just a hangover."

We emerged in another great court, and immediately I caught the smell of flowers. They were blooming in all the gardens. Young children played about in shorts or in nothing at all. There were bathers in the swimming pool and along its edge. Everyone wore gay clothing.

David looked up and so did I, into a blue, wind-swept March sky. Even if you can't see it," he said, "there's a roof made of glass—or what you might as well call glass. This is an enclosed block. There are only eight or ten of them now, but probably all the blocks will be enclosed if the city lasts long enough."

"Let's sit in the sun a while."

David found us comfortable chairs and took off his jacket. It folded into a small package, which he put in his pocket. "If I wanted to startle you," he said, "I'd throw this into a waste basket."

As I followed his example, I replied, "I doubt if I can be startled any more. What is this stuff anyway?" I stroked the smooth surface.

"Plastic material. The garments are molded out of it. One machine can produce hundreds of suits in an hour. It insulates you, and that's why you can be comfortable in the coldest weather if all air spaces are closed."

I sank back in comfort. A group of children came shouting out of one of the doors and ran to the pool. There was a constant rat-a-tat-tat from one corner, where there were fifty

Clothing Center Court

or sixty ping-pong tables. I could look into what appeared to be a great department store, and above it was a broad expanse filled with machines. At my right a circular tower rose high above the roof.

Noticing that I seemed to want something, David asked what I would like and I told him I wished I had my sketching pad. Immediately he went to the store, returning with pad and pencils, and I did my first drawing of the new world.[1]

"Go ahead and talk," I said to David.

He looked about him. "You may have realized that, at this time of year, the sun would seldom shine into this court. So—"

"It's all done with mirrors."

---

[1] The sketches of Braxton were done later. The perspective in this drawing is bad, but I found it almost impossible to get the effect of the twenty-four stories. Also, I made no attempt to include the many people in the foreground.—G.S.

He looked surprised. "Right!"

I leaned back to get a good look at the upper stories. "Now about this clothing?"

"I wasn't joking when I spoke about throwing the jacket into a waste basket. That is what will sooner or later happen to it. When a suit is soiled or the wearer is tired of it, the material is reduced to its plastic state, and new garments are made of it."

"Does everyone wear suits like this?"

"You've seen how it goes. Plastic clothes are supplied by your cooperative, and you wear them for most purposes. But women ordinarily have several dresses, and men may have two or three suits. Those are for the special occasions."

"Do you have to pay for the special clothes?"

"Yes, and they're usually designed to fit the individual taste."

I studied my drawing with displeasure, made a few changes, and then lay idle. After a few minutes I yawned.

"You're about ready for that nap now," David said. "Come on."

While we were on our way to the office, I noticed, above the entrance to an auditorium, "Dewey Memorial Hall," and I said to David, "Not Thomas Dewey, I trust."

"Thomas Dewey?"

"A politician who wanted to be President."

"Of course. No, not Thomas Dewey nor Admiral Dewey."

"John Dewey, then?"

"No, though he is the only one of the three who is still remembered. Several of his books have been translated into

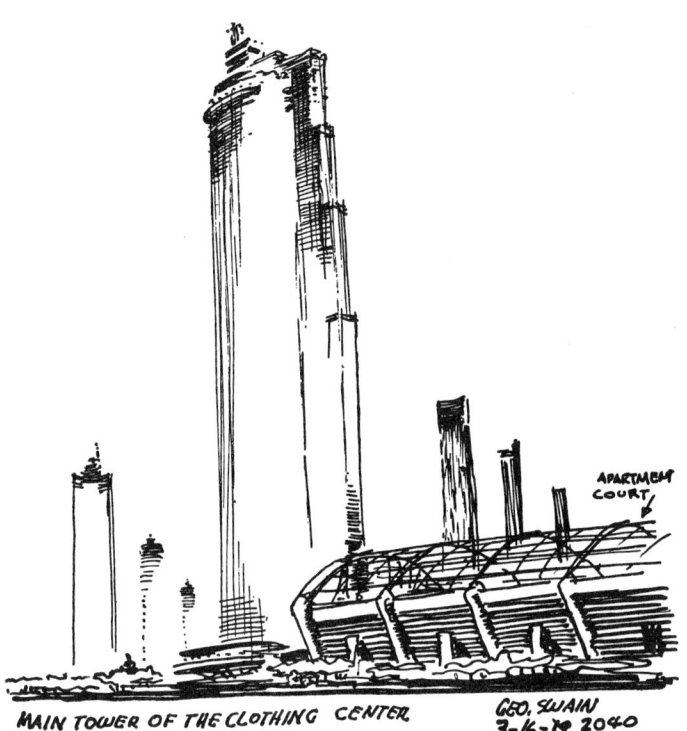

MAIN TOWER OF THE CLOTHING CENTER GEO. SWAIN 3-16-M 2040

English [1] and are read with interest. But this was a later Dewey, a great labor leader of the fifties."

He secured rooms for us, and we took the elevator. Every cooperative, he told me, had guest rooms. I wanted to know what happened if all the rooms were full. "Then you try another cooperative. You'll get taken care of somewhere. It works all right in practice."

I was stunned by the look of the room. It was pie-shaped, opening out from the doorway to the window that stretched from floor to ceiling, and it seemed as if I could walk right

[1] I meant, of course, into Basic English—D.W.

into space. We were high up in the tower, and I looked breathlessly over the city. Whatever David might say, there was nobility, a greatness of human achievement, in this New York.

He took me out on the terrace, and there, in the biting March air, were plants in bloom. I looked closely at one—it probably had a geranium for ancestor—and David showed me how artificial heat was provided. "A gadget," he commented.

As we returned to the room, he said, "You've taken it very well."

"Why shouldn't I? There were people in my day who had no fault to find with things as they were. I wasn't one of them. And they weren't very numerous. A lot of things were obviously bad—depressions, war, unemployment, bad housing, bad health, all the rest of it. And most people were beginning to realize that those things didn't need to be. Even in a smug little town like Braxton lots of us had the feeling that we ought to be making a better life for ourselves. I feel as if I'd been terribly shaken up. I guess I'd become pretty set in my ways, and I don't know how I'll fit into your kind of life. There may be lots of things about it I won't like. But I'm not a fool. I can see that in the big things, the things that hit you in the eye, you've got it all over us."

Embarrassed at having made a speech, I added, "What I don't see is how I'm going to sleep in a room that's as bright as all outdoors and has no shades."

David stepped over by the window and pressed a button. Instantly the room was pitchblack. "Three-way glass," he explained. He pressed another button, and the room was filled with soft artificial light.

"Do you want pajamas?" I nodded. "You'll get used to sleeping without them, but you can have them." He glanced at some papers he had been given at the hospital. "And probably you'd like to brush your teeth. And what about a book to read?" He went to the telephone and gave his order.

Turning back to me, he said, "The room is soundproof, lightproof, and what you would call air-conditioned."

"Tell me," I said; "so often you seem to know what I'm thinking. What do you people know about telepathy?"

"No more than you did."

"But you do seem to know what I'm thinking."

"If you won't be offended, I'll simply say that that's my job. When I undertook this study, I prepared myself for it. I learned everything I could about you and your times. And I've been with you constantly since you woke up—from the very beginning, for Dr. Rosenthal and I could see everything you did and hear everything you said while you were in the examination room this morning. If I didn't know something of the way your mind works, I'd be pretty stupid."

He opened a compartment in the wall and took out a package. "But don't think that I'm the scientist and you're the bug under the microscope. That isn't the way it is at all. I can be your friend, as nobody else in the world can at this moment, just because I do know something about you. And when you know more about me, as you will, I hope you'll be my friend."

He opened the bundle. The pajamas consisted of shorts and a loose shirt—summer material, David called it, giving access to sun and air instead of insulating the body. The toothbrush and dentifrice had apparently been prescribed by the dentist who examined me that morning. The "book" proved to be a roll of film.

David showed me how to use the reading machine. "Don't be alarmed by the book, by the way." He prepared to go. "You sleep just as long as you want to. If you wake up first, come in next door and speak to me. Otherwise I'll call you in a little while. Is everything all right?" He stood in the doorway a moment, reflective and solicitous at the same time.

"I'll be O.K.," I said, and he closed the door.

I undressed, and then found the button that controlled the window. I could look far out into the harbor, for, as I suddenly realized, there was not a sign of smoke in the city, and the air was as clear as that of the Braxton hills. There were boats in the harbor and on the North River, tremendous freighters and smaller craft—and no smoke there, either. On the Jersey shore was another great parkway, and behind it huge structures like those on the island, but not far beyond was open country dotted with tiny houses.

Looking southward, I gazed across the terraced blocks to the tip of Manhattan, where the towers of the Regional Planning Center rose in a gigantic circle. Down the very center of the island was a broad park, with lakes and playing fields. Among the towers that soared near at hand I identified the old Empire State. A large airplane, one of the kind that carried passengers in the wings, flew up from the south and passed directly overhead. I could not hear a sound, and I was

New York City, looking north, hastily sketched on sightseeing flight. Great regional planning center in foreground.

puzzled until I remembered that David had told me the room was soundproof.

I looked for a long time, and then, still restless, got up and wandered about the room, exploring its amazing panels. At last I fixed the head of the bed as David had shown me, darkened the room, and turned on the reading machine. I lay back in comfort as the title page appeared on the screen:

THE FIRST TO AWAKEN

"Night Over Manhattan, an historical romance by Philip Stein." Then: "Dedicated to Our Visitors from the Twentieth Century."

"It was the spring of 1929," the novel began. "Mildred was not a beautiful girl, but she was the liveliest of the jitterbugs, and there was never a time when she lacked for boy friends. Underneath the gay lights of the Sweeney Club, New York's most exclusive speakeasy, the Paradise twins, Delbert and Juniper, sat on either side of her, vying with each other in paying for the Martini cocktails she was delicately sipping through a straw. They were the sons of the city's most aristocratic bootlegger, leaders of the smart social set and members of the Skull and Crossbones Club of Yale."

Fascinated, I read on. It appeared that Juniper had made a hundred grand—Mr. Stein had evidently ransacked the dictionaries of slang—on the stock exchange. Mildred, who became steadily more glamorous and more intoxicated as the chapter proceeded, insisted on dancing a polka with him, and addressed to him staccato sentences in the Hemingway manner. Delbert finally became jealous and flung his way out of the club, knocking down two judges and a police commissioner in his flight.

He took a taxi, and there was a lively description of a traffic jam in Times Square, with Delbert and the taxi driver abusing each other in the language of Jeeter Lester. At last, however, he reached his destination—the home of the Queen of the White Slaves. (Which seemed to be located squarely on the site of Grant's Tomb.) After a great deal of rigamarole, he was admitted to the regal presence.

"In the meantime," according to the second chapter, "three

THE CITY OF THE FUTURE

men were sitting in a coffee shop not many blocks from the Sweeney Club. It was dark and dingy, and the proprietor, who had been gassed in the last war, coughed incessantly. The radio ground out a popular nursery song, 'Yes, We Have No Bananas,' but the three men, hunched close together, paid no attention to it. From time to time they called for more needled beer."

It was exciting in a way, and, in the description of the depression and the organization of Brass Brigade, not too bad. But it was so utterly wrong, not only in hundreds of details but in its whole mood, that I alternately chuckled and snorted. Then I began to wonder: was it any more inaccurate than the historical novels written in my day? Would a Southerner of the eighteen-sixties and seventies have found *Gone With the Wind* any less absurd?

I dropped the cable control, and the light went out. "Good lord," I said aloud. I lowered the back rest. The bed was perfect. Shall I count jitterbugs, I asked myself, or gymbal planes, or coordinated cooperatives? I did not need to do much counting.

IV

CONVERSATION AT MIDNIGHT

WHEN I woke up, there was a gentle light on in the room, and David was sitting by the table, writing in a little notebook. I knew him all right and knew where I was. "Well it looks as if you were able to do with a little sleep," he said cheerfully.

"What time is it?"

"After eleven—after twenty-three, we would say." He held out his twenty-four hour watch.

I got up, used the bathroom, and dressed. "What now?"

"Food."

To my surprise, the restaurant was well filled. "Probably people going on the twelve o'clock shift," David explained.

As we walked along the broad aisle, I noticed waitresses serving the diners, and remembered what David had told me. We glanced into several recesses, but all the tables were occupied, and at last we found ourselves in the open air— or what would have been the open air if the court hadn't been roofed. Here the tables were arranged upon terraces that dropped down to the level of the swimming pool. The lighting in the court gave almost exactly the effect of daylight.

In one corner, under a palm tree, a young woman sat alone over a cup of coffee, reading a newspaper. The waitress, seeing that we could not find a vacant table, beckoned to us, and we sat there. David introduced us to the young woman, and she gave her name, which I did not catch. "I'm glad to see you," she said pleasantly. "Do you work here?"

"No, we're from Braxton in the Northeast District."

"Of course. I ought to have known. I'm very pleased to meet you, Mr. Swain. Did you get here in the daytime? How do you like the city? Don't you think this is a pretty good block?"

My enthusiasm could not have failed to satisfy her. "Are you on the midnight shift?" David asked. She nodded, and he said, "You have twenty-four hour production?"

She nodded again, and I wanted to know how that was decided. She looked at David and then answered, "By the cooperative and the planning boards."

"I'm afraid George doesn't understand all that," David explained. "So far we've just been using our eyes."

She put out her cigarette and drank the last swallow of coffee. "I've got to go now. Would you like to see the paper?"

Many people were filing out of the restaurant, with much laughing and talking. "They don't seem to mind being on the night shift," I commented.

"They probably aren't so keen about it, but it's only four hours after all. They can sleep before or after or both and

THE FIRST TO AWAKEN

have most of the day to themselves. On a four-hour basis there's something to be said for every shift, but I imagine this is the least popular."

"Do the factories in Braxton work twenty-four hours?"

"Only a few departments."

The waitress, a woman of about thirty who wore a brown slack suit, was busy at the tables that had been so rapidly vacated, but in a moment she came forward with menus. She spoke to us pleasantly, and explained to me the nature of a number of dishes I had never heard of.

When she left, I asked David whether she had a four-hour shift. She overheard, and said, "We work from two hours before to two hours after midnight. The rush hours come when the shifts let out, and so we divide the other way. It would be inconvenient if we changed shifts now." She set the other tables in the corner, and then went and sat down by a column.

I picked up the paper. It was only sixteen pages, and of course the first thing that struck me was the absence of advertising. Both the format and the contents seemed rather dull. Thumbing it through, I saw that it was arranged systematically. The first page was given over to what Everett would have called spot news—the sort of items I had heard over the radio in the subway. Then there were pages for foreign news, national news, city news, and news of the cooperative.

David explained that the first few pages were sent out all over the continent from a central news bureau, while district news came from a district bureau and local news from the cooperative itself. "What happens is that a man in the bureau operates a machine something like a typewriter, and the story is set up all over the continent or all over the district, as the case may be. You can have a machine in your home that turns out a paper like this twice a day. In the country and even in the suburbs most homes have such machines. In an apartment house, of course, it's more economical to have one machine that prints for all the residents."

The waitress came back with a seafood cocktail for me and fruit juice for David. I did not like the sauce at first, but gradually I got used to it.

"The paper seems pretty heavy," I ventured.

"It is, and it's meant to be. It's purely factual and as objective as the human mind permits. It's intended to keep us informed, not to amuse us or influence our opinions. I'm not saying those functions aren't important, mind you, but they're taken care of in other ways."

The restaurant was filling up again, and I noticed that the people who mounted the stairs near us or walked along the terrace, all of them presumably direct from a day's work, seemed alert and full of energy. I spoke of this to David. "And a good thing, too," he said. "That means that they can do something in the ten or twelve hours that they have outside of work time and sleep time."

No one seemed in a great hurry. The waitress brought our soup, stopping to say a few words before she took the orders of those at the neighboring tables. David, I observed, liked a leisurely meal, and he ate his soup slowly, commenting once or twice on its goodness.

Making sure that the waitress was really out of earshot this

THE FIRST TO AWAKEN

time, I said, "What rating does she have? She seems a bright woman to be doing this kind of work."

"C rating, I imagine. It isn't a bad job. You notice how efficiently everything is arranged. She has a kind of service kitchen right there, connected, of course, with the main kitchen, and in the midst of the tables she serves. It's relatively easy work, and pleasant for someone who likes people. Probably her husband has a job here in the cooperative, and this is the thing she likes to do best."

"I still think she could do something better."

"Would working in a factory or in an office or teaching school be better? Not necessarily. There's drudgery in every job, George. There never was a task in the world, no matter how fresh and exciting, that didn't involve drudgery. Think of how much hard work and dull routine there is in painting a picture, for instance, or, for that matter, in learning to play a game well."

"You can't abolish drudgery?"

"Of course not. Besides, what is creative for one man is deadly toil for another. What we can do is try to make every job vital and self-expressive for the man or woman who has it. Any really necessary work has possibilities in it for somebody or other."

"It's a nice idea."

"I don't mean that we always succeed, that everybody goes about his job just bubbling over with joy. But we have got away from your idea that it's better to be a bad teacher than a good waitress. And anyway four hours of drudgery never killed anyone. If a man finds little satisfaction in his work, at least he has time and energy left to look for satisfaction elsewhere. Wait till you see a community in action, and then you'll understand. It isn't perfect; don't ever expect that; but it works after a fashion."

We looked up. An attractive couple, dressed exactly alike except that the boy had a black scarf and the girl a white one, were standing near our table. All the others were filled, and the girl, whose dark, oval face was beautiful as she smiled, turned to us: "Would we disturb you? I'm Norah Galt and this is Nicholas Galt."

David gave his name and mine, and they sat down. "You were late getting off," he said.

"No," the girl answered. "I'm on the eight o'clock shift, and Nick's on the four. We were out in the country all after-

Sketches of Clothing

noon, and went to the theater at another cooperative tonight, and now I'm famished. Poor Nick, he's got to go to work at four, but I can have a good sleep."

The boy was moodily studying the menu. Suddenly he looked at me with his intense brown eyes. "You're the man who slept a hundred years, aren't you? Do you want to talk about it or not?"

The way he snapped the question was disconcerting. "I don't mind, but I'd rather ask questions than answer them. For instance, I don't know what you people think about me. In my day, if a man had slept a hundred years, he couldn't keep the reporters off his doorstep. There would be pictures of him in all the papers and newsreels, and probably he'd be interviewed on the radio. Every time he appeared on the street he'd be mobbed."

"Hmmm, do you miss it?"

"Please don't think that. But this morning—yesterday morning, I mean—I thought it had all been kept a secret, and I was delighted. But I have heard my name over the radio and seen it in this paper, and everyone I have met has sooner or later recognized me. And yet no mob scenes."

The girl laughed. "I should hope not."

"But I still don't understand it."

"That's easy," Nick said dogmatically. "Nobody has newspapers or newsreels or radio time to sell. Nobody wants you to endorse toothpaste or—or babies' diapers."

"Nick has studied a lot of history," the girl put in, whether proudly or ironically I could not make out. He snorted.

"It has been a long time," David said gently, "since public interest in private lives could be fostered and exploited for profit." I was amused at the look of disgust on Norah's face. "Long enough," he went on, "so that attitudes have really changed. We have a different sense of what legitimately constitutes public interest."

"Nick is really very curious about Mr. Swain."

"Naturally," said David, "and so are many other people. And every legitimate curiosity will be satisfied. The medical journals will carry reports on the medical aspects of the case,[1] and if anything unusual is discovered, that will be announced in the bulletin. When George talks with the historians, any new facts that emerge will be published. And so on. In the meantime, the feeling most of us have is that he must be allowed to live a normal life. That is why Nick put his question the way he did."

The boy smiled a pleased smile. David went on to make the somewhat alarming suggestion that, if my observations had a general interest, I would have the same opportunities to publicize them as anyone else.

"If you do," said Nick, "for heaven's sake, don't flatter them. They're smug enough already. Give them the devil!"

"Who's 'them'?" David asked.

"The people who run things."

"Nick's a poet," said Norah. "He's always yelling this way at union and cooperative meetings. He got our department to elect him to the administrative committee, but he was such a nuisance they didn't re-elect him."

---

[1] See *Journal of the CMA,* LXXVII, 233, and *Preventive Medicine,* XXXII, 64. Swain's account of his meeting with the historians appears below, chap. x. So far as I know, no contribution to historical knowledge resulted from this. My own report will deal with the psychological aspects of the case.—D.W.

THE FIRST TO AWAKEN

"I wish you wouldn't talk that way, Norah. You feel about this just as I do. The whole cooperative is full of people who can't think of anything but the way the nursery and the restaurant and the schools are run. Honestly, Mr. Swain, they think the millennium has been reached because we have one of the eleven enclosed courts in the city. So long as they can tan their ugly legs while reading about zero temperatures, they're perfectly happy."

"Nice work, Nicky," said the waitress, setting a large, thick steak before the poet.

"He hasn't changed any, Esther," Norah told her.

"He has a point," the waitress replied over her shoulder.

"Of course I have a point," Nick insisted as he set to work on the steak. "These people aren't living; they're stagnating."

I found it difficult to take the remark seriously. Watching the men and women in the restaurant, noticing the eager faces and hearing the snatches of talk, I thought them very much alive indeed. I remembered the workers in the lunch wagons and sandwich joints of Braxton. Some of them, to be sure, were gay, and some were serious. But, especially in recent years, I had seen so many bitter and broken men, paralyzed by defeat. And the people who gathered in the better restaurants to eat the business men's luncheons were rather worse. So often greed and suspicion and fear showed through the pretense of conviviality. So often the kidding became shrill and vindictive. So often serious conversation was nothing but a wail of despair. I warned myself against exaggeration, but I knew that I had looked on the faces of the dead and damned, and there were no such faces here.

"Some of them read your poems," Norah reminded her husband.

"Wait till I get out the new pamphlet. Norah, I'm going to get an A-rating job, so that I can print twice as many in the next edition." Norah shrugged her shoulders as if she had heard that before.

"So poets have to pay to have their poems printed?" I asked.

"Well, you wouldn't expect them to be paid for writing poetry!" Nick exclaimed indignantly.

"They were in my day."

"So?" said David. "Very few of them."

"And they were overpaid," Nick insisted. "I don't care about that. I'm perfectly willing to do productive work, but I've got something to say, and I want people to listen to it."

"People within a hundred yards are listening now, Nicky dear, whether they want to or not."

He lowered his voice as he spoke to me. "You see what I mean. You might be a bad influence. You'll see the big things, the good things, and you'll say how wonderful they are. Then all the smug people will sit back and say, 'See! Aren't we good?' Don't do it!"

He was so eloquent, so intense, as he spoke, gesticulating with his strong hands, throwing back his head, looking at me with such deep earnestness that I hated to disagree, but I could not help reminding him that I knew what life was like a hundred years before.

"All right," he replied, shaking his fork at me. "Sure we've made progress since your time. Heaven help us if we hadn't. But suppose somebody had come into your age from the eighteen-thirties. He'd have seen the skyscrapers and the railroads and the airplanes and the telephones and the radios. He wouldn't have seen unemployment and slums and misery. Well, when he talked about how much progress had been made, don't you suppose the conservatives would have turned his words against the young radicals?"

"Are you a radical?"

"I'm a poet."

"And all poets are radicals?"

The scorn on his face was magnificent. "All true poets," he said with great dignity. Norah giggled.

David once more was conciliatory. "For a great many thousands of years," he said, "mankind has had to devote itself to the simple problem of survival, of keeping the body warm and the belly full. That problem is solved at last—for everybody. What Nick feels, I take it, is that we ought to be getting out of the elementary stage. Life has new possibilities for us, and we ought to be taking advantage of them."

"But we do take advantage of them," Norah broke in. "Most people today want better bodies and better minds."

"They did in my day," I said. "For a while. Then the majority gave up the struggle. They had to. You don't have to."

Nick was sullenly eating his salad. He finished it, and pushed back his chair. He folded his bare, brown arms. "Smugness!" he exploded. "Self-satisfaction! Aren't we wonderful!"

"Nicky, you're frightening Mr. Swain," said the waitress, gathering up our dishes.

"I'm not frightened," I said a little shyly. "I'm feeling at home."

David laughed at that, and even Nick relaxed a little. The waitress came back with our desserts. I had chosen a simple jelly, but David was again eating a rich pastry. "This enlightened age," I observed, not without jealousy, "seems to allow a good deal of leeway in the matter of diet."

"Why shouldn't I eat what I want?" he asked gaily. "I'm healthy. Our grandfathers went through all that nearly fifty years ago. There was a time when people were bootlegging cream puffs and mince pie."

"Really?" Norah exclaimed.

He grinned. "It wasn't quite as bad as that. But it was true that every citizen was given a diet card at his monthly medical examination and had to show it when he ordered his meals. One good result was a fine job of popular education on the question of food, but people hated it, and it wasn't necessary."

"What happens now?"

"You're supposed to have a medical examination once a year, and unless something is wrong nothing is said about diet."

"And everybody eats wisely?"

He took the last forkful of pastry and savored it. "Not at all. There's less indigestion, partly because people know more about food, partly because we eat more slowly, chiefly because there's so much less nervous tension. But people make fools of themselves and have to pay the price. Well, why not? There's an inalienable human right to have a stomach ache."

"Maybe that system was necessary for a while," I suggested.

"There must have been millions of people who had never had enough to eat, and millions more whose meals had always been unbalanced. They couldn't be expected to know what to do when they could have all the food they wanted. That's the sort of thing you don't realize," I said to Nick.

He grimaced, rolling his eyes in mock despair. "You don't have to prove to me that there's been improvement. But because there's been progress in the past, shall there be no progress in the future?"

"What do you write poems about?"

"Discontent!"

"And what do other poets write about?"

"Moonlight," Norah answered, "and daffodils."

"Not about machinery?"

"Sometimes," she replied with a touch of surprise.

"And about ideas," said David, "and people and anything you can mention. And some of it is very bad and some of it is good."

The other tables had emptied, except for another group like ours that was lingering in conversation. The waitress drew up a chair and joined us. "If you weren't so individualistic, Nick," she said, "you could start a magazine. Lots of us would back you."

"So you have magazines?"

"Thousands of them. Almost every cooperative has its own, and whenever a few people care enough about a magazine to spend a little of their income on it, they can start another. Magazines are easy enough to bring out. Getting readers is a different matter."

"Look at the magazine the crowd in Terre Haute gets out," the waitress argued. "Read all over the country."

"And the Jacksonville cooperative's magazine has been famous for years," Norah added.

"I'll stick to pamphlets. And some day my poetry will be in the library of every cooperative on the continent."

I had never known a poet, but I had read enough about them, and Nick seemed the type—with, of course, some special variations. I liked him, but his grimness was sometimes disconcerting. I changed the subject by asking about the publishing system.

David undertook to tell me about the publication of scientific works. These were brought out, he said, by the various scientific bodies, and copies sent to the libraries, universities, and laboratories that would be interested. There was, I gathered, an enormous body of such literature, so that the great problem was to digest and index it. He promised to show me what he called the mechanics of organized knowledge.

"That's easy," Nick broke in. "Now in the case of a creative writer, he has to prove that he's good."

"For a time," David told us, "even after the beginning of socialism, publishing remained an individualistic profit enterprise. But that didn't work. So they tried editorial committees and academies and so on, and that was worse. Now all the while it was becoming cheaper and cheaper to publish a book, and that was what brought a solution."

"It's this way," said Nick. "A writer usually begins by publishing in a local magazine. Then he gets ambitious, like me, and wants to bring out a pamphlet or a book. If he can get subscriptions enough, the cooperative press brings it out for him. But I think that's messy. So I pay for the pamphlets myself and give them away. Sorry I haven't one with me."

"It's unprecedented," said Norah.

"But doesn't that put a terrific burden on the author?"

"Remember what I said about the cheapness of publishing," David reminded me. "The author can type the manuscript himself, and the reproduction costs next to nothing."

"Nick went without smoking for a month to pay for his last pamphlet. Forty-eight pages, two thousand copies. Twelve hundred given away and eight hundred gone back to pulp."

"What about novels?"

"Usually issued on a subscription basis by the cooperative press. A circulation of five or six hundred is enough. Of course, once launched, a novel may sell five or six million copies, partly on film, partly on paper."

"And no profits for the author?"

"Royalties equal to an A-rating income if they're earned—which they seldom are."

I turned accusingly to David. "That reminds me. What about that novel you gave me to read?"

David said soberly to Nick, "I thought he'd be interested in *Night Over Manhattan*. After all, it's dedicated to him."

Nick guffawed, but Norah asked me quite seriously how I liked it.

"It's exciting in a way, but it's full of anachronisms, and somehow it seems phony." After I had explained the adjective, Nick delivered a diatribe against historical romances, and David pointed out that this was one of several books that had obviously been inspired by the news of "our visitors from the twentieth century." [1]

"I've got an idea," said Nick. "Why don't you read all the historical novels about your period and do a whale of a devastating pamphlet?"

"Don't you think there might be better ways for him to spend his time?" Norah inquired softly. "I don't think the book is so bad," she went on. "Of course I don't know anything much about the period, and so the anachronisms don't bother me. It's just written to amuse people, and I think as much can be said for romantic novels as for French pastry."

David laughed, and apropos of Nick's suggestion to me, began to tell of an acquaintance of his who brought out pamphlets against fireplaces. Apparently fireplaces were completely useless, and were even a serious engineering problem, but many people liked them and insisted on having them in their homes. It was another case of society's being productive enough to afford minor inefficiencies. But this old rationalist refused to yield to such prejudices. and hammered away at an indifferent public.

I began to see that the cheapness of publishing constituted a new guarantee of freedom of expression. If, for instance, a scientist was discriminated against by his learned society, or believed he was, he could publish his discoveries at his own expense. Any evil could be attacked in this way. Indeed, as David pointed out, books and pamphlets intended to influence

[1] See the extensive bibliography in *Modern Literature* for November, 2040. There is an interesting essay on the vogue of historical romance in *Revue Philologique*, XI, 333.—D.W.

THE FIRST TO AWAKEN

public opinion were always published privately or by informal groups, and there were a great many of them.

Norah nudged Nick, and they got up to go. We rose with them. The waitress said good-bye cordially, and we slanted across the court. We stood for a moment in the pleasant air, and I looked at the stars through the invisible and incredible roof twenty stories above us. Nick wanted to argue some more, but Norah took him firmly by the arm, and they walked across the court with their arms about each other.

"What a nice couple," I said, "and so friendly."

"New York is gradually acquiring the smalltown virtues."

I asked him about their racial background, and when he shook his head, I said, "You used to be able to pick out the races in New York: Jews, Italians, Germans, Slavs."

"Or you thought you could. Well, you can't any more. The melting pot has done its job."

That reminded me of the way I had been puzzled by the speech of people both in Braxton and in New York, and David explained that a century of radio had largely done away with regional differences.

"So far as race is concerned," he went on, "certain strains predominate in some areas. You could probably find a few people in Braxton who could be called Anglo-Saxon, whatever that means, but most of us are all mixed up."

I wanted to know what had happened to Harlem, and he told me that many Negroes had migrated to Africa in the sixties. "I'm afraid it was hard on the Negroes," he commented, "but good for Africa." A little later more than two million Negroes petitioned for a Negro district, and they were granted a large area in the Deep South. That took another large group of Negroes out of Harlem. The remainder had virtually been assimilated.

As we reached the end of the corridor and stood looking into the street, David took his jacket out of his pocket, unfolded it, and put it on, fastening the cuffs and waistband, and pulling his socks over his trouser-ends. I followed his example. The air was cold on my face as we stepped outside and felt good.

"Do you want to walk a few blocks?"

I nodded, and we fell in step. The walls of the buildings were gently lighted, but no lights shone from within. "Has everyone gone to bed?"

"No. I told you we had three-way windows. They can let light in, or keep it out, or keep it in."

"What has happened to the Negro district—the one in the South, I mean?"

"Still there, and prospering."

"Doesn't it slow up the process of assimilation?"

"That's no objection. Assimilation isn't an end itself. The Negro district, as a matter of fact, is like a lot of other things, like New York itself: if it hadn't happened just when it did, it never would have happened at all. But since it has happened, it goes on, simply because there's no sufficient reason for stopping it, although the reasons for which it was created no longer exist."

I wondered if race prejudice had completely disappeared. David said it hadn't. "You can't make people like each other by law. What we can do, and have done long since, is make race prejudice a purely personal thing. If you have a prejudice, you can't embody it in laws or economic institutions. You can't do anything but nurse it."

Almost silently a great monster passed us, apparently scrubbing the pavement. I asked David where we were going.

"Over to Jersey, so that you can see how this place is kept alive."

"You do hate the city, don't you?"

"Not really; just a little disturbed at your being so impressed by it. But it is a national liability, not an asset. When it was rebuilt, the big idea was to crowd as many people as possible into the smallest space and give them the maximum of gadgets. It was a field day for the architects and engineers."

I could understand that. They had been held down for a long time by the profit system, and had had their best ideas rejected because they wouldn't make money. It was no wonder that they lavished all their ingenuity on what they probably thought would become a model for the world. And I still felt they had done a magnificent job. "How long did it take?" I asked.

"About twenty years. And by the time it was done, people were coming to their senses, and realizing that big cities were as unnecessary as they were unhealthy."

"So there's nothing else like it?"

"Not on this continent, though San Francisco went a long way in the same direction. Barcelona and Athens are pretty bad, and some of the new cities in Africa and Asia."

The street was as quiet as a country lane in Braxton. Remarking that it seemed good to be outdoors for a little while, David led me down a long stairway and onto a platform.

"This is the high speed subway," he explained, "running underneath the interblock system."

A sign flickered, "Brooklyn local," and a train moved silently into the station. A single door opened, directly in front of the one person who was waiting. It closed, and the train went on. "Completely automatic," David said, "controlled by photoelectric cells."

"Jersey City local," the sign read. "Let's fool it," said David, and we moved to one of the places marked entrance. When the train stopped, the door opened, but David held my arm. In about thirty seconds a bell rang gently, the door closed, and the train moved off.

A Brooklyn local went through the station without stopping, because, as David explained, there was no one on the waiting platform.

When we got on the Jersey City train, the first thing I said to David was, "There aren't any windows."

"Why should there be in a subway train?"

There was little sense of motion and none of speed. The few passengers were reading or talking. "The men who designed the new city," David pointed out, "must have suffered at the thought of the hours they had wasted in subways. They not only designed the express system for comfort and speed, but they introduced all sorts of amusements—news flashes, radios, even moving pictures. That's all been allowed to lapse. The engineers simply didn't realize that they were tackling the problem the wrong way. If the money that had been spent on subways in your day had been spent on intelligent housing, New York would have been a good deal better off. But it was impossible in that kind of social organization. Since the economic life of the city has been re-organized, the average citizen is likely not to step inside a subway once a month, and even those who do use it regularly don't mind a quiet fifteen or twenty minutes. They don't have to be amused."

At my suggestion he began to sketch the outlines of the social structure. I learned, what I had already more or less gathered, that the cooperative was the political as well as the economic unit. It was represented on regional planning boards, which in turn had continental representation. There were coordinating boards for the various industries, which might be worldwide in scope if the industry was worldwide.

"But it's so complicated," I said.

He laughed. "Of course. What do you expect? But it's simple compared with the system of controls you grew up under. Let's see, there was the federal government, the state governments, counties, cities and towns, and all the school districts and that sort of thing. Then think of the hundreds of thousands of businesses."

"But a business is a simple thing."

"Is it? With boards of directors, stockholders, bondholders, and so forth? And with holding companies, interlocking directorates, trade associations? I've read some books about the structure of the economic system, and it doesn't sound very simple to me."

I only had to think a minute to know he was right. The control of a little bank like ours and its relation to other banks, to say nothing of its relation to other businesses in Braxton and in the state, had been too complicated for me to understand. Remembering the way the First National Bank of Boston sent out tentacles all over New England, I knew I had been silly.

CONVERSATION AT MIDNIGHT

"I've made our system seem simpler than it is," he went on, "and you won't find it easy to understand the whole story. But it can be understood, and the average citizen does understand it. That's something that couldn't be said a hundred years ago."

Sketches Made at Jersey City Transfer Station

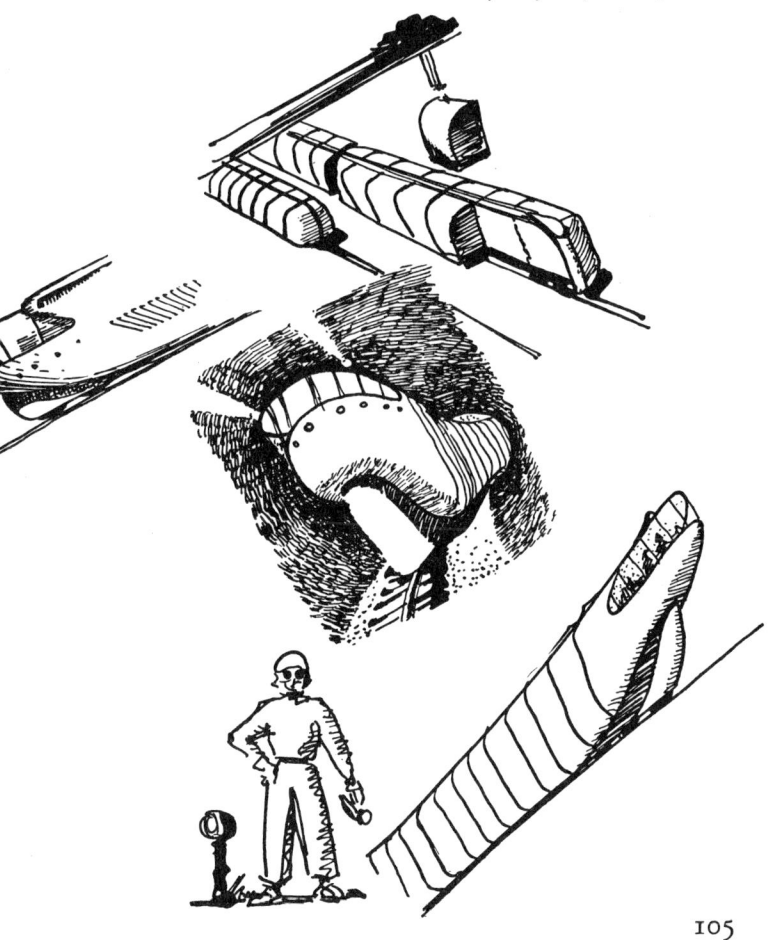

We had emerged in the center of another great block, its court surrounded with stores and offices. We entered an office marked "Transportation Control," and David explained what we wanted to the girl at the desk. She consulted another young woman, and then returned. "You've been here before, Mr. Wilson? You'll look after Mr. Swain and do what the guide says?" He nodded. "We do have to be strict," she apologized, as she made out passes, "but of course we wouldn't obstruct legitimate study."

The guide was as pretty a girl as I have ever seen. The hair that showed underneath her cap was dark red, and she wore her work suit as if she were modeling at a fashion show.

We went through the office and down a corridor, coming at last to an enormous shed. From the bridge to which Margo led us, I looked down on hundreds of trains. Some of them were in motion, but there was little noise, and I could hear clearly the words that one of the workers far below me was calling to another. He was talking about his new baby.

"There's a train due from Omaha on track 79," Margo said. As she spoke, it appeared in the upper reaches of the yards, and in a few seconds the engine was coming to a stop just below us.

"Notice that it's monorail," David said to me. Margo looked surprised, and he added, "Mr. Swain isn't very familiar with these things yet."

She smiled understandingly.

While we were speaking, the sides of the cars opened as far back as my eye could reach, and the contents began to move across the platforms on both sides into the trains that were waiting there. Plenty of men were hurrying about, but all of them seemed to be engaged either in inspecting the machinery or in examining the contents.

"This is tomorrow's meat," Margo said, for my benefit.

"You see," David commented. "New England now raises almost all its own meat, but New York has to transport its supply from the West."

I was beginning to understand his criticism of the city. To take care of its needs, other areas had to specialize instead of developing towards self-sufficiency. Of course, no region was wholly self-sufficient, but the nearer each unit came to that goal, the more local autonomy there could be.

The sides of the train were closing, and the top began to roll back. Tremendous derricks swung great bales from more distant platforms. "Clothing fabrics," Margo said, "and some machinery."

"Dislocates the whole economy," David observed gloomily.

"But surely," I protested, "certain goods can be produced more efficiently in one area than in another."

"That's right. Now tell me what can be produced more efficiently in New York. Besides, don't forget how much we use synthetic products. We're not so tied down to corn belts and wheat belts and cotton belts and oil fields as you were."

Trying to follow what was happening in that shed was like being at one of the big circuses. As in my boyhood, I felt cheated because I could not watch everything that was going on. When my eyes came back to the train beneath us, it was moving out again. "Seventeen minutes," said Margo.

She led the way down the steps. "This is the transfer machinery." She pointed into the pit that the train had just left. "See the rail. These freights run between one hundred and one hundred and twenty miles an hour. That was about one hundred and seventy cars."

I exclaimed at the figure. "There aren't any grade crossings," David said, and she looked puzzled.

She pointed into the train that had just been loaded. Approximately one half of each car was empty. "A car to a block. Roughly five tons of meat for each. There's a southern fruit and vegetable train due in almost immediately."

A bell rang, and she hurried us back to the ladder and the bridge. After the train came in, the process was repeated. Then, while the freight train was being loaded, the trains on either side began to move towards the city.

We watched other trains load and unload, and Margo showed us derricks, transfer platforms, automatic controls, inspection points, and, in the end, so much complicated mechanism that my head whirled. Scores of trains came and left while we looked on.

"How many people work here?" I asked.

"Between two thousand and twenty-five hundred on each of the shifts. This is an unusually large cooperative: about eight thousand transportation workers, six thousand in the offices, two thousand more or less transient train operatives whose families live here, seventy-five hundred service workers, three thousand wives who work elsewhere, and more than ten thousand children."

We had come at last to the end of the shed, and there were more offices and a recreation center. We stepped inside and had some sort of refreshing drink. I can't remember that as a boy I wanted to be a locomotive engineer, but I always admired and rather envied railroad men. And the group of men who were playing games here had the same kind of self-assurance. Their tasks, they seemed to say, were difficult, but they were equal to them. They had their own lingo, too, and their own jokes. More than one looked admiringly at Margo, but that would have happened anywhere.

"We won't have to walk all the way back," she said when we left the center, and she led us to chairs on a beltline. As we sat down, she asked us if we would like to ride on a supply train to the Clothing Center. I was enthusiastic about the idea. She picked up a small instrument on the side of the car and telephoned the office. "Yes, there's a train leaving at six-twenty with a car for C.C.—track 42."

At the track she called an inspector and said good-bye, running up the steps, her cerise scarf fluttering behind her.

"You'll have to step right along," the inspector told us, as he led us down the platform. There was a small compartment at the end of the car, and he warned us to stay there until the door opened at the Center.

Bells rang and lights flashed as the freight train came in on the other side of the platform. Belts began to move, and heavy crates crossed into our car. The bells rang again, and our train moved out, rapidly gathering speed as we went under the river.

There was not a human being in sight, and I grew a little panicky. "Is this an express to our block?" I asked David.

"Watch the car behind us," he answered. It suddenly detached itself, and I caught a glimpse of it as it vanished down a sidetrack. A few minutes later we came to a standstill, and, as the doors opened, I realized that our car too had left the train and reached its destination.

"This way, please," a voice called as we left the car. The boxes and crates were now moving out of the car and into elevators. The man who had spoken was standing at a kind of control board. "Half a minute," he said. The doors closed. "All clear. There's the passenger elevator."

"Home again," said David as we came out into the court. "Are you ready for breakfast?"

V

RETURN TO BRAXTON

IN MY account of the first twenty-four hours after my awakening, I have tried to record every detail that I observed and to report every conversation as nearly verbatim as my memory would permit. At David's suggestion I made comprehensive notes, and I have drawn upon these. But that day still is vivid in my mind. I felt as I imagine a foreign correspondent might feel on his first day in a new capital, or perhaps as an explorer would feel on penetrating territory that white men had never before visited. I thought of myself not as a permanent resident of this new world, nor yet as an isolated exile from an earlier age, but rather as a scout, sent ahead to reconnoiter and report. Try as I would, I could not rid myself of the feeling that I must remember everything so as to be able to tell my contemporaries—my twentieth century contemporaries—about it. Naturally, my attitude rapidly altered, and I became more of a participant and less of an observer. During the week that we spent in New York David systematically showed me the city and helped me to understand the ways in which life had changed. It would be pointless to try to tell everything we did or to repeat the questions that I asked and he so patiently answered. Though my notes are voluminous, I shall make little use of them, drawing only upon the impressions that have remained clear.

David wanted to do some work in the great central library of the Psychological Institute, and I went with him. He took me to what he called the active section, and showed me how, by manipulating keys, he could produce a bibliography of the latest writings on any one of thousands of topics. Since each card contained an abstract of the article or book it indexed, a glance told him what he wanted. Then he turned to an instrument like a telephone dial, dialed a number, and the desired document appeared in a neat little capsule. Taking it to a reading machine, he studied it at his leisure, and if he wanted a copy, photographing was a matter of seconds.

"More gadgets?" I asked.

He was indignant. All this, he said, was essential to modern science. Without such mechanical aids, the student could not possibly assemble and master the data relevant to his particular problem. "It was precisely at this point," he said, "that science was beginning to break down in your day."

I saw the television apparatus that made pictures, charts, and documents available to scholars at distant points, and I discovered for the first time that many book films had a sound track. Listening to a book is, of course, relatively slow, but it does save the eyes.

We went to the planning bureau of the transportation control board. One wall of the central office was an enormous chart. It showed how much electric power would be required for trains during 2040, and how the demand would be distributed over both space and time. It showed how much metal would be required for replacement of rails, how many new cars would have to be built, how many men would be employed. The opposite wall was an equally enormous map of the continent, on which not only railroad lines and terminals were indicated but also each individual train. Both the chart and the map were animated, the map showing the movement of trains, the chart registering changes in estimates, the fulfillment of quotas, and so forth. In the room a dozen men and women sat at desks, watching the chart and the map, telephoning, writing.

I realized that planning, complicated as it obviously was, was less mysterious than I had supposed. Society had had eighty years of experience, and it was no wonder that these people were able to avoid serious mistakes. In the early days, I could see, it must have been different.

In another room I saw a battery of automatic calculating machines, supervised by a pleasant-spoken, gray-haired woman of about sixty. Her job was to adjust transportation facilities to the demand for food, and it specially interested me because of what I had seen at the Jersey City terminal. She showed me how estimates were based on data on population changes, seasonal eating habits, and much else, so that they could tell, almost to a pound, how much of any particular kind of food would be required in a year.

David reminded me that these estimates were prepared by the food planning board and came within the province of this department only insofar as the food had to be transported. I got the point: he was offering another argument for the self-sufficient district.

THE FIRST TO AWAKEN

The supervisor explained the various machines. There was one, for example, on which all the orders of the cooperative restaurants in the city were recorded and tabulated. "Here is yesterday's total," she said, "and here is the estimate. You see, right within five hundred pounds. But I can tell you it doesn't always work out so well, and then I have to get busy."

At the regional center for food planning there were more animated maps and charts, and again I saw how complicated a problem the maintenance of New York's population was. Yet, as I had already suspected, it was easy now compared with what it had once been. The demand for certain kinds of food had actually trebled and quadrupled in a single year in the sixties and seventies. Now the demand was predictable if not steady, and the areas on which New York depended had adjusted themselves to the problems of production.

We saw other departments, and gradually I got a sense of the whole complex machine. As we stood in the circular court of the Regional Planning Center, just in front of the old Sub-treasury Building that still occupied the site of Washington's first inauguration, I gazed at the skyscrapers all around me. "But what a tremendous bureaucracy this requires!"

David smiled patiently. "If I remember correctly, there were a good many office workers employed in this vicinity in your day, and not so usefully employed, most of them, as those you have just seen."

"But that was different."

"Quite. And in whose favor is the difference? As a matter of fact, if you will look at the charts I showed you, you will see that office workers are in about the same proportion to the rest of the working population as they were a hundred years ago. Actually, since the working day is only half as long on the average, fewer hours are spent in offices."

That set me back on my heels, and I asked for an explanation. I got three: efficiency, machinery, and decentralization. "There is no duplication of effort," David pointed out; "nothing is done by human hands and brains that a machine can do as well; and there's only one New York."

This was impressive, but there was still a point on which I was not satisfied. "In my day everybody was afraid of bureaucracy."

"We're still afraid of it, but we have two protections against its dangers—science and democracy. To a great extent the details of planning are worked out according to objective scientific formulas, and the actual operations are largely mechanized. The most power-loving individual would find it difficult to tamper with these processes. Then the broad policies are determined by the people."

It was snowing that day, a nasty March snow, but the street-cleaning monsters went about, sweeping up the flakes and melting them before they could accumulate. "There's no place for snow in a city," David said.

We met Nick and Norah again in the restaurant, and they invited us to a party in their home. Perhaps it would be best if I quoted directly from my notebook:

> Fourteen present. Something good to drink, not entirely unintoxicating. A large room, strikingly and individually furnished, though David said that, except for a few inexpensive items, all the contents were standard equipment.

Much interest in music. Listened to a program of folk songs on the radio, and that started everyone singing. Several songs I knew—old cowboy ballads and that sort of thing. Some very spirited revolutionary songs from the fifties and sixties. Nick played some charming modern songs on the phonograph—steel tape for records.

Got badly mixed up trying to tell about the WPA. They seem to have an exaggerated impression of its usefulness—because of guides, historical documents studies, plays, etc. Happened to mention "Brain Trust," and they could not understand how that could have been a term of derision.

Somebody called Jones got talking about a writer of the thirties and forties called Saroyan. Called him the great neglected genius of my period and compared him to William Blake. Knew little about him but wouldn't have said he was neglected.[1]

Much struck by use of strange colors in decoration of both homes and public buildings. Nick says colors are scientifically determined, though individual taste varies them. Certain colors restful, stimulating, or what not. Lighting used to give variety. According to Norah, texture of materials also plays important part in decoration —grain of wood, weave of fabrics, flow of plastic. Different textures used for contrast and balance. No smooth finish attempted on materials that will scratch; hence things don't show use so much.

---

[1] Swain, I have discovered after some research, is quite right. Probably Jones got the impression Saroyan was neglected from the many letters, half-plaintive, half-blustering, he wrote to the magazines.—D.W.

Almost everybody very tactful. Personal relationships do seem on pretty good level. Little showing off, arguments vigorous but seldom nasty.

Good discussion of American traditions. They are patriotic in a curious way. Know a lot of things about the 19th cent. I never knew.

We all went swimming before we went home. I can't get used to the hours these people keep. They get sleep enough, but they seem to do it when there's nothing else to do. This party began about eleven because some people wanted to go to the theater, and it ended at four, when Nick had to go to work. Norah and another girl decided to go horseback riding before their shift began.

Lots of talk about poetry that was over my head.

There was also, I recall, some talk about art and art museums. The professional artist had disappeared, I gathered, along with the professional poet and the professional actor. That is, no one lived by painting pictures, though there were many persons more interested in art than in anything else. Most people sketched or painted, and fine work frequently appeared at cooperative exhibits.

I had been to the exhibits at the Clothing Center and in other cooperatives. Such an exhibit might include local work or a show borrowed from some other center or perhaps a collection of copies of what we would have called masterpieces. The cooperative gallery, I realized, gave the citizen a chance to see what he liked. With no academic pressure, no excitement over scarcity values, and no political campaigning by schools of criticism, he simply developed his own taste. "A

THE FIRST TO AWAKEN

neighbor of mine," Norah once said, "borrowed for his apartment a Rembrandt, a minor French post-impressionist, and a still life by a member of this cooperative. And he was right. You could see, once he had selected the pictures, that they belonged together."

The cooperative galleries I liked, but I was not so keen about the great art museum, to which Nick insisted on taking me. For one thing, he was not an easy companion, for he made no effort to use language that I could understand. For another, I have never been much interested in the history of art.

One thing I did like, and that is that we had no walking to do. We went into a small room, sat ourselves down in comfortable chairs, and looked at the pictures as they appeared. As Nick had told me in advance, this was a special show he had arranged for me, with the cooperation of the museum's officials. (Anyone could do this if he made the proper arrangements.) According to the program I picked up, the regular shows that week, each of which could be studied in any one of several rooms, embraced such topics as "Paintings by Members of the Birmingham Bessemer Club," "Psycho-Representation Since Van Gogh," "Paintings of the Renaissance," and "Dada and Doodles."

The room, so beautifully lighted, so simple, and so com-

Looking at pictures
Central Art Museum

fortable, seemed incomplete and somehow disturbing until the first picture appeared, and then I realized that that was what I had been waiting for. After Nick had given his little lecture, the curtains dropped, to open again on the second of his series.

I asked, of course, if these were the real paintings, the originals, and I am not likely to forget the disgust with which he looked at me. "When you can tell the difference between these and the originals," he said savagely, "you'll be allowed to examine the originals. Until then these are good enough." I was subdued by that, but he went on muttering, "Damned capitalist mentality . . . value simply because it's unique . . . the picture that matters." Later he relented enough to explain that the reproductions approximated perfection not only in surface color but in texture as well. "Really, George," he insisted, "this concern with originals, for anyone except the most highly trained expert, means nothing when art is separated from money."

Humbly I tried to look at the paintings as they appeared and listen to Nick's comments, but I could understand no more of one than of the other. "The camera," he said, "ended representative painting . . . remained for Picasso to demolish all previous schools . . . a phobic personality, oriented to destruction. . . . Now, when art went back to the people, it went back to representation, but only to leap forward again. . . . The seven principal schools at the end of the century . . . the crypto-symbolic. . . ."

But my exhaustion was obvious "You don't have to like these pictures," he said with resignation. "This is the historic approach to art. This is to help you understand why men painted as they did. If you're not interested, you'd better stick to the cooperative exhibits."

I did go back, though, by myself, to the museum, and sat in one of the groups, reading the very intelligent and informative notes that appeared with each picture. And I did come to feel a direct, simple relationship between the individual and the work of art that I had never felt in the old-fashioned museum. In time, I thought, even I might learn something—but not if Nick was along.

Norah was a better companion. She took me to the cooperative theater one evening, and even explained the jokes to me. I did not understand the play very well, for it was a comedy of manners, hinging on the vanity of a union official who wanted to be elected manager of his cooperative. Much of it, however, was pure slapstick, and I laughed as heartily as anyone at the crazy chase that was the climax of Act II. I was a little shocked to find that various kinds of physical defect were still regarded as funny, but Norah argued that this was salutary, since no one needed to be fat or bow-legged.

The actors were really neither professionals nor amateurs. That is, they all had other jobs, but most of them had had a good deal of experience on the stage. I gathered that many people took part in dramatics, for there were several groups in the one cooperative. Sometimes, Norah told me, a company would have a great success, and then people would come from all over the city to see it, but usually the productions were for the local audience.

That audience interested me. I had met many persons by that time, but somehow I had felt that each of them must be an exception. Now I began to get some sense of what people were like en masse. They were just plain, ordinary people, far better educated than the average person of my day, and with a wider range of interests, but not highbrows. Because most of them took some interest in literature and the arts, I had thought of them almost as intellectuals. They weren't anything like the intellectuals of my day, however. That is to say, they weren't all wrapped up in the arts and their theories about them. They were chiefly occupied with their jobs and their families.

I can't seem to say exactly what I mean. The point is that these people were more like the men and women I had known in Braxton than they were like the Bohemians Everett had introduced me to in the Village. Everett called my Braxton friends Philistines, and so they were, but there wasn't one of them who wouldn't have cultivated wider interests if he'd had a chance.

It wouldn't be right to say that the distinction between highbrow and lowbrow had wholly disappeared, but it certainly wasn't clear to me. Nick was a highbrow, and yet he was a factory worker. Others I met, who had spent more years on their education than he and held more responsible positions, had none of his intense interest in literature. He wasn't typical, of course, and yet his fellow-workers didn't seem to regard him as a freak.

It was all very puzzling. I suppose I had had the vague impression that, once the whole economic level had been raised, everybody would conform to my ideal—a certain type of well-educated, well-rounded gentleman. But it hadn't worked out that way. In some respects this audience was like a typical working-class audience of my day, but in others it wasn't a bit

THE FIRST TO AWAKEN

like that. And what made my problem more difficult was the fact that there really was no norm at all, for individual differences were not merely tolerated but encouraged.

Norah also took me to visit the cooperative nursery, and to my amazement it was more like bedlam than anything I had experienced during my short stay in the new world. Norah laughed at me, saying, "Children have to make a noise."

"But don't you try to teach them to get along together?"

"That's just what they're learning. You can't beat the idea of cooperation into their heads with a club."

After the snow, the weather turned warm, and David, Nick, and Norah suggested that we go horseback riding in the circumferential park. With some shame, I told them that, except for farm horses in my boyhood, I had never been on a horse in my life, and we agreed on a bicycle ride instead. I had always liked cycling, and resented the fact that automobiles had made it so dangerous.

We had a little trouble getting four bicycles, for the good weather had given others the same idea, but two were secured from another cooperative, and we started off across the city. We went under the highway and into the broad bicycle road beside the bridle path. I was excited at seeing the first robin of the year, and we constantly heard bluebirds.

David and Nick rode ahead, arguing as usual, and Norah and I followed. There were hundreds of people out, many of them young but by no means all. A man with a snow white beard swept by us, his brown legs plunging furiously at the pedals, and a good proportion of the horseback riders were women in their forties or fifties. When we had gone round the end of the island and come back on the other side, I was tired but full of good spirits.

I learned my way about the stores in the Clothing Center, and, having collected my weekly stipend, made a certain number of purchases. For one thing, I bought a dictionary, in which I systematically looked up words that were new to me. I also picked up a number of magazines and pamphlets. The latter were usually devoted to propaganda, and it struck me how much better it was to have opinions appearing as opinions instead of being masked as news.

David explained the magazines and pamphlets to me as well as he could, but he did not encourage me to spend much time with them. When we were not making pilgrimages about the city, he led me into conversations in the restaurant or the game rooms, or persuaded me to swim or play tennis, the only game at which I have ever been even moderately good.

We visited schools and libraries and planning bureaus and factories. Everywhere I was impressed by the uses to which machinery was put. I had hated the machines when I worked in the shoe factory, for they seemed to do the only interesting part of the job, and the operatives were merely their slaves. Now such machines had become wholly automatic and workers, if they were needed at all, were needed for their brains. They were the masters.

I spoke of this to David, and we got to talking about the way civilization depended on the machine. "I can't show you where machine parts are made," he said, "for that's all done at the metal centers, but I can show you how they're designed and how they're put together."

So we went to another cooperative and saw dozens of laboratories and room after room of men and women with drawing boards. This was systematized invention. "Our chief effort," one of the men told me, "is to design machines so that they can be built out of standard parts. Otherwise the problem of making machines to make machines would swamp our economy. Even a typewriter has some of the same parts as a power shovel."

"That's why," David said, "when you come to travel round the country, you won't find a separate automobile industry or housing industry or clothing machine industry; you'll find factories for the manufacture of certain types of parts."

This was not the first time he had referred to my traveling around the country, and that night I asked him how much longer we were going to stay in New York. "Have you had enough?" he asked.

"I think so."

He looked up quizzically. "Well, what do you want to do next? You can see the country, or see the world for that matter. Or you might settle down somewhere."

"What do you think?"

"It's your problem."

"It might be nice to go back to Braxton."

Obviously that was the right answer so far as he was concerned. "Good," he said briskly, "we'll leave day after tomorrow."

Nick and Norah and some of our other friends, when they heard of our departure, held a farewell party for us. There was less serious discussion than at the other party. In fact, it was a gay affair, with all of us drinking enough of the delicious wine to forget our dignity. Nick made a burlesque speech at which we all laughed extravagantly. Norah did a dance, very beautifully I thought, and then she came and sat by me while the others moved about the floor in steps that seemed almost as pointless to me as those of my own day. A rowdy square dance followed, in which they insisted I take part, and I did get the hang of it, though I was worn out before it was finished.

It was a good party. I told stories, and they all laughed. I have always thought I told a story rather well, and here was an audience that had heard none of my best ones. Of course, some of them fell rather flat, but the one about the dead horse in the bathtub was a great success.

As we got up to go, Norah made a deep bow, her skirts sweeping the floor, and we all laughed. "Come back," Nick shouted, waving his glass. "Come back in a year's time and tell us what you think."

"Let's get an early start," David said when he left me at my room. Friendly as I felt towards him at the moment, I could not help resenting the suggestion. "We can sleep on the way if we want to," he insisted. "Let's not miss the best part of the day."

He called me before sunrise, and we went to the store for a change of clothes. This was not the first time we had changed, and I had grown quite used to the business of choosing a new outfit and throwing the old one into a container. The cooperative—and this was an innovation that delighted David—had installed showers next to the clothing department, and so we started out with new clothes on clean bodies. David wore a gay suit of mossy green, with an orange scarf, and, emboldened by his example, I had chosen a suit of cinnamon shade and a scarf of green.

We took a crosstown chair car and got out at what seemed to be an underground garage. David signed the register and motioned me into a waiting automobile. "Are we going to drive?" I asked in dismay. "You said we could sleep."

"You'll see," he answered.

We watched the sun rise over Long Island. I was surprised at the number of cars on the road. "Why not?" David said. "This is the pleasantest time to travel."

It took only a few minutes to get out of the city, and soon we came to a large traffic circle. We were taking the shore road as far as New Haven, and David guided the car along the approach. "Do you want to go forty miles an hour or ninety-three?" he asked.

Surprised, I said, "Forty."

Two lanes stretched before us, and we took the outside one. "Now," David said triumphantly, shifting the lever marked "Beam." The steering gear vanished in the dashboard, and he dramatically put his hands in his pockets. I was mystified and a little frightened until he explained the principle of beam control. "This is the greatest improvement in travel," he said, "since the automobile was invented."

I could see what he meant. Unless you are specifically interested in the scenery, travel is always a nuisance. My new contemporaries had evidently found two ways of solving the problem. One was to make travel very fast—for instance, by gymbal plane. The other was to make it possible for the traveler to spend his time pleasantly and profitably. And this had finally been accomplished not only for ships and airplanes and trains but also for automobiles. On a beam highway there was no need for either front-seat or back-seat driving.[1] The car took care of itself, and the passengers were free to do whatever they pleased.

The advantages were obvious, but I could not believe that the mechanism was fool-proof. David insisted on my sitting in the driver's place, and then turned the car onto manual control. My only trouble was in keeping down the speed, and I began to catch up with the car in front. "Step on it hard," David urged, and, though I thought he was crazy, I did. The car, nevertheless, slowed down to an exact forty. I tried going slow but as soon as an auto came close to us, we began to accelerate, reached forty, and stayed there. "This is a forty mile lane, like it or not," David said, as he switched again to beam control.

Reassured enough to relax, I watched the cars passing in the higher speed lane. They flew past us, and that is more than figure of speech, for, with the rear wheels retracted and the steering rudder riding high, they did seem to be machines for the air rather than the land. Unlike our speed, which was arbitrarily determined for the convenience of travelers who wanted to see the scenery, their ninety-three miles an hour was the point of maximum efficiency. Despite their pace, however, they kept a perfectly even course, and I noticed that the people inside were playing cards or reading or writing or otherwise busying themselves.

I was glad to have a chance to see the country. Built close to

[1] This is an allusion to the fact that, in the early days of the automobile, persons sitting in the seat behind the driver often volunteered advice. The term has fallen into disuse, but I believe that the practice is not unknown when cars are being driven on roads that are not beam-controlled.—D.W.

the Sound, the road gave frequent glimpses of the water, and of course there were no billboards to interfere with the view. Many small boats were sailing about, and I spoke to David of the great popularity of boating. He had an interesting explanation. As production, even in agriculture, became more and more mechanized, people sought in sport the direct contact with nature that had largely disappeared from the regular routine of life. For the majority, this desire expressed itself in mild ways, but there were many, especially the young, who demanded a bolder struggle. They turned to the more dangerous sports—to difficult feats of skiing, for example, or moun-

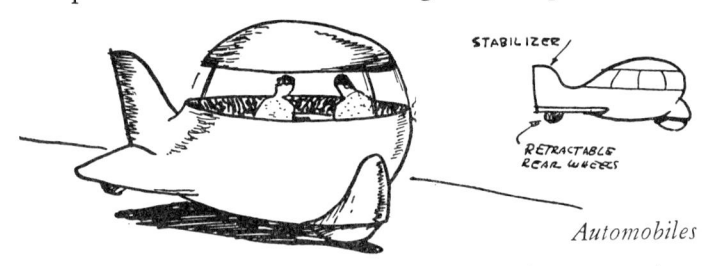

Automobiles

tain climbing. They went on long canoeing trips on treacherous rivers, crossed the ocean in small craft, or experimented with gliders.

The road, which was perfectly straight, now and again took us inland, crossing brooks and rivers and passing through wooded country. I had been struck by the promptness with which we had left the city, but I was even more impressed by the absence of anything that could be called suburbs. We caught glimpses of many towns, usually rather like Braxton, with from four to ten large buildings and a surrounding area full of homes. Bridgeport, I discovered, had completely vanished. Not only had the gloomy factories and the narrow streets been eliminated; there was merely another small town on the site.

Suddenly I was startled by a voice in the car: "Construction ahead; use manual control. Construction ahead; use manual control."

"What happens if we don't? Suppose we were both asleep?"

"Try it and see," David suggested. In a few moments the car came to a complete stop, while the voice repeated, "Construction ahead; use manual control."

"Sit tight," said David, and after a little while a man came and tapped on the window. "Wake up," he shouted, "there's construction ahead."

When David shifted to manual control, the radio voice stopped. As soon as we had gone round the construction, he turned on the beam again.

"Do you have traffic policemen?"

"No. The beam highway did away with them." It was science that had done the trick.

"Do you have any kind of policemen?"

"Several kinds, though we don't call them that. Every cooperative has its inspectors. Mostly their job is to check up on the equipment, but they guard against any kind of human interference, accidental or malicious. Then there are district inspectors, who investigate all irregularities. They work with the psychiatric boards and the cooperative disciplinary committees."

The voice in the car said: "Going off the beam, going off the beam. Turn right for Springfield beam for the north. Straight ahead for Narragansett beam for Providence and Boston. Going off the beam, going off the beam. Turn right . . ."

THE FIRST TO AWAKEN

The voice stopped, the steering gear appeared, the car slowed down. We followed an incline, and made a left turn under the highway. David switched onto the beam again, and we were off.

As we passed through the outskirts of New Haven, I caught a glimpse of familiar towers. "Yes," David explained, "they're still there—a beautiful example of academic Gothic. What a bastard architecture it was."[1]

"What's happened to things like the cathedrals in Europe?"

"Those that weren't destroyed in the wars have mostly been preserved. Some people oppose this. They say that any kind of restoration is bound to be false. Anything we can't absorb into our own culture, according to them, ought to go. But most people want to keep the great buildings of the past, for historical or even for purely sentimental reasons."

He began to look intently out of the window as if he was searching for something. "Did you ever hear of Buckminster Fuller?" I shook my head. "Somewhere along here there is a group of houses that very closely resemble the dymaxion house he invented. There!" He pointed, and I saw what seemed almost like a cluster of tents.

"That's one example of the purely functional house. Mostly, as you see, we haven't got as far away as that from earlier concepts. Still we do think of houses from the inside, not from the outside. A house is something to live in, not something

---

[1] I recommended to Swain a book that deserves to be better known—L. B. Satterlee's *Steel and Stone on the American Campus* (New Haven, 2017). Mr. Satterlee discusses not only the architectural but also the economic and social implications of the Harkness buildings at Yale and similar structures elsewhere. He has a most illuminating chapter on the mental processes of American millionaires.—D.W.

Dymaxion Houses, Fullerton, N. E. D.

to look at. There are schools of architecture that believe dwellings should be adapted to their environment, and there are still a few romanticists who insist on imitating the traditional domestic architecture of a given region. That's all part of a kind of sentimental backwash of the increasing regionalization. You'll see the same thing in art and literature."

"That looks like a typical colonial house," I said.

"Oh, they did very ingenious things in adapting pre-fabricated parts to old-fashioned designs. But the purists are dead against it, and in practice most people don't like the mixed styles."

The sun was bright now, and David asked if I would mind having the top back. "We get ultraviolet rays through the glass," he said, "but I like the sense of being outdoors." The roof rolled back, and I waited for the impact of the wind, but it didn't come. "We use the wind," David explained, "to keep the wind away, by making a cross draft. You'd feel more wind if the car were standing still."

We were silent for a while, and I got out my pad and began to make a few sketches. David watched me, and then began to revise a manuscript he had with him.

I am afraid I have permitted David to appear simply as the person who answered all my questions. It is true that he was amazingly well-informed and incredibly patient. I doubt if anyone else could have helped me so much. He not only could answer my questions; he could understand them. I have quoted him again and again because that is the only way of suggesting how my education took place. But I certainly did not regard him merely as my omniscient guide. He had asked me to think of him as a friend, and it had not taken me long to learn to do so. Though he knew so much more than I, he seemed youthful, and I felt that, for all his erudition, he was full of uncertainties and shynesses. In a curious way, indeed, I felt that we were a good deal alike.

Watching him while I pretended to draw, I was amused at the seriousness of his face. His expressions dramatized every problem of his writing. He would scowl or smile, run his hands through his curly brown hair, fill his pipe and forget to light it, scratch out a word as if he were destroying a poisonous snake, beam as he scribbled a phrase. I thought of him as I had seen him at Norah's party the night before. Some of his reserve—which usually persisted in spite of his complete affability and poise—had left him, and he had been as boyish and as boisterous as the others. I wondered about his wife—with whom, I was sure, he was very much in love.

He looked up suddenly. "Getting hungry? Do you want to

stop somewhere for lunch, or shall we pick it up?" I wasn't tired of riding, and so he ordered lunch for us in a two-way conversation with the beam station at Springfield. "We'll pick it up at Hartford South," he said.

While we signed vouchers for the luncheon, a man filled the alcohol tank. "The car does fifty to sixty miles on a gallon," David said. "We use alcohol because it can be made from annual crops that are grown here in the district. It's not so powerful as gasoline, and gas is still used in the neighborhood of the oilfields, but this saves transportation, and production can be closely adjusted to demand. We have an alcohol plant in Braxton."

As soon as we were on the beam again, David turned over the front seat, and laid out the lunch on a table that rose out of the floor.

"Hartford is a good example of the way cities had to change," he remarked. "You remember, it was an insurance town. Most of the companies went bankrupt during the second half of the depression, and then the government took over insurance. And finally it was abolished altogether."

As usual, both of us ate with relish. "Do you still mind being studied?" David asked.

I thought a moment. "No," I said in surprise.

He smiled with pleasure. "I don't know that I'd want to be studied by anybody but you," I qualified. "You do make it painless."

But he would not agree. He said that I was beginning to acquire their attitude. "The individual's privacy is so much more fully protected that he isn't always on guard. He is willing to cooperate in psychological as in physical study of

THE FIRST TO AWAKEN

himself, for he understands its purpose and something of its methods."

We drifted off into a long talk about psychiatry.[1] I had heard more than one reference to the Dictatorship of the Psychiatrists, and David began to explain. Like most of the sciences, psychology made great advances in the early decades of socialism, and particularly therapeutic psychology. Clinics were widely established and had great success. Not surprisingly, there were staggering problems of adjustment to the new situation, and the clinics developed effective techniques for dealing with them. The psychiatrists, with such extensive opportunities for experiment, reached a point at which they could shape character just about as they pleased.

The next step was to make psychiatric treatment compulsory. Just as everyone had to have a monthly physical examination, he had to consult his psychiatrist once a month or oftener. As David had pointed out before, people were conditioned to like their jobs, no matter how dull they might be. The psychiatrists, in other words, were adjusting people to things as they were, regardless of whether things were good or bad.

"Did you ever read *Brave New World?*" I shook my head. "You ought to. It's an amusing and somewhat shrewd book, written by one of the more fanatical moralists of your time. Fundamentally, of course, Huxley—you know, Aldous Huxley—was quite wrong, for he made the book an attack on any

---

[1] Perhaps at no other point is it so evident that Swain is handicapped by the inadequacy of his vocabulary. I cannot discuss in detail the mistakes that he makes, but I trust that no one will take his remarks as a scientific account.—D.W.

kind of social improvement and glorified suffering for its own sake. The idea seemed to be that if everybody had enough to eat, there would be no place for poets like Huxley. But what I started to say is that conditions were just a little like those described in *Brave New World*. Huxley, however, has a melodramatic revolt against regimentation, and nothing so desperate was necessary. There was a fundamental common sense in the people that kept the psychiatrists in check and finally put them back in their place."

He went on to say what the place of the psychiatrist was. I gathered that, though the change in the basis of property and the improvement in education had eliminated a great deal of crime, there were still offenses against society, and the offenders were given psychiatric treatment. But at the same time the rights of the individual were protected by a kind of jury system. For the rest, men and women went to psychiatric clinics when they chose to. "We know," he said, "that there is no sharp line between normal and abnormal psychology, and we all have our quirks. But then, there are very few perfectly healthy human beings, and yet we don't run to the doctor every fifteen minutes."

Our dishes and eating utensils were all made of a plastic material, and David put them in a bag, to be deposited in a waste receptacle when next we stopped. We had shifted from the Springfield to the Brattleboro beam, and I was looking at the river and the hills. David said, "I'm going to take a nap. Aren't you sleepy?" I shook my head. He swung the seats sideways, so that he had a comfortable couch, and asked me to go on to the Manchester beam when we reached the Brattleboro traffic circle. He was soon asleep.

I took out my notebook and began to write:

If someone had slept from 1840 to 1940, he would have been chiefly impressed, I should think, with mechanical progress. You would have to explain electricity to him, automobiles, radio, everything of that kind. He would have to have a course in science and a history of the industrial revolution.

Now I, on the other hand, am not so much impressed by technological advance. Many of the new inventions are wonderful, and I get excited about them, but the idea of invention isn't new to me. Probably I don't know enough to say so, but my guess is that less mechanical progress has been made in the last century than in the preceding one.

The great change has come in the organization of society. As nearly as I can make out, there is not much left that could be called a government in my sense of the word. According to D., the functions of town and city governments were taken over by the cooperatives. State governments became much less important than regional planning boards, and finally disappeared. There is still a federal government of sorts, but the President is little more than a figurehead, and Congress is a kind of super-advisory council that meets for a few days every three months and discusses general policy. Some people want to abolish the President and Congress, but the old institutions have a certain sentimental appeal.

I realize more and more clearly how important decentralization is. The cooperative has a lot of power because it is in such large measure self-sufficient. It is not wholly independent, however, and so it is represented on the planning council and the other agencies of the district. It also has a voice on the transportation board and the housing board and all the committees that affect it in any way.

Now that I stop to think of it, many of the functions of government in my day were economic—carrying the mail, for instance, building roads, regulating trade, taking care of sewage, providing water, and things like that. And I suppose it is more sensible to have economic bodies to do economic jobs.

Although there are certainly national traditions and a national culture, the nation has pretty well disappeared. That's partly because the regions have taken over so much of its work, and partly because the whole continent is unified. That is, the big planning boards are continental in scope. Canada actually affiliated with the United States in the seventies. Mexico isn't so close to us, but it is part of the same economic unit. The world is unified too, but not to the same degree.

I wonder how it actually works out. Are there still political bosses? Or do high-powered specialists dictate policies? I can't make out. D. talks about science and democracy, but is it really democracy, and who runs the science?

I laid down my pen, and thought a while. This was the way I tried to educate myself. The warning came for the traffic circle, and I successfully got us onto the Manchester beam.

I picked up the pen again, but I was feeling sleepy, and at last I stretched out on the other side of the car.

When I woke up, it was David who was making notes. He seemed in fine spirits, perhaps because of his rest, perhaps because we were getting home. I had less reason than he for being glad, but I did have the feeling that the week in New York had been a kind of holiday and that now life was going to begin for me, though what that could mean in practice I had no idea. I was still a spectator. Plans for the future were inconceivable, and I did not try to make them.

Beyond Manchester, now the planning center for the Northeast District, we were in territory that was very familiar to me. The highway, of course, never passed through towns, but often went close to them, and I tried to identify them, though I seldom succeeded. In some of them fine old churches remained, an occasional old house, perhaps a town hall. Most of the buildings, however, were new.

I spoke about this to David. "Why was it necessary to wipe out whole villages this way?" I asked.

"A hundred years is a long time, George. No matter what happened, these towns would have been rebuilt in the course of a century—if they hadn't just decayed. They've been rebuilt our way that's all."

The country was more sparsely settled than in Connecticut and Massachusetts. Although it was still too cold for spring plowing, there were plenty of signs that these fields would soon be under cultivation. There seemed to be nothing, however, that resembled the kind of farm I had known. Instead, there were long, low structures, usually with silos attached, and there were good-sized fields covered with some sort of translucent material. The soil, I could see, had grown no less inhospitable with the passing of years, and many of the hillsides had been given over to sheep. I had not remembered that the country was so wooded, and after a time I concluded that millions of trees must have been planted a good many years ago.

For a time we ran parallel to a truck road, and I had a better look than I had got before at these giants. There were fewer trucks, David said, than in my time, partly because the railroads had been made more efficient, chiefly because of decentralization, but in such a district as New England they were generally used. Largely automatic, they moved at a steady speed, well out of the way of passenger traffic.

David said, "We leave the beam highway here. Don't you want to drive?"

I took the steering gear. The road was broad and fast, but, unlike the beam highway, it followed the natural contours of the country. We were about five miles from the town, and soon I could see the hospital on the hill. We curved around it, and there was the town itself. As I cut down the speed, the rear wheels dropped, and we coasted easily towards the center.

It didn't look so strange now. There was the airport from which we had left. There was the auditorium. There was the old safety tower. I crossed the bridge and drove into the court in front of the apartment houses. "Just leave the car by the twelfth entrance. Come on—we're home."

VI

I FIND A HOME

I SPENT that night and the next in one of the guest rooms of the Braxton cooperative apartments. I met David's wife, Nathalie, and their three children. Nathalie, dark, sharp-eyed, quick-tempered, frightened me a little. Always cordial towards me, and often prompter than David in understanding my difficulties, she was so impatient with him that I was alternately embarrassed and indignant. The slowness of his speech, with the faintest suggestion of a downeast drawl in it, seemed to irritate her, and she often completed his sentences for him, snapping out the words he was getting ready to speak. They were obviously fond of each other, and he seemed used to her manner, but I was ill at ease when I was with them.

The oldest of the children, a boy of eight, as dark as his mother, I liked. To use an old-fashioned word—old-fashioned even in my time, I mean—he was manly. We talked together, and he showed me his games and books and told me about his school. His sister, on the other hand, who was six, seemed

I FIND A HOME

to me as thoroughly spoiled as any child I had ever known.[1] She was impudent in a highly intelligent way, exacting, and quick to pout and cry if her will was thwarted. The baby was a healthy, impersonal animal of whom I saw practically nothing.

Except for Everett I never had many friends, and after Elsie's death I was terribly lonely. I think that has to be said so that those who come after me will understand that I was not a stranger to lonesomeness. If I had been, the first days in Braxton might have been unbearable. Perhaps those who awaken later will make friends more rapidly than I. I am glad, however, that I did not expect too much. I was alone in this new world, but the sensation was not too distressing, for it was a familiar one. I was alone in the world I had left.

Of course I had David, and, like his great-great-grandfather, he was a sturdy bridge between my solitude and the throng of men and women who were there roundabout me. Yet, seeing him with his family, hearing him speak so intimately of experiences and interests in which I had no share and could have none, I felt that David was my friend only by an effort of the will and the imagination. I cherished that effort but resented the necessity for it.

David knew all this, and would doubtless have found a way sooner or later to meet my difficulties, but it was actually Nathalie who suggested my going to live with the Waldmans. I had asked David how it happened that some people lived in

---

[1] Although Swain volunteered to omit these and later passages about myself and my family, I regard them as an essential part of his story. It is, however, necessary for me to record my disagreement with some of his statements.—D.W.

the cooperative apartments and others in single houses, and he had replied that some preferred one and some the other. He was explaining how the balance was maintained when his wife suddenly said, "Wouldn't the Waldmans like to have George live with them?"

That is how it happened. The Waldmans were people of my age or a little older. Victor worked in the assembling plant and Agnes in the sports goods factory. They had two children at home—Abraham, who was sixteen, and Roberta, who was eleven. Timothy, the oldest, was studying in Cambridge. There had been a girl, Freda, between Abraham and Timothy, but she had been killed that winter in a skiing accident in the White Mountains. That, I afterwards realized, was why Nathalie had suggested my going to live with them.

David drove me to their home, nearly a mile out of town, that afternoon. From the street the house was inconspicuous enough—long and low, almost like a wall. Not only were there trees and shrubs and gardens all about it; there were shrubs on the roof, and in the very center, near the familiar power unit, was a greenhouse.

We swung up the drive, and left the car under the shelter. The door slid back, and there stood Victor Waldman, big and red-cheeked, his hand outstretched in welcome. "A fine idea," he said in his hearty voice. "I hope you'll like it here."

As we walked along the corridor, I had a glimpse of the kitchen, and then we were in the living room. There was glass on two sides, looking into the garden and orchard, with a good view of the hills beyond. The other walls, which, as I soon learned, hid radio, television, and phonograph, as well as tables and equipment for games, seemed simple panels

The Waldman Living Room

of natural wood, and the fixtures appeared to be made of warmly gleaming copper.

Real wood was burning in the fireplace, which projected a little distance into the room, with a kind of built-in seat along one side. After we were seated, Victor sank back in a huge armchair, only to lean forward again and operate a small pump. This pneumatic chair—a survival from an earlier period, I discovered—was his particular joy, though he could not sit in it five minutes without changing the pressure. At last he was satisfied, and lit his pipe.

Elsie and I had always liked a cozy room, and both in the apartment houses and in homes like the Waldmans' the rooms had at first seemed to me almost too spacious. They always looked large, no matter what the actual dimensions, and they usually were good-sized. Gradually, however, I was losing the sense that I must be shut in and protected. This room, for instance, though one felt it was almost a part of the garden outside, pleased me at once, and I sensed, as I could not have done a few days earlier, that it was homelike and comfortable. It had little of the style of Norah's apartment or Nathalie's, but it fitted the easy-going, open-handed way of living that I immediately associated with the Waldmans.

Victor seemed delighted with the idea of my staying with them. If I found it satisfactory, he said, there was no reason why I could not have a room of my own designing added to the house. In the meantime there was Freda's room—which, he said sadly, was just as she had left it.

After David had refused insistent invitations to stay for dinner, Victor took me to my room, urging me to arrange my things in any way I pleased. (My "things"—all the personal possessions I had acquired—were carried in a small handbag.) The room had obviously belonged to a young person, but it would have been hard to say whether the occupant was a boy or a girl. I looked at the equipment of the long table-desk, explored the panels a little, and studied the reading-machine. The closet was full of skis, snowshoes, skates, tennis rackets, golf clubs. Over the bed was a bookcase, and I looked with curiosity at the contents, for I had come to understand that one bought only books of which one was very fond. There were several books on sports, beautifully illustrated, an anthology of poetry, a volume of Shakespeare's plays, five or six rather formidable discussions of scientific principles, and a few novels.

I was to hear much about Freda before I left the Waldman household. Nothing had reconciled her parents to her death, and nothing ever would. Whether she had been as beautiful and brilliant as they said, I could not know, but I knew well enough how dear she had been to them. Not having been a particularly religious person myself, I have never known how actual a consolation faith in immortality might be. Certainly the sorrows of my church-going friends seemed like the sorrows of the rest of us, except that they had words to repeat and we did not. The Waldmans had no words. They faced the bitter fact that something full of beauty and energy and intelligence and love had gone from the world. Their lives went on, but never without sorrow.

Victor Waldman brought his wife to my room as soon as she came home from work. She was on a twelve to four shift, and he on an eight to twelve. Most of the Braxton industries, as I had already learned, worked on a twelve-hour basis, though there were some processes, of course, that required continuous operation. In the summer the day ran from six in the morning to six at night, instead of from eight to eight. Vacations, which were a month long, were spread throughout the year, so that approximately one-thirteenth of the working force was always absent. That fraction always bothered me, but it seemed to give no trouble to the planning board. And, indeed, the thirteen-months year was no more of a problem for me than the duodecimal system, which it took me weeks to master.

Agnes Waldman was built like her husband, and was as rosy-cheeked. I was surprised to find her wearing a plain, ample dress. Later I discovered that she always changed as soon as she got home. "Pants are all right for the gazelles," she would say, "but not for a big ox like me." I did not say so, but I thought she was right.

That afternoon she invited me to come down to her kitchen while she got dinner. I had never been inside a private kitchen, and I was glad of the chance. David had scoffed at the idea of family cooking, and had even looked up a quotation from Sir Thomas More: "It is both ridiculous and foolish for any to give himself the trouble to make ready an ill dinner at home, where there is a much more plentiful one made ready for him so near at hand." But I found that many women and not a few men cooked because they liked to. The meat and groceries section of the cooperative store was good-sized, and offered the same variety of foods as was available for the cooperative kitchen. The Waldmans, moreover, had their own supply of fresh vegetables, not only in season but out, for the greenhouse was equipped for chemical agriculture.

I could see that Mrs. Waldman liked nothing better than the preparation of a meal. The kitchen was surprisingly simple, chiefly, I discovered, because the equipment was all built into the walls. As Agnes stood in front of the curtained windows, everything she needed was within easy reach, and her hand moved from lever to lever with unhesitating speed.

Yet, mysterious as the equipment was to me, it struck me at once that I might have been at home in my mother's kitchen. No doubt there were gauges and thermometers and testing devices hidden away in the cabinets, but Agnes preferred to rely on old-fashioned methods, for she tasted and stirred and pondered and exclaimed, just as my mother had always done, frowning and smiling by turns, with neither her hands nor her tongue ever quiet. She had put a comfortable chair for me where I would be out of the way, and I could relax and watch and listen.

She was a good cook and a good housekeeper, fastidious for herself but never fussy with others. If one of the children tracked in mud, she unostentatiously got a mop and cleaned it up. It didn't, I must say, seem hard work, for the floors,

Agnes' Kitchen

though they were as soft to the feet as oriental rugs, could be readily washed, and there were no cracks or corners to hold the dirt.

Housekeeping had been beautifully simplified, and how Elsie would have rejoiced in it. Less mechanized in the Waldmans' home than in the apartment houses, it was no great problem even there. In the first place, there was so much less dirt, because of the way the house was heated, because of the way things were made, because of the complete elimination of smoke and soot in the city. In the second place, the floor and walls and furniture were so designed and constructed as not to hold the dirt. And finally there had been a wonderful invention. Agnes would pick up a room, putting away loose papers and everything of that kind. Then she would shut the door, and turn a special control on the air-conditioning machinery. There would be a miniature whirlwind in the room, sweeping every particle of dust or ashes into its vortex, and suddenly the whirlwind would be sucked away. Of course, Agnes would then appear with a dust cloth, but it was quite superfluous.

Even in preparing a meal, as I saw that first afternoon, she made more work for herself than was necessary, simply because she liked to. The equipment of the kitchen, Abraham Waldman told me, was all old-fashioned, for the revolution in domestic cooking had stopped with the drift to cooperative restaurants. She had the new type of ray oven, but she seldom used it, preferring the familiar electric cooker. The stove, the dish-washing machine, and the refrigerator had been there ever since her marriage, for, as I had learned, what was not made to be quickly destroyed was made to last. The dishes, for example, were all unbreakable, and they had lasted all these years, though dishes in the restaurant served but for a single meal because it was more economical as well as more sanitary to melt them down and make new ones.

The entire energy for the operation not only of the kitchen equipment but also of the ventilation system, the lighting, and all the various little devices was furnished by a small power plant on the roof. This worked—in some way that I never understood, though both Abraham and his father explained it again and again—by the direct extraction of energy from the sun's rays. I know that it had something to do with chlorophyll, for I remember David's saying on one occasion, "There was a chemist in your time who was doing excellent work on chlorophyll. He gave it up to become president of Harvard University. From every point of view it was a mistake."

As Abraham insisted, this was not the most economical way of creating energy, but it was effective for domestic pur-

I FIND A HOME

poses and small industrial units, and did away with the cost of carrying electric current. It was Abraham also who helped me to understand that heating was no problem, even in New England winters, because the houses were so perfectly insulated that the heat of the human body was adequate. Indeed, according to him, the air-conditioning plant was usually engaged in lowering the temperature rather than raising it. Lighting, too, required little energy because of the use of fluorescent paint.

Abraham came into the kitchen that afternoon, while his mother was getting dinner and talking to me. He was a gangling boy, though I could see that he might fill out to his parents' dimensions. He was shy enough at our first meeting, but I quickly discovered how vocal he could be. At first I thought he would surely become a great scientist, but afterwards I realized that I thought so merely because his scientific knowledge was so much greater than mine. As a matter of fact, he knew no more than the average boy of his age, and perhaps he was not far from the average in most ways. At twenty or twenty-one he would be much better educated than college graduates of my day. He would have advanced in his understanding of the sciences, which already seemed so amazing to me, would have a working knowledge of history, would understand the productive system. His aptitude for music would have been encouraged, and he would have some taste in art and literature. That would be enough for him. It would make him a useful and potentially a happy citizen. Probably he would be rather like his father, a sound member of society, doing his job well, taking a strong interest in his family, unambitious and happy.

Freda, I gathered, had been different. She had a passion for science that was stronger than her other passions—for sports, for dramatics, for poetry. She would have chosen the difficult road of advanced study and research. As David's story had already made me understand, students—and, indeed, all those who took the quest for knowledge seriously, whether they were officially enrolled as students or not—had no four-hour day. Within the limits of physical strength, and with due provision against too narrow a specialization, students lived in and for their studies. That was the career Freda would have elected.

That was also likely to be Roberta's course, though I scarcely guessed it when she first bounced into the kitchen, a dog under one arm and a kitten under the other. She seemed then merely a charming butterball, who ran about the room, tasting food and chattering even faster than her mother. She wore blouse and shorts, and her stocky legs were deeply tanned. All of the children and most of the adults were brown, and to see that shade in March, when I remembered the pallid faces with which we had come through a New England winter, was a satisfaction.

I cannot say that the meal, when it was finally put on the table, was any better than those I had eaten in the restaurant. In fact, I could not see that there was much difference. But I liked the sense of eating in a home again. Mrs. Waldman went on talking, interrupting whenever her husband tried to ask me a serious question. Roberta had her questions, too, but Abraham was mostly concerned with making sure that I understood where they got their power, how their paper was printed, how the beam highways operated, and other mechanical

I FIND A HOME

details. I must say that, though I became bored by his insistence, I learned a lot from him.

Almost every day, so long as I stayed there, I had breakfast and dinner with the Waldmans. Victor and Agnes had lunch at the cooperative—separately because of their working hours—and the children were at school. Breakfast was always early, not merely because Victor went to work at eight but also because it seemed to be the rule in the family, as in most of the community, that the hours around sunrise were not to be wasted. If we were staying at home in the evening, the Waldmans usually were in bed soon after nine, and if for any reason they stayed up later, they managed to find time for naps the next day.

While we ate, there was no jumping up or clearing away for Agnes to do, for she served the meal from what Abraham called the suspensor. Wheeled to the table, it kept the food at the right temperature and the proper succulence—not only relieving the housewife but solving the problem of dilatory children and late guests. Indeed, with its aid Agnes could and sometimes did prepare and serve a whole meal either in the dining room or in the garden.

That evening, after the disher had been set to work, we went into the living room, and Victor got a baseball game by television from California. Television had improved greatly, and the images were almost as clear as in a good moving picture. Baseball also had changed, and, though I was never a fan, I was distressed by my inability to follow the game. As I had already learned, all kinds of sports were popular. The emphasis was on playing rather than watching, but there were thousands of spectators at this match.

THE FIRST TO AWAKEN

After a time, with Victor and Abraham absorbed in the game, and with Agnes calmly embroidering, I stopped looking at the screen, finding Roberta and her pets more entertaining. The Boston terrier, ears pricked up, was stalking the yellow kitten, who played his part by pretending complete indifference until the dog was almost upon him. Then he would whirl, a white and yellow paw in the air, and the terrier would back away, legs spread and stomach on the floor. Finally the dog gave up, and stretched out by Roberta, his eyes almost closed. The kitten rubbed against my leg, jumped to my chair, and leaped to the bench. Roberta looked up at me with mischief and laughter in her eyes. The kitten walked casually along the bench until she was directly over the dog, whose head lay between his paws. Experimentally she reached down, tried again, and then smacked his twitching ear. Instantly he was on his hind legs, barking madly as she made a leap over his head and landed on Victor's stomach. Startled, he bounced in his chair, and Abraham scolded Roberta, while the rest of us laughed. This was home.

I settled into a quiet sort of routine during my first week at the Waldmans'. In the morning I read the bulletin and studied. After lunch at the cooperative, I either walked about the countryside or went with David to the tennis courts, which were still under glass. In the evening I talked or played games with the Waldmans or went out with them.

I spent much time listening to the radio. In New York I had scarcely been aware that the radio still existed, but in Braxton I realized its importance. If in its economic life the town had become largely self-sufficient, in its cultural life it was linked with all the rest of the world. I particularly liked the musical

I FIND A HOME

programs that I got, without visual accompaniment, on the radio in my room. There was not an hour of the day or night when I could not get fine orchestras, choruses, and soloists from every part of the earth. Somehow it seemed to me that I had never had a chance to listen to music before, and I learned to like many of the older composers I had once regarded as dull as well as a few of the moderns.

Victor liked to follow sports by television, and Agnes was fond of plays, especially the more sentimental kind. (Her taste ran to romance, and she warmly admired *Night Over Manhattan*.) There was a long-drawn-out historical play, broadcast from London, that she followed nightly for weeks. Occasionally, however, she would sit spellbound through a performance of Shakespeare, and often, when I was watching some modern play, she would come and sit down—for just a moment, she would say, but usually she sat to the end.

Television had been so successful that, together with the rise of local dramatic societies, it had supplanted the movies. Films were, of course, used for educational purposes, and there were some film clubs that made excellent pictures, but Hollywood was no more. Occasionally old pictures were shown, but the audience as a rule laughed so heartily, not merely at the costumes and scenery but also at the situations and ideas, that the few admirers of the cinema, who insisted on its validity as an art form, were discouraged. "Movies are silly," said Roberta, who had seen one of the supposed masterpieces of the forties, and most inhabitants of Braxton agreed with her.

Characteristically, though he preferred sports broadcasts himself, Abraham insisted on my getting some of the educational programs, and I was glad he did. There were, for example, illustrated lectures on science that did more for my education than a whole library of books. The historical studies seemed to me rather tedious but not without value for me. All such programs were quite serious and systematic, and, as I quickly found, it was a mistake to tune in on a series whenever it happened to take my fancy. They were obviously planned on the theory that the spectators wanted to learn. If they didn't, there were plenty of other programs.

When Victor was at home and wasn't watching some game, he loved to talk. He asked me many shrewd questions, and his answers to my queries sometimes seemed to me a little sounder than David's. Our conversations were by no means purely intellectual. He was fond of reminiscences of his boyhood, which had been in no way extraordinary but was not without interest for me. He also liked to discuss his grievances, which were many. Any break in the efficiency of the community—even a slight mistake in filling his order at the restaurant or a five minutes' delay in the beginning of a class—infuriated him, and a blunder at the factory would keep him grumbling for days. It was rather boring, but he was fundamentally so good-natured that I never minded.

Because he was so fussy, I never ventured into the greenhouse, though he had offered to initiate me into its mysteries. But as it grew warmer, I began to work a little outdoors, raking away leaves and puttering with the shrubs.

One morning a tall, fine-looking man came across the lawn. His hair and beard were white, but his step was so agile and his face so alert that I thought he could not be much over sixty. His clothes had the appearance of rough tweed, and he wore a sombrero instead of the conventional cap.

I FIND A HOME

"You're George Swain, aren't you?" he said. "I'm Simeon Blake. A beautiful morning, but if I were you I shouldn't try to force the season. We'll have snow again." We talked for a time about gardening, and when he left he invited me to walk with him the next afternoon.

Impressed and curious, I asked Nathalie Wilson about him when I met her for lunch. "Oh, Simeon Blake," she said. "There's a story for you. A fine figure of a man, don't you think?" I agreed, and she went on: "The most romantic character in Braxton. Over seventy-five now. Born on a farm over in Deerfleet, educated here in Braxton, became an engineer. He must have been one of the best, too, for he was on the New York City engineering board before he was thirty. He was a driver—tremendous energy and great imagination. But he came too late."

"What do you mean?"

"New York was practically finished."

"And no more super-cities."

"Correct. Simeon turned to the Mississippi control project. That was being completed, too, but he produced new plans, and they were adopted. When he had finished that job, he offered the continental power board a plan for tapping the heat within the earth. They said that there were sources of energy enough available for all conceivable needs in the next century, and turned him down."

I could guess that he hadn't liked that. Even in a few minutes' conversation I had felt how warmly and naturally his friendship went out to people, but he wasn't a man I should have cared to cross. "What happened next?"

"He was invited to help with the Sahara reclamation project, and again he revolutionized all the plans. He was the obvious person to take charge of the Chinese flood-control, irrigation, and power program. He simply made over the whole economic life of eastern Asia, and they say he is still one of the great Chinese heroes."

No wonder I had felt that this was somebody out of the ordinary. "But that isn't all," Nathalie warned me, warming up to her subject. "About twenty-five years ago he came back to America to stay. He announced that the day of the engineer was over. What remained to be done in the world anybody could do. In the engineering line, that is. But in the field of economic re-organization, barely a beginning had been made."

"But that's extraordinary, Nathalie. Surely by 2015—"

"No, and not by 2040. Anyway Simeon saw there was a job to be done, but first he had a lot to learn. So he took a routine position in the planning office. I'd like to have been here, for he turned things topsy-turvy. They elected him to the cooperative board, and then he went to the district committee. Five years later he was heading the world-wide committee on education, and did a wonderful job coordinating research, libraries, exchange fellowships, and things like that."

"What's he doing in Braxton?"

"He resigned five or six years ago. Said it wasn't good for men to hold positions of responsibility when they were getting old. Said that, with the extension of the life-span, there was a grave danger of our getting a gerontocracy—a government of old men. There was a great reception for him when he came back to Braxton to live."

"But good Lord, a man like that must do something."

"He does plenty. He has two or three inventions that he

works on. He's learned Greek and Latin and reads the classics every day. He's perfecting a new kind of graphic representation of statistical concepts. And, because he thinks he should do his share of useful work and loves horses, he puts in a four-hour day at the Braxton stables."

Victor came into the restaurant, fresh from his shift, and sat with us. He and Nathalie talked further about Blake, and their talk sounded a good deal like hero-worship.

This was the day that Victor had promised to take me round the assembling plant. I knew that it was a kind of regional service station. That is, it was not an assembling plant for automobiles alone or for radio sets alone or for kitchen equipment alone. It served all those purposes and many more. Standard parts came from the various mining centers, in accordance with planning estimates, and were here incorporated in whatever it was the community needed.

Having seen the plant many times from the outside, I expected it to be light and clean, but I had had no idea that a factory could be so quiet. The central department was filled with huge and fantastically shaped machines, many of which were in operation, but the great room was rather quieter than our bank. Along the high roof, supported on curious columns, smaller at the bottom than at the top, giant cranes moved almost silently, Victor scarcely had to raise his voice as he explained the functions of the various machines.

Victor stepped up to a girl who was studying a blueprint. "What are you working on this afternoon, Sally?"

"Automobile engines."

He leaned over to examine the adjustments she was making in the machine. "Every spring," he explained to me, "we put new engines in about a quarter of the cars in the district. Of course there have to be some replacements at other times."

I did some calculating. "How long does a car last?"

"Twelve to twenty years."

We went along to another machine. The mechanic grinned at Victor. "Can't you stay out of this place?" he asked.

"This is where I was working this morning. We're making housing parts out of reclaimed metal." He pointed out the window. "We have our own small-size blast furnace and rolling mill."

A woman came down the aisle with papers in her hand. "Where's Carter?" he asked her, after he had introduced us.

"He's taken a gang out to the southwest farm center to install the new blowers."

"Tell him to be sure to come round tonight."

We walked through the other departments, and then took the tunnel under the river. The alcohol plant was completely automatic. It was surrounded with tall towers for the storage of the vegetable products, and with tanks for the storage of the alcohol. Pipe lines, Victor told me, led to the filling stations of the vicinity.

Crossing a court, we came to the woollen plant. I had already seen the large flocks of sheep in the vicinity, and I knew that a hardy breed, something like the Australian Merino, had been developed. Victor showed me how photo-electric cells were used to sort the wool. The finer grades were then sent through a process of cleaning, drying, and spinning, and made into woollens and worsteds. The coarser grades were immediately given chemical treatment and were used in the building industry. In the weaving rooms I saw beautiful cloth

I FIND A HOME

that would be used for all sorts of special purposes. Because of the general use of plastics, the whole textile industry had become marginal, but nothing was overlooked that could be economically used. On state occasions many Braxtonians wore suits or dresses that had come from the backs of their own sheep.

Braxton was much prouder, however, of its sports goods factory, for its products were shipped all over the country. I have spoken of the new forests I had seen on hills that had been stripped bare long before my time. From hickory and maple and ash the factory made skis, snowshoes, tennis, squash, and badminton rackets, baseball bats, and every other type of game equipment that required wood. Many of the workers were highly skilled, and some of them had originated important changes in design.

It was nearly four, and we waited till Agnes appeared in a group of about a hundred workers. Few of them seemed in a hurry to get away, and I recalled our rush from the shoe factory once the whistle had blown. A certain number got into cars and drove away, presumably to their homes. Others lingered in the clubroom. The majority went to the apartment houses on the other side of the river.

We sat in the clubroom for a time, and two of Agnes' fellow-workers came to join us—a young man named Tom and a girl whose name I did not get. There was a good deal of banter, but Tom seemed seriously interested in getting me to talk, and I found myself describing my work in the bank. In spite of their knowledge of the past, they had certain misconceptions, or so it seemed to me, and I tried to explain as well as I could the status of the white-collar worker.

This seemed a good time to explore certain problems that had been troubling me. They wanted to know why I had worked in a bank, and I wanted to know why they worked at all. I could understand the incentives that operated with persons like David and Nathalie or even Nick and Norah, to say nothing of Simeon Blake. But these were average citizens, with no particular intellectual interests and no high ambitions. I thought I knew the answer, but I wanted to be sure.

As the ensuing conversation showed, it seemed so natural to them to hold a job that they had difficulty in understanding my questions. In the first place, they had been brought up in the tradition that everybody worked. The greatest effort was made to see that each person found a job that suited him, and obviously they did not feel tied to a particular machine or a particular factory. You could argue about what job you would take but not about whether you would take a job at all.

Part of the explanation was that life was almost unthinkable outside a cooperative. It was true that no one would be allowed to starve, even if he flatly refused to do any kind of work, but to people like the Waldmans and Tom and his friend such a life seemed unbearable. Membership in the cooperative gave them not only food and shelter and clothing and a host of luxuries but also social status. They belonged.

Victor, when he got the point of my questions, was aghast. His house, his garden, his clubs—he couldn't imagine living without them. "Besides," he said, "I like my job."

"And wouldn't you feel cheap," said Agnes, "if you couldn't belong to the cooperative? Why, you couldn't eat in the restaurant or go to the theater and the meetings. It wouldn't be any fun."

I FIND A HOME

Tom was thinking. "In your day a man wouldn't go to the poorhouse unless he had to, would he?" I shook my head. "Well, it's like that today. People want to be free, and they want to be respected, and they want to have lots of good things. And that means taking a job. If I get what you're driving at, there's no problem there at all. Practically everybody is willing to work. Our problem is getting everybody to work efficiently."

That was the second question I wanted to ask.

Victor got excited about this. "You're right, Tom," he shouted. "It's the slackers we have to look out for."

"Like Mike Marvin,[1] eh?" said Tom's companion, nudging Agnes.

There was a good deal of talk of Marvin's case and of the discussion of it that had gone on in a union meeting. It was with this kind of problem that the unions seemed chiefly to deal. As a consumer the citizen was represented by his cooperative, as a producer by his union. Unions checked production quotas with the planning boards, supervised working conditions, and were responsible for employment policy and labor discipline. They sometimes resorted to fines and other punishments, and in the last resort they could fire a man.

"One thing you want to understand," said Agnes, "is that, in most kinds of jobs, a man either does his work or he doesn't. And if he doesn't do it, the whole department is thrown off, and everybody kicks."

"But take that lad Newton in my factory," Victor broke in. "He sends in word that he's sick. The doctor goes to see him

[1] For obvious reasons some names have been changed.—G.S.

and finds there's nothing wrong. I tried to get the union to act, but they wouldn't do a thing."

"What happens if a man is fired?"

"He goes round to the vocational guidance office and gets another job. Or else he's just out."

"Well, suppose he's out," I persisted. "Would he be forced to leave his apartment?"

"If he wasn't married, yes. If he was, and his wife had a job, he could stay. That is, if his wife would let him. But he couldn't eat at the restaurant or use any of the cooperative buildings."

"Suppose his wife chose to support him?"

"She'd be a fool," said Agnes.

"And he'd be a laughing stock," Tom added.

"And would a woman under the same circumstances?"

They all nodded.

"Suppose a man wants to move away from Braxton?"

"Who's stopping him?"

"It isn't quite like that, Tom," Agnes said. "You can't just walk out on a job. You aren't supposed to go unless there's somebody to take your place. Unless, of course, the union sees it's an emergency."

"But you can walk out if you want to. Jenny Pritchard did. Fell in love with a fellow she met on her vacation and went to Boston with him."

"Love is like that," Tom's companion said. "I don't think Jenny was half as bad as Bill Douglas two years ago. He'd been talking for a long time about going to a warmer climate, and that winter he just took a car and cleared out. Took a car, too. Can you imagine that?"

I FIND A HOME

We talked a little about the business of moving from one cooperative to another. Officially it could only be done with the consent of both cooperatives, but actually if a man had private information—say, from a relative—that there was no shortage of jobs in the place he wanted to go, he seldom bothered to wait for the formal approval. Again I could see that there had once been rather strict regulations, but they had fallen into disuse.

We came back to the subject of discipline. Agnes insisted that, if a man liked his job, there would be no difficulty. Victor, in his grumbling way that meant so little, wanted the unions to take stronger measures. I gathered that the problem was by no means solved. The great majority of workers did their jobs efficiently and uncomplainingly. The work was interesting in itself, and they valued the respect of their comrades. A few people gave trouble. Some of these were maladjusted and found their way sooner or later into the hands of a psychiatrist. Others were misfits, and did well enough in other positions. The remainder were brought in line by public opinion and by union discipline.

"Do you ever have strikes?" I asked. It appeared that there had not been a strike in Braxton in thirty years, but they belligerently asserted their right to strike. I was surprised. "But wouldn't you be striking against yourselves?"

"No, against the planning board. Believe me, they can't put anything over on us."

"Do they try to?"

"They haven't lately, but there's that man Lister—he's a trouble-maker."

Their militancy seemed to be a hangover. In the early years

Sketches of Houses

I FIND A HOME

there had been many conflicts between the planning boards and the unions. Sometimes the planners had been at fault, with their ambitious projects and their desire for regimentation. Sometimes the unions had been jockeying for a privileged status. It had taken many decades to evolve a sound technique, and even now, when it had been accomplished, the workers did not intend to surrender any of their rights.

"Things go along well enough," said Agnes comfortably. "Let's eat."

We were having dinner at the restaurant that night because Agnes wanted to go to the theater, and I had promised to attend a class with Victor. As usual just before and after dinner, the recreational rooms were full—though, for that matter, it was seldom that they were not in use. I wandered about as I had come to love to do. There was a basketball game going on in one part of the gymnasium and a gym class in another. The pool was full, and the squash and handball and tennis courts were all in use. Talkative groups occupied the corridors and smaller rooms, but the reading rooms, where men and women bent over books and magazines, were quiet.

There was a hobby exhibit in one room and a new collection of paintings in another. I strolled in to look at the paintings, but, though much of the work interested me, I was thinking chiefly of the people. It had suddenly struck me how good-looking most of these men and women were. Not beautiful; I don't mean that; but healthy and self-respecting and pleasant to look at. In New York this hadn't impressed me so much, for, like all provincials, I had always thought of New Yorkers as being smart, but here in Braxton, where I had seen so many drab persons, it was something to think about. Though there still seemed to me something ludicrous in the way clothes were made, I couldn't deny that there was more variety than there had been in my day. People took satisfaction in the dozens of little ways in which individual ingenuity and taste could show themselves. They thought about physical appearance, too—good teeth and good complexions and good figures. They insisted on exercise and sunshine and proper food and sleep.

The store was well filled now. In the clothing section, which was the busiest, there was much laughing and talking. A group of young people were standing around the book and magazine counters, arguing with the clerk and with each other. As usual, I was impressed by the number and variety of toys, toilet accessories, and personal knick-knacks that were on sale. Many of these were made in their homes by people who lived in the remoter parts of the district or by Braxtonians who spent their leisure time in that way. Compared to books and magazines, or to the various items of household furnishing that were on sale, they seemed expensive, but I realized that this was because they were outside the mechanized system. Noticing a brooch that I thought Roberta would like, I bought it.

After dinner Victor took me to the classroom. Many classes were held every evening, organized either by various cooperative committees or by independent groups. This was a class of workers in the assembling plant, and I was particularly interested in it because Nathalie Wilson was the teacher.

There were, I counted, sixteen men and seven women in the room, in addition to Nathalie and myself, and I was surprised to see that Victor was by no means the oldest. Nathalie spoke for about fifteen minutes at the beginning, summarizing the ground that had been covered at previous sessions and

I FIND A HOME

stating the theme of the evening's discussion. She spoke clearly and simply, although there were references to processes and formulas and measurements of which I was ignorant. The idea of planning and even its general principles she took completely for granted, but she often referred to the historical development of those principles, sometimes going back to my own time.

The course had been going on all winter and had apparently covered the more important phases of continental and regional planning. That evening the class was considering the specialized industry, using the sports goods plant as an example. Nathalie unrolled a series of flow charts, showing how its products were distributed. She then gave a simple account of bookkeeping in a cooperative system—a subject that naturally appealed to me. I began to see that the cooperative was conducted on the most businesslike basis. I also realized for the first time that it was not in the strictest sense self-supporting, since it received special allotments from the continental planning board. Or, to be precise, it shared in the allotments granted the whole Northeast District, which was less rich in natural resources than the continental average. It had, in other words, a constantly unfavorable balance of trade, for which the board compensated.

The discussion was on a high level, for the men and women knew what they were talking about and they wanted to learn what she could teach them. I could see that this kind of adult education was one of the foundations of the new democracy. I liked the atmosphere, too. None of the students seemed to feel that there was any difference between them and Nathalie, either on the ground that she was acting as teacher or on the ground that she was a scientifically trained employee of the planning board and they worked in a factory. In my day manual laborers treated an educated person with a mingled reverence and contempt. Here they were all workers together.

There was one unpleasant note. Early in the evening a young man raised an objection to a point Nathalie made about possible changes in public demand. Nathalie answered him very well, I thought, and two others supported her argument. But the youth was persistent, and during the next hour he constantly recurred to his criticism. Nathalie was not only patient herself but restrained the impatience of the others. "Damned show-off," Victor muttered to me as we went out. "I'll fix him." I wondered how, for it seemed to me that I had encountered that young man's ancestors more than once, and I had never known them to be fixed.

We went round to the theater for Agnes. The play had not ended, and we stood at the back of the crowded hall. It was a verse drama of the Elizabethan period, and, if the lines were not always spoken to my taste, the spirit was perfect. The girl who had the leading part was lovely in her ruffs and stiff brocaded skirt, and the boys were handsome in doublet and hose.

There was great applause when the curtain came down. Agnes had tears in her eyes as she came to meet us, and she sighed more than once as we walked home, at her suggestion, under frosty stars.

VII

HOW IT ALL HAPPENED

IF I was spending the early evening in my room, Roberta was likely to come in, hoist herself up on the desk, and talk to me for an hour at a time. She was almost as voluble as her mother, and her lively tongue ran from arguments in the classroom to questions of cooperative policy and from misfortunes of the hockey field to proposals for the exploration of interstellar space. Abraham tired me out, but Roberta constantly entertained me. What she learned touched her imagination, and her imagination made something new of it.

History fascinated her, and, since I was reading a good deal of history myself, we often talked about our lessons. Either because of a peculiar aptitude or because of her teachers' skill, she had a kind of perspective that I found it hard to acquire. She had critical sense, too, and I liked the way she prefaced most statements by saying, "I think," or, "We think," or occasionally, "They think."

"I think," she said one evening, "that the greatest inventors

THE FIRST TO AWAKEN

in history were the man who discovered how to use fire, the man who first learned how to plant a garden, and the man who first tamed animals. That was the beginning of civilization. Who do you think the greatest inventors were?"

I admitted that I had never thought about it quite that way.

"That's the way things started," she went on. "Civilization hasn't really lasted very long, has it?"

We went on to talk about the industrial revolution. She saw quite clearly that capitalism had been necessary, and she protested when I spoke bitterly about the capitalists. "What else," she said, "would you expect the capitalists to do? But we do think a lot of other people were stupid."

"What people?"

She looked up at me impudently. "People like you, George, people who were being hurt by capitalism. Why didn't you get rid of it?"

I'm afraid my explanation seemed pretty lame, and I hastened on to ask her some questions of political theory. I wanted to know what she was being taught about our form of government.

"By your time," she said, "you couldn't have both democracy and capitalism."

"But we did have democracy."

"Now, George, that isn't so. Did you have as much political power as the men who owned the bank? Did they have as much political power as the men who owned the corporation that ran the shoe factory? Why, you've told me about these things yourself. What is that place down near New York that you said everybody made such a fuss about? You know, Jersey

HOW IT ALL HAPPENED

City. Well, you said the other night that during the strike Braxton was just like Jersey City."

I had said that, and it was true. In fact, the more I read and thought about the twenties and thirties, the more I wondered how much democracy we had really had. For instance, I'd just been reading John Steinbeck's *The Grapes of Wrath.* Everybody was talking about it during the autumn of 1939, but the Braxton library refused to put it on its shelves, and I never felt that I could afford to buy it. So I had had to wait a century to read it. I had been terribly moved by it, all the more because I knew that there had been, so to speak, a happy ending.

That book had started me thinking. What had democracy meant to the sharecroppers? To some of them, perhaps, the idea had meant a great deal, but the reality was pretty empty. I thought of the lies the people of Braxton had been fed by the *Voice,* and I wondered how anybody could expect democracy to function when such sheets were the sources of the voters' information. I thought of the way the shoe company had bought town officials, imported their own thugs, and been able to call out the National Guard. Braxton, with its town meeting in which everyone could speak his mind, had seemed on the surface a perfect example of democracy, but when it came to a showdown, the will of the people hadn't amounted to much.[1]

I was genuinely puzzled. Our democracy had certainly functioned badly, and yet at the time I had felt that it was our only hope. For all its imperfections, it was infinitely preferable to the totalitarian systems that existed abroad, and I said so to Roberta.

"Why didn't you use it, then? Why did you let people take it away from you?"

"Don't blame me; that was after my time."

She thought a moment. "But it was beginning to happen in your time, and what did you do about it?"

There wasn't much I could say to that, and she scampered off to listen to a favorite radio program while she got ready for bed.

From reading and conversation I had got a reasonably clear understanding of the events of the first two-thirds of the nineteenth century. I found that, in order to understand what had happened after 1940, I had to go back and discover what had happened before. I had to see the process of growth and decay as a whole.

The United States had been, so far as natural resources were concerned, the most fortunate country in history, for

[1] Although the general character of the period is well understood, some readers may think that Swain is exaggerating. They are advised to look at the reports of the Subcommittee of the Committee on Labor and Education of the United States Senate—known as the La Follette Civil Liberties Committee. A critical analysis of its findings was published a few years ago—*Economic Power and Political Democracy,* by Rose E. Marcus and associates (Washington, 2029). For contemporary discussions see the bibliography in this book.—D.W.

within its own boundaries it had almost everything that was essential to the building of an industrial civilization. It was no wonder that industrialism had made rapid progress and that the nation had become fabulously rich. Not everyone, to be sure, had shared in that wealth, but almost everyone could hope to get a share sooner or later.

From the very beginning of the industrial revolution, however, there had been periods when the nation seemed unable to take advantage of its wonderful natural endowment. Two hundred years ago, for example, in 1840, when there was a whole continent to be exploited, the country had been paralyzed by a depression. And these depressions recurred more or less regularly.

A few people began to suspect that there was something wrong with capitalism itself, something in its nature that caused it to break down every ten or twelve years. Early in the game there were men and women, like the Brook Farmers and John Humphrey Noyes and Fanny Wright, who wanted to get away from capitalism altogether and set up colonies that were run according to idealistic principles of equality and justice. Most of these colonies didn't work very well, and anyway they had no effect on the growth of capitalist industry.

Then, towards the end of the nineteenth century, there were people like Howells and Bellamy who wanted to remake the whole system. Americans were beginning to hear about Karl Marx,[1] and Eugene Debs and Daniel De Leon led the Socialist Party and the Socialist Labor Party. Before the First World

[1] Not many persons heard about him. I knew nothing about Marx until Everett discovered him after the depression, and even then my impression of his theories came from Everett's somewhat jumbled arguments.—G.S.

THE FIRST TO AWAKEN

War there were at least a million people who voted for a Socialist for President.

It was not only workers who were getting worried about unemployment and low wages; the middle class was upset. My father, for instance, was nothing of a Socialist, but he hated the trusts, and he was a great admirer of Teddy Roosevelt. The trusts were getting bigger and bigger, and a lot of people realized that there was less and less opportunity to get rich. They had no desire to get rid of capitalism, but they did think it ought to be regulated in some way, so that the little fellows would be taken care of.

There had been several reform administrations—Theodore Roosevelt's, Woodrow Wilson's, and Franklin Roosevelt's. I saw that they had all defeated themselves. It was not until they had themselves surrendered to reaction that a reactionary administration drove them out of office. But why had they become reactionary? The wars had something to do with Wilson and the second Roosevelt, of course, but they were not the whole explanation. The whole explanation, as I had suspected in 1940 and now saw clearly, was that capitalism could not be reformed.

As Dr. Carr had said, change was overdue in the thirties. After the first war we had kept our factories booming by giving Europe money with which to buy our goods. But we had paid for that policy in 1929, and there was no such easy way out of the depression that followed. I still admired FDR and felt that he had saved us from chaos in 1933, but I could see that such measures as his, admirable as they might be in themselves, could never have brought full employment and raised the national income to what it ought to have been. I was glad

HOW IT ALL HAPPENED

I had voted for him in 1932 and again in 1936, but my trust in his program was a little silly.

One thing was true: each reform administration had an educational value. Somehow I had always felt that we of the Tavern Club were very bold in entertaining doubts about the capitalist system, and probably that was boldness for a bank teller, but I now realized that our questions were being asked by millions of Americans. That was one reason why, though Mr. Roosevelt was doing his best to save capitalism, the capitalists hated him.[1] They felt that he was undermining faith in their system. In a way they were wrong, for events were creating the disillusionment, but in a way they were right, for the New Deal measures were an admission that the critics of capitalism had a case.

The process, however, worked both ways. When the New Deal failed to solve the problems of economic breakdown, and the Democratic administration lost its crusading fervor, there was disillusionment with reform as well as with capitalism, and the result was an apathy of which the reactionaries took full advantage. In the election of 1940, one of the most crucial in all American history, the electorate had no real choice.

The situation made me wonder about the weaknesses of organized radicalism. Surely by that time there were millions

[1] This seems to me doubtful. The capitalists resented Roosevelt's measures insofar as they directly reduced their profits and privileges. Also, they genuinely believed that, if they could have a free hand, prosperity would return. Throughout this account Swain shows his inability to understand the capitalist mentality. On the one hand, he seems to regard them as unmitigated villains, and on the other, he attributes to them a far-sightedness of which they were certainly incapable. Naturally, they acted according to their interests as they understood them.—D.W.

of people ready to voice their approval of any reasonable alternative to capitalism, and yet this powerful sentiment found no effective expression. There were a few Socialists in Braxton and, it was said, one or two Communists. I knew little about them, but it seemed unlikely that either party would ever exert an important influence on American opinion. I knew enough, even in 1939, to discount much of what I read in the papers about the Communists, but I had always felt that America was very different from Russia. As for the Socialists, in Braxton at least they were too much wrapped up in themselves and their doctrines to have any effect. I feel now that I ought to have found out more about both parties, but I don't know that it would have made much difference.

I wish I could understand more clearly why socialism—with a small s—made so little headway. Was it because its advocates were so tangled up in doctrinal disputes among themselves? Or does the explanation lie in the skill with which it was discredited by the apologists for the status quo? Or perhaps people could only learn from events—from a worse depression, from the growth of fascism, from the example of Europe. Certainly today the advantages of socialism are so obvious that it is hard for me to remember why we held back.

Going back to 1940, I now see that among the leading capitalists, those who were capable of doing any thinking whatsoever, there were two schools of thought. One group, looking at Germany and Italy, believed that fascism was the only solution, and secretly supported various demagogues. The other did not like fascism, for they had seen it get out of hand in Germany, and they did not believe it was necessary for America. They thought that the country could still be sold a

HOW IT ALL HAPPENED

business administration, and they were proven right in 1944. At once they consolidated their gains, putting safe men in strategic positions from which they could not be ousted.

Conservatives and radicals alike were influenced by what was happening in Europe and Asia. Even before I went to sleep, some students of international affairs were predicting a fifty years' war. It was not quite so bad as that, but there was a solid decade in which the war of nerves never ceased and the war of guns repeatedly flared up. As a matter of fact, I discovered that historians tended to treat the fighting that went on from 1914 to 1972 as one continuous war, and it was just as well to take the broad view, for the details were infinitely complicated.

At the beginning British statesmen hoped to get rid of Hitler, make peace on the western front, and start a united crusade against Soviet Russia. Hitler was again placed in the best bargaining position, since he could come to terms with either Russia or the Allies. For a time the Allied statesmen seriously considered risking public indignation at home by withdrawing their demand that Hitler must go and renewing the policy of appeasement, with the anti-Soviet crusade always in mind. Then, when Hitler refused to rise to the bait, they even considered fighting Germany and Russia simultaneously, counting on the aid of the United States.

For more than a month after I went to sleep the fighting continued to be predominantly on the diplomatic front, but then the war spread to both north and south, and the small nation vanished from the face of Europe. I had seen the beginning of that process, of course, but I had not dreamed of the way it would be carried to its tragic conclusion. And

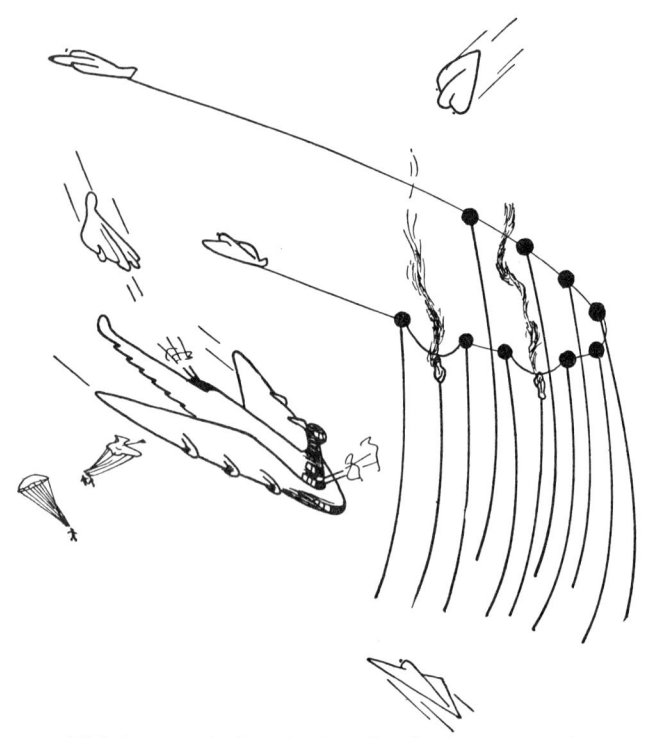

This is a purely imaginative sketch of an air battle, c.1950, based on my reading. It shows an air cruiser being driven into a Goering net by interceptor planes of the amoeba type.

then, when it was concluded, when the small countries had all been gobbled up, there was again a freezing of the lines, a relapse into what had begun to be called the Sitzkrieg. After all the death and destruction, the two powerful blocs that faced each other were nearly self-sufficient, and neither was willing to begin the ultimate and decisive slaughter.

I have tried to memorize the events of the next few years, but the story is too complicated for me to keep it in mind. I know that Italy made a separate peace with Germany, and that it subsequently joined the Allies again. I know that Russia and Japan were almost constantly at war. I know that there were revolts in Bohemia and Poland. At intervals there was heavy fighting on the western front, but the position of the lines was never seriously changed. Once Hitler decided to risk everything by bombing Paris, but the retaliation was so terrible that he did not repeat. From month to month people said that the real war was beginning, but always they were wrong.

Meanwhile the standard of living sank all over Europe, and particularly in Germany. The war machine was somewhat more adequately supplied after the Balkan coup, but the people went hungrier and hungrier. No one could have believed that human beings could endure what the Germans suffered. But still they hung on.

The break came in 1948. Realizing that he had been beaten in the war of attrition, Hitler began the Blitzkrieg that had been feared for so many years. But he had waited too long. His regime collapsed as the Kaiser's had thirty years before. Soldiers and sailors revolted. The hungry people swarmed into the streets. Hitler committed suicide.

Germany, Russia, the Baltic states, and part of the Balkans now formed a solid anti-capitalist bloc. Economically they were all exhausted, and Russia, which had preserved its military strength, was at war with Japan. Nevertheless, the Allies hesitated to strike, for their own populations were growing restless. They sat tight behind the Maginot Line and gave Japan what help they could.

I had never known much about Soviet Russia, but I had been prejudiced against it by stories of the cruel methods used by the Bolsheviks to maintain their power. The alliance with

THE FIRST TO AWAKEN

Germany had been a great shock, and the invasion of Finland was even worse. But now, looking back, I can see that, however wrong the methods used, something was gained. The whole history of the Soviets was, as Dr. Carr might have said, an example of the clumsy way in which mankind progressed. Just as the French Revolution, despite its excesses, helped to liberate Europe, so the Russian Revolution began a new and better era.

As a matter of fact, the history of the middle decades of the century—like the history of almost any other period, I am afraid—was not reassuring reading. Gains were made, but only at a terrible price. When change came, it came fiercely, for it had been fiercely resisted. I had been wise when I stretched myself out on Dr. Carr's operating table.

There is no doubt, however, that the overthrow of Hitler did release a new kind of revolutionary energy, which was felt as much in Russia as in Germany. The Soviets had been fighting so long merely to hold what they had gained that they had forgotten the dreams of the October Revolution. Now men were dreaming again of the better world they could build.

The character of the war had made it possible for the United States to remain at peace. On the other hand, the fact that it was a war of skirmishes and brigandage had cheated Wall Street of the war prosperity to which it had looked forward. Great fortunes were made, to be sure, but war orders never brought anything like recovery, and by 1941 employment was again falling off. The depression of 1943-44 may in part have been maneuvered for political ends, but that of 1947 was bona fide. Unemployment was almost as widespread as in the early thirties, and the relief program adopted by the coalition of

HOW IT ALL HAPPENED

Republicans and conservative Democrats was a long way from adequate.

With the new alignment that resulted from the German revolution, international issues again became of first importance. The State Department was in the closest touch with the Nicolson government in England, and there was a clear understanding that, when France and England launched their attack on Germany and Russia, they would have the financial and later the military support of this country. England, meanwhile, was again trying to secure the support of Italy, but Ciano was having an even more difficult time than his father-in-law, and he frankly warned the British that the regime could not survive more than six months of war.

It was two years before England was ready to strike. Socialist Germany, working frantically at the terrible task of reconstruction bequeathed it by Hitler, was not prepared. The Westwall cracked, and at the same time Japan made new advances in Siberia. The American press had already launched its new campaign for American participation, and President Leland, the conservative Democrat who had been re-elected in 1948, was doing his best to encourage the war spirit.

Then, in the spring of 1951, just as it seemed certain England would succeed in establishing puppet governments in Germany, the Balkans, and the Baltic republics, and as American capitalism was ready to throw American manpower into the final struggle against Russia, revolution broke out in India and China. The Chinese people quickly disposed of their Japanese rulers, even defeating the troops that were withdrawn from Siberia. The Indian revolution was less successful, but it forced England to patch up a series of peace treaties in Europe.

THE FIRST TO AWAKEN

There were three candidates in the American election of 1952. Leland, running for a third term, pointed to the partial recovery that had resulted from war orders. Mayor Gaderick, for the second time the candidate of the progressive Democrats, offered a kind of modified New Deal platform, promising to revive the National Labor Relations Act, restore the old provisions of the Wages and Hours Act, take steps to recapture the TVA from private enterprise, and initiate new housing and health projects. It was not a very bold program, and certainly not an adequate one, but it had the support of the greatly weakened trade unions.

The third candidate was Tim McKinstry, once one of Henry Ford's service men and more recently mayor of Detroit. McKinstry, candidate of the newly formed American Party, denounced Leland's war policy even more strongly than Gaderick, and called for peace, national self-sufficiency, and old-age pensions. Although he was careful to avoid any suggestion of anti-Semitism himself, all the anti-Semitic organizations supported him. McKinstry Clubs sprang into existence all over the country, and particularly in those communities in which the Ku Klux Klan, the Christian Mobilizers, the Liberty Boys, and similar organizations had prospered. Negroes were beaten; stores owned by Jews were looted; union headquarters were raided; and in a few instances Catholics were attacked. McKinstry did his best, however, to restrain anti-Catholic demonstrations, for he had been guaranteed what was still called the Coughlinite vote,[1] and his roaring denunciations of Great Britain were finding favor among the Irish.

[1] I doubt if this term was used as late as 1952, for Father Coughlin, a Catholic priest and demagogue, had been discredited more than ten years

HOW IT ALL HAPPENED

From the point of view of 2040, the election of 1952 seems one of the more puzzling incidents of American political history. One fact is clear: some of the most influential capitalists withdrew their support from Leland and gave it to McKinstry, and without the money and the newspapers and the radio stations they put at his disposal he would never have won. The problem is that of motives. Did Wall Street decide that the British Empire was finished and might just as well be deserted? Did the support of McKinstry indicate a determination to abandon the fight on the larger front and make a last stand for capitalism here? Or did Wall Street have reason to believe that Gaderick was stronger than his supporters imagined, and did they turn to McKinstry as their only hope of beating him? Was McKinstry from the first Wall Street's man, or was he bought during the campaign? These were questions I could never answer.

In any case Tim McKinstry, mouthing denunciations of Wall Street, was elected with Wall Street support. Within six months it was apparent that, whatever the intentions of American capitalists, British capitalism could not be saved. British troops were withdrawn from India, and the rival parties fought out their differences. Ireland, South Africa, and Egypt proclaimed their independence. England, under an ineffectual Labor Party government, became to all intents and purposes a satellite of Socialist France, and large sections of the upper classes migrated to Canada and Australia, which were semi-fascist.

earlier. See Samuel Rugg's *Causes of Anti-Catholicism in the Twentieth Century* (Boston, 2016). However, the Catholic group that supported McKinstry was much the same as that which had followed Coughlin.—D.W.

THE FIRST TO AWAKEN

Capitalism had now been destroyed throughout the whole sweep of Europe and Asia, but that did not mean that peace was immediately restored. The principal governments made peace with each other, but each was engaged in civil war at home. The age-long persecution of minorities had left such a heritage of hate and suspicion that desperate reactionaries found it easy to stir up nationalist sentiment. Then, when the minorities had won their independence, they were egged on to war against the socialist capitals. Banditry flourished, and the difference between banditry and rebellion became less and less apparent. All Southeast Europe was in turmoil, and it was seldom that the larger nations enjoyed peace.

Gradually, however, progress was made and order restored. The German-Russian alliance stood firm, and, despite the ravages of war, the two people worked together to raise the horribly debased standard of living. The Scandinavian countries, though they had long been the principal scene of war and had lost much that had been gained in earlier decades, still had the rudiments of a great cooperative movement, and reconstruction came more rapidly there than elsewhere. France led the way for Spain and Italy.

The United States was the last stronghold of capitalism, and even there capitalism scarcely resembled the models of the classical economists. Big business, frightened to death by what was happening in Europe, permitted McKinstry to follow fascist lines. Business rejoiced, of course, when he suppressed all the various parties that could be said, by any stretch of the imagination, to advocate socialism. Business also approved his legislative program restricting union functions and his use of the McKinstry Clubs to capture the unions.

But business was not so well pleased when he limited their profits and imposed a system of bureaucratic control. Nor did they enjoy paying tribute to the gangsters that he put in charge of the unions. Nevertheless, as business saw the situation, it was McKinstry or nothing, and they preferred McKinstry.

Cut off from foreign markets, and suffering from its internal disorganization, the American economy was staggering, and McKinstry's economic advisors, including some of the shrewdest men in the country, were called in and put to work. The pension plan, which had been so useful to him in his campaign, was shelved, and in its place was put a pretentious program of social reconstruction. This turned out to be little more than a series of work camps, paying starvation wages, but it was introduced with much adroit publicity, and for a time it added to McKinstry's popularity. And that he was popular at first, if not with a majority then with a large minority of the American people, seems certain.

His brighter advisors saw well enough that autarchy would work only if accompanied by the more equitable distribution of income, and, indeed, I gather that many of them were sincere in the opinion, which they so often expressed, that they were going to reconstruct the national economy. His political entourage, on the other hand, was interested solely in jobs and power, and his Wall Street supporters were determined not to lose control. There was a constant pulling and hauling. McKinstry levied tribute on business for his political needs, and he also forced some concessions to appease the populace, but he could not check the growing disintegration of production by half-way measures. As discontent mounted, his only answer was repression.

With the approach of 1956, many reactionaries argued that there should be no election. McKinstry himself was probably in agreement, for his clubs were agitating for what they called a constitutional dictatorship, and several magazines that opposed Big Tim were raided and their editors beaten. In the end it was the more astute financiers who stopped this plan, chiefly, I assume, because they thought the election campaign would help to keep McKinstry dependent on them.

McKinstry had succeeded, where everything else had failed, in unifying the socialist movement. There were still little groups of pure doctrinaires who propagated the true word as revealed to themselves, but they did not count. The great majority of socialists, whatever their particular programs, supported the underground Democratic League. Throughout the cities of the East and Middle West, McKinstry Clubs, in cooperation with the police, beat and arrested thousands of League members, and the League had to function as revolutionaries had functioned in Czarist Russia and anti-fascists in Nazi Germany. In parts of the West, however, the League was working openly.

Since there were only two legal parties—the American Party and the Democratic Party—the League determined to capture the latter. By this time millions of workers, farmers, and people of the middle class, who had supported McKinstry four years earlier, were turning against him. The League was unquestionably strong enough to nominate and elect its candidate.

McKinstry seems to have held a conference with his most powerful supporters, in the course of which he insisted that only a dictatorship and the immediate suppression of the opposition would suffice. The supporters, however, had another plan. With the aid of the McKinstry Clubs, they took over the whole machinery of the Democratic Party, and proceeded to pack the convention. It met in a Detroit auditorium, guarded by Federal troops, and nominated on the first ballot Mark Leland, who was somewhat less popular with the electorate than Herbert Hoover had been in 1932. Meanwhile, the American Party, meeting in Buffalo, nominated McKinstry in one of the most tumultuous and carefully planned demonstrations ever staged.

After this piece of fraud, the Democratic League came close to a schism. The more impetuous and desperate members—and conditions were becoming very desperate indeed for millions of people—demanded an armed uprising. Even on the executive council were men who, much as they hated the prospect of violent revolution, doubted if the suffering people could be restrained much longer. By now socialism was obviously succeeding in parts of Europe, and the socialist temper in America was becoming more militant. McKinstry, however, still had the whole military machine in his hands, and, with the weapons of destruction developed during the war, it seemed clear that even a successful revolution would leave the country devastated. The more moderate opinion won out, and the advocates of immediate action agreed to cooperate.

Despite Leland's unpopularity, McKinstry took no chances, and his racketeers stuffed ballot boxes and broke voting machines and terrorized boards of election. Inaugurated for the second time, he promptly forced Congress to do away with itself and made the Democratic Party illegal. It was a time for strong measures, for unemployment was still growing, and the relief problem had become insoluble.

The depths of disintegration reached in the later fifties were beyond anything I had conceived of. In Everett Wilson's papers I found a number of letters written at this time, and they revealed as nothing else could the extent of the breakdown. Here, for example, is a letter from a Braxton boy of nineteen or so to his younger brother:

New York City
July 8, 1957

Dear Rodney,

I got here last night, and I think I did pretty well, because as you see it only took me two and a half days. Of course, in spite of all the work Dad did on the car, it broke down before I had got fifty miles. It was the front axle. I knew it was no good to try to find a garage so I looked around for a blacksmith. I finally found one who thought he could fix it, but I want to tell you we had a hell of a time. I had to do most of the job myself.

Well, that took almost all day, but I thought that maybe I could get to Brownsville before night and stay with Cousin Mattie. But then I ran out of gas. I hadn't seen a single gas station all the way that was open. I walked into Limerick, about three miles, and asked all round. Everybody said I couldn't get it except from Martin Fay, who is a Big Shot here—you know what I mean. I finally went to him, and he charged me a dollar a gallon. I got two gallons.

HOW IT ALL HAPPENED

I stayed at a farmhouse that night. I tell you, the farmers are lucky. Especially now that crops are beginning to come along a little bit. It was funny, though, to see a lot of machinery standing around rusting. They just can't get gas to run it. This guy had dug out a lot of his grandfather's stuff, I guess, and was using that. He has a horse and a mule. It was kind of funny too to see electric light fixtures and ice chest and all that sort of stuff—no good now.

Gosh, the roads are terrible. When I got down into Connecticut, it was queer to see four-lane highways that were rougher than our street. In Springfield I swapped the eggs and stuff for gas. You can do that in cities. People will give you most anything for food.

I had a kind of adventure. I was stopped monkeying with the carburetor, and I saw two guys come out of the woods. They looked pretty tough, so I got my gun and just stood there watching them. Pretty soon they started walking the other way. Everybody tells me about holdups. I'm glad I know how to shoot.

Well, I got here, and I suppose the thing Mom and Dad will want to know is, did I get the job? Well, I did. Uncle Dan took me right to the store, and I started work right off. I guess I'm going to like, and, as Uncle Dan says, I'm awful lucky. New York is a funny place, though. It makes you kind of nervous like to see folks standing round so peaked looking. It's still a gay place though, but I guess it takes more cash than I'll ever get to see the sights.

Well, this is a longer letter than I ever wrote before, so I guess I'll close. Give my love to everybody.

> Your loving brother,
>
> Cal

Every kind of public service had suffered. For example, a great many schools had closed, and people were saying it was enough if children learned to read and write. As the letter shows, highways had fallen into disrepair, and all kinds of travel had become difficult. There were still rich men. In fact, there had been a whole new crop of profiteers, and people who had money spent it freely. New York was indeed a gay place, for a few people. But the average American saw his standard of living go lower and lower.

As usual, an undernourished population became apathetic, but there was still a good deal of fight left in the American people. There were violent demonstrations in many cities, put down with great loss of life. In California there was a pitched battle that lasted for days. In northern New England, in the vicinity of Braxton, farmers organized and broke up the McKinstry Clubs.

The truth is that the United States was too big a country to rule by force. The Democratic League began to conceive of a new strategy, simply taking over areas in which McKinstry forces were weak. A great section of Iowa and the Dakotas, for example, virtually seceded from the union. So did the Northwest. So did parts of Texas and Oklahoma.

As this happened, McKinstry tightened his grip on the industrial East. And it would be wrong to suppose that he did not have a popular following. His work camps, bad as they were, were better than starvation. The army, which he naturally enlarged, was well fed. And there were good pickings in the McKinstry Clubs. He was frankly anti-Semitic now, and the pillaging of the Jews enriched his followers. He was calling for a war on Mexico, and the revived armament industry was beginning to reduce unemployment.

Meanwhile life was taking a new form in the seceded areas. I gathered that Everett's daughter was secretly in sympathy with the rebels, for I found several letters written her by active workers in the Democratic League. One of these was from a young woman who had apparently had a narrow escape and had been smuggled out of Boston by the underground organization.

Sioux City, Jan. 5, 1958

Dear Marcia,

It is wonderful out here, and you're not to believe a word the papers say, especially your father's. People are really living here. My mother came from this marvelous corn country, and it seems as if I were coming home. I had expected to find the farms well organized, but I had not been prepared for the city. All the factories are running now, and new ones are being built!! And they are all operated on a cooperative basis, as are the stores.

Of course, some things are hard to secure—coffee, for instance, and you know I like coffee. Sugar I don't mind so much; at least it's good for me to go without it. These things are smuggled in sometimes, in spite of McKinstry's guards, but they're expensive. Gasoline is one of the problems, but as soon as Kansas comes in with us, which we expect to happen any day now, we can get it all right.

I met Rutherford Jones the first week I was here, and last night I heard him speak. Marcia, he is a great man, and I am sure he will be the first president of a socialist United States. He has a plan all worked out, and as soon as we can take over the East everything will be all right.

The people here are fine. My only criticism is that some of them are so delighted with what they've got here that they don't take any interest in the rest of the country. They do not realize that their safety depends on getting rid of McKinstry altogether. He does not dare attack now, but no one can tell what may happen.

Tell R. and G. to keep up the good work. I shall be coming back one of these days, though I don't suppose I'm likely to see you before the happy day. Do anything you can for the bearer of this letter.

Yours,
Claudia

Thus the forces were arrayed against each other by the beginning of 1960. The Democratic League controlled the entire country west of the Mississippi. McKinstry had stopped talking about Mexico, and it seemed certain that his huge army was to be used against the League. The League also had its armed forces, but they were poorly equipped in comparison, chiefly because Jones, its principal spokesman, insisted that it must at all costs raise the standard of living. Many members felt that he was short-sighted. They wanted a powerful army ready either to defend their territory or liberate the people of the East from McKinstry's power. Jones, however, still held that war would devastate the whole country, "If the people of the East are not with us," he said, "we shall be defeated whatever we do."

His program was not so impractical as it sounded. He had his representatives everywhere in the East, and he knew what was happening. Munition workers were engaging in systematic sabotage, though scores of them had been shot. There were strong League centers in every city, and even in the army. The people of the East were bombarded with socialist propaganda, not only from the League's radio stations but also from the capitals of Europe. Socialist successes in Europe, indeed, were one important source of Jones's confidence. Although there was still fighting going on in various countries, others were able to point to their achievements, and could promise the fullest cooperation to a socialist United States.

On September 28, 1960, McKinstry proclaimed himself Perpetual President. On October 5 it was announced that he had resigned. Actually he had been shot by what was journalistically known as the Praetorian Guard, an organization of men who had fled before the advance of socialism in Europe. They had been organized and equipped by six or seven of the most powerful and resolute financiers and industrialists, and they were reaction's last resort. Taking command of the regular army, they seized the principal cities of the East, and established a man named Caspar as dictator.

The rest of the story is one of bitter but, fortunately, not very prolonged fighting. If the reactionaries could have relied for supplies on any other country, they would have had a

THE FIRST TO AWAKEN

better chance, but Canada was also in the midst of civil war, and there was no other nation to which they could turn. For a time their military training and equipment gave them the advantage, and the anti-fascists suffered horribly. Detroit, Pittsburgh, and Boston, all of which had been captured by the democratic militia, were cruelly bombed, and everywhere there was a bloody crushing of resistance. But within a few weeks the Praetorian Guard had shot its bolt. The democratic army became better organized and better equipped—both because it was aided from the West and because it succeeded in capturing stores of munitions. (The taking of Springfield, in which Everett died,[1] was one of the more dramatic incidents.) At last the reactionaries made a desperate stand in the South and were defeated.

The council of the Democratic League proclaimed Rutherford Jones head of the provisional government and announced plans for a constitutional convention. The decision to hold the convention was made only after a prolonged struggle. As might be expected, the bitterness of civil war did not readily recede, and there were many Leaguers who favored a dictatorship. Jones and his group stood out for a more magnanimous policy. "If," said Jones, with uncommon frankness, "I honestly believed that there was a danger of a revival of the Praetorian Guard or of the McKinstry Clubs, I should be the first to recommend drastic measures. I do not propose to see what we have won taken away from us by a ruthless minority. If I have anything to say about it, the leaders of

[1] In his papers is a note to his daughter, the last, presumably, that he ever wrote. It ends: "I'm on the right side at last. We'll give 'em hell."—G.S.

the recent counter-revolution will never have another chance to threaten our peace and security. But I will not tolerate punitive measures. I will not tolerate the unnecessary use of force. If I must err on either side, I shall err on the side of magnanimity. Better a weak government than one that abuses its strength. Better the risk of failure than the certainty of tyranny. We were a free people in the past, and we must not surrender the freedom we have regained."

Again this seems to have been good political sense. Eighty or eighty-five percent of the people were on Jones's side. The League enjoyed prestige because of its military victories in the East and its economic successes in the West. The people were ready for some kind of socialism, and his plans were the most convincing of those presented. There was some confusion in the course of the elections to the convention, but it was certainly a more representative body than that which met in 1787.

Jones was elected President under the amended constitution, and put into effect what had long been referred to in League propaganda as Plan X. Much of the machinery of socialism, badly as it had been abused, had been brought into existence in the semi-fascist period, and all the basic industries were so thoroughly disorganized that nationalization was an economic as well as a political necessity. Simultaneously with deliberate inflation and the fixing of prices, relief rates were established on a high level, the states were given grants to implement the various pension plans that had fallen into the discard, and wages were raised. The demand for consumers' goods of every kind was unprecedented.

For the moment Jones did not bother those capitalists who

had not actively supported the rebellion, beyond establishing the wages they must pay. The others, more numerous and more powerful, had either been killed in the civil war, or fled the country, or been arrested. Workers were already managing many factories, and this became the rule in all businesses that had been abandoned. The organization of cooperatives, which had been so successful in the West, was rapidly extended to the East, and the damage wrought by the civil war was repaired with surprising promptness.

As President Jones persistently warned the people, inequalities and injustices could not be immediately eliminated, but for most people the rise in income was so great that they were willing to be patient. Having succeeded in putting the productive resources of the country to work, the administration could devote itself, drawing upon the experience of Europe, to the creation of an efficient socialist order. I gather that life in the sixties was rather uncomfortable, but it had its heroic aspects, and it laid the foundation for the complete reconstruction of American life.

Abraham liked to talk about the Technological Era. The building of New York seemed to him a magnificent enterprise, and he was full of enthusiasm for the development of the power system, the creation of the highways, the perfection of stratosphere transportation. I realized, of course, how much the civilization of the year 2040 owed to the technicians, but I came to share some of David's prejudice against mere size and efficiency. In the seventies and eighties production seemed to be the end of man, and though, by the standards of my lifetime, David exaggerated the degree of regimentation, there was no doubt that life in 2040 was a great deal pleasanter.

If there had been a constant struggle to maintain a high productive level, the technicians might have retained their dominance, but they created the age of abundance and themselves became, so to speak, victims of technological unemployment. That, to be sure, is too strong a statement, for, as David had pointed out again and again, we depended all the time on technical knowledge and skill, but it is true that, when production became relatively so easy, it was hard to convince people that that was all that ought to concern them. The technicians had to give people what they wanted; they could not dictate to them what they ought to want.

That, of course, was the upshot of my history lesson. I had come into a world in which the economic problem had been satisfactorily mastered for fifty years. I was surrounded by men and women who not only had never known capitalism but had been spared the experimental stages of socialism. They were the outcome of a new way of life, and I had a chance to see what that life had done for them.

VIII

PROGRESS OF AN EDUCATION

ONE NIGHT at dinner I said, "Roberta, we're both being educated, but I'm afraid I'll never catch up with you."

She giggled, but I meant what I said. As first I had felt that education must have made a phenomenal advance, and so in many ways it had, but the real point, as I was gradually learning, was that its task had become much simpler. I tried to think back to 1940. Suppose I had then had a daughter of eleven or so, Roberta's age, what problems would we have been facing? For example, was her education intended to help her get ahead in the world or was it supposed to make her a useful member of society? That question would have been meaningless to Roberta and her parents. To all intents and purposes, and with only minor exceptions, she could "get ahead" only by being useful. I knew now that ambition had not disappeared, nor selfishness, but they were pretty successfully harnessed to social ends. When Roberta discovered what she wanted to do, there would be a chance for her to do it.

Moreover, because the society to which Roberta belonged was intelligently organized, it was easy to understand. She knew exactly what her father did and why, and she saw how his job was related to all the other jobs in the community. That was not because she was uncommonly bright, but because Braxton formed a reasonable pattern. In the same way she learned economics, which had always been a puzzle to me, as easily as she learned her way home from school. Every experience she had added to her knowledge of the world.

Probably I would have been scrimping and saving so that my daughter could go to college, though I could not have known whether she was fitted for more advanced education nor whether what she learned would benefit her. Roberta would have as much education as she was willing to work for. College would never seem to her merely a place to have a good time nor yet a path to social prestige. Till she was nineteen or twenty she would find learning a not too painful process, and she would have a healthy social life with her contemporaries. Thereafter, though it was never put so baldly, she would have to prove that she could contribute more to society by continuing to study than she could by productive labor. I gathered that there were occasional tragedies, when ambition outran ability, but ordinarily the discipline of higher education discouraged those who were not fitted for it.

In my own youth it seemed to me that fully half of my school hours were spent in purposeless studies. Nobody ever told me why I had to take these subjects, and I felt, probably quite rightly, that nobody knew. Roberta always wanted to learn whatever it was she was studying, not because of some pedagogical magic, but because her studies grew out of her life. Mathematics and the sciences were keys that opened doors right there in Braxton. History was the story of her own past. Geography was the planning of trips she would some day take. Spelling and grammar—a good deal simplified, I admit —were tools for communication.

As I realized when I went to school with her one day, Roberta was brighter than the average child, but, though I saw some relatively stupid children, I never saw the two expressions I remembered so well from my own school days —blank bewilderment and bitter resentment.

The school itself was so designed as to give a sense of freedom. Instead of being the rigid, blocklike structure I was used to, the building was spread out in an irregular and indescribable pattern. The rooms were of various sizes and strange shapes, and many opened directly onto gardens and playground. The decoration of each room was not merely designed but also executed by the children who worked there, and the color schemes ranged from the somber to the gay and even garish.

Braxton Elementary School No. 7

PROGRESS OF AN EDUCATION

It took me only a little while to understand how directly Roberta's experimental attitude towards life could be traced to the classroom. Yet there was no emphasis on novelty for its own sake. I was puzzled on discovering a group of younger children building a tower that was bound to topple—and did in my presence. "They may as well learn," said the teacher, "that the discoveries of the past can be used to save time and energy and pain. Nothing should be accepted uncritically, simply because it belongs to the past, but they mustn't get the idea that what is old is necessarily wrong."

In Roberta's history class there was a discussion of heroes. From my own era the only persons to figure in the talk were Ford and Lenin, and it amused me to see how much both had been romanticized. The girl who admired Ford looked on him as a pioneer of mass production and therefore a man who had helped lay the foundation for the socialist commonwealth. The devotee of Lenin, on the other hand, talked of his conspiratorial years and made him a kind of Robin Hood.

Scientists, inventors, engineers, poets, revolutionaries, and athletes were mentioned before the class was over. I was surprised to find so much emphasis laid on individual heroes, and said so to the teacher, a young woman named Margaret Bryan, whom I had occasionally met at the cooperative. She was not at all apologetic. "This is the age for heroes," she said. "They'll learn—some of them already know—that no great change can be attributed to a single individual, but the last thing we want is for them to think that the individual doesn't count. They have to realize that it is important for men and women to be brave and resourceful and self-sacrificing and wise. We can still use a few heroes, you know."

THE FIRST TO AWAKEN

It was this young woman who was responsible for the most extraordinary experience of my first few months. I spent part of almost every day at the library, which was not, of course, a great research institution, but, because of the use of films, housed in small space an extensive collection. Margaret frequently came into the library after school, and several times she suggested reading that I was glad to do. One afternoon she brexed [1] in with her tennis racket under her arm. Apparently she merely wanted to look up some reference, for a few minutes later she was rushing out again. She saw me and stopped. "I suppose you've read your own obituary?"

"What?"

"Haven't you? I should think you'd want to." She went to the stacks and came back with a roll of film. "Here's the *Voice* for 1940."

She left, and I sat staring into the reading machine, as the familiar headlines unwound before my eyes: a neutral ship sunk, victory by Finnish troops on skis, a blast for the third term, a blast against the third term, the meetings of the Rotary club and the various church societies, the advertisements of the stores where I had shopped, the reports from a score of neighboring towns of who was ill and who had visited whom. And then I saw the headline, "Bank Employee Dies Suddenly," with underneath it a picture of me in uniform taken when I

[1] This, so far as I can detect, is the first instance in the entire manuscript of Swain's using a word that was not in use in the nineteen-thirties. In speech, by this time, he was using many such words, chiefly, of course, names of things that have come into existence in the past century, but also other expressions that are now common. I have devoted considerable attention to this question of vocabulary in my forthcoming report.—D.W.

returned from France. I could not help shivering a little as I went on and read:

> The body of George Swain, for nearly twenty years a teller at the Braxton National Bank, was discovered yesterday afternoon on Putnam's Hill. Dr. Carr, distinguished Braxtonian and cancer specialist, who discovered the body, pronounced death due to heart failure. Funeral services will be held tomorrow at the First Congregational Church, Rev. Alvah B. Lawton, D.D., officiating.
>
> Mr. Swain was a veteran of the American Expeditionary Force, having served in the Yankee Division, and saw action at Chateau Thierry. After leaving the army he entered the employ of the Braxton National Bank.
>
> It has been ascertained that Mr. Swain telephoned the bank yesterday and said he would not be at work that morning. It is believed that he was feeling ill and that that is why he went to walk. Death was apparently instantaneous.
>
> The deceased was the son of the late Martin Trelawney Swain, for eight years principal of the Braxton High School and widely respected in educational circles throughout the state. Mrs. Swain, the former Elsie Harrington of this city, died three years ago. She had been prominent in the social life of Braxton.

In a curious way I was touched by this. It was just what I would have expected if I had ever stopped to think that an obituary must have appeared, and yet, conventional as it was, it carried me back to a world that day by day I found it more difficult to remember.

Abstractedly I turned the film, noting how easily life in Braxton had gone on without me. Then suddenly my eye fell on a poem of three short stanzas, with the title, "To a

THE FIRST TO AWAKEN

Comrade," and underneath, "In Memoriam, G.S., died March 8, 1940." It was signed, "E.W."

Everett, to my way of thinking, was never much of a poet, but that did not matter. He had felt deeply enough to write this, and even, in spite of all his cynicism, to publish it. And I, living in the world of his great-great-grandson, was reading it.

> Our songless time no hero sings,
>   Nor hero sees or knows.
> We cannot hail him while he lives,
>   Nor mourn him when he goes.
>
> Our faith is small, our hope is thin,
>   Our feeble vices thrive.
> Yet men have walked on humble streets
>   Who kept a dream alive.
>
> We bludgeon dreams, and I had tried
>   All tricks men know to slay.
> I thought them dead but now perceive
>   They lived until today.

With trembling hands I copied this. Suddenly the librarian was upon me, horrified, I suppose, to see anyone engaged in copying. Embarrassed, I refused her offer to show me how to make a photostat, and she went away. But I was a little ashamed of myself, for she had always been as kind as she could be, and, as I got ready to go, I stopped by her desk. She said nothing about the photostat, but remarked brightly, "Isn't Margaret Bryan a lovely girl?" I agreed that she was, and to my amazement the librarian blushed. Bewildered, I fumbled with my papers and left.

PROGRESS OF AN EDUCATION

I had an engagement with David that night, and of course showed him Everett's poem. We talked about it for a long time, for somehow he had overlooked it when he was going through the files of the *Voice*, and it seemed to have for him almost the personal significance it had for me.

As I was leaving, I remembered the librarian's behavior and described it to David. He burst into laughter. "I know what's on her mind," he said, "even if you don't. You've read *Looking Backward* and *News from Nowhere* and books like that, haven't you? Well, so has she—in your honor, I imagine. I know because we talked about it once. Now in those books the hero always falls in love with some utopian damsel. Well, Miss Telfer has picked out Margaret for you." He laughed again. "You could do worse, you know."

Though I saw David only two or three times a week, I knew that he was continuing his observations.[1] I seldom thought of this, however. I regarded him as the oldest and most helpful of my friends. In Braxton it was easier to see him as a person rather than as embodied omniscience. He went about his work in his serious, conscientious way, and whenever I stopped at his office, it was filled with persons who were consulting him. He talked to them in the same level, sober manner he used with me, and I could see that they liked him. He would go to infinite pains to revise a time study or check the analysis of an industrial process, and the workers were almost invariably satisfied with his conclusions.

It was David who suggested that I grow a beard. I don't

[1] Swain proved more and more cooperative and more and more interesting. In the appendix of my report I shall print the tests I used. Note particularly Chart 47a—"An analysis of Changes in Social Orientation."—D.W.

know how he guessed that I had always wanted one, but I always had, and seeing so many bearded men of all ages had rekindled the ambition. Yet it would have taken a long time for me to work up my courage if David had not casually said that most men grew a beard sometime in their lives, and he wondered how I would look with one. I think I looked rather well, and certainly it was a relief to dispense with shaving. I had never got used to the arc brush, and had stuck to the old-fashioned electric razor, even though it took so long and had to be used every day. Victor had laughed at me, but now I could laugh at him. Agnes approved, saying she would want Victor to have a beard except that he looked enough like a gorilla anyway.

It was David also who reminded me that I would do well to have another medical examination, and suggested my going to Dr. Rosenthal, since I already knew him. The doctor found nothing startling. "You probably have a higher immunity to most diseases than the rest of us," he said, "since you have been exposed to them more. We shall have to watch out for influenza, though, for the virus has taken a new form since your time, and I doubt if you are immune. There are also certain diseases of the nervous system that have developed in more recent years. In fact, I would recommend a series of inoculations."

When I happened to remark that the doctor's job must have become a good deal easier, he disagreed with me. He admitted that the raising of the standard of living had eliminated much disease. "The number of days lost as a result of illness," he said, "has been reduced to about ten percent of what it was a century ago and this in spite of the fact that at that time many people were not under medical care when they should have been. Improvement in living conditions is responsible for a large part of this gain. The rest we owe to the elimination of tuberculosis, the virtual elimination of cancer and venereal diseases, and the effective control of diseases due to filterable viruses."

"But that's what I mean," I said. "There can't be much left for you to do."

He began to tell me about the tasks of preventive medicine, about the organic disturbances that nobody understood, about the constant vigilance against epidemics, all the more dangerous because they had been so long absent from the world. "There is so much for us to know," he said. "No doctor in your day could be expected to diagnose half the ailments he ran into, and he didn't try. He said a few consoling words, left a few pills, and hoped for the best. We feel that there must be a scientific treatment for every ill, even the so-called imaginary ones, and when we find areas in which we are still ignorant, as we do, it haunts us. We have cooperative clinics, but a man doesn't dare specialize too narrowly. You can't divide a field into seven or eight parts without losing something."

At the same time I went to the oculist and the dentist. I had always been proud of not having to wear glasses, and it was a comfort to discover that I still did not need them. Being without them, however, was less of a distinction than it had been in my time, for it was much easier to avoid eye strain, and some defects of vision could be corrected by diet or exercise. Most persons, moreover, who had to wear glasses all the time had them fitted to the eye-balls, so that they were incon-

THE FIRST TO AWAKEN

spicuous. A few of my friends regarded this as an unnecessary bother, but only a few.

In the dental clinic Dr. Bross studied my X-rays, saying, "Not so good. But we can do a job of patching." While he worked he watched a kind of moving picture of my jaw that showed him exactly what he was doing. He talked about control of decay through diet and glandular treatment. "But there's still plenty of old-fashioned plugging up to do," he said cheerfully, manipulating his strange instruments. The experience was not pleasant, but at least there was no pain.

The dentist seemed an affable young fellow, and I asked him some of the personal questions I liked to throw at my acquaintances. "Don't you mind having a low income rating?"

"Lord, no. I don't have time to spend the money I get."

"But wouldn't your wife like to have more money?"

He smiled. "My wife works in the assembling plant, and has a B rating."

So my education progressed. Merely living in the Waldman family taught me much, and my debt to David was incalculable. But more and more I found myself turning to Simeon Blake.

He had kept his promise to take me to walk, and as good spring weather began we walked often. With his fine square shoulders thrown back, his beard glistening, his open jacket flying, he set a pace that was almost too much for me. Usually I called for him at the stables, and he talked about the good points of the horses. After a time he even overcame my timidity enough to give me riding lessons, and though I was always awkward on horseback and tried in vain to imitate his nonchalance, I came to enjoy a mild canter.

PROGRESS OF AN EDUCATION

We talked about many subjects. Simeon smoked large and strong cigars, and after I had come to know him well, I asked him about this and about the contemporary attitude towards smoking and drinking.

"So you thought a perfect society would eliminate the minor vices? An almost-perfect society did, but we've learned better since then."

"Prohibition didn't work?"

"Not prohibition. We had subtler methods. In the seventies and eighties drinking was increasing. People had more leisure and more money. Most of the drinking was cheerful and relatively harmless, but drunkenness wasn't unknown. We engineers couldn't stand it. It wasn't efficient, and we wanted efficiency at all costs. So we turned to the psychologists and the physiologists. They were as conscious of their new power in those days as we were, and they were glad to oblige. They devised a cure for alcoholism, and then we called in the publicity boys to make every American who liked to drink think he was alcoholic. After that success, they turned to smoking."

"Puritanism revived?"

"No. Well, yes, in a way. I suppose that control over personal habits is always exercised by a little group of fanatics who love power and are able to create new patterns of social approval and disapproval. And like all puritanical reforms, this had some justification and some good results. But in time people began to learn that we were efficient enough to be able to afford some inefficiency. We were sacrificing to efficiency not only the minor vices but also many of the major virtues."

As always when he was talking earnestly, his pace quickened. When I caught up with him, I said, "But isn't life too easy? Won't self-indulgence soften the fiber of the race? I mean, there used to be a lot of talk about survival of the fittest and that sort of thing."

He looked down at me and snorted. "Use your eyes," he said. "Look at those young people—hard as nails. Look at the game of tennis those two women are playing, and they're over fifty if they're a day. Get your friend Wilson to tell you about life in the Arctic Reclamation Corps. You'll find soft people, yes, but fewer, I swear, than ever before in history."

Comparing his fine physique with my own gangling frame, I wished I had kept my mouth shut. "Talk of survival of the fittest," he exclaimed. "When have the men who drove themselves like slaves ever been fit, and how long have they survived? How many of the business men of your era died at fifty of apoplexy! And what of the factory hands who were thrown out on the street, warped and rotted in their forties? No, no, George, it was when we treated ourselves like machines that we endangered the race, not when we started treating ourselves like human beings."

"But aren't there people who smoke too much or drink to excess?"

"To be sure, my boy, to be sure. And we could stop them if we wanted to. But we believe—most of us at any rate—that a man has a right to make a fool of himself if he chooses. We will protect ourselves from the consequences of his foolishness, but we will not protect him unless he asks for protection. Nine times out of ten a man who is injuring himself by eating too much or drinking too much will have sense enough to see a doctor. If he doesn't, that's his business."

"But suppose a man comes to work drunk?"

"His fellow-workers will take care of him. If it's an accident, they'll kid him a little and let it go at that. If it's a habit, they'll probably tell him he can either see a psychiatrist or quit. If he quits, he's left alone unless he's in danger of becoming a public nuisance."

I still felt that he was being a little casual about the whole problem. "You don't feel that excessive drinking is abnormal?"

"My dear George, of course it's abnormal. But we're all abnormal in one way or another, and a good thing too. What's a norm? It's either an average or an arbitrarily fixed standard. We could choose a norm and then use every psychiatric resource to make people conform to it. But do we want everybody to be alike? We went a little way with that experiment, as I can remember, and it was a failure."

"So you decided that you shouldn't interfere unless the welfare of society was endangered?"

"Oh, more than that. That's a dangerously broad concept, the welfare of society. The burden of proof is now on society's side. It has to be proven not only that other persons are injured but that they are injured in some serious way."

"Suppose a man beat his wife when he got drunk."

"Well, she isn't economically dependent on him. She can leave him. And if she chooses to stay with him, in spite of the beatings, isn't that her business?"

"But if a man abused his children?"

"That's different. Then he would either have to consent to the proper psychiatric treatment or the children would be taken from his care."

THE FIRST TO AWAKEN

We were cutting across the square in front of the cooperative restaurant. "The system works badly," he said, "but better than any other we have devised."

Another time we talked about eugenics. I had gathered from David that there was no attempt to tell people whom they should marry or how many children they should have, but I had seen several references to eugenic principles in magazines I had picked up. "We might do something with eugenics yet," Simeon said reflectively. "It's a bit premature perhaps."

"Premature?"

"It's foolish to talk about eugenics until you know what's in the race. We've begun to find out. You see, George, a hundred years ago it was impossible to tell what differences between people were due to environment and what to heredity. Now everybody has more or less a fair chance. If children seem stupid, at least we know that it isn't because they are undernourished or need to have their adenoids removed. We're getting rid of accidental differences, and so we can look for fundamental ones. For the first time it means something to ask whether one stock is better than another."

I could understand that. I had always been sure that there were greater capacities in most of my fellow human beings than had a chance to express themselves. Elsie's father would sometimes say: "Those Dagoes aren't good for anything but digging ditches," or, "All a Canuck can do is run a machine." I knew he was wrong. I knew that some of them could have become musicians or scientists or bank presidents if they'd had a chance. I was always being surprised by the broad interests of people who had had no formal education, and by the wisdom they showed, too. I had never doubted that there was talent of a high order that my society didn't know how to use.

That is one reason why I adjusted myself fairly easily to the people of the new Braxton. The kind of uncertainty I had felt for a time in New York left me. These were just ordinary people, only they'd been given a chance. It didn't amaze me that a workman like Victor knew a good deal about agricultural chemistry, or that Agnes was interested in the drama, nor was I surprised at the brightness of their children. Perhaps I hadn't been so clear about it before, but I did know that these possibilities existed.

"We know a good deal now," Simeon went on, "about the mechanism of heredity, and if we wanted to breed human beings as we breed domestic animals, for particular qualities, we could probably do it. But we want something a damn sight more difficult to get."

We were walking along the river that day, and up and down the valley tractors were doing the spring plowing. As well as I could remember, much of this land had been played out in my day, and I spoke of this to Simeon. I knew that science had made land productive that had once been useless, but it seemed to me that even so it would be cheaper to import crops from more fertile areas.

"We had a choice," he answered, and I realized that I had heard that phrase many times. "A hundred years ago it was impossible to raise good crops here and expensive to import them from the West and South. Today transportation is cheap, and at the same time fair production is possible. Fifty years ago the tendency was still in the direction of regional special-

Stockton Corners Farm Center

ization, but science made regional differences less and less important, and in the end the social factor was decisive. This is at least a workable democracy."

Our path carried us near one of the country highways, and perhaps a dozen cars drove up and stopped. Simeon said it was the four o'clock shift at the agricultural station. "Don't the farm workers live here?" I asked.

"Some do and some don't. They have the same choice as factory workers. I imagine these men live in the apartment houses."

Blake was a man easy to identify, and one of the workers waved to him from a distance, calling his name. We walked over, and I was introduced to him and some of his companions. We talked for a few minutes, and then they took their places on the tractors, while the men who had been working either entered the farm center or drove away.

We walked for a little way beside the road. "Are you game for a couple more miles?" Simeon inquired. I nodded.

The houses, pre-fabricated like those in the city, had the same variety of design and the same look of comfort. The barns seemed rather like small factories than like the barns I remembered. I commented on the cattle, which a hundred years of breeding had made magnificent creatures.

In some areas workmen were taking down the great sheets of stuff like cellophane that had so puzzled me when I first saw them. It was under these that winter farming was done, not on the same scale as summer farming but in sufficient degree to supply Braxton and the neighborhood with fresh vegetables.

The newly turned soil smelled good, and, taking deep breaths, I said to Simeon, "Not all the poetry has gone out of farming."

To my surprise he answered, "Most of it has, though."

"What do you mean?"

"Farming isn't a direct struggle between man and nature any more. These workers are skilled mechanics, who deal with machines, not with nature. Their work goes on in spite of sun and wind and rain, and they even pay little attention to the passing of the seasons. Poetry, like religion, grew out of man's humility before forces he could not control."

"So what do poets write about now?"

"About man and nature, mostly. The weak ones write about man's contact with nature where he has tamed it—you know, gardens and pretty sunsets. The strong ones explore that area in which man still confronts nature directly—within himself."

"And religion?"

He shrugged his broad shoulders. "There are still churches."

"There are?" I said in astonishment.

"To be sure. There is still a Pope, who still claims to be infallible. There are some of the old Protestant denominations and some sects that sprang up in the twentieth century. But all the churches put together play so little part in the life of a community such as Braxton that you didn't know they existed."

"And religion?" I repeated.

"Something that was part of religion—many would say the most important part—is still alive." He shrugged again. "You can call it religion if you want to."

"It's funny that I hadn't thought about churches before."

Simeon led us straight through one of the new forests and up a long hill. "As an institution," he said carefully, "the church served many needs, some of which had nothing to do with religion. Even a hundred years ago the majority of Americans got along without the church. And today most people find that what the church used to do is better done by other institutions. That isn't to deny that the churches did much that was good."

"And much that was evil," I put in.

He nodded solemnly.

"But what about religion itself?" I persisted. "I mean creeds—God and immortality and all the rest of it."

"No amount of argument ever shook anybody's faith, but,

as I said a moment ago, man's steady conquest of nature changed the intellectual atmosphere. That change had begun long before your time. The deism and rationalism of the eighteenth century were the result of two hundred years of scientific progress. The confidence they expressed in man's powers was premature, and that is why there was the revivalism of the next seventy-five years. But science went on, and organized religion fought a losing battle. It is still fighting it. At times in the twentieth century it seemed to be gaining, but the tide has been ebbing for fifty years now. Yet who can say what a great disaster would do?"

"And what do you believe?" I asked boldly.

"Pretty much what you do, I imagine, George. Man is on his own in a universe that wasn't designed for his particular benefit. That universe is full of mysteries and always will be. Man will never wholly understand it, nor will he ever succeed in adapting it perfectly to his desires."

"But what is the end of life?"

"What we make it."

We had come to the top of the hill, and in the center of broad fields I could see what appeared to be an old-fashioned farmhouse with a ramshackle barn. "Why was this left?" I exclaimed.

"You'll see."

There was smoke—old-fashioned smoke—coming out of the chimney, and soon I could see a man chopping wood in the backyard. "This is Bill Jenks," said Simeon with a grin, "the man who doesn't belong to the cooperative."

Bill looked up and came towards us, shouting at Simeon, whom he evidently recognized. He was over seventy, and his unkempt hair was gray, but his tanned face was almost unlined under the grizzled stubble. His pants, I felt sure, had originally come from the cooperative molding machine, but they were stained beyond recognition. His patched shirt might have been bought at Sears Roebuck.

He greeted Simeon cordially, took one of his good cigars and lighted it, and, when he had been told about me, said cheerfully that I was a damned fool. In the house the floors were dirty and the ceilings covered with cobwebs. The bed, piled high with old-fashioned comforters, was unmade. Something was boiling on the stove.

He took us out to the barn, to get Simeon to look at his cow. She was a nice creature, well kept, and Simeon slapped her flanks and praised her. Chickens were running about, and there was a mangy horse in the stall. A patch of land beside the barn had been plowed, and the plow was lying in the yard. There was a kind of chuckle down deep in Bill's throat as he talked about the winter. "I came through all right," he said triumphantly.

Simeon told me about Bill as we walked back to Braxton. More than thirty years ago he had quarreled with his wife and moved out of the farm center. He had found this abandoned farm, fixed it up, and lived there ever since. "Where does he get his supplies?" I asked.

"What little he gets, he gets at the cooperative store. You can't imagine, George, what a nuisance he is to the bookkeepers." Simeon laughed. "When he got his cow, for instance. He carves toys and stuff out of wood, and he had saved quite a lot of money. But there was no price on cows. Cows simply weren't for sale. It was a crisis." Still laughing, he mimicked the conversation between Bill and a clerk. "Bill got his cow."

"It seems pretty heroic."

"Now, don't romanticize, George. He's just a stubborn old fellow, and there's no sense in your thinking about him as a second Thoreau or anything like that. He has a narrow, uncomfortable life, and he's just sustained by the thought that he's still getting even with his wife and with all the rest of us, whereas actually he couldn't get along without us. Don't misunderstand me. I like him, and I think it's good for the red-tape boys to have to deal with exceptions. But I can't let you make a hero out of him."

There were thousands of such persons scattered through the country. Although the desperate conditions of the breakdown and the civil war had sent most people flocking into the cooperatives, a minority, accustomed by then to a self-sufficient life on a low level, refused to join. At first they were subjected to some pressure, but as time went on the matter seemed less and less important. By now, as Simeon said, most cooperatives would go out of their way to help these individualists.

Every time I talked with Simeon I learned something new, and each meeting is clearly recorded in my mind. It was one day when we were riding together on a beautiful bridle path that he began to speak of old age. "Men grow old," he said. "I have grown old. As we conquer disease, there are more and more old people. What are we going to do about them? There is work for them, to be sure, so long as health remains, and comfort when health goes, but is that all we can do for them and all they can do for us? I have seen civilizations in which the old were held in respect for their wisdom. Our civilization did away with that kind of veneration, long before your day, and rightly, for change came too fast. The old men's wisdom could not solve the young men's problems. But civilization does not change so quickly now. Is it just a prejudice of my own age, or may it be true that the experience of seven or eight decades could teach us something? I resigned from the educational planning board because I feared that I might become a brake on progress. I was right. I was formed in an earlier world. But does that mean that there is no service I can render?"

I did not want to seem to be a flatterer, and so, instead of saying what it was in my heart to say to him, I remarked, "Most of the older people I have met appear to be happy."

"On the whole. Never underestimate what has been done. No insecurity, no fear of poverty or helplessness. And best of all, work for everyone who can do work and wants to, no matter what his age."

"Don't people ever retire? I mean, not merely to take another job, as you did."

"To do what? To sit in the sun and twiddle their thumbs and be taken care of? Some people think they would like that, but nine out of ten either go back to work or throw themselves into some hobby that is more exacting than a job. The tenth is usually a sick man. If a person retires at sixty, as anyone can do, it is usually because there is some non-productive work that he is interested in—writing or study or scientific experiment. That is all to the good, because such work often proves valuable and because an older man who isn't doing his job well is always a problem."

He began to gallop, and I followed along as best I could.

PROGRESS OF AN EDUCATION

When he slowed down again, and I had come abreast of him, he said, "There was a man in the district planning board when I went there, only sixty-eight and he loved his work. But he was making crucial mistakes. I had to tell him, and he was a broken man, of no use to anyone. How much better for him and for us if he'd stopped earlier."

We turned back towards the town. "I shall live a long time yet, and so long as I have health of body and mind, I am glad. But if my life is to be so long, I want it to be good for something. I should like the end of my life to be as useful as the middle years, but if that is to be true, my usefulness must be of a different kind. There is so much still to be done."

"So the world isn't finished," I said jocosely.

"Finished! We haven't begun yet. Change may be slower, more orderly, but change there will be. And perhaps it should not be too orderly. Often I think how much the Technological Era accomplished. Rationalism was rampant in those days. We made plenty of mistakes, but we did things that needed to be done, things that perhaps could not have been done if men's minds had not been well shaken up. How we smashed through prejudices! One after another we put through reforms that men had talked about for decades, even centuries: introduced the duodecimal system, adopted the thirteen month calendar and the twenty-four hour clock, simplified spelling, created three international languages—Basic English, Basic German, Basic French. We unified the sciences, abolished the great plagues, remade education. We changed the world."

I was surprised, for I had gathered from Nathalie, as well as from Simeon himself, that he had come to think the technologists were wrong.

"Do you still believe, George, that right is to be found only on one side and wrong on the other? No, we were right, and our opponents were right. We had to push as far as we could, but of course we had to be stopped. If civilization is a balance of forces, the forces must be there. Who was responsible for the slowing down of technological reform? Some wise men and a host of lazy ones. Could the lazy men, or even the wise ones, ever have given us what we have today? No, George, never. There had to be men like them, or we would have gone on to destruction, but there had to be men like us."

This was a puzzling conception, and I tried to apply it to the understanding of my own period. "Did there have to be crooked politicians, then, as well as reformers?"

"Indeed there did. The crooked politicians, as you call them, were usually effective organizers and men who got things done. Left to themselves, they were an evil, but so the reformers would have been—if they ever had been left to themselves."

"But the struggle between capital and labor—"

"Was a good thing, a force for progress, so long as the capitalist really functioned. Of course, when he ceased to do anything but sit on his money bags he had to go. The nature of the conflict shifted."

"I see no signs of conflict now."

"You may not have looked far enough. I admit, though, that this is a period of relative calm. It may last a long time, but it will not last forever. We haven't come to the end of human history, my boy."

"But what kind of progress can we expect now?"

"Kinds we don't expect."

I thought of Nick and his dissatisfaction. "Will progress come from the poets?"

"Perhaps; at least it will come from men who have the power to envisage new possibilities. They will make us realize that we have wanted something all along, only we haven't known what it was."

We came to the top of a rise, and there the town was before us, and I felt as I had on that first morning when I looked down from the hospital roof. I still couldn't believe that all this had happened to so ordinary and colorless a person as myself. "What a marvelous adventure!" I said.

"You knew none of the other men?"

"No. I was the only one from Braxton. A man named Tillset, from New York City, is the next."

Simeon nodded. "A scientist," he said, "and apparently a good one. A disappointed man like yourself, cheated of due recognition, driven from his job. It's going to be interesting, isn't it? Eight months from now you will be an old citizen. Perhaps you can help him as nobody could help you."

"It is a pity," I said impulsively, "that Dr. Carr is not here in my place. He could do so much more for you than I can do."

Simeon gave me a friendly look. "I doubt that. I confess that I'd like to have known Carr—a strange personality, I should say. You, George, if you won't be offended by the term, are a representative character, and that is your value."

We came to the stable. The man who took Simeon's place on this shift apparently never had a thought beyond his work, to which he was devoted. He respected Simeon's knowledge of horses, and it would have seemed fantastic to him that any other knowledge Simeon had could be more important. He and Simeon talked professionally about a mare that was sick, and then we left.

"You must travel," Simeon said, as we approached the Waldmans' house by way of the old orchard. "The world is still wide, though only a few hours separate us from the most distant parts, and there are still many kinds of people in it. Good night."

IX

THE COURSE OF JUSTICE

ONE bright May morning I was taking a sunbath when the telephone sounded. As usual, because I received so few calls, I had forgotten to connect the extension, and I ran to my room. It was David, reminding me that the disciplinary committee of the cooperative was to be in session that evening. I arranged to meet him for dinner at the restaurant.

In preparation I studied the brief notice in the Braxton pages of the bulletin. It began by listing the panel—some twenty well-respected citizens—from whom the committee would be chosen. Then followed short summaries of the three cases to be heard. The first was a criminal case, the only one to occur since my arrival in Braxton. The second involved charges of disruptive conduct brought by the executive committee of a union against one of its members. The details of the third startled me: two members of the planning board charged a third with incompetence. Evidently this was why David wanted me to be present.

The Braxton planning board was composed of five members. Three of them were heads of the three principal departments: processing and production, agricultural production, services and distribution. The fourth was the cooperative's representative on the district planning board. The fifth, the only one to be elected by popular vote, was the general manager. These were the most responsible officials of the entire community, and for two of them to bring charges against a third at a public trial was almost unprecedented.

David seemed in no hurry to finish dinner. "The first case is just routine," he said.

There were not fifty people in the room when we slid into our seats. In the front, around a large table, a dozen or so men and women sat at ease, some of them taking notes, others speaking to each other in conversational tones. Before I could gather much of what was being said, the woman at the center of the table rose. "Fellow citizens," she said, "sudden death is always a tragedy, and peculiarly so if it comes at the hands of another human being. We have all expressed our sorrow and given our sympathy to the family of Barry Masters. The young man who committed this crime has foolishly attempted to deny his guilt, but we of the disciplinary committee feel that the evidence is overwhelming. Dr. Sidley, who has been in charge of the case, has reported fully on the psychological causation and on the appropriate methods of treatment. We have no hesitation in turning the offender over to the Permanent Committee on Crime, and we adjure the committee not to release him until it is sure beyond the shadow of any doubt that he is not a danger to society. We hold the committee responsible for the protection of us all and for the restoration of Thomas Bennington McClain to health and usefulness."

This last, I suspected from the tone in which it was spoken,

Lister speaking, first day of trial.

was a kind of formula. I had just succeeded in identifying the criminal when he walked from the room, a man on either side of him. The three judges rose and left the table, and the witnesses either found places in the audience or left the room. The secretary rose and began to call the committee for the next case.

Everything went so smoothly that it was a minute or two before I could force myself to realize what had happened. In something less than half an hour a man had been tried for murder, found guilty, and sentenced. There were many serious faces in the audience, but no one seemed greatly agitated, and there was no scurrying of reporters to provide sensational headlines for the morning's papers.

"I don't understand," I said to David.

"This is the simplest kind of case," he whispered. "It's really handled by the psychiatrists, and the disciplinary hearing is just to protect the individual in case they should be too hasty. The next case will be more interesting."

It took a few minutes to select the committee because one person named to it declined to serve on the ground of personal interest in the case. As soon, however, as the two women and the one man were installed at the table, the secretary read a statement of the case, and the chairman called on the spokesman of the union to present the charges. A great stocky fellow, whom I had several times met in Victor's company, got up. He was a man who owed his popularity in his union and in the community in no small measure to a witty turn of speech, and the audience laughed uproariously as he described the defendant's behavior. The defendant—a Frank somebody-or-other—had always been quarrelsome, he said, but was otherwise a good worker. On this particular occasion he had got into an argument with another of the men and punched him in the nose. The victim had fallen against a machine, and, though he had been in no personal danger, his fall would have stopped production if it had not been for the quickness of hand of a bystander. At a meeting of the union it had been voted that Frank should either put himself in a psychiatrist's hands or leave the shop.

"I thought unions settled questions like this," I whispered.

"This man appealed," David whispered back. "Shhh."

The chairman having called upon him, Frank rose in his

place and looked about the room, half-sheepishly, half-defiantly. A man well over fifty, with gray hair and sharp blue eyes, he was rather slight, but I could see his muscles under his dark shirt, and I did not think I should like to be punched by him.

"Frank," said the chairman, "I guess we all know that you've been in fights before." There was a snicker from the audience. "Do you deny that you're a troublesome character?"

"I stand up for my rights."

"Do you deny that your action on April 27 threatened production?" Frank shook his head. "Then what have you to say for yourself?"

Frank looked around. "I say that Fred Douglas deserved a good poke in the face." He sat down.

The judges conferred for a few minutes, and then the chairman said, "The facts seem to be essentially as stated by the union representative. If anyone wishes to contradict any statement that has been made, this is the opportunity."

A man a good four inches taller than Frank and perhaps fifty pounds heavier rose from his place in the audience. "I'm Fred Douglas," he said. "Frank says I deserved a poke in the nose. I told him he was a stubborn skunk, and he was, too. I was just following the blueprint, and he says, 'I've been setting up this machine for twenty years, and I guess I know how to do it.' 'Why, you stubborn skunk,' says I, and he pops me in the nose. Anybody knows I could make mincemeat of him, but he caught me by surprise, and I fell against the machine. What I say is, he's a dangerous man to have around, popping people in the nose when they aren't looking."

One of the judges spoke to the chairman, who then said, "Frank, what we want to know is why you won't go to a doctor."

Frank rose again. "I've had my physical examinations same as everyone else, and except for that I've never had cause to see a doctor. I don't like those fellows, poking around and asking fool questions. Besides, I don't see any reason for not hitting a man like Fred Douglas. I wouldn't want to be the sort of a man who wouldn't do something like that when it was necessary."

The judges conferred briefly, and the chairman announced: "It is our opinion that Frank should not be required to consult a psychiatrist, though we strongly recommend his doing so. On the other hand, we do not believe that the union should be forced to tolerate a worker whom it finds uncongenial and disruptive. We urge the union to give Frank another chance, but we leave the matter in its hands."

He sat down and a second judge got up. "Though Frank has been known for years as a belligerent person," she said, "this is the first time he has ever appeared before a disciplinary committee. The reason is that, in spite of his temper, he is a good workman. I agree that he would do well to see a psychiatrist, and his prejudice against doing so is absurd, but I hope the union will not keep too rigidly to its decision."

"Are there any further comments?" the chairman asked. "If not, the case is closed."

It was ten minutes of twenty-one. As the three judges left the desk, there was a turning of heads, and I looked around. Erect in the doorway stood a man with red hair and a red beard. With a cape thrown loosely over his shoulders, and with a sheaf of papers held under one arm, he slowly stared up and down the room. Then, taking even, firm strides and holding his head high, he walked to the table, spoke curtly to the secretary, and found himself a chair. This was Mike Lister, the board member who was charged with incompetence.

As the new committee was being chosen, other persons crowded into the room, until at last there was not a vacant seat. The chairman called for order, read a statement of the case, and asked for the presentation of charges. A mousy little woman in her late forties began to speak, fumbling now and then through the papers before her. It was Marjorie Leroy, whom I had several times met at the Wilsons'. For all her drab, fussy ways, she had a national reputation, and no one questioned her fitness to serve as liaison officer between the Braxton cooperative and the district planning board.

It was hard for me to follow what she said, not merely because of her language, which was highly technical, but also because of her dull, monotonous way of reciting facts. She began by speaking of the harmony that had always existed in the meetings of the Braxton board until Lister became a member, and, despite her unemphatic way of talking, there was a touch of vindictiveness in her voice when she mentioned his name. Since that time, there had been constant discord, with the result that sessions had been prolonged and business left undone. Furthermore, complaints had been brought to the board that Lister was high-handed and dictatorial with his fellow-workers, and these complaints he had refused to discuss. Finally, there had been difficulties in his own department, that of processing and production. An accident in the woollen rooms had never been adequately accounted for, nor had the breakdown of a battery of plastic molders. These matters, which obviously concerned the entire board, had been concealed as long as possible from the other members, and their insistence on discussing them had been treated as impudence.

If Marjorie seemed like the traditional old maid schoolmarm,[1] the board member associated with her in her complaint was as robust and forthright as a person could be. Dan Rose, manager of agricultural production, had been himself a farm worker and had come into prominence as head of the farm workers' union. Although he had to rely on his assistants for expert scientific knowledge, he was valued for his practical skill and managerial ability. For the most part he simply echoed Marjorie's charges, and the chairman once or twice warned him against repetition, but he did give a more vivid picture than she had of the chaos at board meetings, and he was more concrete in describing the accidents that had occurred in Lister's department. Several times he alluded, with some bitterness, to Lister's pre-occupation with the experimental station, and the chairman finally asked him if this was relevant. "I don't know whether it is or not," he shouted. "That's something for the investigators to find out."

While they were speaking, everyone glanced frequently at the man they attacked. He sat quietly in the front row, his face now and then lighting with anger or what seemed to

---

[1] Throughout the nineteenth century most school teachers were unmarried. By Swain's time this lamentable state of affairs had been to some extent remedied, but the spinster teacher remained the symbol of frustration, desiccation, and obstinacy. For the benefit of readers in other parts of the country it may be worth pointing out that Mrs. Leroy is the mother of five children.—D.W.

be amusement. Every now and then he glanced at his papers and made a note. His whole bearing was confident, and he seemed eager for his chance to speak.

As soon as he was on his feet, I realized that he was a natural orator, though he deliberately adopted a conversational tone and made only the most reserved gestures. "I am accused of incompetence," he began, "though I think my accusers could find a better word for what it is they really hold against me. I shall spend little time in discussing the details of the case. The investigators—for I am sure there will be an investigation—can determine whether I did so-and-so on such-and-such a date. No, what is involved here is fundamentally a question of policy. I have my conception of what the Braxton planning board should be doing, and my colleagues have theirs. It may be that I have been mistaken in some of the means I have employed, but if that is all that is wrong, the charges that have been brought against me are greatly exaggerated. If, on the other hand, my aims themselves are wrong, the charges are much too mild."

He went on to describe his career: advanced study at Harvard, Munich, and Moscow; three years as a productive worker in the South; two years in the planning department of a southern cooperative. Then Braxton had sought a man who was trained in chemistry and economics to manage its experimental station. He had applied for and been given the job. "During four years there were no complaints," he said, knowing well that few persons in the room could be ignorant of the brilliant record he had made. His promotion to a managerial position, though he spoke of it modestly as a surprise, had been almost inevitable.

"Prior to this time," he went on, "I had had no more responsibility for the shaping of policy than any other citizen. When, however, I was asked to join a policy-forming body, I took my responsibility seriously." He ran his fingers through his gleaming hair. "I had had special kinds of experience, just as the other members had, and I drew upon them. I thought it no crime to have opinions of my own or to express them. I had expected disagreement, but I had not anticipated bitter, intolerant opposition. In the eyes of my colleagues I was apparently guilty of heresy because I ventured to criticize practices that have been followed and ideas that have been held during the past three or four decades. When I endeavored to exercise the power with which I had been entrusted, certain of the workers in my department accused me of arrogance and refused to carry out my instructions. When I presented my views to the board, I was denounced as an obstructionist."

I find it difficult to recall, and quite impossible to convey, the impression that he made upon me. He spoke with such fire, so well restrained, and with so little rancor. "My colleagues have referred to the experimental station. I will not conceal from you the fact that I have constantly pleaded for more attention to this important part of our community life. Do I call it a part? It is the very source of our corporate well-being. Far from trying to conceal from you my interest in the work that is being done and could be done in the station, I want to tell you all about it. That, indeed, is why I have asked for a trial, instead of simply accepting the fact that I am persona non grata with the other members of the board, who are sound citizens doing sound work."

He described the achievements of the station—his own

THE COURSE OF JUSTICE

achievements, of course, though he did not say so—and indicated some of the projects he would like to see undertaken. "But do not suppose," he insisted, "that I am concerned with the station alone. For me that is merely a symbol, a symbol of the progress that we have it in our power to make. Do we want progress or do we not? I do, and I think you do. If I were to follow the tactics of my colleagues, I should call them blind bureaucrats and enemies of advancing civilization, but name-calling does not appeal to me. I content myself with saying simply that my views deserve a hearing. When time after time I have been outvoted, I have never complained, but I have refused to keep silence. Now they are trying to muzzle me."

There was a murmur almost of applause as he gathered his papers and took his seat. Even the committee seemed impressed. They spoke together for a moment, and then the chairman, announcing the appointment of investigators, adjourned to the second evening following. As we left the room, it was obvious that people were taking sides, for I heard many phrases: "Lister is right." "You can't do anything with trouble-makers like that." "Dan Rose is a practical man; I've worked with him and I know."

Thoughtfully, I followed David to his apartment. Some time earlier I had asked myself whether science and democracy had really solved the problem of economic and political control. Now it seemed to me that I might be on the verge of discovering the answer. Even in my own time, as I have more than once said, most people were decent most of the time. I think I should have been willing to swear that there were not a dozen really vicious persons in the whole town of

THE FIRST TO AWAKEN

Braxton, and yet a mob of nearly a hundred men had raided CIO headquarters, behaving as Hitler's bullies were reputed to behave. It took the strike to show me what potentialities there were, for good and evil, in the hearts of my fellow-citizens. Even at this time the trial did not seem of comparable importance, but I thought that it might give me the same kind of insight.

I wanted to know what David was thinking, but first there was something else I had to get said. "This will make a good chapter in my book," I remarked as casually as I could.

"Yes, indeed."

I was taken aback, for I had expected at least an expression of surprise. "It's your fault," I said sheepishly. "You started me taking notes, and now Simeon wants me to make a connected story."

"Why not? You'll see things a little more clearly, and it will be a great help to me and my associates. Also, it ought to be useful for those who are yet to awaken."

"Exactly the three reasons Simeon gave."

He did not notice my touch of exasperation, but went on, "You can use some of the sketches you've been making, too. Oh, I thoroughly approve." [1]

Before David could get our drinks, Nathalie had come in from her class, and was asking about the trial. "Get George to tell you," he called.

She was much amused by my description of Frank's be-

---

[1] I did not want to seem too enthusiastic, for I feared Swain was thinking in terms of twentieth century authorship and publishing business. Both Blake and I visualized an autostatic edition of a hundred copies or so, for neither of us foresaw the wide appeal of Swain's story.—D.W.

havior, but when I got to talking about the Lister case, I noticed the scowl gathering that always alarmed me. I suppose I had made it clear that I had become one of Lister's staunch defenders. In fact, I remember saying, "I don't see how they had the nerve to bring him to trial."

Discreetly changing the subject, I began to talk about the committee's procedure. Like most laymen, I have always distrusted and resented the technical jargon of the courts and their utter disregard of common sense. I had felt that these things could be done in a simple and straightforward manner, and my experience that evening seemed to bear me out. I had to admit, though, that the higher educational level made a considerable difference. This was a public that could read or listen to arguments and understand them. Moreover, to a degree simply inconceivable in my day, there was an agreement about basic principles that simplified the whole procedure. Braxton was now truly an integrated community.

David was interested in these impressions of mine, but Nathalie insisted on discussing the subject of Michael Lister. "You've made up your mind already," she said, "and the facts aren't in yet."

I felt that she must be right, but for once I was willing to argue. "It's so clear," I boldly anounced. "It's just a case of bureaucracy, of people in a rut, unwilling to recognize new ideas."

Before Nathalie could put her irritation into words, David said gently, "If it's as simple as all that, don't you think other people would have seen what was happening before Mike Lister came along? I've never denied that people love power or that they get set in their ways, but I do believe we ought

THE FIRST TO AWAKEN

not to jump at conclusions. Tell me, what do you think has happened?"

This wasn't so easy. "Well, more or less what Lister says. Marjorie is the kind of person who believes that whatever she does must be right. Her mind is closed to any new ideas. Rose I'm not so sure about, but it seems to me that he's the kind that gets power and hangs onto it."

"How does he hang onto it?" David asked. "By giving out bribes? What can he bribe people with? By handing out soft jobs? There aren't any soft jobs, and anyway the vocational bureau and the union check all appointments. By protecting his favorites? Possibly, though it would be difficult to conceal a clear case of incompetence. I'm not saying, George, that a power-loving man couldn't entrench himself, but I do want you to realize that it's harder now than it was in your day. That's why we insist on seeing the evidence."

"Rose is a shrewd manager," Nathalie said sharply, "and Marjorie is one of the best-trained planners in the country."

"Then what is Lister?" I inquired. "I'm willing to admit that I may have been too hasty in forming a judgment, but you seem to have formed a judgment too. By your theory Lister must be what somebody in the corridor called him— simply a trouble-maker."

"I think George has a point," David said.

The door opened, and a girl in nurse's costume walked in. "Oh," she said. Then, a little accusingly, "You haven't switched off service."

"I'm very sorry. Will you forgive me?"

"The baby is crying."

As Nathalie hurried to the adjoining room, with an impatient word for David in passing, the girl left. "What kind of gadget is this?"

"Didn't you know? The children's rooms are wired for sight and sound connections with a central office, and we switch them on when we go out. It's better than taking them to the nursery."

Nathalie came back, still frowning a little. "I know Lister only slightly," she said slowly, as if trying hard to be just. "His record in the experimental station was excellent, and I don't doubt that he's able enough in his own way. Some of the people who work with him feel as you do. In fact, to many of the young people in his department he's a hero. My own opinion is that he is one-sided and that he hides his defects by romanticizing himself as a pioneer."

"Aren't you passing judgment again?"

Nathalie flushed a little, and we managed to change the subject. As I left, I encountered one of our neighbors, who drove me home. She was an admirer of Lister and spoke of his defense with enthusiasm.

Before I went to sleep, I wrote an account of the trial in my journal, and perhaps a paragraph or two may be worth quoting in order to reconstruct my mood of that moment:

> Once in a long while I have the feeling that everything is topsy-turvy, and that is the way I felt tonight. Lister is the kind of man I admire, progressive, courageous, independent. He says just what he thinks, and he doesn't care who disagrees. The Wilsons may praise Marjorie and Dan, but it strikes me that they are old fogies. The

whole town needs to be stirred up by somebody like Lister.

What puzzles me is David's and Nathalie's attitude. I have thought of them as intelligent young radicals, but this seems to have been a mistake. For all their intelligence, they defend the status quo. Perhaps it is a bad thing to have life run as smoothly as it does today. I felt tonight that I was more radical then they. That is, I can see the need for change more clearly. That must be because I am used to thinking in terms of change, whereas they have grown up in a society that is almost—but not quite—perfect.

Late as it was when I went to bed, I got up at sunrise to have breakfast with the Waldmans. The weather was still a little cool, but after a few minutes in the sunshine I unloosed my jacket. Agnes was presiding as usual over the suspensor, and Victor was reading aloud from the morning's bulletin. Abraham listened with his solemn expression, while Roberta danced about, vegetable juice in one hand and toast in the other.

They wanted my account of the trial, and I told them about it, but, having learned my lesson, I concealed my own opinion. They were less reticent. Victor said sternly, "I've never quite trusted that fellow Lister," Agnes nodded agreement, and he went on, "We've all seen men like that, and I won't say they never have any good ideas, but you can't do anything with them. You know, you've got to have teamwork to get anywhere."

"You just like to do the same thing over and over again,"

said Roberta, sitting on the arm of her father's chair. "The troublemakers make progress."

"The troublemakers make trouble," Agnes pronounced.

"Lister has the right idea," Abraham broke in. "We're not trying to find out what we could really do with our resources."

"And what do you know about it, young man?"

"He spoke to our class just last week. All the managers come every year. He was the only one who could recognize a new idea if he saw it."

"That's what I don't like," said Victor, "going round and stirring up a lot of children."

I chuckled. "Isn't he silly?" Roberta asked me.

"He does sound like some fathers I've known, good patriots who were scared to death of subversive ideas."

"We have a right to know what kind of cooperative we're growing up in," Abraham insisted, very reasonably it seemed to me.

Victor got up to leave for work. "I'm not against change," he said, "but I want orderly change, planned change. I learned in school, just as these children are learning, that life is a process. You can't stand still, George, I know that as well as you do. But you can have change without getting into a mess."

I doubted that. At least I was inclined to believe that a mess might be necessary every now and then. I felt rather smug, for it seemed to me that everything Victor and Agnes said strengthened my case against David and Nathalie. The Waldmans were fine people, but you couldn't really expect them to understand the need for change. I was delighted when Roberta said, "Maybe it's almost as bad to move ahead in a rut as it is to stand still in one."

Plan, the installation, and view of the interior of my new room. The circles in the ceiling are the new ray curtain—on the same principle as the house of rays.

That was an important day in my new life, for I was at last to have a room of my own. I had been perfectly contented in Freda's room, and I would never have risked hurting the Waldmans' feelings by suggesting a change. But they had begun to talk about the change as soon as it seemed clear that I was likely to stay with them. I could see that they did not want to yield to sentiment, and also that they took pride in my having the best that Braxton could offer, and so I agreed.

If Agnes had not gone with me to the Bureau of Home Extension, I should have been hopelessly lost, for the variety of panels and parts was overwhelming. Gradually, however, Agnes managed to make clear to the girl in charge what kind of life I led, and we worked out the plans for my unit. It included an extension of the corridor, bathroom, sleeping alcove with temperature-controlled bed, and study. The floor panels contained the heat elements, and the ceiling the light elements. I chose the simplest type of information panel—television, clock, weather report, etc.—and an elementary research and writing panel. I had some difficulty in getting an old-fashioned bathtub, but the kind of unit I wanted was finally located.

Not without some signs of emotion Agnes packed away such of Freda's possessions as she was keeping, and I gathered my belongings together in another room. Agnes was still engaged in unnecessary cleaning when the man arrived to disconnect the wires and pipes and all connecting links. A few minutes later a tractor with a power arm came up the drive, and the sections were swung out of the way. The truck drove up with the new units, which were put into place, and the old parts were carried off to be reconditioned.

I talked for a few minutes with the man who made the necessary connections. Complicated as the business seemed to me, it offered him no problem, and he talked cheerfully as he worked. He was full of ideas about his job. At first, he said, the single house had been almost prohibitive, and the only way of solving the housing problem was to build large apartments, which could be economically lighted and heated. With the utilization of solar energy, however, half the battle had been won, for now few wires or pipes had to be brought in from outside. Better insulation, moreover, had made the cost of heating four walls inconsiderable, and there was plenty of cheap heat available. Foundations were still something of an expense, but the construction of the floor panel made the simplest foundation practical. And now, with the use of standard parts in the various sections, the building and maintenance of a single house had become economical and easy, and, for the time being, most expansion came in that way rather than through the building of new apartment houses or the enlarging of old ones.

My conception of a ray-house, showing this device in action.

I had thought that I had nothing new to learn about gadgets, but I was mistaken. The next afternoon I drove with Simeon Blake to an experimental station operated in the interests of the Arctic Reclamation Corps. While Blake was in conference, a friendly guide took me around the grounds. In the middle of a field were four posts, almost as if someone were starting to build a house. "This," he said, "is a house of drafts. It's the same principle as is used on automobiles, except that a motor is required." He pressed a button, and let me feel the wind that made the four walls and the ceiling. "It's useful in exploration. You just carry this compact apparatus, and then wherever you stop you have a shelter."

He also showed me an apparatus of rays that served the same purpose. I was a little skeptical, but he quickly demonstrated how easily the temperature could be raised within the enclosure.

On our way back I talked to Simeon a little about the Lister case, but he seemed uninterested. "Wait till the facts are all in," he counseled.

"But the principles?"

He looked at me speculatively. "Don't rush ahead, George. Wherever something is built, something else is blocked." I did not understand what he meant just then, and I was rather disappointed at his failure to see the case as I saw it.

THE COURSE OF JUSTICE

As we came along the river into Braxton, we saw scores of young people in canoes and row-boats, and there were several eight-man shells out. Half a dozen baseball diamonds were in use, and heaven knows how many tennis courts. It was the warmest day we had had, and part of the restaurant roof had been rolled back, so that the hardier diners could catch the last hour of sunshine. Simeon, as usual, was in favor of the open air, and so we sat, almost over the river, watching the boats come and go.

A group of young men and women, most of them in shorts, came laughing and chattering down the boatrun. A boy and girl began loading a canoe, with enthusiastic but disorganized assistance from the rest of the group. At last they took their places, and, amid shouts and cheers, paddled away from the dock. It was easy to gather from the talk that they had just been married and were starting on a canoe trip.

The bulletin had announced that that evening the disciplinary committee would meet in a larger room, and it was a wise precaution. Simeon had not cared to attend, and I looked about for David but could not see him. A number of persons called greetings to me as I stood in the doorway, and at last I went and sat with Margaret Bryan. She, I gathered, was at least mildly a Lister partisan.

I looked about the room, and as always when I saw a large group of my fellow citizens together was struck by the color of the scene. Many of the women, as often in the evening, wore dresses of their own design and making. Though I was told that there were currents of fashion, I could never detect them. There were short, sleeveless dresses, not unlike those my contemporaries had worn for sports, robes that were almost classic in design, embroidered peasant smocks, and austere suits. Many women, of course, were in slacks or shorts, but here too there was more variety than was common during working hours. Most of the men wore the familiar coats and trousers, but occasionally I saw a cape or even something that looked like an informal dinner jacket.

They were certainly not all built like gods, but hideously misshapen figures were rare. Some of the older men were stout, but it was unusual to see a heavy paunch. My contemporaries, I suspect, would have put the average age of the group some ten years lower than it actually was.

As the permanent secretary summarized the proceedings of the previous session, Margaret whispered a few words about the investigators. The disciplinary committee maintained a permanent staff, including psychiatrists, students of legal history, and authorities on evidence. In addition it drew upon members of the statistical bureau for fact-gathering. Thus the citizens who were called upon to act as judge and jury had the benefit of expert advice. The investigators, she said, were supposed to collect the demonstrable facts.

The first investigator reported on the records of the board meetings, and it appeared that Marjorie and Rose had scarcely exaggerated the storminess of the proceedings. Another tabulated the opinions of the men and women in Lister's department, bringing out the sharpness of the disagreements. A third had begun analyzing the statistics of production when there was a little commotion. Lister was coming in, accompanied by a young man. "Billings," Margaret whispered. "He has Lister's job as manager of the experimental station."

Lister walked with his head high, but his companion seemed troubled.

The investigator went on, speaking calmly. Excitement was growing in the room, and, unable to understand, I looked questioningly at Margaret. "There were shortages in supplies for several departments," she said tensely.

The investigator sat down, and, as usual, the chairman asked if there was disagreement. Lister was on his feet in a moment, repeating, even more eloquently, the defense of himself he had previously made. The chairman stopped him. "Do you deny the existence of these shortages?" The arm he had dramatically raised fell to his side. "No," he said quietly. Then the fire came into his face again, but the chairman would not let him go on.

Completely bewildered, I listened as attentively as I could to the next report. Investigation of the experimental station apparently showed that it had been supplied with materials in excess of its quota. Margaret looked horrified, and the shock had quieted the whole room. The investigator went on. The manager of the experimental station, she said coolly, had falsified his credentials when he applied for the job. Before the murmur of incredulity and resentment, Billings grew pale, and Lister dropped his eyes.

When, at the conclusion of the report, the chairman spoke, it was clear that he was struggling against indignation. He and the other members of the committee proceeded to question Lister, Billings, Marjorie, Rose, the heads of the departments involved, and several of the employees. The questions were asked and answered in a tone of profound seriousness, though occasionally there was a note of defiance or of shame.

While the committee conferred, there were hushed, breathless discussions all over the room. At last the chairman rose. "The facts established," he said, "appear to be these: First, Michael Lister diverted from the departments for which they were intended supplies that he used for the unauthorized expansion of the experimental station. Second, the foremen of these departments were so lax that they did not check their consignments with the planning schedules, and therefore did not detect the shortages, though at least two accidents resulted from them. Third, Howard Billings was appointed to a position for which he was not qualified. For this appointment Michael Lister was primarily responsible, but neither the union committee nor the vocational office seems to have made an adequate effort to investigate Billings' record. Fourth, Billings forged papers to secure his job, and in the job connived with Michael Lister to divert supplies to the station. Fifth, when Billings went to Marjorie Leroy and Dan Rose and offered to give them evidence against Lister if they would protect him, Billings, they agreed to do so.

"The seriousness of these offenses is apparent to all. We agree to censure Mrs. Leroy, Mr. Rose, the six foremen previously named, and all employees who may be revealed by subsequent investigation to have played a part in this scandal through either intention or negligence. Disciplinary action will be taken with regard to Lister and Billings after psychiatric consultation. The committee stands adjourned."

Instantly Lister was clamoring to be heard, and the chairman restored silence. "No member of the planning board," Lister shouted, "can be removed against his will except by vote of the entire cooperative. I demand a meeting of the cooperative. I will make my defense to the people."

The chairman turned in bewilderment to the experts, one of whom came forward and spoke to him. "Mr. Lister is right," the chairman said. "Due notice of the meeting will be given in the bulletin."

"Let's get a drink," I said to Margaret as we went out, and I noticed that the idea had occurred to others. When we were seated in the recreation room, I sighed and turned to her. "For God's sake, tell me what it's all about."

She smiled, but I could see that she also was disturbed. "Mike Lister," she began, "took supplies that were intended for other departments and turned them over to the experimental station. And the foremen were so lax that they never noticed."

"I get that. But what did he get out of it?"

She was puzzled. "The station is his pet. I suppose he has some big experiment on that he wants to push."

"Is that all?"

Again she was puzzled; that was bad enough to her.

"Now what about Billings?"

"He seems to be the kind of man who has always got along by playing on other people's weaknesses. I don't know how he met Lister, but he must have sized him up pretty well. Lister appointed him, of course, because he could run him. Billings probably made Mike think he was his disciple, but what Mike really wanted to do was keep his hands on the station."

I could hear fragments of similar conversation from all around us. "How did Lister think he could get away with it?"

"That's just it. We've all become so easy-going that people

don't check carefully any more. Probably he knew he'd get caught sooner or later, but perhaps he thought that if he'd finished his great experiment, people would forgive him. I still think he's sincere, you know."

She powdered her nose, and patted her bolero jacket. "What I don't understand is why Billings went to Marjorie and Dan."

"That's easy," I told her. "He was after Lister's job."

She looked at me in astonishment. "Why, of course," she exclaimed. "He knew Lister would never inform on him, and he thought they'd get Mike out on the simple charge of incompetence."

"Probably," I added, "he thought his record was so cleverly falsified nobody would ever find out about him. That may have been a smart bit of detective work."

We walked along the corridors together, and then across the river to the apartment house in which Margaret lived. I stroked my now not wholly discreditable beard. "What does this make me?" I asked. "I was convinced that Lister was the apostle of progress, and so in a way he is. I was convinced that there was bureaucracy, and I wasn't far from right. Yet Lister, who was my hero, turns out to be the villain of the piece."

She laughed. "You objected to my teaching the class about heroes. I object to your making Mike Lister a villain. He's a good man, though I now see that he's one-sided and pretty much of a romantic."

"Just what Nathalie said night before last. What do you suppose will happen to him?"

"Unless the psychiatrists find something seriously wrong,

he'll probably be made manager of the experimental station. Why not? There's where his talent lies, and we can use it."

As I drove home, I took comfort in thinking I was not alone in having made a mistake. Certainly the affair was a blow to the smugness of the Waldmans and the Wilsons, for, if I had been partly wrong about Lister, they had been partly wrong about Rose and Mrs. Leroy. Only Simeon, who had urged me to wait for the facts, had been proven wholly right.

"This is not," I wrote in my diary that night, "even an almost perfect society, but it seems to be a reasonably sensible one."

X

I SPEAK MY PIECE

MARGARET was right about Lister's sentence: the disciplinary committee recommended his dismissal, subject to the approval of the cooperative meeting, and his re-appointment as manager of the experimental station. Billings was placed under psychiatric care. June 24 was the date set by the policy committee for the convening of the cooperative membership.

For several days the trial was discussed everywhere I went. Victor fussed and fumed over the shocking state of affairs, and Agnes tranquilly pointed out that everything was all right now. Roberta and Abraham, on the other hand, quickly forgot that they had been mistaken about Lister and rejoiced in the shake-up that was taking place. Their attitude, I discovered, was not uncommon. Most of Lister's adherents, though they disapproved of his actions, were rather pleased by the revelations that had been made.

Meanwhile life went on as usual in Braxton. People went about their work, ate their meals, played their games, fell in love, gossiped, quarreled, and made merry as they had always done. A community of some sixteen thousand persons, much as those persons might talk, could not be deeply or long affected by the misdeeds of a handful of men and women.

I was thinking a good deal these days about the normal course of life in the year 2040, for I had received three invitations to appear in my role of citizen of the twentieth century. One was from an eminent historian at Harvard, one from a club to which Roberta belonged, and the third from the educational committee of the Braxton cooperative.

As I have already said, I was puzzled at first by the attitude people took towards me. There can be no question that, in my time, the bedside where I awoke would have been crowded with reporters and photographers, and for a day or two the papers would have been full of my pictures and my opinions, real or invented by some ingenious reporter, on every subject under the sun. Over the radio and in the newsreels millions would have heard me say a few well chosen words on the progress that had been made in the preceding century. Perhaps, if news had been running low, some paper might have paid me to sign my name to an autobiography composed by an overworked hack. After a sensation of a week or two, I should have been heard from only when a reporter was assigned to collect opinions of representative citizens and chanced to think of me as a possible source of wordage. I should have been wise, therefore, to take advantage of the sensation while it lasted by going after a job as anti-anachronism expert for historical movies or signing a contract to plug some cereal over the radio.[1]

[1] The incredulous reader is referred to the work cited above, Bayle's *The Vanishing Newspaper;* also to my footnote on page 47. Swain is being ironic, but the exaggeration is less than one would think, for his awakening

THE FIRST TO AWAKEN

Of course, nothing like this happened in the year 2040, and I gradually learned that David was right when he said there was a new respect for the individual. People did think it extraordinary that a man had slept for a hundred years, and they did want to know what I thought about them and their civilization, but they kept their curiosity within the bounds of good manners. If I seemed inclined to talk, they listened eagerly and asked a great many questions, but they seldom pressed me. Looking at the various items and articles that had appeared about me before I awoke, I found in all of them the assumption that, whatever else was true, I must have a chance to live my own life. Of individualism as a shutting away of the self from others, or as an attempt to impose the self on others, there was relatively little, though the Lister case showed that something of the kind persisted. Individualism, however, as a development of the self and its potentialities flourished. There was a general belief that everyone had a right to be a little queer, and I benefited by it.

would have been made a sensation by newspapers eager to increase their circulation. It is actually true, for instance, that "autobiographies" of celebrities were written by anonymous journalists. This was picturesquely known as "ghost-writing." It is also true that the collection of the opinions of various notorious persons on various sensational subjects was encouraged not merely to fill space but also to influence the views of the general public. I quote from a contemporary source: "The public generally does not know that every newspaper office has a standing list of wind-bags who will express opinions on anything for publicity's sake. Twenty-five cents in telephone calls from any newspaper office will create a 'public clamor.' " On the subject of historical motion pictures, it is well known that producers went to great pains to secure accuracy in minor details, though quite willing to falsify major historical trends. Finally, see below, page 266, on the subject of radio advertising. To "plug" is to advertise in a persistent and even ecstatic manner.—D.W.

The three invitations indicated a growing realization that I was now sufficiently at home in the present so that I would not feel exploited if asked to talk about the past. I thought I should accept them all, but I went to consult David. He had seemed rather distraught in recent days, and talked vaguely about going away, and I assumed that some problem of his work was bothering him. Much interested in the requests, he asked if he might go with me to Harvard.

It was a week later that we set out, traveling by automobile. David wanted to stop at the regional college in Concord, and I spent an hour or so wandering about the campus. It was about as large as the college in Braxton, and served an area of about the same size—that is, the towns within a radius of fifty or seventy-five miles. The regional colleges, which were sometimes old schools and sometimes new, were open to every youth, and attendance, if not exactly compulsory, was almost universal. The students were relatively young, being graduated at the age of eighteen to twenty, and there was a good deal of what I would have called college life—sports, dramatics, dances, and that sort of thing. The subjects were those considered fundamental, and, as I think I have already pointed out, the student graduated with a sound knowledge of the past, an ability to find his way round his own world, and some understanding of himself and his potentialities. The more I learned about the regional colleges, the more I became convinced that they were the greatest educational achievement of the new age. In my day educators had discovered how to make learning an exciting process for the very young, and now the discovery had been extended. Perhaps because I had myself been cheated out of college, I had always felt that there was something almost romantically attractive about college boys and girls, and that feeling revived as I watched these youngsters walking about under the new-leaved trees. And they were not less attractive in the classroom, much as their seriousness amazed me.

David left the highway to show me the old textile cities—Manchester, Lawrence, Lowell. Of course the textile industry as I had known it had vanished. "I suppose," I said to David, "that the movement to the South continued because it was more economical for the factories to be near the source of raw material."

"That isn't why they were going south in your time," he pointed out. "They were looking for cheap, unorganized labor." After a moment's thought I knew that he was right. He went on to say that, with the widespread use of plastic materials for clothing, cotton had come to have its chief use in building.

The power of the Merrimac was now transformed into electricity for a large area. The factories by the river had long since disappeared, and their places were taken by apartment houses, recreational centers, and single homes. The ugly old cities were pleasant towns now, not unlike Braxton. Their industries were diversified, and their populations, dwindling in my time, had fallen to twenty or thirty thousand apiece as people had spread into the country.

Boston also had changed. It was nothing like New York—no great skyscrapers, no tremendous blocks. The old State House still stood on Beacon Hill, and some of the narrow, winding streets were almost unchanged, though they were closed to automobiles. In the North End were apartment houses, the smokeless factories of the new day, and great parks built around the old historic landmarks.

Boston seemed to care more for the past than New York. At the foot of Beacon Hill, near the Charles River Basin, was what was called a living museum. A group of houses from the eighteenth, nineteenth, and twentieth centuries, which happened to fall within the same block, had been preserved, and their occupants, obviously with great satisfaction to themselves, lived as nearly as possible the lives of their ancestors. It was growing harder, I learned, to find persons who wanted to live that way, but at first there had been long application lists. I was rather proud of myself when I walked through the twentieth century apartments without a pang of nostalgia.

Boston was not so large as it had been, but it was still a sizeable community, divided into several cooperatives, and all about it were what had been the suburbs, now independent, self-sustaining communities rather than merely places where Boston workers came to sleep. Large districts had been entirely cleared of their tenements and turned over to modern farming.

Like everyone else in New England, I had visited Harvard more than once, looking at the glass flowers and wandering in and out of the labyrinths of brick, but as we approached it along the Charles I could not have recognized it. What I saw was simply a large cooperative block, built in the style to which I had become accustomed, somewhat irregular in shape and dominated by an impressive tower. Inside, too, it was rather more like a small edition of a New York block than anything I had considered academic. There was a terraced restaurant,

University Hall, Harvard, drawn from the portico of the new Memorial Chapel.

built close to the river. There were recreational rooms, apartments, and offices. But instead of factories, there were laboratories, museums, libraries, and classrooms.

This was the real Harvard, but the old Harvard had not completely disappeared. In fact, the western half of the Yard was, according to Timothy Waldman, exactly as it had been in the nineteenth century, with the old buildings, the beautiful elms, and the graveled paths. But this was purely a tribute to the past, for the buildings served only as historical museums, despite every effort to find a more active function for them.

The other half of the Yard was unrecognizable, for Widener had vanished and the new Memorial Chapel had gone the way of its predecessor. Widener, Timothy said, had proved utterly unpractical, and the library was now an integral part of the block. The chapel had been torn down only a few years before, though the revolt against it, on architectural grounds, had been gaining for years. Now there was a great new auditorium, built in celebration of the University's quadricentennial, and Timothy showed me with some amusement the plaques commemorating the three memorials whose place it had taken.

Timothy, forewarned by Roberta and his mother, had come to our rooms that first evening. In appearance he made me think of Abraham, and he had the same serious manner, though of course he was more mature. He took me about the university the next morning, and frequently acted as my guide.

Harvard had become the chief center of advanced study in New England, though by no means the only one. I soon learned that, with means of transportation so easily available and with the elimination of academic competition, no university felt obliged to teach every subject under the sun. On the contrary, if a student wanted to study Sanskrit, there was nothing to stop him from going to the University of Calcutta or the University of Leipzig, both famous for their Sanskrit scholars. A physicist might find that a man in Oslo or in Peking was working on just his problem. A historian might travel to Rome or Leningrad to consult with a specialist in his field.

To my unscholarly mind Harvard seemed to provide every facility for scholarship. It took me some time, however, to understand the organization of the place, which existed for learning, not for teaching. The instructors in the regional colleges knew how to teach, but if a young man or woman submitted to the discipline of higher education, he was expected to study. He became a sharer in a cooperative enterprise.

I could never distinguish between instructors and students, and in a sense there was no distinction, for the instructors were all men and women engaged in some kind of enterprise and the students were associated with them. The instructor helped the student to find the particular job that he wanted to do, and guided his preparation. Thereafter they worked together.

Timothy wanted me to meet Dr. Birchall, one of the world's outstanding mathematicians, and with some trepidation I agreed. As we walked into the room, the first thing I noticed was a tow-headed boy, stretched flat on his stomach along the floor. Around him were three or four young fellows, and there were two or three older men and a couple of girls sitting about, either working at tables or listening to the discussion. The tow-head was speaking in an excited falsetto, with a slightly Germanic accent, and every once in a while he would draw a diagram on a big sheet of paper at his elbow, and everyone would crowd around to look.

Nobody paid attention to us, and Timothy motioned me to sit down and wait. After a few minutes an older man, whom I supposed to be Birchall, noticed Timothy and nodded. Then, after looking more closely at me, he nudged the lad on the floor with his toe. The baby face was turned towards me, the blue eyes staring. He blinked, smiled, jumped to his feet, and introduced himself with elaborate apologies. That was Birchall.

Insisting on our all having coffee together, he tried to engage me in conversation, but it was hopeless. As I told him, I was as ignorant of the science of my own day as I was of the science of his. He shook his head pityingly, and then said that perhaps I hadn't missed much. I gathered that all of them felt that science had been in a bad way in the thirties and forties. They spoke with regret of such men as Eddington, Jeans, and

Millikan, praising some of their work but lamenting their willingness to substitute mysticism for the scientific attitude. Birchall said that science in my day had been ready for another great advance but had been held back by the general social disorganization. As a matter of fact, in his view science seemed to have more to do with social conditions than I, thinking of scientists as independent of time and circumstance, had ever supposed.

The university, I quickly realized, was not isolated from any phase of contemporary life. From its faculty came scientific discoveries, long-range plans, new insights into the past and new conceptions for the future. There was the closest relationship between the universities and the planning boards, and instructors often served as consultants or even as members. Students not only went out from the university to take part in productive enterprise; workers came to the faculty and students with their problems. Even in Cambridge the old town and gown feud had become meaningless.

Birchall, as I soon discovered, was freer from pedantic notions and manners than many of his colleagues, but it was impossible for the grosser forms of pedantry to thrive in that atmosphere. An instructor could easily become wrapped up in his job and convince himself that his particular bit of knowledge was indispensable to progress, but he was certain to be brought back to earth by his student-associates. I encountered one white-whiskered old philologist who insisted to his disciples that they were doomed to ineffectualness unless they knew Norse, but such eccentricities seemed to be regarded as merely amusing.

Certainly I became very conscious of my own shortcomings

and once more hoped that Dr. Carr had included better informed persons among my successors. The historian whose guest I was obviously despaired of extracting anything useful from my dull brain, and I don't know why he should have expected to, for he knew far more about my period than I or most of my contemporaries. I did catch him in a minor error, but that was slight consolation.

At a kind of seminar that he arranged I spoke, at his suggestion, on my own political and social views. I told why I favored the New Deal and advocated a third term for Roosevelt, why I wanted us to keep out of the war, what I thought about Hitler and Stalin and Chamberlain and Mussolini, how I had become interested in the CIO. I was prepared to defend my views, but there were no attacks. Instead, everyone sat and nodded his head, as if I had said exactly what he expected me to say. And no doubt I had.

I had a much better time with a group of students and teachers who were interested in the literature of the twentieth century. We sat in one of the tower rooms, looking across the Charles to the kindergarten and playground, and talked informally over beer and sandwiches. Though I still felt ignorant, I was glad that I had read as much as I had, for I managed to take a not too discreditable part in the discussion.

After some talk about my particular tastes and the interests of the general reading public, they began to ask specific questions. There was one girl who had been reading Faulkner, Jeffers, Caldwell, and others, and she wanted to know if there really had been so many warped persons as their work suggested. What could I tell her? I recall defending Faulkner once when Everett, then in his more radical phase, denounced him as a pathological degenerate, and I had tried to read *Roan Stallion* aloud to Elsie, only to be stopped before I had finished a hundred lines. Yet I knew that nothing could be more absurd than to regard their characters as widely representative. I tried to say, out of my sketchy knowledge of their work and my confused thinking, that they expressed a state of mind even if they did not describe an existing condition, and I guess my inquisitor was satisfied.

Another student asked if people had really talked like the characters in Hemingway's novels, and I had to reply that I had never known anyone who did, but his clipped dialogue nevertheless sounded right to me. Never having read *Finnegans Wake*, I could answer none of the questions that inspired, nor had I anything to say about Proust or Thomas Mann. I could explain, after a fashion, why there had been so much excitement over *Gone With the Wind*, for I confess that I was enchanted by it.

There were many questions about publishing as a business enterprise, and there I was completely at a loss, for I knew nothing about it. Why had so few people read books? Was it because they were so expensive, and if so, why were prices so high? What function had the book reviewers in the daily newspapers performed? Why was it that so many obviously worthless books had been so highly praised? What was the significance of the popularity of detective stories? How had there happened to be so many books when authors were so poorly paid? Why had Upton Sinclair published his own books? Had people really been so regimented that they preferred to have books selected for them by an editorial committee?

THE FIRST TO AWAKEN

It was a good group—most of them young, with three or four persons of my own age or older. Two or three expected to teach literature; several were historians; others had a less professional interest in the subject. All of them had read more and read more thoughtfully than I, and of course their standards were very different from mine, but they seemed to have a real interest in my opinions. The girl who had asked about Faulkner—her simple, friendly manner reminded me of Margaret Bryan—wanted to find out how my taste had compared with that of people in general.

"Oh," I said, "I was somewhere between highbrow and lowbrow."

That took some explaining. The distinction meant nothing to them, and I found it rather hard to see why, for they had damned various contemporary novels and plays and poems as wholeheartedly as Nick had done. Gradually it dawned on me that the whole character of the reading public had changed. Everybody had a decent education and everybody had a chance to read books. That didn't mean at all that only literature of the very highest quality was read; if I could judge from what they said, many third-rate books were written and circulated. But a first-rate author had a chance to speak to all the people, for all the people could understand him. They had the same social and cultural background, shared the same assumptions, worked in the same kind of world. First-rate authors were rare enough, but when they appeared, they didn't have to write for little highbrow coteries.

One of the older women, who had served as editor of a highly regarded cooperative magazine, asked me what I thought of their authors. I had to confess that I didn't know yet. There was simply too much that I couldn't understand—more in literature, somehow, than in life. This struck them as natural, but they urged me to make an effort to overcome the handicap, and thus began a perfect bedlam of an argument as to what authors I should start with. It was fun to listen to, and I made a few notes that have since proved useful.

Some of the group walked along with David and me as we went to our rooms, still arguing about this poet and that novelist, and it reminded me of the long talks Everett and I had had. There was moonlight over the Charles, and we strolled along the river for a few minutes. "I'm terribly ignorant," I said to David.

"They didn't have to listen," he replied. "You all seemed to be having a fine time."

The eminent historian had arranged a luncheon for me, and this I particularly dreaded, but it went rather well. He spoke on myths of the twentieth century, and there were references to Veblen and Arnold and other contemporaries of mine of whom I had scarcely heard. He asked me if most people had not been convinced that every politician was a crook and that democracy was nevertheless a great success. He also commented on the popular notion that America was a religious nation, offering some statistics on church attendance.

But the best discussion was on advertising. What they all wanted to know was whether I and my contemporaries had accepted the claims the advertisements made. Had we really believed that the same cigarette could be both a stimulant and a sedative. Had we expected to be restored to health by this or that breakfast food? What had we made of the rival claims of automobiles, laxatives, whiskeys, shaving creams, cameras, toothpastes, cough drops, and radios?

I said that I thought most people had developed a healthy skepticism about advertising and then they wanted to know why it had paid. I couldn't tell them.

In answer to a question I described advertising on the radio. In the months just before I went to sleep, I had listened a good deal to war news, and so I was able to give them a graphic account of the way the praises of gasolines, patent medicines, and cigars had been mingled with accounts of air raids, the sinking of ships, and the maneuvers of troops.

You must remember that this was a group of historians who had spent much time with newspaper files. One of them had even gone to the trouble of studying the editorial columns of the Braxton *Voice*. How well I recalled those editorials as he quoted them—always praising democracy as an abstraction but always trying to eat away whatever rights the average man had. Day after day Old Winfield hammered away at the Reds —meaning anyone who questioned the sanctity of the profit system or the wisdom of the Republican Party. The historian wanted to know what influence those editorials had had. I wondered. Most Braxtonians read no other paper, and if they did chance to subscribe to one of the Boston sheets, they got exactly the same opinions thrown at them. Perhaps few of them read editorials, but that day-after-day repetition must have had some effect.

Someone wanted to know about the influence of advertisers on editorial policy, and I had nothing concrete to say, though I remembered Everett's cynicism. Someone else asked about columnists. Why had such persons as Walter Lippmann, Hugh

Johnson, Boake Carter, and Westbrook Pegler been taken seriously. I didn't know. Perhaps they hadn't been. But why, then, had their columns been printed in so many papers?

There was a bright young fellow, a bit of a smart aleck but quick and amusing. "Did you ever go to a night club?" he asked me suddenly.

"Once or twice."

"You knew you were being overcharged for your food, liquor, and entertainment, none of which was first-rate. Am I right?"

"I guess so."

"Then why did you do it?"

I honestly didn't know. Stupid as I knew the whole business to be, it had somehow seemed rather splendid to be acting as if money had no importance for me. I even tipped the hat girl a quarter, though I was perfectly well aware that the greater part of it would go to a syndicate that was getting rich out of suckers like me.

"Advertisements that nobody believed and that nevertheless sold goods; columnists whom nobody respected and everybody read; night clubs where people paid to be cheated. It all fits together, doesn't it?"

I could only defend myself by saying that very little of the life I had led seemed sensible while I was leading it, and I could not be surprised that even more of it appeared insane now. As a matter of fact, I rather liked the boy for treating me and my contemporaries as the damn fools we so obviously were. The others were too understanding and polite to suit me.

All in all, in spite of many embarrassing and even humiliating moments, it was a good trip. The new Harvard came to

THE FIRST TO AWAKEN

seem very attractive to me, from the outside, so to speak, as well as from the inside. Standing in the Yard, I would sometimes look at the old buildings and then at the new, and I could recognize a kind of harmony between them, for both were built to serve human needs and not to impress hoi polloi.

David and I didn't spend all our time in seminars and classes, for we visited Concord, swam at Revere Beach, watched a baseball game, and otherwise amused ourselves. Then there was a Yard caretaker, a member of the policy committee, who told me that the cooperative was one of the oldest in the country, having been founded, in a rather differ-

A view of the Vislet Factory. Note the river front is reserved for the Cooperative's recreation buildings.

ent form, in 1882. He was very friendly, insisted on my having dinner with his family, and gave me some slips for Victor's garden.

Yet I was glad to be back in Braxton. The Waldmans welcomed me with honest warmth, Simeon Blake came round to invite me to ride with him and tell him all about it, and at lunch there were friendly faces and cordial invitations to sit with this group or that.

The evening I got home I went to Roberta's room to ask her some questions about the approaching meeting of her club. When I found her wrapped up in a blood-and-thunder tale that I had just happened to look through at the library, I was a little shocked. She was so darn sensible and level-headed, along with all her liveliness, that I couldn't quite imagine her relishing so absurd and bloodthirsty a tale. I said nothing to her, but I did speak to David. He refused to get excited, and after a while I decided he was right. I had read hundreds of such books, and had grown up well-behaved to the verge of timidity. The children of my contemporaries had listened to ghastly serials on the radio, and probably suffered no permanent damage. Children still craved a robust diet, and after all they had the digestions for it.

I speak of this here because it would be so easy to give the wrong impression of Roberta as I saw her in action with her club. She warned me that she and her friends would not let me off so easily as the Harvard experts had done, and she was quite right. After we had had lunch in the school restaurant, we went out into a quiet garden, and the inquisition began. If the scholars had been able to take the absurdities of my era for granted, these boys and girls were not so urbane.

THE FIRST TO AWAKEN

Knowing enough to recognize the ridiculous aspects of my old life, but not enough to be able to explain them, they could not restrain their indignation, and, in the friendliest way possible, visited it upon me.

At Roberta's suggestion I was to describe a typical day. "Well," I began, "I'll take a day three or four years before I went to sleep—while my wife was still alive. Now you stop me and ask questions whenever you want to. We got up about quarter of eight."

"Why did you get up so late? Wasn't it a nice day?"

"It was a very nice day, but we always slept as late as we could. Before I got dressed, I went downstairs to fix the furnace, and Elsie got breakfast."

This required a little discourse on the subject of heating houses, and I found myself involved in a detailed description —hilarious from their point of view—of our home. I also had to explain why we didn't have any children and what we ate for breakfast.

"Then," I continued, "Elsie drove me to work and went on to her own job." I answered a question about the private ownership of automobiles. "The bank opened at nine, but we had to be there earlier to have everything ready." For a moment I was almost homesick. I could see the little bank so clearly. It was little and friendly, and in the fifteen or twenty minutes before the doors opened, before either the customers or the big shots had arrived, there was good-natured kidding and laughing. Then Big Joe would ostentatiously strap on his revolver, while we put our name-plates in place, and the day had begun.

The children had a rough idea of the role of money in our

economy, but I lost them and myself in a discussion of loans, interest, discounts, savings accounts, checking accounts, and balances. In the end one thing was clear: a ten-year old could give an adequate description of their monetary system, whereas I made a botch of describing the conditions under which I had worked for almost twenty years.

When the morning was at last behind me, I described the business man's fifty-cent lunch at the Royal Cafe. The food wasn't very good, I admitted, and the conversation was even poorer, but it was a break in the day.

One of the children wanted to know what my wife was doing all that time, and I tried to tell them about the general attitude towards women who worked. Many women worked in the shoe factory when it was booming, but they were looked down upon by people in my class. In Braxton it was still heresy for a married woman of the middle class to have a job, and Mr. Harrington had been horrified when Elsie took the position in the relief office. When I heard how they snorted at that, I didn't tell them that I also had had my qualms.

When we got on to the subject of relief, they really went to town. God knows I thought I had seen the full absurdity and tragedy of poverty in the midst of abundance, but I had not begun to explore the subject. These boys and girls could not make themselves believe that people had been jobless while factories stood idle. Their minds rejected the notion that people could have gone hungry while food was being destroyed, or could have been cold for want of clothes that were piled high in warehouses. I have never seen so clear an example of the difference between knowing a thing and realizing its implications. They knew everything I was telling them, and yet they had never before been forced to imagine what life under such conditions had been like for real human beings.

One boy, for example, referred to a picture of a Hooverville they had recently seen. "Didn't you know how to build better houses?" he asked incredulously.

"Of course they did," a girl replied superciliously; "it was the system." But what the system meant to them, except sheer craziness, it was hard for me to conceive.

The question they asked again and again was, "Why did you put up with it?" I tried to explain that many people believed this was the way things had to be. Not only the people, I said, who were doing rather well under the profit system, but lots of people who suffered. They had had it drilled into their heads that any attempt at change would only make matters worse. The newspapers they read, for instance, told them every day that business men had to be left alone or there would be even lower wages and greater unemployment. I quoted not only my father-in-law, who hated "that man," meaning President Roosevelt, but also some of the people on the WPA that Elsie talked with.

Remembering the discussion in Cambridge, I told them about the editorials in the Braxton *Voice*. The idea of propaganda did not bother them, for they thought it natural that a man should try to influence other people, but they were shocked when I said that these editorials were not recognized as propaganda. "Of course a business man would say he ought not to be interfered with," one girl pointed out, "but why should the workers believe him?"

I got back to my day in Braxton, and, after finishing my account of my work, met Elsie and went shopping. This suggested many practical questions about the kind of goods that were available, the prices, the variety, and so forth, and in due season we touched on advertising. Less polite than the Harvard experts, they roared as I set forth the alleged merits of the different kinds of breakfast food. One, I said, would make you thin, another make you fat. They would enable you to get good marks in school, play championship baseball, be successful in love, or talk the boss into a raise. I scored my greatest success with this account, and I am sure the children never understood how little I was exaggerating.

They thought it appalling that Elsie should have had to get meals when she didn't enjoy cooking, and I could see the realization dawning that meals in my day weren't as easy to come by as a glass of water. Having adjusted themselves to the idea of our backwardness, they weren't surprised that dishes had to be washed by hand, and they seemed to find no particular virtue in my having done the job almost every night.

They wanted to know how we spent the evening, and as I described our meager range of opportunities, I fully grasped for the first time the wealth of choices offered to the citizen of 2040. Indeed, I ought to say that, if the children were getting a new understanding of the twentieth century, I was achieving a deeper realization of the twenty-first. Though I had been in the new world but three months, I was already beginning to take things for granted. These gasps and giggles made it clear to me how great the change had really been.

Though I had finished my account of the day, they did not want me to go. Not all of their questions, to be sure, were on the highest historical plane. They wanted to know what children wore and what games they played. Many of our games

THE FIRST TO AWAKEN

had survived, at least in modified form, but I made a date to teach them duck-on-the-rock and run-sheep-run, and I told them about Hallowe'en—an indiscretion for which I may yet have to answer to their parents. If I had been a cowboy or a coal miner or a steeplejack, they would have been delighted as I could not possibly delight them. One of the littlest ones had got it into his head that I lived in the days of the Indians, but the others laughed at him so that he blushed and pretended he had been joking.

Roberta seemed to be the leader of the group, though she was not the oldest, and she maintained order whenever restraint was necessary. That was fairly often, for, after the children had been laughing at some absurdity that I recounted, it was easy for them to go on to giggles and pinches. Roberta was something of a giggler herself, but she always found a good question to start the discussion going again.

It was she who asked me about war. "You were a soldier in the First World War, George. Why did you fight?"

"I was drafted, but probably I would have volunteered sooner or later. You see, I believed my country was in danger and I had to defend it. I was a sucker, Roberta."

"The country wasn't in danger?"

"Not any part of it that concerned me. A couple of million men like me got into uniforms and drilled, and some of us went over to France and fought. That's all right. I'd do it again for something I really believed in. There are things that are more important than a man's job or his family or his life. But while we were fighting or getting ready to fight, a few thousand business men were getting richer and richer. And they made their money out of us. We didn't have decent camps or decent uniforms or decent food or decent guns. Why? Because these business men were grafting. You might get the idea that in a war the whole nation makes sacrifices. That isn't so. Most people make sacrifices, but a few people don't. And those people get rich out of the sacrifices of the others."

I must have spoken rather heatedly, for one little boy said solemnly, as if to re-assure me, "We don't have wars nowadays. We think it's a silly way to behave." He looked around and added, "We do have fighting, though. Bud and Cliff were fighting this morning, and that's why Cliff's handkerchief is all bloody."

We were still arguing about human nature and war when Margaret came along and rescued me. She suggested that we play tennis with Nathalie and David, and I was glad to have some sort of recreation.

These two sessions prepared me for the third and most important. The educational committee of the cooperative was holding a series of lectures and symposia on the subject, "What Can We Learn from the Past?" and they had come to my period. A history teacher from the regional college spoke first, giving in fifteen minutes a brilliant account, or so it seemed to me, of the decline of capitalism and its consequences.

Then a technician, one of the many highly skilled mechanics on whom the smooth functioning of Braxton life depended, talked on science and invention. A woman of fifty or so, she had made the history of invention her hobby, and, though she spoke hesitantly, she gave a good account of the conflict between science and profits. She praised our scientists and inventors for what they had done in the face of great obstacles, and she warned against depending too much on planned invention, pointing out that unpredictable discoveries could be made by men and women who ventured out of familiar paths.

This was the first time I had ever had to speak in public, and as the third speaker rose I fumbled nervously with my notes. He was a manuscript processor and a very good talker. He talked, however, about his own century rather than mine, and his theme, often repeated and ingeniously illustrated, was that times had changed less than everyone thought. There had been, he granted, a certain improvement in the mechanics of civilization, and various elementary problems, which ought to have been solved centuries earlier, had at last been taken care of. This was a good thing but scarcely cause for universal rejoicing. Man, still a barbarous creature, little removed from the animals in his needs and desires, blundered his half-tragic, half-comic way through a hostile universe. The absurdities of the twentieth century had only yielded to the absurdities of the twenty-first, which were less apparent because everyone was used to them. Human limitations remained what they always had been and always would be. Each generation felt superior to its predecessors, and none with justice. "I ask my friend here," he concluded, bowing in my direction, "whether he and his contemporaries were not quite as happy as we. There was a proverb in his day: the more things change, the more they are the same. We should be a wiser people if we remembered that."

He sat down with a smug look, and there was applause. Suddenly I made up my mind, and stuffed my notes into my pocket. As I rose, I felt confident of what I had to say, and my nervousness left me.

I SPEAK MY PIECE

"Friends," I began, "you have been asking what you can learn from my period. Frankly, I don't think that you can learn much. I think that mine was a mean age. Capitalism had its great days, but they were over before I was born. I don't want to flatter you. Like our last speaker, I'm against any idea that we've reached utopia and there's nothing more for us to do. But I don't want you to underestimate what's been done in the last century. I know what I'm talking about, and I say that the gains that have been made are real gains. The last speaker asks if my contemporaries were not as happy as you, and I say, 'No!' You are happier people, better people, wiser people.

"I imagine there is nobody here tonight who doesn't have congenial, interesting, useful work. You don't know what a blessing that is. Millions of my contemporaries couldn't find work at all, and millions more, myself included, never found jobs for which they were suited.

"I know that nobody here has the slightest sense of economic insecurity. You don't even understand what the words mean. But in my day everybody was scared, from the bottom of the economic scale up almost to the very top. Millions, as I have said, had no jobs at all, and didn't know when they might lose the meager charity that kept them alive. Those who did have jobs feared to lose them. Even people who had good incomes lived in dread of a poverty-stricken, miserable old age. Fear, usually suppressed but sometimes breaking out into sheer terror, ruled that society. If you had done nothing but destroy that fear, there would be what our friend calls 'cause for universal rejoicing.'

"Our friend says that man is still a tragic figure, and perhaps he is right, but you know nothing of the man-made tragedies with which my age was haunted. You read your histories, but can you picture to yourselves what fascism was like? Can you conceive of thousands upon thousands of people being beaten, tortured, degraded, killed, merely because of their race? For that matter does the good American word 'lynching' have any meaning for you? Can you see in your mind's eye a black body, mutilated and writhing in agony, being given to the flames?

"You read of labor spies, but do you know the sickening feeling that comes when you dare not speak your mind to the man who works beside you? You read of strikes, but you have never had your nostrils stung with tear gas nor felt policemen's clubs upon your heads. If you should hear of men being shot down in cold blood in some backward part of the world, you would be horrified, but I can remember when American citizens died at the hands of American police for the crime of asking for a living wage.

"Yes, there are still tragedies, but you know that the woman you love will never die of starvation, will never be raped by some man in uniform, will never be blown to bits by an enemy bomb. You know that your son will not be killed in battle nor come back to you with his lungs rotted out by poison gas.

"Your children will never lack food or clothing, nor will they ever know what it is to covet an education they cannot have. They may fall ill, may even die, but you will never have to endure the bitter thought that they could have been saved if you had had money to pay for the right kind of doctors and medicine. You will never know what it is to see one man squandering upon a single night's entertainment money that could mean health and comfort and life itself to your family.

"No one of you will ever be cursed and persecuted because of his color, his race, or his religion. No one of you will ever have to rot in jail for a crime he didn't commit—or, for that matter, for a crime he did commit. You can't imagine. A man in my day might steal millions of dollars that had been entrusted to him and never go to jail at all. Or he might be sentenced for a year or two, whereas some boy from the slums would get ten years for taking a joyride in an automobile that didn't belong to him. Also, do you realize that men were jailed on account of the ideas they held, not only in Nazi Germany but right here in the United States?

"If I had a map of old New York here, I could point to certain spots and say, 'A boy born there is going to end up in jail if tuberculosis doesn't get him first.' And do you realize that men had jobs that they knew, absolutely knew, were killing them, and they kept on working?

"The last speaker says that mankind is as mean as it ever was. My friends, he doesn't know what he's talking about. You're not angels, oh, no. But I have seen a man lie and steal and betray his fellowmen for a job that paid less than $20 a week. Right here in Braxton I saw men I knew, decent men, go out armed with clubs and axes and guns to injure other men and destroy their property. Why? Because their jobs or their profits were at stake.

"There are meannesses you never dreamt of. You look with contempt on liars and cheats, but I tell you that in my day the truth was a luxury. Our friend will say that men are still capable of such baseness if they are driven to it. I am sure he is right, and that is just what I am talking about. You aren't driven to that today. It isn't by sermons that man gets better but by the kind of progress you have made. There's both good and evil in man, and you have the kind of society in which the good has a chance. I mean it when I tell you that you are better, wiser, happier. You can afford to be. And because you've never had to lie and cheat, to torture or be tortured, to kill or be killed, you can grow in ways of truth and humanity.

"Perhaps the kind of skepticism our friend has expressed is healthy, but don't let him deceive you. Someone says that struggle is man's destiny and his salvation, and that's right, but don't underestimate what you have already won. I tell you that if my contemporaries had been able to conceive of such a society as you now have, they would not have rested until they had destroyed the cruel, crazy system under which they lived. You will say that you have made no more than a beginning, and that is what I would want you to say, but do not forget that it is the beginning of a new hope for mankind, such a hope as never dawned on our horizon. You have not reached utopia; you will never reach utopia; but don't jump to the conclusion that the struggle is futile.

"This isn't what I had meant to say, and probably I've been too emotional. Please forgive me. But in the three months I have lived among you, you have given me your friendship, and I have tried tonight to pay some small part of the debt I owe you."

There was a good deal of applause, and they seemed to mean it.

XI

DESIGN FOR DIVORCE

THERE were many favorable comments on my little talk, and I was amused to find that it was quoted by both sides in discussions of the Lister case and the approaching town meeting.

I resumed my pleasant routine of study and recreation, and I turn to my journal to remind myself of what I was doing. The entries are not exciting, but they bring up agreeable memories:

> Read the article on the origin of life in the World Encyclopedia. Listened to lecture in elementary biochemistry from the University of Chicago, and watched two experiments. Lunch with the Careys. Walked with Roberta et al. Read "Frenzy," by Carl Ballard. I like his poetry better than most. Listened to Brahms' Symphony 1. Went to historical pageant with Margaret B. Very amusing. . . .
>
> Made notes and wrote a few pages in my book. Missed biochemistry course. After lunch visited restaurant kitchen. A marvelous place; the chef is a chemist and the cook is an engineer. Had my beard trimmed. Very warm;

wore shorts in public for the first time. Played tennis with David, winning two sets out of three. Dinner with the Mellons at their home. Played gaperdee. . . .

Wrote a little, read more in encyclopedia, and listened in to lecture. Letter from Norah; Nick is bringing out a new pamphlet next week. Saw David and George K. at lunch. Went to playground and talked with Peter. Simeon and I went canoeing. Got a new dalkin. Listened to baseball game for a while, and then read *Titus Andronicus* for the first time. To bed at nine. . . .

Victor goes to work now at six, and we are getting up before five. Agnes leaves a second breakfast for me in the suspensor, and I eat it about ten while listening to the lecture. Got five pages written this morning. Took a nap after lunch and then went with Abraham to visit the vislet plant. Started for a walk with the Dell twins, but it began to rain. Saw revival of Shaw's *Major Barbara* from London and thought it very funny.

June has always been a lovely month in our part of the country, and it seemed delightful to have as much time as I wanted for rides and hikes and canoe trips. There was never any difficulty in finding a companion, for, if my adult acquaintances could not spare the time, Roberta and her friends were always ready for any kind of outing after school hours.

Not far from the school was a fine playground, with every facility for organized games and with woods and fields and a small pond as well. Here, though the children were well guarded against any kind of danger, they had the sense of being entirely on their own. I liked to chat with Peter, the old man in charge, and often I would arrive a few minutes before school was out, talk with him until the children arrived, and then watch him as he allocated tennis courts and rowboats, appointed guards for the beach, handed out baseball equipment, and adjudicated disputes. When that was done, I would either continue the conversation or lead a small expedition into the hills.

Roberta had once asked me my birthday, and I had told her it was the twentieth of June, but I had forgotten all about that when the day came round. I suspected nothing, therefore, when I was told there was to be a picnic. We drove to a favorite spot of mine, a waterfall, and there were Simeon and David and Nathalie and their boy and a couple of Roberta's playmates. Agnes produces a cake with forty-four candles, and there was a little pile of presents at my place. We toasted marshmallows and sang songs and were all very juvenile.

After a while the adults were worn out, and we sat talking together while the children played on the edge of the water. Simeon and David somehow began to talk about travel, and Simeon's descriptions of the places in which he had worked were always fascinating. Even Victor, who had often called travel foolish and could be persuaded only with difficulty to

Interior of the Universal Factory

make a trip to New York or spend a summer fortnight at the shore, was interested, and it was he who finally said, "George, you ought to take a trip around the world."

I don't know why it should have been so staggering a suggestion, for David had several times referred to my traveling when I had got used to the new life. But, put so concretely, it did seem a startling idea, and then, almost immediately, a very attractive one. Before I knew it, we were discussing my itinerary.

When David asked me to have lunch with him the next day, I thought he wanted to discuss the trip to which I had so suddenly committed myself, and so he did, but I could see that there was something else on his mind, and as we sat over our coffee he finally brought up the subject that was troubling him.

"You've never thought of marrying again, have you, George?" he asked.

I shook my head. Of course I had thought of it, but not as something I was likely to do.

I was willing to tell him in detail just how I felt about marriage, but I quickly saw that it was his problems, not mine, that he wanted to discuss. He began by talking about marriage in general, saying little that I didn't know. As with almost all my observations, I had slowly modified my judgments. At first I had felt that all the problems of sexual adjustment that bothered people in my day were solved. Then I realized that there were such things as domestic quarrels, infidelity, and conflicts between parents and children, and I began to wonder if there had been much change. Slowly I became able to see what had changed and what hadn't.

By and large personal relationships had altered less than

DESIGN FOR DIVORCE

economic and political institutions. The most important changes, indeed, were those already under way in my own time. Even when I grew up, Braxton was sufficiently industrialized so that the family was no longer an economic unit, and the century had merely made that condition universal. In the same way the economic independence of women, which had gone a long way by 1940 and had pretty well revolutionized marriage, was now complete. Finally, contraception had been perfected and made generally available, so that procreation, which was largely voluntary for the upper classes in my day, became wholly so for everyone.

There were new attitudes, and yet, when I analyzed them, I found them less different from my own than I had supposed. It was true, for example, that premarital experimentation was largely taken for granted. But many earlier societies had tolerated experimentation in men, and some had tolerated it in women. In the nineteen twenties and thirties there had been much talk about the new freedom, and I suppose fewer women, if not fewer men, were virgins when married. Yet anyone who had grown up in a small town and seen something of rural customs, as I had, was not likely to assume that his generation was pioneering in unconventionality. I also knew that in my time infidelity was not limited to Bohemians, though it was perhaps only among Bohemians that it was a major topic of conversation. In 2040 people acknowledged its existence without particularly approving. It often involved unhappiness, but it was something that happened, and not a subject for prudish head-shakings, lascivious whispers, or public boasts.

In short, monogamy was the rule, though a rule that was

THE FIRST TO AWAKEN

only approximately followed. There had, to be sure, been some significant changes. Both prostitution and venereal disease had virtually disappeared. Better education and a clearer understanding of glandular functions had eliminated most types of what we called perversion and many minor maladjustments. And there was no such thing as illegitimacy.

Marriage was taken seriously, and there was a kind of tacit agreement that a relationship outside of marriage was preferable to a marriage too hastily entered upon. At least in Braxton the various examinations and declarations of intentions involved a delay of several months, and this was regarded as wise. If two persons decided to be married, it was usually because they wanted to have children, and the raising of a family was a responsibility not to be lightly undertaken.

At first I was surprised at the eagerness with which most couples looked forward to having children, but I remembered how much Elsie and I had wanted a baby and how terribly unhappy many of our friends had been because they felt they could not afford to have one. With child-bearing rendered completely safe and largely painless, with all economic problems taken care of, with every opportunity being given to the woman to continue her career after pregnancy, there was nothing to discourage couples from having three or four children, and most of them did. Larger families were something of a problem, for the organization of the community was geared to a gradual increase of population, but there were no insurmountable obstacles, and I knew several families in which there were six or seven children.

Nothing is harder to measure than happiness, but I am sure there were more happy marriages than in my day. I attributed

DESIGN FOR DIVORCE

the improvement partly to better sexual adjustment and partly to the lessening of economic tensions and pressures. If it is true that in my day economic necessity often kept families together, it was only at the expense of considerable suffering, and in the social class to which I belonged insecurity brought separation more often than unity.

One thing was clear, namely that people could get married and could have children if they wanted to. The prerequisites of a happy marriage, so to speak, were denied to no one. Whether a given couple created on this basis a satisfactory life together was their problem. They were better fitted to do so than most people in my day had been, but there was no easy recipe for happiness.

That was what David wanted to talk to me about. Psychologist that he was, he was almost as embarrassed in discussing the subject as I should have been, but at last he managed to make me understand that he and Nathalie were considering a divorce. Beyond that he would say little, for, as I gathered with some difficulty, he wanted me to talk the matter over with both of them.

"We could go to a psychiatrist," he said apologetically, "but somehow that isn't what I want. You're a friend of ours, and yet you can be objective about the business. Let us both talk to you, and then you say just what you think."

Divorce, I knew, could be obtained by mutual consent if there were no children. If there were children, however, their interests were put first. Fifty or sixty years earlier, as David had told me, the care of children was increasingly left to institutions, but, with the growing revolt against the mechanization of life, there had come to be more emphasis on the home. Now institutional care, though probably better in many respects than care in the home, was a departure from the norm and therefore regarded as bad for the children. For that reason the home was to be maintained unless the continuance of the marriage was likely to be worse for the children than its dissolution would be.

In practice this meant that hasty divorce was impossible. If a couple persisted in wanting a divorce over a period of a year, it was almost automatically granted, and it could be granted sooner on the recommendation of a physician or a psychiatrist. But the community, though it denied no one the right to a divorce, did insist on canvassing the possibilities of a different adjustment. The fact that divorce was on the decline could probably be attributed largely to the avoidance of the kind of marriage that was bound to collapse, but the remedial work of the domestic clinics had something to do with it.

Although I now got along very well with Nathalie, I was still uneasy when she and David were together, and this was a particularly delicate situation. When I entered their apartment that evening, full of misgivings, David had just laid down a book and Nathalie was writing at her desk. She wore a white blouse and white shorts, very effective on her dark skin, and there was no denying that she was a handsome woman. Her walk was light and graceful and full of poise, and, though she was scarcely up to my shoulder, her back was so straight and her head carried so high that once more she overawed me.

The baby and his sister were in bed, but Everett, the eight-year-old, came in to ask some questions and say good night. He shook hands with the cordiality that seemed so natural to him, and said, "We had lots of fun at your party." Then he added, speaking seriously and directly, "I wish I had heard the speech you made. Everyone says it was very good."

After he had left, Nathalie said, "This is a great favor, George." There was something like tenderness in her voice and yet, it seemed to me, just a touch of mockery.

She stretched herself out on a comfortable chair and looked at David, who was still walking about the room. "I'll begin," he said. "The first day we met I told you that I began studying to be a protein chemist at Dartmouth. I fell in love with a girl here in Braxton, where I had grown up, and she married someone else." He was speaking in the matter-of-fact tone he used when he told me about economic organization or the state of science, but I realized that it was something of an effort. Suddenly I understood how sensitive he was, how truly he could be said to be a poet, though so far as I knew he had never written a line of verse, and I felt stupid for not having understood this before.

"I joined the Arctic Reclamation Corps," he went on. "Lots of boys of twenty do that, not because they've been disappointed in love but because they want physical exertion and adventure, something to test their strength and courage. It's a rough, hardy life, and that's just what I wanted."

Nathalie's expression was difficult to fathom, a little amused, I thought, but not contemptuous or impatient. David stared hard at her. "I had a wonderful three months. Then Nathalie arrived with a statistical survey. There were quite a few girls around the camp, but there were twenty boys for every girl, and Nathalie was very popular. I fell in love with her. I was barely twenty-one, remember, and Nathalie was almost as beautiful then as she is now."

He paused again, but Nathalie said nothing. "I was determined to marry her, though I couldn't believe that she would ever look twice at me. I surprised myself. No rebuff could stop me, and I plotted and intrigued like an infatuated Machiavelli, and my campaign began to succeed. We danced together, became partners at games, had long talks, and I proposed marriage. She refused me time after time, but I persisted, and at last—why I still can't tell you—she consented."

He took a cigarette and leaned against the wall. Nathalie smiled. "David is protecting your sensibilities, George. Let me tell you what happened. My father was an engineer, Mexican by birth, probably with some Spanish and some Indian blood. I was born in South Africa, and by the time I was twelve I had lived in eleven different countries and knew six languages reasonably well. My father finally settled down in one of the great mining fields of western Canada. After my regular education, I spent two years at the University of Calgary, studying economics. I liked men. I mean, I liked to sleep with them. There are girls like that, just as there are boys like that. I don't think it was because I had a sense of inferiority or craved power or anything like that. It was physical and, if I may say so without shocking you and David, healthy."

I was shocked, quite unreasonably so, but I tried to conceal the fact. "I didn't crave a lot of attention," she went on. "In fact, I spent less time thinking about boys than most girls of my age. I was a serious student and a good one. But I knew what I wanted, and my wants were pretty physical."

David looked morose, but whether because he disapproved

of her talking so frankly—and I have modified her language —or because he was jealous in retrospect, I cannot say. She interpreted his expression as I did, for she said, "We agreed to be honest. I'm not defending what I did, and I'm not apologizing for it. I did nobody harm, not even myself. However, there was a student of psychiatry who kept telling me that my promiscuity was a sign of psychic disorder. Of course he was trying to frighten me into marrying him, but I was foolish enough to be impressed, and I left the university and went up north.

"Things went on just about the same up there. David wasn't the only man I was seeing, and on the physical level my relations with him were less intimate than my relations with some of the others. That wasn't my fault, by the way."

"It was mine," David broke in, coming forward, so that he stood facing me, with his back to Nathalie. "I wasn't what you would call a prude, but what I felt for Nathalie was so utterly different from what she felt for me that there seemed something incongruous in the idea of a sexual relationship between us. Jealous as I was, I admitted even then that it was all right for her to sleep with men who were as casual about it as she. I know I was stupid about the whole thing, but I was young and just a chemist, and I had a point, which she wouldn't see and still won't."

He was pretty grim, but Nathalie smiled as she continued: "I liked David, liked him very much. He wasn't—and isn't— an ordinary kind of person. I'm afraid you've seen me grow impatient with him, but I am tolerant now compared with what I was in those days. He seemed so naive, and at the same time he had a way of making simple things complicated.

He was always seeing problems where there weren't any, or I thought there weren't. I may have been reckless about sowing my wild oats, but I had no intention of going through life being promiscuous. As a matter of fact, the idea of marrying David occurred to me almost as soon as I met him, and no other man had put that idea in my head. But he made it all so damned difficult. He insisted that I ought to feel something that I didn't feel and didn't really believe he felt. So I told him no again and again, and went out with other men even when I didn't much want to."

"Then why did you marry me?" David demanded, turning to stare at her.

"Because I couldn't stand your mooning around all the time," she answered, and there was a cruel snap in her eyes.

He went and stood by the window, looking out at the little terrace and the late June twilight beyond. Embarrassed, I fumbled for a question to ask. "How did things go after you were married?"

He turned, unhappiness in his eyes, and Nathalie, almost as if in apology, spoke first: "Very well, at the outset. I don't know what David thought, but I liked it, and found I'd missed a lot. The relationship was warm and intimate and many-sided. David is nice, and there was so much to talk about, and the baby was exciting. Oh, we did fight, for David fights too, though you may not believe it—fights by sulking, by being so damn scrupulously reasonable, by never forgetting anything. But they weren't serious fights."

David seemed about to reply, but checked himself. I began to see the whole situation, but I had to keep on asking questions to try to relieve the tension. "Is the trouble that you're interested in different things?"

"Oh, no," David answered promptly. "That makes for a good marriage. And it isn't jealousy," he went on after a moment. "I got over that pretty well."

"And have had little enough cause to be jealous," Nathalie added.

"No, the trouble is that I rub Nathalie the wrong way. It sounds silly, but it's true. Just as she says, I'm always worrying about problems that don't exist for her."

"And then I have to take him down a little. So I say something mean, and he is filled with righteous indignation and sulks."

Not quite honestly I said, "It doesn't seem very serious."

"But it is!" they cried together.

"David isn't getting his work done," Nathalie went on. "He always has this problem on his mind."

"And Nathalie isn't happy except when she is working."

"We've gone into this before, and we can't have these periodic crises. It's not going to be easy for either of us, and it seems wretched for the children, but we can't go on."

David leaned against the wall again, his face full of gloom. "We've always said that two sensible people ought to find some way of getting along together, but we've given it a try for ten years, and it doesn't work."

"It isn't . . ." I said hesitantly, "there's not . . . I mean. . . ."

"Oh, no," they chorused again.

I tried to think. Perhaps there was something I could say. My helplessness must have appeared in my face, for David woefully shook his head. "There you are. I knew it was futile."

"But you are the one who wanted to call George in," Nathalie told him sharply. "That's always the way. I don't care what we do so long as we stop talking about it. Anything is better than always gnawing away at the problem. George can't tell us anything we don't know, and we owe him an apology for making him listen to all this nonsense."

"All right," said David wearily, "I apologize. I guess you've done all you can, George, just in listening to us talk. Thanks."

As we sat in melancholy silence, the room gently filled with music. "Oh," Nathalie exclaimed, "the Budapest Quartet. I forgot the radio was set for that." We listened to the whole sonata, each of us occupied with his thoughts.

When I got up to go, Nathalie said, "Have you spoken to George about Friday?"

"We're having some people in—a kind of farewell party—if it's all right for you. You might come around early and talk with us first. Maybe you'll have some ideas."

Nathalie looked at me with just a trace of a smile, and I had to admit to myself that David was a comic figure as he stood there, his head bowed, his face furrowed. But I was sorry for them both.

I thought of the matter often in the next two days, taking the problem on a long, solitary walk, as I had occasionally taken problems of my own. I had known of one or two such cases and read of many more: two wholly admirable persons who somehow damaged each other and did not belong together. The more I thought, the clearer it seemed to me that separation was the only answer. I pitied young Everett, but I thought the little girl's spoiled manner might be explained by the friction between the parents, and of course the baby would know nothing about it. It was tragic for David, who, I felt, was in a way destined for tragedy—a poet, as I had said to myself before, condemned by his sensitiveness to dissatisfaction with the world and with himself. Nathalie would suffer, too, but she had the strength to bear suffering.

The problem was still on my mind when the night of the cooperative meeting came. Part of the restaurant, several of the smaller halls, and some of the game rooms had been made into one large auditorium to accommodate the ten or twelve thousand people who were expected. The restaurant and stores closed early that evening, and no one was kept away by work except the few persons who volunteered for vital services.

However indifferent the people of the old Braxton had seemed to the broad issues of the nation and the world, they had always shown good sense in dealing in town meeting with matters that intimately concerned them. Disillusioned as I had become with the actual operation of democracy, I never lost the feeling that my fellow-citizens could govern themselves if they had half a chance. Their decisions often rested on what seemed to me the wrong premises, on too narrow a conception of their own and the town's best interests, but they were seldom taken in by the slick politicians who orated at them. It was not incompetence but the crack of the economic whip that made slaves of them.

I had always rather relished the old town meetings, and I was looking forward to this session. When, however, I saw the great hall filling with people, I wondered if the cooperative would ever be able to transact its business. If, I thought, everyone insisted on talking, we would never get anywhere, and I remembered how our town meetings were plagued year after year by long-winded egotists who had nothing to say but loved to talk.

The problem, I soon realized, had been faced long ago and in effect solved. The bulletin had printed the resolutions prepared by the disciplinary committee and the counter-resolutions offered by Lister. Several pamphlets had appeared, arguing for or against the expansion of the experimental station. The citizens considered themselves well informed, and they did not intend to tolerate windbags.

The meeting began promptly at nineteen o'clock. The chairman of the disciplinary committee read the resolution calling for Lister's demotion, and to my surprise there was no discussion. Victor, who was sitting beside me, showed me how to operate the buttons on the arm of my chair, and, though I had not intended to vote, insisted that I had a right to and should. When the presiding officer called for the vote, it was recorded automatically on the scoreboard over his head. Out of more than ten thousand votes, there were only sixty-eight against demotion—the last dogged expression, I suppose, of the loyalty the man had aroused among certain of his followers.

He was on his feet as soon as the vote was recorded, apparently undismayed by the outcome, which he must have expected. In support of his resolution, which called for a large increase in the appropriation for the experimental station, he spoke with all of his old fire. His argument rested on the fact that chemical industry had become basic in the new economy, and that it was precisely in this field that a revolution was overdue. His opponents would say, he pointed out, that the great research laboratories and university faculties were taking care of the problem, but it was in its relation to the small community such as Braxton that chemical industry was most significant. It was too easy to sit back and say that the high and mighty authorities were at work and all would be well. Each community had to make its own contribution. Moreover, each community had to look out for its own interests, and our problem was what we could do for ourselves, not what the Continental Committee on Chemical Industry could do for us. We were a self-governing cooperative, and if we saw a chance to raise the standard of living in the near future, we ought to do it.

There was solid applause when he sat down, and Mrs. Leroy seemed ill at ease as she rose to answer him. She ridiculed what she called his pretensions, his belief that he could do more than the organized scientific bodies, but the audience clearly did not respond to this argument, and she shifted her ground. Suppose, she said, Mr. Lister did succeed in making some astounding discovery. Did that mean that Braxton would be turned into a paradise overnight? On the contrary, as every citizen must know, to say nothing of a former member of the planning board, the gradual adoption of new techniques was the only way of avoiding exorbitant costs of obsolescence. Moreover, Braxton could not make these great advances of which Mr. Lister had spoken until the rest of the district was adjusted to the changes involved. She was as enthusiastic a supporter as anyone of the experimental station. It not only served a vital need in the daily life of Braxton but played its part in the general progress of science. The gains, however, that could result from an increased appropriation could not possibly outweigh the losses, for there would have to be either a great increase in production or a drastic restriction of consumers' goods. With the vast machinery for research and experiment in the country—and she for one had great confidence in our scientists—it was folly for a single community to expose its citizens to inconvenience and possible hardship.

For the first half hour or so after the discussion became general, the argument proceeded skillfully, opponents meet-

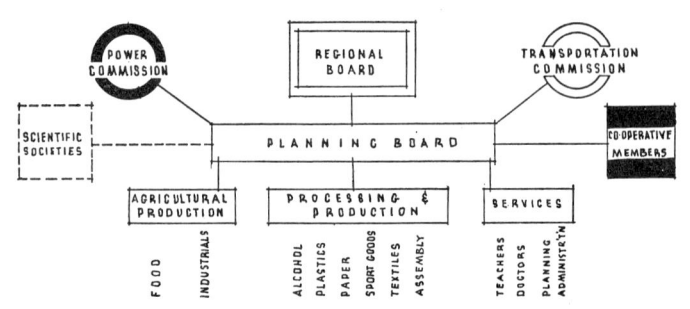

An attempt at self-education in the structure of control—from my notebooks.

ing each other squarely and the issues being more and more clearly defined, but in time speakers began to repeat each other, and the audience grew restless. Finally, as a young woman from the store was speaking, there were cries of, "What's your point?" and "That's been said."

The chairman politely interrupted her. "The citizens," he said, "want to know if you have anything to add to the arguments previously offered."

"Yes, I have," she cried defiantly. She began again, but there were smiles on the faces all around her, and she sat down in confusion. I turned to Agnes: "That's kind of tough. No wonder the poor girl couldn't remember what she wanted to say."

But Agnes had no pity: "Then she ought not to have tried to say it."

There were still speakers and eager ones, but they were more careful to be brief and pertinent, and those who wandered were quickly checked. At last everyone seemed satisfied, and the chairman called for summaries. This was one of the best things about the whole procedure. A young man rose at a table where he and others had been taking notes and outlined the essential arguments that had been given for Lister's resolution. Then a young woman did the same for the opposition. Both statements were applauded and deserved to be.

The vote was some six thousand against and three thousand for the resolution. Most of the voters, it appeared, now regarded Lister as something of a fanatic, and they were unwilling to give him the free hand that he was in effect demanding. On the other hand, the size of the vote for the increased appropriation indicated the strength of his appeal.

When the vote was completed, several persons rose and asked for the floor. All of them, it seemed, wanted to offer compromise measures, and the chairman, in defiance of what I had known as parliamentary procedure but with good sense, allowed each to make his resolution. Then, after reading the resolutions carefully to the voters, he said: "Friends, it's getting late. I have no authority and no desire to limit debate, but I think everything has been said on the subject that needs to be said. I think we all know which of these propositions we favor. And if nobody wants to talk, we can get the voting over with and go home."

If anyone had been planning to make an oration, the applause must have discouraged them. The vote was taken by a process of elimination, the least favored proposition being dropped each time. But, because of the voting buttons, it took only about fifteen minutes to settle the question. Proposals for more moderate increases in the appropriation were all defeated, and finally it was a choice between referring the question to the regional planning board and appointing a special

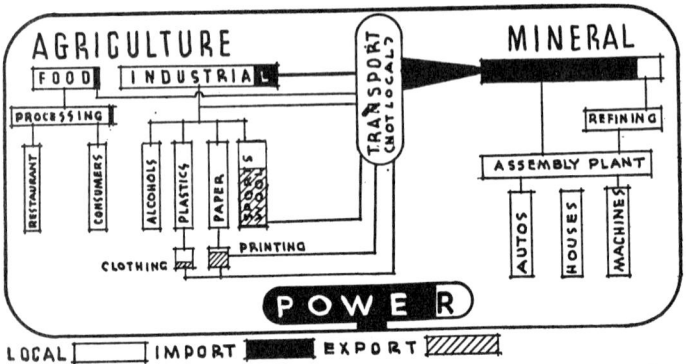

An experiment in making a flow chart, showing production in Braxton.

committee to investigate the practice in other cooperatives. The latter won.

Partitions rolled back, and the ten thousand people quickly vacated the hall. Groups sauntered through the corridors to their apartments, hundreds of cars moved away in all directions, and pedestrians strolled under the rich foliage of elm and maple.

The Waldmans were well satisfied with the outcome, though Victor had voted to consult the regional board.

"They'll see," he said; "it'll have to go to the regional board in the end. Gee, I'm sleepy."

Doubtless he went to sleep at once, but I was exhilarated by the meeting and sat for a time making notes. I had seen the new democracy at work, and I had no complaint to make. After I lay down, I thought about David and Nathalie.

When I reached their apartment the next evening, they began talking about the meeting. Both of them seemed very gay, and I admired their courage. We sat on the terrace, and the conversation flickered from the baseball game going on below us to the light on the hills to the latest gossip in the planning office. Patiently I waited for them to bring up the subject I had come to discuss, but neither of them did, and at last I said, "I've been thinking about what you told me, and I suppose that divorce is the only way."

They stared at me as if I were insane. Then David grunted and mumbled, "We really shouldn't have bothered you, George," and Nathalie said with a smile, "We were just feeling a little low. It was ridiculous for us to talk about divorce."

They were nowhere near so embarrassed as I, and I had no difficulty in changing the subject. Nathalie was in high spirits all through the evening, and I noticed how tenderly David looked at her.

It was a good party. We played something a little like charades, and both Simeon Blake and Margaret Bryan were very clever and as amusing as they could be. Everyone offered me plenty of good advice and wished me well, and it struck me, with some surprise, that I should be sorry to be leaving Braxton for more than a few months.

Walking home with Simeon Blake, who scorned automobiles for anything less than five miles, I thought with pleasure of the good friends I had made. Thinking of the Wilsons reminded me of my anti-climax, and I said, "You know Nathalie and David pretty well. Have they ever—they don't seem to get along very well some of the time."

His laughter rolled up and down the street. "So they've been asking you whether they ought to get a divorce or not. They go through that every six months or so. But they haven't yet, and I've stopped worrying about it." [1]

---

[1] This chapter is of interest chiefly as revealing Swain's attitude towards institutions and customs that we take for granted. I hope it is not necessary for me again to warn the reader against accepting his account of conversations as wholly accurate. Inevitably his reporting is colored by pre-conceptions of which he had not wholly freed himself. Anyone who is familiar with Dr. Binder's classic work, *The Pathology of Capitalist Decay* (Boston, 2009), will understand what this implies.—D.W.

XII

ADVENTURES OF A GLOBE TROTTER

I'M NOT going to try to describe everything I saw during the three months I spent going round the world. It will be enough if I set down some of the experiences that throw light on the way people were living.[1] My notebooks and sketchbooks are full, but I shall rely chiefly on my memory.

The Waldmans were all a little solemn at breakfast the

---

[1] In suggesting to Swain that, while writing, he keep in mind those who were yet to awaken, we thought that it would be easier for him to organize his impressions if he felt that he was speaking to his contemporaries. Obviously it would have been impossible for him to write for us, since we find commonplace precisely what interested him. In other words, to act as an interpreter one must understand the persons for whom one is interpreting. Swain's account has greater meaning for us because he does not have us in mind. In general this chapter is written in the same terms, and much that Swain says is familiar to every schoolboy. But the careful reader will detect a certain ambiguity, for at moments Swain seems to have a modern audience in mind, and quite unconsciously he begins to write of our life as if he were part of it and not merely a spectator. This interesting phenomenon is dealt with at length in my report.—D.W.

Gravity Airport, Melbourne

morning I set out, though it was obvious that Roberta was envious and Abraham was thinking of the time he would set out on a similar adventure. Agnes, sentimentalist that she was, was almost in tears, and I blinked a little when she said, "It's going to be hard, having an empty room again."

Certainly a late June morning was no time to leave Braxton, which had never seemed so beautiful, and I could easily have backed out at the last moment. David called for me and drove me to the airport. He had made all arrangements, securing for me, through the educational committee of the Northeast District, the full privileges of a traveling student. I could travel anywhere and be fed, clothed, and provided with a place to sleep. The few personal belongings I found it necessary to carry with me were held in a little bag the size of a brief case.

David himself was so happy and so full of enthusiasm on my behalf that I forgot my touch of homesickness. Both he and Simeon Blake, as well as some of the acquaintances I had made at Harvard, had given me introductions to dozens of individuals in the countries I planned to visit. They assured me that my student's card would bring me a welcome anywhere, but I was glad not to have to trust myself to that alone. I wasn't actually apprehensive about the trip, for, having survived my voyage into a new century, this seemed a mere outing. For months I had been depending on luck and the friendliness of the people among whom I had been thrown, and my experience had been happy enough so that I was willing to continue on that basis. But I was casting myself loose from an environment that had become familiar and pleasant to me, and I had my little shivers of doubt. I have never been a bold person.

David shook my hand warmly, and I hurried aboard the Boston plane. Several of the passengers I knew slightly, and we talked together during the brief trip. They were quite unexcited by the news that I was going round the world, and the realization that this was no longer a rare excursion helped to put me at my ease.

When the transcontinental local left Boston, it was towed by two powerful little tug-planes, which detached themselves and flew back after we had reached our flying height. My nearest neighbor began to talk with me, and I found that he was a representative of the continental transport union. I had made up my mind to conceal my identity, and when he asked me what I did, I told him merely that I was a student. He looked at me quizzically, and I have no doubt that he put my age at fifty or more. To be sure, students of fifty are not unheard of, but he asked the logical question, "What have you been doing?" He was not being inquisitive but merely friendly, and there was nothing I could do but tell him the whole story. Subsequently I discovered that, if an acquaintance seemed likely to be boring, the easiest thing

THE FIRST TO AWAKEN

was to say that I had had a long illness, which brought a look of pity and put an end to questions. Most of the time, however, I told the truth, for that was the only way I could learn what I wanted to know.

David had smiled when I told him I was going to start off by seeing Niagara Falls, but I had a little list of places I had always wanted to visit, and I intended to let nothing stop me. I am glad I persisted, for the falls are more beautiful than I had imagined. During the era of technology nobody cared about the sight-seers; power was all that mattered; but, as power became available from so many new sources, the hydroelectric plants were dismantled, and now the whole volume of the river pounds over the precipice. And since the engineers, in the interests of their power project, stopped the recession, the full grandeur is there and always will be.

I spent a happy afternoon at the falls, saw them illuminated that evening, and stayed the night at a youth hostelry within earshot of the gorge. I met a couple of youngsters there, industrial workers from Rhode Island, spending their vacations in travel, and we set out together for Chicago. Chicago is smaller than New York, but, I think, more beautiful, especially as one comes towards it over the lake. The twenty great blocks lie along the water's edge, and from the air one sees broad avenues stretching as far out on the prairie as the eye can reach.

Saying farewell to my friends, who were going directly to California, I took a plane for New Orleans. I am glad David and Simeon insisted on my seeing the South. Industrialization rapidly accelerated after the beginning of socialist planning, and the result has been an amazing transformation of southern character. The general use of air-conditioning and the introduction of a different diet have turned the southerners into an energetic people, and New Orleans reminded me a little of New York in my own day.

After I had been taken to see innumerable land reclamation projects, power plants, factories, and industrialized farms, I began to wonder if something could not be said for the leisureliness I had always associated, rightly or wrongly, with southern life. To suggest this, however, anywhere between San Antonio and Charleston, is heresy. I could not even admire an old mansion, of which many are preserved, without someone's showing me photographs of the sharecroppers' cabins that were once the disgrace of the South.

I spent more time in the Southern District than I had expected, but it was worth it, and I shall always be grateful to the acquaintance in New Orleans who insisted on my going to Birmingham. This is the center, as David had told me, of the Negro area. In one of the richest mining areas of the country, its factories produce the finest precision instruments in the world, and its university is famed for scientific research and technical pioneering.

Perhaps one reason why I liked Birmingham is that its inhabitants took so much interest in me and my views. They are proud of their achievements, and rightly so, and they welcomed me as one who can testify, however inadequately, to the progress they have made. Refusing to lecture, I did give an interview to the cooperative magazine, the first interview I had been asked for and the only one I gave in the United States. Most of the Negroes I talked with admitted

THE FIRST TO AWAKEN

that there is no necessity now for them to have a district of their own, but it is likely to go on for a long time. White people come to study at the university, and, as a matter of fact, there is no discrimination against white engineers or workers, but assimilation, if it happens at all, will not happen for centuries.

I was entertained by the dean of the university, an anthropologist of international reputation, who talked to me about the culture of the district. He said that at first the Negroes tried hard to maintain a specifically Negro culture, and he told amusing stories of the absurd lengths to which some of the patriots went, but as prejudice decreased and economic pressure vanished, the attempt to maintain artificial differences was given up. What the Negroes had to contribute, he said, has gone into American culture, and they see now that that is their culture too. There are, I think, some special traditions and customs and ways of speaking, but they are regional rather than racial and no more marked than, say, the cultural peculiarities of New England.[1]

I flew from Birmingham to Mexico City, which, knowing that Mexico was part of the continental planning unit, I expected to be like Boston or Chicago or any other northern city. On the contrary, I found the architecture, the culture, and whole attitude towards life as different from what I had learned to know as anything I saw in Europe or Asia. To

[1] Many readers from outside New England will be surprised by this, since it is generally held that New England has more unique qualities than any other region and that its speech is particularly easy to identify. See Mark V. Hyman's *Culture of the Northeast* (St. Louis, 2037). It must be remembered that Swain is himself a New Englander.—D.W. (And so, in case anyone has any illusions about it, is David Wilson.—G.S.)

some extent Mexico began its industrialization under the influence of socialist ideas, and the upheavals in Europe and the United States permitted it to continue its development without much outside interference. Since the people became wiser and wiser in assimilating industry to their own character and needs, there was no such frantic scramble to raise the standard of living as took place in the seventies and eighties in the United States. Efficiency has never been regarded as the highest virtue in Mexico, and is not today. Most cooperatives prefer six hours of leisurely to four of intensive labor. Agriculture has been mechanized so far as the major cooperative units are concerned, but agricultural workers still hold tracts of their own, which they cultivate according to their own tastes. Everywhere you find the old and the new blended together, oxen and tractors plowing almost side by side, women in machine-molded slacks or shorts weaving blankets in traditional Aztec designs, modern automobiles parked in front of adobe houses.

After the strenuous days I had spent in New Orleans and Birmingham, Mexico City was agreeably restful. It is the most fascinating city I visited. Along its great squares and wide streets, which still empty at the hour of the siesta and fill again towards evening, the low, spacious buildings are bright and airy. Shops open on the street, and the windows are gay. Public buildings are more ornate than any I have seen in the United States.

With Camilla and Luis Azada, to whom Nathalie had given me an introduction—I think they are second cousins of hers—I walked or drove about the city, stopping for a drink at sidewalk cafes, visiting museums, looking in at theaters

THE FIRST TO AWAKEN

and music halls. They took me to see the cooperative factories and apartment houses and anything else I wanted to look at, but they did not wear me out with sight-seeing. In fact, they were constantly urging me to relax, and I found it easy to sit in their garden and look at Popocatepetl and dream. I do not wonder that so many northerners visit Mexico every year.

More than once I was a little embarrassed at knowing no language but English, not because I needed other languages but because I seemed so much more ignorant than the Mexicans, who could speak my tongue. As I discovered, one can very comfortably travel around the world even if English is the only language he speaks, but most people know two or three of the basic languages in addition to their own. With the basic languages one can conduct any kind of business, take part in scholarly deliberations anywhere in the world, and carry on a conversation with almost the first person he meets in the streets of Shanghai, Murmansk, or Addis Ababa.

Knowing that Wichita was the center of the continental planning boards, I rather expected it to be like the Washington of my day, only, of course, in better taste, and, as the plane from Mexico City dropped to the airport, I was disappointed to find that it looked like any other medium-sized city, with office buildings and apartment houses of the simplest functional type. I recalled something Simeon once said: "The old state sought both to intimidate and flatter the citizen by a display of grandeur. The new machinery of group administration is—machinery." Wichita wasn't very impressive, and I soon lost the romantic notion that this was the spot on which the destinies of the continent were settled. Vast as the coordinating agencies are that have their center here, it is the local cooperative that is the significant unit. The planners do not command; they obey; at most they recommend.

Elsie and I had often talked of going to Yellowstone Park and the Grand Canyon, as well as to Niagara Falls, and I visited them both, with considerable satisfaction. Nor was I the only one who found them worth visiting, for I encountered plenty of tourists. Most of them were traveling by automobile, and one young couple, with whom I went horseback riding at Yellowstone, were scornful of my using planes. They painted such an attractive picture of their trip that I made up my mind that another year I would really see the country.

Chiefly because Abraham had urged me to, I stopped near Tucson to see the rocket station, where the three hundred and something attempt was being made to reach the moon. I had no idea that the rocket itself was so large or that the preparations had to be so elaborate. There was no use in my trying to understand the technical problems involved, but I marveled at everything, and meantime studied with some amusement the men who were so wrapped up in this experiment. They tried to tell me of the advantages that would result, but I could see that actually they were driven by the idea of doing something that had never been done before. The idea, moreover, had a wide appeal, for funds were provided by voluntary contributions, which came from all over the world. The actual release of the rocket, which I and several thousand other people had hoped to watch, was postponed, and I was in China when I learned that there had been another failure.

Hollywood was another place that Elsie and I had always wanted to visit, but there was no Hollywood now. As a whole, however, California was no disappointment. It is such a rich and populous state. San Francisco, which was built at about the same time as New York, is almost as large as that city and even richer in ingenious gadgets. David would disapprove, and I was less enthusiastic than I might once have been, but it is a staggering as well as a lovely city.

In spite of everything that has been done to offset the disadvantages of the New England climate, life in California is easier and fuller, and I can understand why so many people choose to live there. Yet I prefer the deep, fresh green of a New England spring to the luxuriance of the Coast, and I would not willingly choose never to know another New England winter. Fortunately other people feel as I do. The migration to California ended many decades ago, as life became better organized in less favored regions, and an occasional visit seems sufficient.

For the first time in my life I had crossed the continent, and, though I knew how little of it I had actually seen, I was rather pleased with myself. It seemed good in a way to be traveling in space, for most of the time I simply forgot that I had been asleep for a hundred years and took in new impressions as any traveler might do. It was, for example, no more phenomenal for me to be boarding a gymbal plane, which I did for the first time at San Francisco, than it would have been for me to take passage on a luxury liner in my own day. I was a little nervous, but simply because I didn't know my way round, and after we had risen into the stratosphere, I fell asleep.

I liked the Hawaiian Islands, as almost everyone does, and I was glad to spend five days there. Though the islands have long been independent, there are still close ties to the United

Moon Rocket, Tucson, S. W. D.

States, and English is the predominant language. The Hawaiians, even more than the Mexicans, take life easy, and I could gather that life today is nearer to what it was before the coming of the white man than to what it was in my day. In Mexico the people are determined to keep the machines in their place, but in Hawaii they just don't care, and why should they? Electrical power is produced in abundance, but it is used for domestic rather than industrial purposes. There are some factories, but it is not easy to get people to work in them, even when large bonuses are paid. Horses are used more than automobiles, and on some of the islands there are no roads on which a car could travel.

I was discussing this with a man I met on the beach, and he said, "Ah, yes, but you ought to go to Tahiti or Samoa or some place like that. I spent six years on one of the Friendly Islands, and I'd be there yet except that my wife couldn't stand it. This is our compromise."

According to him, the South Sea Islands, never more than

superficially touched by civilization, were left almost completely alone during the later phases of the European wars and revolutions. A polyglot population drifted there and found life pleasant, even threatening to fight when the representatives of the world planning boards finally got around to visiting them. The planners at that stage of their work fretted and fumed, but there was no possibility of using force, and the islanders were left alone. "It's marvelous," my acquaintance said. "You plant a little garden if you want to, fish a little if you feel like it, and that's all there is to it."

His wife, who joined us, told a different story. On their island there had been no doctor, though there was one on a neighboring island who came by motorboat—old and given to breakdowns—when word could be got to him. There were no schools for the children, the food grew monotonous, there was nothing to read and nothing to talk about.

The husband shrugged his shoulders. "What I don't understand," he said, "is why everybody in the world doesn't want to go there. In fact, some of the islands have had to restrict immigration. Beautiful climate; food lying around for the asking; clothes unnecessary. Lord, I'd like to go back."

Most of the islands could be reached only by boat, and, much as I was tempted, I did not want to prolong my trip. Instead, I took the gymbal plane to Melbourne as I had planned. Simeon had talked to me a great deal about Australia, for he had had a share in the reclaiming of its deserts. After its brief fascist phase, the continent had attracted the more energetic Englishman and an organized attack upon its resources had soon made it one of the richest areas on the globe. Because the development took place under socialist conditions, there had been no wasting of power, fuel, and minerals, but everything had been made to contribute to the growth of a balanced, efficient economy. Where once there were only the few great cities along the coast, now there are hundreds of busy communities in the interior, and patriotic Australians insisted on my visiting some of them. Though I was later to see instances quite as striking, this was my first observation of socialism on the frontier, so to speak, and I found it exciting.

I have said little about the persons I was meeting from day to day, for it would take many volumes to do them justice. They were, I scarcely need say, of all kinds, good tempered and bad, thoughtful and inconsiderate, interested and bored. I told my own story again and again, not only because most people wanted to hear it but also, as I have said, because that was the best way of making them understand what I wanted to know. Most of them were kind, and I wish I could express my gratitude to all the hundreds of new friends I made.

But I must say something about John Ling, the young Chinese with whom I became acquainted on the flight from Melbourne to Canton. There was an interesting group of passengers: two professors from the University of Brisbane, bound for the University of Lassa in Tibet; an official of the world bureau of mines, a Russian returning to his office in Siberia; seven or eight students of as many different nationalities; and a dozen others with whom I did not become acquainted.

Then there was John Ling, who, in the breeziest manner possible, came and sat beside me at dinner, told me he knew who I was, and delivered a lecture on China. He was twenty-four or five, had studied in America and in Europe, and told me that he was on his way to becoming the world's leading authority on radium-bearing minerals. China, he said, was the greatest country on earth. "It is lucky for you that the old days of conquest are gone, for we could rule the world—if we wanted to."

A little irritated, though chiefly amused, I said, "What do the Japanese think about that?"

"The Japanese? Who are they? They conquered our country, but we absorbed them, and one day there was no more Japan. But there is always China. Do you realize how many

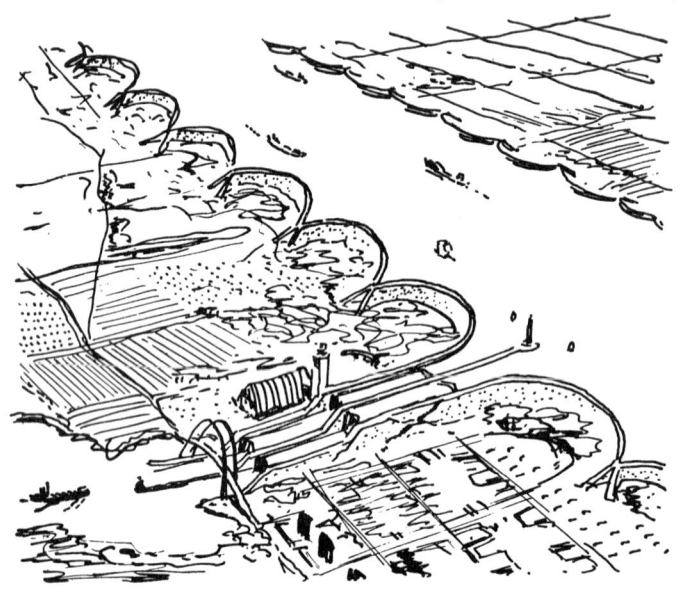

Yangste River Flood Control. The plan for elevating the river above the surrounding countryside was made by Simeon Blake.

of the great inventions were made in China? We laid the foundation for the industrial revolution centuries before it happened."

"Nevertheless, it happened in Europe and America, and had to be exported to China."

"An accident of history. This was the country to which industry belonged, and now we have proven it. Wait till you see our cities, Mr. Swain—the largest, the most modern, the best lighted, the most beautiful in the world. Why, in New York there are a few blocks under glass, but in Shanghai every apartment house has a protected courtyard, the smallest of which is sixty acres."

I was taken aback, but, as I later learned, he was not exaggerating. "Why shouldn't we be the greatest industrial nation?" he challenged me. "We have the resources and the manpower. Ah, manpower. Did you ever read about the poor, patient, plodding, fatalistic coolie, who would live on a few handfuls of rice and work like a horse? Well, he doesn't live on rice any more; he lives well; but he still works like a horse. We're all coolies now; we all work like that. In America the four-hour day and talk about three hours. In China the eight-hour day, and you can't drive the men away from the factories. You think things are happening in Australia, but wait till you see China."

John was so enthusiastic that he insisted on acting as my guide in Canton, and then accompanied me to Shanghai, Hankow, and Peking. Always he was at my elbow, singing China's praises, and I couldn't dislike him. Nor could I dislike China. Having lived for some months in a society that was beginning to regard mechanical efficiency merely as a means,

THE FIRST TO AWAKEN

I found China bewildering, exhausting, and terribly alive. Whatever is produced elsewhere in the world is immediately duplicated by the Chinese. They have longer and wider and faster beam highways than the United States, larger units of agricultural production than Australia, more airplanes than the whole of Europe. Every factory is equipped with the latest machinery. The machinery, by the way, is silent, but the factories are noisy because work is performed to the constant blasting of loudspeakers. Skyscrapers stretch floors above the Empire State, and there are restaurants that can serve twenty thousand persons at a time. Rivers have been changed in their courses, the Desert of Gobi has been made to blossom, and engineers are smashing at the Himalayas to change the climate of the interior provinces.

John regretfully left me at Peking, for he was headed for Gobi, and I flew back by way of some of the anshrel cities of the interior. Everywhere life is on the move. At the universities I saw some of the millions of young people who are eagerly preparing themselves for their tasks, and I heard children in the nursery schools taught that they must be ready to contribute to the great destiny of the Chinese people. John Ling was right: after centuries of misery, the Chinese finally discovered the machine, and they are still intoxicated by the discovery.

I flew from Yunnan to Calcutta and thence to Lucknow, Delhi, and Lahore, and back to Bombay. Brought up as I was, I knew of India only what I had read in Kipling's stories. Kipling was, I know, a thoroughgoing imperialist, full of talk about the white man's burden, and if I had ever had any notions about the supremacy of the white race, I should have lost them by this time. Yet the vividness of Kipling's descriptions had left its mark on my mind, and it was his India I was looking for. I saw something of it, too. Many people still traveled by foot, and, much as times had changed, the throngs on the highways reminded me of *Kim*. Native costumes survived, and one could pick out tarbush, turban or khoka. I saw water buffalo, elephants a-piling teak, oxen in the fields. I visited mosques and temples and tombs, was taken by efficient guides through rajahs' palaces, and witnessed the beginning of a tiger hunt.

India has had a long struggle. After British rule collapsed, the rival sects and races and parties fought among themselves, and the country broke up into many small districts. Around most of the larger cities the beginnings of a socialist economy were established, but these communities were constantly harassed, and it was almost all they could do to survive. The rural population was devastated by famines, plagues, and religious wars, and it was not until the World Council of Socialist Republics was finally created that anything like order was achieved. The council proceeded cautiously, for the peoples of India, like the other peoples of the world, were very much afraid of tyranny and unwilling to sacrifice any of their independence. However, through famine relief and the furnishing of supplies for reconstruction, the council encouraged the spread of socialist order, and at last peace was achieved.

This was not much more than thirty years ago, and the three decades have given time only for the most elementary kind of rebuilding. Although some of the cities are developing the new type of planned industrial organization, the chief effort is still simply to raise the general standard of living. The aims are scientific agriculture, safe and sanitary factories, decent housing, universal literacy, and adequate medical care. A more highly industrialized civilization, for which India has all the natural resources, will probably follow, but that is in the future.

In one thing India has continued to excel all through its difficult decades: its universities are its greatest pride. Not only in philology and history but also in the physical sciences their faculties are world famous, and the Indian student looks with some contempt on his European or American colleague.

Perhaps China had worn me out. In any case I felt below par most of the time I was in India, and I was not sorry to be on my way to the West. I changed planes at Addis Ababa, and, having sympathized with the Ethiopians in their struggle against Italy, I was glad to see the grandeur of the old capital. I went on to Egypt, of course, to see the pyramids. For a time I was vaguely disappointed, and I could not understand why, but then I realized that in all the pictures I had ever seen they were surrounded by sand, and now they were in the midst of green fields with trees all about them and vines running up the sides.

Of the Sahara there is little enough to say except that it is a rich and fertile region, with a large and apparently prosperous population. The Bedouin has become agricultural and industrial, and camels are for the most part seen only in zoos. It is magnificent but not romantic.

There was a young engineer at the city of Abd-el-Krim who urged me to go with him into the Kamerun Mountains. "You're taking too soft a trip," he told me. "There's still adventure left in the world. Why don't you see some of it?"

He talked well about the history of Africa. Emancipated by the revolutions in Europe, the more advanced colonies made rapid progress, but the backward areas relapsed into barbarism. Many Europeans believed that the Council of Socialist Republics ought to use its police force to civilize the natives, and the problem was complicated by the discovery in some of the barbarian areas of minerals the industrialized world very much wanted. In the Kamerun Mountains, for example, was a great deposit of beserium, the essential element in the alloy that gives building materials a uniform coefficient of expansion. The old arguments for imperialism were raised, and it was said—truthfully according to the engineer—that the people would be happier under an enlightened foreign administration than they were under their own chiefs. The decision finally was reached that emissaries should be sent to try to persuade the inhabitants to accept the council's representatives. The engineer said with a wink that, surprisingly enough, those areas with valuable minerals had all accepted the offer, whereas most of those that had no such resources had stubbornly clung to their own rulers. I suppose it was bound to happen that way, but I am glad that there was at least a gesture of idealism. There are areas in Africa—and in Asia and South America as well—where people can be as primitive as they choose. I suppose they won't survive indefinitely, and probably it is mere sentimentality to give any encouragement to ignorance, superstition, and cruelty, but it is better for us to have to try persuasion and kindness rather than to rely on force.

South Africa, the engineer said, has had a strange history.

Both gold and diamonds lost their value after the revolutions, and, despite efforts to increase their use in industry, the mines were closed down. There was much suffering, but in time a varied industry was established and a mechanized agriculture, and South Africa prospered once more. Then, just at the end of the century, rich lodes of uranium minerals were discovered, and the emphasis again fell on mining. This time, however, they managed to avoid the disorganization of a boom, and, though the economy is unbalanced, it is not dangerously dependent on the mines.

From Carthage, once more a great city and a major port, I took a plane to Italy. Here I realized for the first time the difficulty of reconciling a proper regard for the monuments of the past with concern for a satisfactory life in the present. Europe, too, had its technological era, when the engineers were all for efficiency at any cost, but the Italians, proud of their history, had fortunately resisted the new vandalism. The people had simply insisted that the engineers must find a way to give them all the benefits of industry without destroying the ancient structures, and enlightened opinion throughout the world backed them up. It took some ingenuity, and many problems have never been satisfactorily solved, but at least the old Italy, the Italy I had come to see, is still there.

I visited Naples, Rome, Florence, and the other principal cities, and turned myself for a time into an old-fashioned sight-seer. And what wearisome business that is! But exciting business, too, and rewarding.

I was in Rome for two holidays, one religious and the other secular. With thousands of other tourists and spectators, I went to the Vatican to watch the solemn procession. There did not seem to be many of the devout, but they went through the old ritual with sincerity and dignity, and at moments I was deeply moved. Since the schisms of the mid-century, when many Catholics broke with the Vatican because it was so unpleasantly involved in secular politics, the popes have set a model of simple piety and scholarship. Despite their attacks on the growth of paganism, which naturally dismays them, Catholics do not quarrel with the cooperative socialism of modern society, and, though they are a dwindling band, they are not without honor and respect either in Italy or elsewhere.

The celebration of the anniversary of the overthrow of fascism was more colorful and more popular. Great throngs marched to the Monte Avetino, bearing banners with pictures of Garibaldi, Matteotti, Garino, and other revolutionary heroes. There were mass gymnastic demonstrations, speeches, and songs, followed by the most elaborate and the noisiest display of fireworks I have ever suffered through.

After the fireworks the crowd broke away from the field, cheering and shouting, and somehow I found myself caught up in the hilarious mass and pushed along in the direction of the Coliseum. A little frightened, I tried to escape, and elbowed my way, despite good-natured protests, until I reached the outskirts of the throng. I saw a doorway just ahead, and, when a new surge of the crowd brought me close to it, I made a jump, ran up the three or four steps, stumbled, twisted my ankle, and almost fell.

There was a voice speaking Italian, and I looked up to see a young woman smiling at me. "Oh, you're English," she said, "no, American. Are you hurt?"

THE FIRST TO AWAKEN

Rubbing my ankle, I said I thought not, but I could not bear my weight on the foot. "Just wait till the crowd goes by," she urged, and we both sat down on the steps. She was an American, too; yes, and she came from the Northeast District. And from Braxton! I placed her; she was the Bensons' oldest daughter, who was studying archaeology in Rome. And she placed me. We sat and talked about the town and all its people until suddenly I noticed that the streets were bare. In no time she had found a service car and taken me to my hostelry, where she insisted on the doctor's coming to look at my ankle. He strapped it up, and Mary promised to visit me the next day.

She was a first-rate guide, and she drove me through the city and the suburbs and taught me more of ancient history than I had ever expected to learn. Just this personal touch, I realized, was what I had been craving, and perhaps I exaggerated my lameness in order to be babied.

Mary was going to Greece in a few days, and I postponed my departure in order to go with her. We took the tourists' low-flying plane, with transparent bottom and sides, and, though I was nervous and a little squeamish at first, it was a beautiful trip.

As we flew over Athens, however, I looked at Mary in amazement, and she burst out laughing. No one had told me that it was a city of skyscrapers, that one of its principal groups of buildings had been modeled upon Radio City. I knew, of course, that the Balkan Republic had had a great boom in the twenty-first century, but I did not know what the boom had done to the life of the country.

"It's the greatest architectural joke of the age," Mary said.

"For hundreds of years the architects of western Europe and America couldn't get away from the building designs of the ancient Greeks, and now the modern Greeks borrow from us."

They had borrowed more than our architecture, I discovered, for George F. Babbitt would have found congenial spirits in Athens, Sofia, and Bucharest, though, having no real estate to sell, these Balkan Babbitts could not be quite so objectionable as their prototype. I paid little attention to them, however, for Mary was willing to continue her lectures on ancient history.

I did allow myself, against my better judgment, to be taken to a meeting of an antiquarian society in Sofia. The rooms were full of the most hideous stuff I have ever seen, and it was only with some difficulty and considerable chagrin that I identified the chrome pipe chairs, skyscraper bookcases, and grotesque lamps as products of the nineteen twenties and thirties. My attitude infuriated the curator until Mary explained that I was objecting to the ugliness of the articles. Then he brightened up. Of course they were ugly. That was why he and his colleagues collected them. But they were so significant! And didn't I have to admit that there was a strange charm—yes, he would even say beauty—in their very grotesqueness? By that time I was ready to admit anything, but my visit, from the society's point of view as well as my own, was a horrible failure.

Mary was so friendly and helpful, and reminded me so strongly of the people I knew and liked at home, that I hated to leave her, but I was already behind schedule, and, bearing messages from her to her family and friends, I took the plane to Odessa and thence to Moscow. I felt at home in Russia.

THE FIRST TO AWAKEN

It is a big country, like my own, and it seems in about the same stage of development. Its industrial revolution began later than ours but moved faster, and Russia, like the United States, has had its era of technology and recovered from it. People put in their four hours a day efficiently and then proceed to enjoy life. The inhabitants still feel a deep pride in theirs having been the first nation to adopt socialism, admitting the shortcomings and mistakes of the early decades but boasting of the achievements. I had never said harsher words about the Soviet Union of my day than I heard in Moscow and Leningrad classrooms, but the heroes of the revolution are everywhere honored.

Everyone in Moscow and Leningrad urged me to visit some of the new cities in Siberia, but I was growing weary of travel, and I went on to Berlin. I liked Germany, too. I could never reconcile the horrors of fascism with the peaceful, home-loving, philosophical Germans of my acquaintance, nor do I understand to this day how such a people fell victim to Hitler's savage demagogy. But the Germans I met in Vienna, Munich, Berlin, and Leipzig were like the Millers and Keimses and Steubens I had known in Braxton. They, too, had mastered the machine long since. The old word that Dr. Carr occasionally used, Gemütlichkeit, took on a new meaning for me.

In Leipzig I went to call on the Barths, a family I had met in Shanghai. They were getting ready to take a leisurely boat trip on the Rhine, and finally succeeded in persuading me to join them. There is no sense in my trying to talk about the beauties of the Rhine or about the pleasures of a cruise after travel by plane. I liked the Barths, and I was glad to have a chance to talk with Herr Barth because, as a member of a world committee on population problems, he knew all about the long history of struggles between nationalist groups.

At first every group, however small, was granted the fullest cultural autonomy, and then, as the socialist organization of production and distribution made decentralization possible, economic regions were established to suit the traditions and language of the inhabitants. But, as the old nationalist demands were satisfied, they became less urgent, and regions were frequently reorganized on a more rational basis of geography and economic resources, and national boundaries lost their importance. In certain areas—notably the Basque Country, the Macedonian district, and the North of Ireland—patriots still make propaganda against this tendency, but their cause is hopeless.

Herr Barth lectured me on national characteristics. They exist, he said, because different areas have gone through different developments, but one talks about them only with the greatest caution. The Balkans, for example, show the effects of a comparatively recent industrial expansion. Scandinavia has had a long tradition of cooperation. Italy has its past kept constantly before its eyes. But these differences are purely historical, and the old racial theories have been banished along with other superstitions.

I left the Barths and went on into France. Aside from the obvious things in Paris, I remember chiefly the hospital, for I was sick there. The doctors, who of course knew all about me, were delighted to get me in their hands, and they had a field day, but they did cure me, and they made me very comfortable while I was in bed. The illness was reported in the

THE FIRST TO AWAKEN

Braxton bulletin, and Simeon immediately radioed half a dozen of his friends, who came and amused me and took me around the city when I was well.

Lying in bed, I thought about my trip. I realized that even in my day a traveler might cover thousands of miles and never see anything to criticize. But I had done what snooping I could, and I had never seen anything worse than a street fight or a bunch of boys hooting at a drunk. There were no signs of poverty, no slums, no beggars, no people in rags. I remembered what a labor leader said just before I went to sleep: "Give every man a decent job at decent pay, and we'll be on the way to solving all our problems." It wasn't quite so simple as that, but fundamentally he had been right.

Whatever else might be true, the economic system did work. I have given no idea of the variety of economic organizations I encountered. I have simply tried to distinguish between unindustrialized areas, those in the process of industrialization, and those that have, in a sense, completed the process. It would be pointless for me to try to state just what proportion of production is socialized in each region, where and to what extent and how a free market is maintained, how cooperatives are organized in various parts of the world, and what forms of political and economic control are maintained. It is enough to say that decentralization, which has been made practical through the progress of science and the consequent perfection of synthetic substances, has reduced the necessity for control on a continental or world scale. There are, to be sure, many planning boards and bureaus concerned with the larger areas, and sometimes they exert a degree of pressure, but they have pretty well learned from fifty or sixty years of

ADVENTURES OF A GLOBE TROTTER

experience how to reconcile the interests of the different sections. I don't mean to say that there is no conflict, but there is an adequate machinery for dealing with whatever conflicts arise.

All of this was brought home to me when I arrived in London. England, to put the matter briefly, has become a museum. In the later stages of the wars and revolutions, when the Empire had fallen apart, British industry disintegrated, and there was mass emigration. The remaining population adopted a kind of socialism—a most British kind—which persists. Parliament still rules—House of Lords and all—and there is still a king. The people support themselves by farming or fishing and by the tourist trade.

London is an extraordinary city. Forty years ago, when the population was already less than a million, a law was passed that every building built since 1776 must be destroyed unless the necessity for its preservation could be demonstrated in a court of law. Such building as has been done since is in the Georgian or Tudor style, and the architects and builders are very skillful. The city is beautiful in its own antiquarian way, but to my tastes dreadfully uncomfortable.

One of the most amazing things is that there are a handful of families still living in bombproof shelters. Their grandfathers and great-grandfathers got used to these underground homes during the days when London was in constant fear of raids, and the descendants have gone on inhabiting them. Many people disapprove, on the ground that, being products of the twentieth century, the shelters ought not to be preserved, but they are inconspicuous, and by now they have a certain quaintness of their own that justifies them.

Tourist Cruiser, Liverpool, England

The rural areas are organized according to a plan that friends of mine described as essentially Tory socialist. That is to say, counties and towns are nominally ruled over by hereditary lords and squires, who are expected to keep up the old traditions. The real administrators, however, are the elected representatives of the cooperatives. So perfect is the agreement as to the desired way of life that there is no conflict.

Without the influx of tourists the economy could not possibly be sustained, but, thanks to tourist credits, the regions are able to import whatever they need to supplement their own produce. There are, of course, strange paradoxes, for the country has not been completely untouched by the progress of science, but little machinery is tolerated. Even the number of tourists to be admitted at any one time is limited, lest an excess of foreigners disrupt the national life.

For the tourist it is a paradise, a constant pilgrimage from one historical or literary shrine to another, with nothing to distract the attention. I did a pretty thorough job—London, Oxford, which has gone back to the seventeenth century curriculum, Stratford, the Lake Country, the Scottish Highlands, and all the rest of it. If the English had their way, travel would probably be by stagecoach, but the wishes of the tourists have to be consulted, and there are fast, comfortable busses. I did not see all I wanted to see, but I saw all that I could take in.

I tried to talk with some of the Englishmen I encountered, but it was hopeless. Even when I pointed out that I had been born in the nineteenth century, they persisted in regarding me as a parvenu. The tourists, on the other hand, most of them from the United States and the other English-speaking countries were a friendly lot, well-informed, eager, and often amused at what seemed to be the consciously archaic ways of the natives. We sometimes sang or played games in the busses, and I had many pleasant talks with fellow-countrymen.

Back in London, I tried to make up my mind what to do next. Friends urged me to visit Iceland and Spain and Finland and Palestine and South Africa, but I wanted to go home. It seemed to me that I had been footloose long enough, and I doubted if I was capable of digesting any more new impressions. Suddenly I decided to telephone David. I had been surprised when he called me in the hospital in Paris, and I had never used one of the calls to which, as a traveling student, I was entitled. Now it seemed foolish not to avail myself of my privileges, and I put the call through at once.

I got him at his office, asked him about himself and his

family and my other friends, and then told him what was troubling me. He said, "Well, for heaven's sake, come home then. You can go again, you know."

That settled it. But first, on another impulse, I went back to France to visit the battlefield of Château-Thierry. The caretaker of the cemetery was in his nineties, and he, too, had fought near that site, though in another and even deadlier war. We talked for a long time—about war and progress and human nature and his friends and my friends, the dead and the living. Then I took a gymbal plane for Boston.

XIII

HAIL AND FAREWELL

THOUGH I had seen thousands of communities not unlike Braxton, I could recognize the outlines of the town from the air—the way it lay along the river, the shape of its hills, the position of its buildings, the flow of its roads. This was home.

I had been round the world, and, though the trip had been orderly enough, it had not been without its adventures. I had seen many countries, talked with many people, eaten strange foods, looked at the great monuments of the past and the present. I knew more now about the world of 2040 than I had known of the world in which I was born. As I slipped on my jacket, I examined myself in the mirror. Yes, the tall, thin man with the brown and gray beard, with the deep-set, puzzled brown eyes, looked like a traveler. His shoulders were a little stooped, but he held his head well, and the eyes had a sparkle in them.

I had half expected David to be at the airport, but I had not expected the little delegation—David and Nathalie, the whole Waldman family, and half a dozen other friends. Roberta threw her arms around me and kissed me, and Agnes followed her example.

They were full of questions as we drove to the Waldman house under the beautiful foliage of a New England autumn. Agnes had cooked dinner for the whole crowd, and, as Victor leaned back and lit his pipe, he said, "There, I bet you haven't had a meal like that all the time you've been gone!"

In the living room we sat with the half-light coming in on us through the scarlet leaves. There had been meals, I could have told them, as good as Agnes' dinner, but no room quite like that room.

On their insisting, I began to tell my story, but there were so many interruptions that my travelogue never got beyond Niagara Falls. They were not interested in the world but in me. Even Nathalie seemed pleased to have me back.

I asked about Simeon Blake, and they told me that he was away for a few days at a conference in Pittsburgh. There was other news: who had had babies and of what sex; the honors Timothy had won at Harvard; a new record established in the canoe regatta; a serious accident on the Blaine farm; the death of my old friend, the caretaker of the children's playground; and a number of marriages. Nathalie had made some important contribution to the science of statistics, and David was getting on well with his study of the Swain case. Margaret Bryan, who had been invited to read a paper to a teachers' conference, asked me if I would look at it. Roberta had spent a month at a girls' camp and boasted of being able to swim half a mile and tie thirty-two knots. Abraham, who had worked for six weeks on a fishing schooner, looked stronger and more mature.

Affairs in the cooperative were about as usual. Lister was doing good work in the experimental station and saying privately that, even with the meager resources he had, he would produce revolutionary results. The specialists in agricultural pathology had been in a dither over a strange blight on potatoes, and a new design for snowshoes was causing trouble at the factory. The committee to study other cooperatives, which had not yet brought in its report, was being criticized for its slowness. Delbert, the sculptor who was doing the relief on the facade of the new primary school, had fallen from the scaffold, and though his assistants were going on with the work, the dedication had had to be postponed.

It was good to hear all this talk of trivial, intimate things, which interested me more at the moment than problems of world policy. Those problems, of course, came in for their share of discussion, and I was asked my opinion on what was happening all over the globe, but we constantly came back to Braxton and its affairs.

That evening, after all the guests were gone, I was trying to organize the notes I had taken on the trip. Victor, who had been out to take a last look at his greenhouse, came and stood in the doorway a moment. "Seem good to be home?"

"It's swell." He said good night, and I began to get ready for bed. I felt relaxed. There was no more struggling to assimilate new impressions, no more striving to grasp strange concepts. I was back where I belonged. That was the phrase I used to myself, and it startled me so that I sat down on the edge of the bed. It was true: I belonged.

The next few days were busy. David had left a little pile of pamphlets and books and magazines for me to read; Roberta insisted on my visiting her school; Victor wanted me to see a new machine; on an unseasonably warm evening the Wilsons took me for a picnic. But the pleasantest moment was when I heard Simeon Blake's voice. Just arrived, he came over for an early morning walk. "It's good to have you back, George," he said. "I'm old enough not to like to have friends too long out of my sight."

We started along our favorite route, up the hill and along the ridge back of the hospital to the woods. "Did you enjoy it?" he asked. "Did you really have a good time?"

"Marvelous, but I can't tell you how glad I am to be home."

"That's fine. Learn a lot?"

"Mostly how ignorant I am. Sure, I learned a lot."

"People pretty good to you, George?"

"Splendid, most of them. Answered all my fool questions and took good care of me. Your name worked wonders all over the place."

"You once asked me if the world wasn't finished? What do you think now? Still plenty to be done, eh?"

"More than I dreamed."

"That's the beginning of wisdom. Did you ever read any of the utopias—you know, Morris and Bellamy and Wells and the rest of them?"

"I've read *Looking Backward* and *News from Nowhere.*"

"The trouble with the utopians is that they tried to produce a finished system. They had it all figured out—pulled the perfect society right out of their own skulls. There is no perfect society."

HAIL AND FAREWELL

"But there are better and worse societies," I said staunchly.

"Oh, right; quite right. No question about that."

"Somebody or other said, I forget who, that if his lifetime of effort brought socialism ten minutes nearer, he would be satisfied. I think Bellamy and Morris helped, just a little. Even you can't realize the paralysis that overcame people a hundred years ago. If they had only had a vision of the kind of world they could build out of the materials that were lying all round them, you'd have had a cooperative society, not ten minutes sooner but a generation sooner. The world might have been spared two or three of the most miserable decades mankind has ever spent. I know men can't run ahead of history, but we were running behind history. Everything was ready for change and we didn't know it."

Simeon stopped to talk to a tractor driver who was harvesting corn. "What ever happened to the stone fences?" I asked as we went on.

"They went into roadbeds or foundations years ago, and the woodchucks went back to the tree roots. So you think people needed a vision of what was possible?"

"Didn't they? Tell me, do you believe that change had to come the hard way, with war and revolution and bloodshed? Wasn't there an alternative?"

"Apparently not. You can't argue with history, George. People had to be thoroughly fed-up, made utterly and intolerably miserable, before they would act. That's the way it happened, you know."

I did know it, but I thought I had a point, and I tried to find a way of stating it. "It's easy to say that now," I finally said, "but put yourself back a hundred years. Speaking as of 1940, would you still say there could be no choice, no possibility of a sensible, peaceful, intelligent reconstruction of society?"

As usual when he grew interested in the conversation, he quickened his steps. "That's different. History makes man, but man also makes history. There used to be a saying, you can't make a silk purse out of a sow's ear, but of course you can if you know how. We say that the kind of people who were living in America in 1940 were bound to go through the upheavals of the fifties. And that, as you justly point out, is what we have to say after the event. But suppose we ask ourselves how the situation would have had to be altered to make a different outcome possible. That's what you're driving at. If people had been only very slightly different—and for all we know, the right kind of political leader or the right kind of book might have done the trick—then it's easy to imagine a quite orderly reorganizing of the social processes. A scientist discovers something about the world that changes man's relationship to it, and that in turn changes the world. That might have happened in the field of social policy. In a sense it did happen, for our revolution would have been as bloody as any in Europe if we had not learned from Europe's experience."

"Then if you had been living in 1940, you would have tried to make people see that change was desirable and possible."

"If I had seen it myself."

"And of course you would have."

I was panting now, for we were climbing, and I stopped to look down into the valley. There is nothing in the world, to me, lovelier than our New England autumns. A sheep came and stared at us as we sat on the rocky ledge. "I suppose," said Simeon, "you have made your case for utopias, though I don't put much stock in that kind of political astrology. Either the author or reader would have been foolish to take the details seriously. Who would venture to guess what Braxton will be like a century from now? Not I. Yet I dare say the character of change is more predictable now than it used to be."

"I don't suppose anybody did take the details seriously," I persisted. "It was just the idea that mattered, the idea that men didn't have to be slaves."

He kicked a pebble so that it rolled down the slope and the sheep went back in disgust to join the flock. "I wouldn't guess about Braxton a hundred years from now," I said after a little silence, "but I can't help wondering. Do you imagine people will be happier?"

He leaned back on his arms. "Happiness? You have said yourself that nothing is harder to measure. Do you know why? Happiness is the foam on the crest of a breaking wave. It's a by-product. It's the mark of an achievement, not the achievement itself. We could make everybody in the world perfectly happy. With drugs, my boy. Drugs that are well known. They make you think you are a pretty splendid person and everybody else is just as good. There is no hangover and no let-down. But would you suggest that all we have to do to achieve utopia is to turn out these drugs in sufficiently large quantities so that everyone would be constantly under their influence? It's one way perhaps, but I'd just as soon let loose a blast of lethal gas that would painlessly wipe out the human race. How about it? Would you exchange weeks of such bliss for the moment that came when you found your friends at the airport the other day? No, George, you don't get anywhere talking about happiness."

I lay back and felt the sunshine on my whole body through the summer fabric. "Our problems weigh upon us as much as yours weighed upon you," he went on. "I don't deny that we have a greater chance for happiness, for that would be silly. There is a story that turns up in some book of memoirs. A college president, traveling through the South in the thirties, said, 'I wonder if the poorest of these sharecroppers is not a happier man than I.' His companion replied, 'If a starving man can be as happy as a well-fed one, you're probably right.' You see, the college president had never known what it means to go without food, whereas he knew all too well the worries of administering a great university. His problems were more complicated than the sharecropper's, and therefore he felt that he was the less happy person. Yet, if he had suddenly been put in the sharecropper's position, he would have known degrees of misery that he had never dreamed of. It does him no great credit, by the way, that he couldn't see this. You would expect the sharecropper to suppose he would be perfectly happy in the president's shoes, but an educator ought to have a little more imagination.

"We are all given to talking about the happiness of children, forgetting that their worries are as urgent as our own, trivial as they seem to us. Don't misunderstand me, George. I am not saying that the gains of the last century—or the last ten thousand years—are inconsiderable. I don't agree with that young whippersnapper who spoke with you at the symposium. But you mustn't let this happiness business confuse you. A man who is being tortured will find happiness in the cessation of the torture, but an hour later he will be thoroughly miserable because his stomach is empty. Fill his stomach and he will be unhappy because he is not free. Free him and he will worry about the state of his health. Cure him and he may agonize because he can't get the last line of a sonnet. My point is simply that you can't apply a subjective test. The man who is fretting over a line of poetry will be convinced that he suffers as much as the man in torture. But of course we know that it is better, from the point of view of civilization, for men to be worrying about poetry—or about the conquest of knowledge or the organization of society—than for them to be worrying about their bellies and their jobs."

As we got up and took the path into the forest, I said, "I still believe that there are more happy people than there were a hundred years ago. There are conditions under which happiness is simply impossible."

"I wonder."

"Yes, there are. Conditions of the man himself. You don't know how many men and women got warped and twisted by the society I grew up in. I don't mean merely the jobless and the underfed. I'm talking about men and women in my own class. Liars, toadies, bullies. That strike I've talked about so much; I can't make you see what I learned from it. A minister perjuring himself in his pulpit; an editor giving out orders for lies and more lies; a doctor betraying his sacred oath. How they must have hated themselves and all humanity. There was a little fellow who worked in the bank, and he was so gentle that his wife had to drown the kittens their cat was always having. Yet he was there with a club, and he hit a girl who worked in the union office. What do you suppose that did to the rest of his life?

"I go about the streets of Braxton, and I know that the

men and women I see are better people because they have never had to do such things. Look at the forester over there. He has never had to cringe before a boss, never had to lie to hold his job. He has never been bullied and doesn't feel that he has to bully others. He has never had to choose among evils but always among goods. Of course he is a better person and a happier one."

Simeon leaned against a tree, shading his eyes so that he could watch the skillful movements of the man in the oak. He smiled a little. "I know him, and he is an acutely unhappy man. His wife left him six months ago, and his oldest son was a failure at the university."

He shouted a greeting to the man in the tree and spoke for a few minutes to his companion on the ground. As we went on, I said, "He may be unhappy now, but he has had happy moments in his life, and there is still a chance of happiness for him in the future. His life isn't ruined."

"Of course, of course. I'm only trying to make you see, George, that there are still disappointments, and they seem to be bitter. Men are disappointed in love, in their ambitions, in their children. There is still disease, you know, much as we have done, and there is still death.

"You once said you were surprised at the pessimism in so much of our poetry. But we can afford to be pessimistic. In your day most pessimism was a man's apology for his own failure, an attempt to impute to the defects of human nature sins of which he knew he was guilty. As you have said, many of your contemporaries had to think badly of mankind or find themselves unbearable. Today we are beginning to be strong enough to face our limitations. We know that ours is a species just sufficiently adapted to the world in which it finds itself to permit survival. The world was not molded to our hearts' desires, nor, much as we may modify it, are we able to shatter it to bits and reshape it to our ends. What we have achieved, we owe to a long and perilous struggle, and that struggle has to continue. If man has greater powers for good than most people in your day were able to believe, he also has greater potentialities of evil than the unthinking citizen of today imagines. It is well for the poets to remind us of the horrors of which mankind has been guilty, lest we forget to preserve the conditions that have done away with them.

"Many people a hundred years ago believed that they were witnessing the end of civilization. People often believe that in an age of rapid change, but perhaps your contemporaries were nearer right than our know-it-all historians would admit. Mankind may have come very close to the brink of self-destruction. Don't forget that when you talk of roads that the race might have taken.

"Well, the era turned out to be a beginning, not an ending. But only a beginning. A very wise man of the nineteenth century said that, once man was freed of bondage to his belly, once it became relatively easy to take care of the physical needs, civilization could begin. How true that is you know better than I. But remember that it is merely a start that has been made. History is ahead of us, not behind. Thousands upon thousands of years were spent in the building of a foundation, and, now that it is finished, we must realize that it is a foundation and nothing more. No one feels more acutely than I how good it is that we are reaching out to new ideals, but new ideals bring new possibilities of failure. The struggle is never over.

"I don't know why I talk this way, George. Everything you have been saying is right, and I was with you one hundred percent when you made your speech last spring. I'm glad that you're here to say such things. But I have a queer feeling this morning that I must make you look more to the future and less to the past. Perhaps it is because your period of apprenticeship has come to an end. You are one of us now, and you must stand where we stand.

"Most people are no more concerned about the future than most people were in your day, and that is right. Life has to be lived in the present. But there have to be and there always are persons whose minds range beyond the satisfactions and disappointments of the moment. In your day only the pampered minority had the opportunity to embark upon the contemplative life, and they entered it with all the corroding prejudices of their upbringing. Today we are more fortunate. Our thinkers come out of the people, for there is nowhere else for them to come from, and if they are strong, they think of and for the people. We need thinkers like that."

We stopped to watch a doe and her fawn playing in a glade. "I have spoken of death," he went on. "There are those who think we can abolish death, and, if we can, doubtless we will, for that is how man is made. But death has not been abolished yet, and premature death, as it has become rarer, has become more tragic. Nothing but time, I fear, has ever consoled man or woman for the death of a loved one, and the death of such a girl as Freda Waldman would have brought sorrow in any age, but I know that I suffered the more deeply because her promise was so great and her fulfillment of it so almost certain.

"Of the death of men and women who have lived out their days there is nothing to say. I can tell you, though, that even at my age death is inconceivable. I know that there will be a world when I am no longer part of it except in some chemical sense, but I do not believe it. I do not see how you can love life and not hate death. Perhaps when it is ready to happen, I shall be ready for it. There is little wisdom in fearing death, but none in welcoming it."

I had said nothing to interrupt him, and we had walked rapidly through the forest, across the further ridge, and down into the valley of the Braxton River. The hospital came into sight, and I said, "A little less than two months and you will have another man of my century among you. I wonder what he will think, and whether my little journal will be of any use to him." I had looked up what I could find on Tillset, and I thought he might well be both flattered and embittered by the articles that had appeared after what was supposed to be his death.

We left the river bank and cut across the playground. With some trepidation, I revealed to Simeon my little secret: "Well, here is where I start work tomorrow."

Half a step ahead of me as usual, he stopped short and looked into my face. "By gad," he cried, "the very thing! How did you do it?"

I had simply gone to the vocational guidance office and told them I wanted a job. The girl brought out a folder and studied it.

"Were you really expecting me to come looking for a job?" I asked her.

"Well, you're in our files like any other citizen."

She ran over various possibilities: a clerical job for which my bank experience might fit me; a position in the store; another clerical job that it would take me six months to prepare for. We discussed my qualifications and interests. "The doctor,'" she said, "reports that you ought to spend as much time as possible in the open air. It isn't vital, he says, but desirable. Now there's that place at the playground, and we could take on a man at Deering Crossroads farm, or there ought to be something opening soon in one of the outdoor services that wouldn't be too difficult."

As soon as she mentioned the playground, I knew what I wanted.

While I told the story, I watched Simeon's face, but I could not interpret his expression. "It isn't much of a job," I said, "but I do seem to get on pretty well with kids, and somebody's got to do it. Of course, it does seem as if there ought to be something—that I ought to make a more important—I mean, after all the trouble everyone has taken." I gave up the attempt to apologize for the humbleness of the task I had chosen, and rushed on: "But the most important thing, it seems to me, is to do something useful and to belong. If I can't make a great contribution, and I guess I can't, I want to make a little one. I want to do my share."

"Why, of course," said Simeon, his eyes sparkling and his hand firm on my shoulder. "What do you think we've been educating you for?"

We had lunch together, and then I went home to write down what I could remember of our conversation. I was amused to see that I had to go back and strike out several words that would be quite unintelligible to those who are yet to awaken. Roberta and her kitten came in before I had finished, and waited patiently—or as patiently as could be expected—for me to come and play croquoits.

As I put away my papers, Roberta said seriously, "Now that you're getting a job, I suppose you'll be getting a wife and a home of your own."

"I might," I said casually.

"Well, of course we'd hate to have you leave us, but I guess it would be the right thing for you to do."

Utopian Literature

AN ARNO PRESS/NEW YORK TIMES COLLECTION

Adams, Frederick Upham.
President John Smith; The Story of a Peaceful Revolution. 1897.

Bird, Arthur.
Looking Forward: A Dream of the United States of the Americas in 1999. 1899.

[Blanchard, Calvin.]
The Art of Real Pleasure. 1864.

Brinsmade, Herman Hine.
Utopia Achieved: A Novel of the Future. 1912.

Caryl, Charles W.
New Era. 1897.

Chavannes, Albert.
The Future Commonwealth. 1892.

Child, William Stanley.
The Legal Revolution of 1902. 1898.

Collens, T. Wharton.
Eden of Labor; or, The Christian Utopia. 1876.

Cowan, James.
Daybreak. A Romance of an Old World. 1896. 2nd ed.

Craig, Alexander.
Ionia; Land of Wise Men and Fair Women. 1898.

Daniel, Charles S.
AI: A Social Vision. 1892.

Devinne, Paul.
The Day of Prosperity: A Vision of the Century to Come. 1902.

Edson, Milan C.
Solaris Farm. 1900.

Fuller, Alvarado M.
A. D. 2000. 1890.

Geissler, Ludwig A.
Looking Beyond. 1891.

Hale, Edward Everett.
How They Lived in Hampton. 1888.

Hale, Edward Everett.
Sybaris and Other Homes. 1869.

Harris, W. S.
Life in a Thousand Worlds. 1905.

Henry, W. O.
Equitania. 1914.

Hicks, Granville, with Richard M. Bennett.
The First to Awaken. 1940.

Lewis, Arthur O., editor
American Utopias: Selected Short Fiction. 1790–1954.

McGrady, Thomas.
Beyond the Black Ocean. 1901.

Mendes H. Pereira.
Looking Ahead. 1899.

Michaelis, Richard.
Looking Further Forward. An Answer to *Looking Backward* by Edward Bellamy. 1890.

Moore, David A.
The Age of Progress. 1856.

Noto, Cosimo.
The Ideal City. 1903.

Olerich, Henry.
A Cityless and Countryless World. 1893.

Parry, David M.
The Scarlet Empire. 1906.

Peck, Bradford.
The World a Department Store. 1900.

Reitmeister, Louis Aaron.
If Tomorrow Comes. 1934.

Roberts, J. W.
Looking Within. 1893.

Rosewater, Frank.
'96; A Romance of Utopia. 1894.

Satterlee, W. W.
Looking Backward and What I Saw. 2nd ed. 1890.

Schindler, Solomon.
Young West; A Sequel to Edward Bellamy's Celebrated Novel "Looking Backward." 1894.

Smith, Titus K.
Altruria. 1895.

Steere, C. A.
When Things Were Doing. 1908.

Taylor, William Alexander.
Intermere. 1901.

Thiusen, Ismar.
The Diothas, or, A Far Look Ahead. 1883.

Vinton, Arthur Dudley.
Looking Further Backward. 1890.

Wooldridge, C. W.
Perfecting the Earth. 1902.

Wright, Austin Tappan.
Islandia. 1942.